*Three Views of Crystal Water*

Also by Katherine Govier

**Novels**
*Creation*
*The Truth Teller*
*Angel Walk*
*Hearts of Flame*
*Between Men*
*Going Through the Motions*
*Random Descent*

**Short Stories**
*The Immaculate Conception Photography Gallery*
*Before and After*
*Fables of Brunswick Avenue*

**Travel Anthologies, editor**
*Solo: Writers on Pilgrimage*
*Without a Guide: Contemporary Women's Travel Adventures*

# Three Views
# Of Crystal Water

## KATHERINE GOVIER

HarperCollins*PublishersLtd*

First edition

HarperCollins books may be purchased for
educational, business, or sales promotional
use through our Special Markets Department.

HarperCollins Publishers Ltd
2 Bloor Street East, 20th Floor
Toronto, Ontario, Canada
M4W 1A8

*www.harpercollins.ca*

Library and Archives Canada Cataloguing in
Publication

Govier, Katherine, 1948–
Three views of crystal water : a novel /
Katherine Govier.

ISBN-13: 978-0-00-200589-0
ISBN-10: 0-00-200589-1

I. Title.

PS8563.O875T47 2005      C813'.54
C2005-901514-4

HC 9 8 7 6 5 4 3 2 1

Printed and bound in the United States

Drawing by Rex Nicholls

Typeset in Meridien by Palimpsest Book
Production Limited, Polmont, Stirlingshire

Transparent things, through which the past shines.

*Vladimir Nabokov*

For my mother

# PROLOGUE

It is a warm day, late in the season; the sky is clear and the sea is calm. We will dive in the deep. We meet early at the shore with our baskets; when we come back they will be full of abalone, if we are lucky. And we will be lucky, I feel it.

We women carry the lunch, and the men and boys bring little braziers to light in the centre of the boats. Although the day will be hot, the deep water will be so cold we will have to warm ourselves every hour.

We set out, boats behind the boats, towed by the two fishermen who have motors; four and then four more fishing boats sally forth in two obedient lines. We travel nearly a mile before the motors slow. As one we turn our heads to look back where we have come from. Our island lies behind, a saddle-shaped disk, low in the centre and higher at each end. On sharp, clear days in late summer it appears to have jumped off the surface of the sea: there is a little space under it, as if it were floating on an invisible cushion. But today the air is slightly misty and the summer island, as we call it, seems half sunk in the distance.

We have arrived at the deep fishing grounds, a semi-circular cluster of islands called the Watchers. Our lines of boats pass between two rough cones that erupt from the glass-topped sea. She is at her most docile – turquoise, almost flat, but moving in the long soft swells that are memories of a storm far away and days ago. Yes, the sea has memory: you can read it if you learn the signs.

Tamio unties us from the boats in front and behind. Because I have no brother, no father, no husband here, my boatman is Keiko's nephew. He has only a shy smile for me and no words. He stands, holding the oar that fits into the little cut in the stern.

1

When he has poled us to the diving spot I remove my *yakata* and stand, wearing only the thong the *ama* call the 'black cat'.

The other women are not concerned to show their bodies. It is a matter of no importance to them; nearly naked is the way they have always dived and is the best way to dive. But I am unused to it, as I am unused to much that is custom in this place. Tamio looks down with covert curiosity: does he think a white woman's nipples would be different? He holds the waist belt with its charges of lead to make me sink. But I don't want it yet. I tuck my *tegane* into the thong where it crosses the small of my back. The knife makes me a little braver. I loop another rope around my waist, this one sixty feet long and heavy. Keiko's nephew checks the knot. This will be my lifeline.

I keep my sights on the neighbouring boats. Hanako is in the nearest one; she is sixteen and an apprentice diver too, but we both know she will be very good one day. Hanako's mother Maiko is just beyond: she is one of the best divers in the village. And Hanako's grandmother too will dive today. She is fifty-five and has been diving for nearly forty years, since she was Hanako's age. Grandmother loves to dive. She could have retired but she did not want to. She says she would have nothing to do all day and that she would miss the rest of us.

I keep my eyes on Hanako. When Maiko and Grandmother jump off the sides of the boats, she jumps. When she jumps, I jump.

I see Hanako's feet leave the boat. I see the side rock down with the pressure of her jump, and then bounce up as her weight leaves it. I see her arms go up, in that gesture of submission one makes before entering water.

I see the hair lift off the back of her neck and fly into the air. I see her head enter the splash her feet made and the water close over it. I open my mouth, fill my lungs, and follow.

Oh, the shock of entry. Every time, it is as if I've never done this thing before; never left the safe air and gone feet first into this cold, wallowing, two-faced, foreign element. I call it alien, although in the sweet state it is what nourishes me and even fills my body: aren't we ninety per cent water? But I fear this part of me. It is a world unto itself. I also adore it. Water is seductive, silky to the skin, welcome in its chill when the sun is burning. Endlessly lovely: sometimes a scroll, its lines of foam columns of script telling an ancient tale; sometimes a healer. It soothes, offering weightlessness and dream in exchange for consciousness.

But try to enter it! Its surface is a pane of glass I shatter at my peril. It stings. Its weight exaggerates any insult. It bulges and caves into great troughs. It tosses me like an angry parent. It sucks me down.

Bodies of water, we call them. Fresh, salt, dead, alive, still, fast-moving, tidal, land-locked. I know little about those other bodies which span the world, but I can tell you that the sea I plumb is a trickster. Lashing at the black lava rocks, tasting of the mysterious living things, shot with sunbeams or sunk in massive gloom, it is bitter to the nostrils and stinging to the lips. I've seen rock cliffs under water that trail air bubbles out of some crevice as if they were breathing.

But today the water is perfect. It is pale, silvery turquoise. Whoever named the aquamarine must have been looking at this water on just such a day. It gives me no shock. It fits over me gently. My feet, like arrowheads, make their bite and my body sails down their stream of froth. Easily, I stop my downward motion and with one strong scoop of my arms send myself back up to the surface. When I break it I shake the hair out of my eyes and little drops of sea water fly in bright radiance around my head. My friends, the other girls and women, bob on the surface, laughing to each other. They purse their lips then and make the mournful whistle they call the *ama-bui*. Then, silently, simply, they give a nod to their *tomahi* and bend, break the water with their faces and neatly tuck down.

I will do the same. First I fill my lungs with air. They expand in my chest, and for once there's no tightness, no tension. I tuck my head under, jackknife at the hips and strike out with my legs while using my hands and arms to dig a downward path. It seems easy to drift head down toward the forest below. I pass startled small fish and see the shadows of larger ones flit beyond the corners of my eyes. Ahead of me, below are the tips of the tallest seaweeds and coral. The weed is a magnificent lime colour, and the coral wears new white and pink blooms. Today it's all open, showing its heart to the penetrating sun, the magical ringmaster down here. Down further, twenty, twenty-five, thirty feet, I enter the green forest. The light-filled strands drift alongside my body but they don't alarm me. I'm used to their touch. I can see, ahead of me, white sand and black rocks. The rocks lace the sand's edges and promise a deeper place. I turn, and begin to swim along the sand floor. I can see crabs, and pink and purple suction cups on a tapered arm as an octopus suddenly retreats from my path.

Now the water darkens, over this valley in the sea floor. In a little crater I'll find what I am looking for. My lungs are half empty. But I know how much air I have and can ration it. Rushing will not help. But neither can I waste time. I swerve, pushing the water away from my path first one way and then the other, hanging upside down, my hair below me like tassels, I thrust my hand into the crack, and feel for the rough edges of the shell. Holding on with one hand so that the drifts of water down here, like winds above the surface, don't carry me away, I reach to the small of my back and bring out my knife.

It's really as much of a crowbar as a knife, this tool that centuries of diving has developed. It fits into the cracks between the rocks and, because it has a bend in it, even slides under the edge of the rough shell. I slice sideways with as much strength as I can muster, although I have no earth to brace myself. It cuts the muscle that holds this shellfish to the rock.

This is the trick. I place my free hand on the knife. Kicking with my feet I slash, hard. This is my special cut. Guide with the right, power with the left, I repeat to myself. The abalone detaches. Holding it in my left hand I replace the *tegane* behind my belt with my right. Then I kick again, trying to plant my feet on sand. But a surge of motion, like a sleeper's unconscious roll, takes me sideways and I lose my grip on the shell.

My lungs warn me; there's not much time left. The surge relents and I tumble back to where I started, and in the little release of pressure that comes from the water's movement, I get my feet down and both hands in the crevice. The abalone comes away, leaving a small storm of protest on the sand floor. Creatures hiding in its lee roll away and the sand itself flies up in protest.

Cradling the razor-edged shell against my chest, I try not to cut myself. I tug on the rope which disappears above me into the column of blue. I feel like a monk at the base of a bell tower, pulling with all his might to make the bells swing. But their clappers are stopped.

I wait for the return tug from above. I hang on to my rope and my shell and try to rise. I cannot see him there in the little leaf-shaped boat shadow that floats over my head, but I hope the boatman is pulling hand over hand, as fast as he can, so that the rope comes in and falls at his feet in expert circles. I can see, shooting up from the clouded depths, my friends rising too, like slim angels called to heaven.

# VIEW 1

# 1

## *Mei*

### Attacking from in front

So this is how it began.

Vera, bereaved, a slip of a girl, stood in a slanting rainfall on the quay. The year was 1934 and she was thirteen. It was a romantic moment in what she hoped would be a romantic life. This little girl, who was me, but has now become, with the perspective of twenty-five years, a stranger called Vera, was waiting for her grandfather. She had loved him for her whole life, a love renewed on his infrequent stops from the sea to dry land, and now she would be his. He was an elusive man, James Lowinger, the pearl merchant, a wild, imposing man whose portrait, a painting of a white-whiskered Poseidon braced against the mast in a tearing wind, dominated the parlour Vera shared with her mother, Belle. But he was coming home.

The *Empress of Japan* slid into its berth, high-bowed and with attendant pomp. With a great rumble and sigh the engines stopped, and the porters began to run up the long ramps pulling their wheeled carts. The passengers leaning over the rails waved to loved ones below and then began to walk unsteadily down the hypotenuse to terra firma.

No waves for Vera.

On she stood in the cold, under her umbrella. She looked and looked, clutching her skirt with her free hand, waiting for the White-Moustached God to make his appearance. At length he did so at the top of the ramp. There he was, just like his portrait, ruddy and bewhiskered. He waved. She looked over her shoulder. To whom was he waving? She looked back. He was waving to her. She was amazed he recognised her. Then he turned his head to speak to the tiny person who stood beside him.

A woman. In a kimono.

Vera was not entirely surprised. Her mother had made reference to James Lowinger's travelling companions, biting her lip. Her grandfather and the small Japanese woman came down the hypotenuse. Vera didn't give him a chance to speak first. She stepped forward.

'Grandfather,' she said.

'It is really you, my dear?'

'Yes it is. It's Vera.'

He appeared astonished, and delighted. 'Vera. My darling.' He opened his arms.

'Grandfather,' she said warningly, 'I have to tell you.'

He opened his arms more widely.

He wasn't listening. She had to stop him. 'Grandfather, Mother died.'

He started, but did not lose his composure. The wind-roughened cheeks twitched; neck sinews stood out over his starched collar; hands clutched, probably involuntarily, at his trouser legs in a gesture eerily like her own; the ruddy colour drained from his face.

'She did what?' He said this in a thin voice of incredulity.

Vera could see that he wasn't comprehending. He had trouble with the verb, the 'action word', they called it at school. It was throwing him off.

'She died. She's dead,' Vera amended.

The hand went to pull his moustache. 'I see,' he said.

He saw, but what did he see? Did he see Vera, child of his child, bereft and soaked to the skin and all but transparent with grief?

Or did he visualise, in that instant when he knew she was gone, his beloved daughter Belle? Did Belle's shortened life

10

from the moment of her birth inscribe itself in his mind? How he held her in his arms, in Yokohama, when his wife handed the baby over without a word? How he tried, but not hard enough, to keep her with him in Japan? Did he think of the first time he lost the girl to his wife? Or the second to marriage? Or the third to Vancouver, Canada, a beautiful city with a view to the Orient?

Or did his mind trip, as his foot tripped – over the grief struck grandchild, and his dead daughter – and stumble on the wife who'd given them to him? Did he think of Sophia, whom he had replaced with this young, Japanese woman?

Vera did not know. James Lowinger recovered his balance and put his foot down on dry land.

He was not at ease there. His life was water. One bit of land or another was much the same; it was not-sea. The news had caught him at the moment of landing, of crossing over from water to earth. All of his life, crossings had marked him – going from island to boat, from boat to mainland. Ramps and bridges were the same. He tripped, he lost his footing. All went into flux, his language, his understanding, his memory.

The Japanese woman caught his arm.

He turned to her. She stood there not getting a word of it. He was unsteady; her arm was holding him up. He hardly knew this little girl, though he recognised her, could not miss her, with that white hair. She was strangely personable, for a child, and too much like his wife for comfort.

'This is my granddaughter, Vera,' he said. 'Vera,' he said, 'this is Miss Tanaka. Keiko.'

Miss Tanaka, Keiko, was younger than Belle. Younger than Belle had been, rather, because now it is clear that Belle was never to grow old. Vera was as much a surprise to Keiko as Keiko was to Vera. A surprise and yet not a surprise: James Lowinger was a man who had secrets. He gave nothing away, until he had to. The day before, carelessly, as land came into view, he had told her: 'Oh Keiko, by the way. A long time ago I was married in Yokohama. My wife was English. She left me

11

and took our child to England. Belle married a bounder; he's left her I imagine. She has a child, my granddaughter. I wired them, that we were coming.'

But he hadn't wired *we*. Only *I*.

As her grandfather and Keiko stepped off the gangplank, Vera was conscious of herself as a girl needing to be rescued. She had been brave for long enough. She hoped to let down for a bit. When their feet touched terra firma and she had delivered her news she offered up both arms in her grandfather's general direction, for an embrace. She made the same undiscriminating gesture to the unknown Japanese woman. Then, turning toward home, she worked her hand into her grandfather's, the one that was not carrying the valise, and allowed a few tears to fall.

They found a taxi that would carry their trunks and she gave the address of the little house on Ivy Street that had been Belle's, that still was Belle's. When they arrived, the three of them climbed slowly out of the cab and the driver helped unload the baggage, very little, really; the rest would come later. They made their way up the narrow pavement. And all the while Vera was taking the measure of this man, who was pretty well her only chance for being looked after in the world.

The main event was his moustache, which was waxed and hence pointed at its extreme ends. Or should we say moustaches? A plural will give more a sense of the presence of this accessory. They started under his nose and stood out thickly over his upper lip. When the lip ended (although you couldn't see the corner of his lips, but you knew there was one) the moustaches swooped down, then up and curled back upon themselves, spiralling into smaller curls. This stiff upcurl happened well beyond his cheeks and reminded Vera of the things on the ends of the curtain rods that her mother called finials.

The finials were not white, not like his beard, and not like his hair, but rather an orangey brown. Moving inward, from the tip, the moustache hairs were a dried auburn and tobacco colour, then a dark brown turning to slate grey, and finally at the root, white. He'd been young when he grew the curls, she supposed. One day, she supposed, his moustache hair turned white. One particularly tempestuous day on the high seas.

The swag of the moustaches also left to the imagination the shape of her grandfather's upper lip. It might be a villainous thin, hard lip, or it might be, and she suspected it was, a soft, full, sweet-shaped upper lip. Vera would never know. The face was blustery, and had high red cheekbones. His eyes were a beautiful blue, but one of them had a white cast over it. His chin was long and came to a thoughtful point; there was impishness to the lines around his mouth, which showed they'd been made from smiling. He wasn't as big as Vera had expected: the chest inside his double-breasted navy jacket must have shrunk since the jacket was purchased, and his long sea legs, that Vera imagined would have bestraddled the deck of the bucking frigates the way a cowboy bestrode a horse, did not seem steady. His knuckles stood up, his fingers were as long as a pianist's, and they waved, sensing things. But his voice, now that he had regained it after the shock of her announcement, was powerful and commanding. Keiko circled in its gusts trying to go respectfully behind him while he tried to herd her in front as if he needed assurance that she was truly there.

Vera produced her key and opened the door, and her grandfather and Keiko were impressed with her competence. They gave each other a look: see how she manages!

And then they entered the door of the house, and disappeared.

And silence descended. For days.

The neighbours who had helped Vera bury her mother poked their heads out of their doors and conferred over the rhododendrons. The trio had been seen. What could it mean? Was the curious little kimono-clad woman a housekeeper? They watched the house. But for some reason, maybe because the Lowinger-Drews kept strange hours, or maybe because each of the three exited singly and deliberately tried to pass unnoticed, the other inhabitants of Ivy Street rarely caught a glimpse of the girl, her grandfather, or the mistress. Because that was what had been determined: the little woman was more than a servant. At night when the lights were on in the house and the curtains unpulled, the pair had been seen, nuzzling. Kissing over the kitchen sink. It was shocking for such an old man. And such a young woman; hardly more than a child herself, much more like a companion for Vera.

'Well that's nice isn't it?' said a kinder soul. 'She needs a playmate.'

'Of course, you can never tell with Orientals, they don't seem to age.'

They liked Lowinger and they called him Captain. He walked down the street, and his eye was caught by every dog or squirrel that crossed his path. He chuckled and was entirely lost in the creature, until it was out of sight.

'He's very charming.'

'And there is money.' He was thought to have accumulated a fortune as a pearl merchant, on top of the one he inherited from his father from the same business. But some doubted the veracity of this. Inquisitive housewives smiled on James Lowinger and opened their mouths to speak, but words failed and they faded behind their front doors. Were they scandalised by this Japanese woman in her kimonos? Or just shy, as shy as Keiko herself? There was little censure spoken in the corner grocery store; James Lowinger excited no real disapproval for his flagrantly irregular life. Perhaps a little envy, was all. If he hadn't come home with an oriental woman, who took tiny steps because the folds of her kimono draw together at the knee, they'd have been disappointed.

What they didn't know was that Keiko, despite her demure and inarticulate manner, her lowered eyes, was no timid Japanese mistress. She was an *ama*, a diving woman.

For a while life changed little on Ivy Street. Vera still walked to school in the mornings, but the housewives did not call out to her, or if they did it was with a kind of pity. It was not only Keiko who was strange but she, Vera, who became strange by her association with the Japanese woman. And the bravery she affected when her mother died stuck to her. She wanted to lay it down but she could not. She still had her friends in the school-yard. Sometimes after school they all went to buy a soda pop. She was held in a certain awe because of the tragedy of her mother's death, and its odd denouement. She didn't talk about it, but one day the minister stepped out of the manse and said: 'Is Captain Lowinger in town then for a few months? Will he be stopping here, with you?'

Vera said she didn't know.

In front of her grandfather's mistress, Vera was polite and excessively well behaved. This nuance was lost on Keiko, as Japanese children are usually well behaved, but Vera meant it as a hostile gesture. It was to show Keiko that she was a guest and not part of their household at all.

There was another change: instead of going home after school, Vera went to her grandfather's place of business. It was on Homer Street, down by the water. She took the streetcar to Granville, and over the bridge to the Gastown, on the water-front. Gastown was the oldest part of town, the port, where the old light standards had once been gas lamps. The lights were left on all day, but they were far apart, and small; often the fog and rain made the street very dark. You could smell the kelp and the oil that mingled at the dirty edge of the water.

That November Vera walked through late afternoon gloom in delight. When her mother was alive she was never allowed to come down here alone. There were fish and chip shops and bars. And there were sailors from all over the world, in their white clothes, sometimes their blue clothes, with weathered faces and strange tongues. At any time of day they might spill noisily through the doors of a bar; they might be asleep standing up at a bus stop. They lived on another timetable, they'd crossed the date line, the equator, the Tropics. They'd be looking for sex, her mother had told her. Vera knew not to catch their eyes,

15

never to look at them directly. As she walked quickly down the street they might look at her, but she was too young and too thin to be of interest.

Out of range of roving sailors, Vera slowed to look into the dark entrances of hotels. The sexy women limping in high heels, were in there often. Farther along the street were women who looked tired, handing out tracts about God and Jesus Christ. There were shops selling seashells, plastic flowers and postcards of the Lion's Gate bridge. There was a hat shop that belonged to her grandfather's friend. A furrier with buffalo coats, a hardware shop, a shop selling steel-toed work boots and checked shirts. There were jewellers, traders, importers, exporters. And then there was Lowinger and McBean.

Vera had never seen Mr McBean; his only appearance was in the firm's name. He might be fictitious, a title only, like the 'Captain' in James Lowinger. Her grandfather was no sailor, but a trader in gems, pearls in particular. He and his father before him travelled all over the world, hiring luggers and diving men to search for pearls. But the pearls were gone now. The company had bales of fabric and crates of dishes packed in wooden cases, *goods*, as they were called.

There were a few steps up from the street. There was a door with a top half of frosted glass. She opened this door and right in front of her, so she couldn't slip past unseen, was a little office with shipping schedules pasted all over the walls, presided over by Miss Hinchcliffe. Hinchcliffe was at all times erect and mannerly, as if her respectability were at issue. Why she was not Mrs Hinchcliffe, Vera did not know. She was certainly old enough to be married, and there was an inviting vigour in her form that was more like the sexy women than the missionaries. Still, she imagined that no man was polite enough to meet Hinchcliffe's high standards.

'Hang up your coat! Wipe your shoes! Put that wet umbrella in the hall!' were her usual first words, followed by, 'So, we are to be favoured with your presence again today are we?'

'Hello, Miss Hinchcliffe.'

16

There were maps on one wall and a black telephone and metal filing cabinets. 'Captain' Lowinger's office was beyond, in a room with a window of pleated glass through which Miss Hinchcliffe could keep an eye on his shadowy form. When Vera opened the door she would see him seated, smiling, behind a perfectly clear desk. There were no piles of paper and no calendars with dates circled, no complex timetables. His wooden desk had a green leather top and he had a lamp with an emerald shade. To one side was a set of brass scales that was used to weigh pearls, and the corn tongs to pick up the gems. There was nothing else except, in the corner on the floor, a typewriter. She could only assume that in this office, unhampered by physical records, Captain Lowinger conjured magical fundamentals that were then subject to mental administration.

The action was all on the walls, which were decorated with woodcut prints on rough yellowed paper. The pictures were of tall women with fleshy faces and chopsticks in their hair. There was a Japanese name for them: *ukiyo-e*. But Captain James called them his Beauties. His Beauties stood around like a picket fence, to keep out the world. Each one existed on a blank background as if she were completely alone in the world. She might have been a model on a ramp. Each one had a slouch, an over-the-shoulder glance, and dainty hands and feet which appeared as afterthoughts from under great swirls of decorated fabric. Each sumptuous kimono was patterned with mountains and rocky streams, shells and flowers and leaves. Each Beauty's body cut a figure like one of those giant letters on the first page of an old book, a decorated L or S or F. They were a veritable alphabet of women.

But they were unreadable. They had their backs to the room, and their eyes cast down, thoughts lost in the folds of their wraps. Everything about them was secretive, held in, padded, even their faces, which appeared to have no bones. They were white and soft and disturbed only by the thinnest fine painted lines to suggest eyebrows, nose, cheeks. Only the lips, red and rounded, were defined. But they were closed.

Her grandfather was not always alone amongst his Beauties. When Vera arrived, he might be talking to an urgent man in a blue serge cap who he called Skipper. Or he might be listening to a visitor who took pulls on a pungent-smelling pipe, sending clouds of smoke into the room, behind which the Beauties faded perceptibly. This visitor might be telling a tale, complete with grand gestures and occasional whispers, and sidelong glances through the door to where Miss Hinchcliffe would type with renewed energy. On these occasions Vera would go back to the warehouse and walk up and down the rows of bales of fabric, feeling them with her fingers. Or she'd peer into the fragile crates filled with dry grass and wonder if there were pearls inside. She might look at the life-sized kimono doll and take all her clothing apart. There were little spikes that went into her hair, and tight wrappings around her middle. Her feet had one split instead of toes, dividing the white cotton foot in two, so that it was like a dainty hoof. They'd been specially designed to fit into the thongs of the platform slippers she stood in.

If his visitor were a persistent one, Vera repaired to the big cutting table meant for fabric with its low-hanging light in a metal shade. She was allowed to open certain wooden boxes and take out the prints one by one and look at them.

She stared and stared at the *ukiyo-e*. The people were so very, very strange. Most of them looked like women, but only a few of them were, according to Vera's grandfather. Everyone wore a robe, often with a skirt too. The ones with swords were men. The ones with make-up and hair piled in knots and smirky smiles, who looked very much like women, were also men: they were actors who played women's parts. It was hard to find the real women. But Vera grew skilled at it. They were softer, and smaller, and less obvious about it.

They were usually shown among other women, fixing hair or serving tea. It was peaceful as they went about their lives inside squared timbered rooms. Sometimes they travelled with their companions, poled along in a banana-shaped boat by a man in a loincloth. If the weather was good and the current was with them, the boatman leaned on his pole, lazily. They glided through such scenery! Mountains and hillsides were cut by a slanted path, where trees attended in stylish attitudes, with clumps of branch here and there like soft clouds.

But there were days when rain came down aslant like a torrent of nails. There was snow too. The women were never dressed for it. For one thing they had bare feet, with a thong between their first and second toes, and square sandals like little benches, to prop the foot up high off the ground. The snow fell heavily, loading their pretty, papery umbrellas with inches of white. It covered the slated tile roofs and stayed in a thick layer on the branches and even stopped, mid-fall, in the air, a white dot carved in the print and coloured in. The snowfall was a kind of burial, but the figures were bright and graceful, as if for them to withstand this final curtain was effortless.

The snow in the pictures was so sad, cold and exquisite. The difficulties were borne lightly, gaily, as if everyone knew it would melt tomorrow. As if everyone knew that the tea house was around the next bend. The cherry blossoms would soon be out. The people would be flying their kites, which they did all together, an entire street of people. Or standing on a shore with a picnic basket looking expectantly to a nearby island.

There was snow sometimes in Vancouver, but it rarely stayed more than overnight. Vera's mother had had the same delighted attitude to snow, an attitude that was also a denial. She could just as easily have said, 'Let's go for a walk with our bare-toed shoes and our thin umbrellas and the little white split-toed socks!' That would have been on her gay days. Other days she was a sleepwalker.

And the pasty faces, the swollen cheeks, the lost features of these women were her mother's.

But this was a thought Vera did not like to have, and she pushed it away.

The devils – or men – in the *ukiyo-e* world simpered and hunched their shoulders and curled their toes. Their eyes were black marbles in wild open Os. They had huge dog faces with curled-back snarling lips and mad, crossed eyes, and eyebrows that make an angry V in the middle of their foreheads. Their hair was tied up in knots on the top of their head, and they often had a rope over one shoulder. One had a blue bow at his waist, the tassels dancing at his knees. His five fat fingers spread out in astonishment as he looked down and off to the right: something was there. He too had bare feet and carried two curved swords.

Once, her grandfather came out of his office and stood beside her. He smiled as she looked from one print to the other.

'Why do you have so many?' Vera asked.

'They used to be easy to find. No one put any value on them,' he said. 'I sent them home over the years. I don't know if your mother ever looked at them. And now – I look. There's always something new to see.'

'Do people buy them?'

'Oh they're not for sale, not for sale, Vera,' he said. And he laid his finger alongside his nose making a joke of the secret. 'If anyone knew they were worth money, my creditors would have them in a flash. We'll just keep them here, where only you and I can look.'

This day, when she got past Hinchcliffe, her grandfather was tapping on his typewriter. He asked her to wait in the hallway. She knew that when he let her in, the typewriter would be back on the floor and any evidence of paper would have vanished. Once in a while he spoke of a book. Vera hoped he would write it. She wanted to know all about his adventures. Sometimes at night in the house on Ivy Street he told stories. But, he said, any book would put him in a conflict between truth and loyalty. 'That be very interesting,' said Keiko, who was learning English.

Vera went to the measuring table and stared for a long time at a print where a child with a net was out in the darkness with a woman, her mother or a nanny. There appeared to be an official nature to the relationship, but then this was true of nearly all the pictures and nearly all the relationships. The little girl reached with her net trying to catch the little lights that were in the air, like stars come down to dance over the tips of the grasses.

'Fireflies,' said James Lowinger. He placed his hand on her shoulder. It was heavy but it was gentle. 'They're catching fireflies. The Japanese love fireflies. Do you see how the artist has tried to make them shine? It is a very fine print.'

She saw that there was a round hole in the darkness and then little sparks of yellow that radiated from this white spot. She leaned back against her chair and the back of her head rested somewhere in the middle of his chest.

'Did you ever see them catching fireflies?' she asked.

'No,' he said. He laughed. She loved the way he laughed. It was uncomplicated, amused. 'Even I'm not that old. This was a long time ago. Before I ever went to Japan.'

Her grandfather shifted the paper, and found another. His fingers touched the dry, stiff yellowed paper with care.

'Look,' he said.

Water was everywhere, everywhere in this land of extremes, of cloud-like blossoms floating in the dry arms of trees, of shores littered with shells and crabs, of people standing on a shore looking out to an island, carrying what she took to be picnic baskets. She grimaced over the working men, their loincloths high over knotted thighs, who poled the boats upstream in a gale.

Tiny, almost comic figures engaged in Herculean tasks amongst giant waves, in deep gorges among mountains with white and black gashes down their pyramidal sides. Small, determined, they fought on.

'Is Japan still like that?' Vera asked.

'I don't think so,' he chuckled. 'Not the last time I checked.'

But he didn't sound very convinced.

The world of these pictures, which Vera took to be the world of her grandfather's business, and of his romance, was far away in the distance, but at an unspecified place in time. Perhaps it

21

still existed. It was like the world of fairy tales. It was like a per-formance. Vera wondered who had made the pictures, which were like records of all that went on. She thought the picture world was his secret world, the one he might be writing about.

Someone was always watching this world. The artists who made these pictures peered through timbers, branches, and windows to frame a view; they hid behind fence poles and horses' back ends. They stood in corners so that they could encompass a whole line of warehouse roofs descending a hill, or let the bent branch of a tree swirl over and under the scene to frame it. And the people knew they were being watched. They were like actors in a play. They knew they were exquisite. They made processions and fought battles. They toyed with the idea of removing their costumes, but they never actually did. There were a few pictures where the women let the kimono slip off one shoulder or even off both. They raised their hems in certain cases to do unspeakable things. She liked them even more for that. Those prints she looked at furtively, blushing.

Of course she knew her grandfather had been a pearl merchant. But as closely as she scanned the pictures, Vera could see nothing to do with pearls. Water pictures she examined carefully for clues. But then – in a special bottom drawer – she found the seashore prints. The diving girls in their fire circle by the beach. Bare-breasted, with fabric looped over their hips, long-haired and long-bodied. Like sloops, an easy curve from chin to hip.

Then one day, Vera stumbled across the octopus. Good grief, what an idea, what they might do with those tentacles. She was horrified, put down the pictures and leaped out of the room with her face blazing.

More often than not, when Vera arrived after school, her grand-father was waiting for her. He stood up in his courtly way and they went out, telling Miss Hinchcliffe they'd only be a few min-utes. He took his umbrella from the stand and opened the wooden door with the frosted top half, paused on the top step to see if it was raining (it was), took Vera's arm and descended to the street. On the pavement, they turned right. The flatiron building filled the end of a block where two streets angled together, which was why it was called a flatiron: it was triangular. At the bottom of it, just below street level, was a triangular coffee shop. There were windows on either side, one looking on to Homer Street and the other on to Water Street: the café was only ten feet wide at its widest. At the narrow end it came to a point in two windows. At the wide end was a curtain.

As soon as they stepped in from the rain, Roberta appeared from behind the curtain.

'Captain Lowinger,' she said, gravely, as if he'd come to church, 'and Miss Vera.'

'Hello, love,' Captain Lowinger said. 'We'll have coffee and an order of cinnamon toast, with extra sugar.'

They sat. Their faces looked out on to the pavement just at the level of people's feet. Now Vera had the tall, rumbling figure all to herself.

Vera's mother had raised her on tales of James Lowinger's adventures. It was as if Belle had been planning all along to abdicate and leave the girl in his hands, as if she had guessed that the fact, and possibly *only* the fact, of Vera's existence would be powerful enough to draw in James Lowinger from his perennial sailings around the South Seas, to rein him in just as his great strength was waning, so that he would be safe at last and seated, facing her, pouring milk in his coffee and muttering that he needed a spoon.

'My grandfather needs a spoon,' Vera said, raising her voice to hail the waitress. Roberta was a capable woman past thirty with a dreamy streak, often discovered, as now, with her gaze out of the window into the ankles of the passersby.

'Where's my cinnamon toast and where's my sweetheart?' he said, looking up plaintively for Roberta, his hand on the tabletop, his neck curling forward from rounded shoulders. 'I might die waiting.'

'We can't have that, can we?' said Roberta, plunking the plate down in front of him.

'Cut or pick!' he said to Vera.

It was his game. The first time they played it she'd been small enough to sit on his lap, and he was visiting the house on Ivy Street. Belle had cooked an uneven number of breakfast sausages.

'We'll divide them.'

Hamilton was travelling but that wasn't unusual. In fact it was preferable. Her grandfather wanted to pass on tricks of the trade, and he never wanted to pass them on to Vera's father. 'That's what the pearl traders do.'

'What do you mean?' Vera had asked that first time.

'Cut means you divide them, and let me pick which portion. Pick means you pick, so I cut.'

Vera couldn't decide. She had gnawed at her pyjama sleeve. She had quivered. He had watched her and smiled as she stared at the prized sausages. If she cut, she could make sure the halves were exactly even. But if she let him cut, he'd have to try to make them even too. But he might make a mistake. Then one half would be bigger, and she could have it.

'Pick!' she had said.

'Smart girl!' he had roared, and laughed so that his moustache ends wobbled, which made her laugh. 'The picking price is always higher than cutting price.' He had divided the sausages meticulously, leaving one end of the extra longer than the other. 'Now which do you want?'

Vera had giggled and giggled, picking the bigger portion.

He had set her back down on her own chair.

'Last time I did that I was sitting on the ground in Bombay in one of those low little shops the Indians have. There was some oily meat involved as I recall, that I sopped up with a piece of delicious bread hot from a stove. The merchant laid out his pearls on the back of his hand.'

'Did you cut or pick, Grandpa?'

'I picked. I always picked. And then you know what I did? To bargain with him on the price, I covered my hand with a

24

handkerchief and put out my fingers to say how many hundred rupees I'd pay. Five fingers, five hundred. Whole hand, one thousand. Half a finger –' he made as if to chop off the end of his finger '– What do you think?'

'She doesn't like arithmetic, Father,' Belle had said. She was formal with him.

'Well I do!' he had said, spearing his sausages and wolfing them down whole. 'I like arithmetic these days because I'm making money.'

Today, Vera looked at the four half slices of toast.

'It's cut already,' she said.

'You're right. I'll have to let you pick then.'

He smiled. His ruddy skin was growing whiter, and beginning to shine like the inside of a shell. His face was clearing of the weather burns and tobacco stains of decades; he was being tamed. Was it his nearness to an end that made him flirt with girls and waitresses? A growing lightness in his life, that was really an acceptance of death that made him so attractive? They were all in love with him – Hinchcliffe, Vera, Roberta. He was powerful but childlike, immense, and visibly incompetent: he trembled and knocked over the cream pitcher. His body leaked and crumpled. He burped and gagged, laughed gently at himself.

'And by the way,' Vera said. 'You won't die. Not if I can help it.' She did not think it would happen, ever. Perhaps because her mother had fretted about it so much: he'll be lost at sea, he'll catch beriberi, and he'll come home to die. But he had proven very durable.

'Today in school we talked about pearls, Grandfather.'

'I don't know why you would. There are no more pearls in the sea. They've all been snapped up, every last one of them. Every self-respecting wild oyster has cashed in his chips,' said Lowinger.

'I don't believe that there are no more pearls,' she teased.

'You have to believe me, I'm your grandfather.'

25

She pouted. 'Then tell me about them.'

'Pearls are not my favourite topic, Vera dear.'

'But they are mine.'

'Are they, my dear?' Busy with his cinnamon toast. 'Are you catching the disease then?'

Vera crossed her narrow feet and took a strand of her white-blonde hair to curl around a fingertip; her stubborn adolescent expression gave way to the blank, childish look of she who expects a story.

'Is it catching?'

'Oh, highly contagious, my dear. You want to stay away.'

'But don't you think I've already been exposed?' Her mother had sent her around to the neighbours to sit in the rooms of the children who had scarlet fever and rubella, so that she would catch them and get them over with. So that if she got them later in life they would not kill her.

'Is that your excuse? Well, it was mine too.'

There was silence for a few minutes while he tore off ragged bits of his sugary toast, piece by piece, and popped them in his mouth.

Then, 'Do you even know what a pearl is?'

'I do.'

'You don't.'

'I do.'

'Then tell me.'

'Pearls are formed inside the shell of an oyster when it is irritated by a grain of sand. That's what they told me at school.'

'It is not that simple. There are as many explanations put forth for that, my girl, as would take me all day to tell.'

'Then tell me.'

'A pearl is nothing but the tomb of a parasitic worm.' He declaimed with a half smile that made the handlebars of his moustache twitch:

> *Know you, perchance how that poor formless wretch*
> *The oyster gems his shallow moonlit chalice?*

26

*Where the shell irks him or the sea sand frets*
*He sheds this lovely lustre*
*On his grief.*

'Who wrote that?'

'I don't know.'

'What do they teach you at school? No proper poetry either I see. It was Sir Edwin Arnold. And do they tell you that a pearl is the result of a morbid condition?'

'No.' She knew she had got him going.

'They don't. All right. Do they tell you then what Pliny said about the pearl?'

'No, Grandfather.'

'Well, they should then. Pliny thought, you see, that pearls were the eggs of the shellfish. That when it came time for these oysters to bring forth young, that their two shells, which are normally closed up tight, only a little gap there for the eyes to look out, you know, that the shells would part and open wide and a little dew would come in. And that this dew was a seed that would swell and grow big and become a pearl, and that the oyster would then labour to deliver this pearl, at which time it would be born, as another oyster.'

He chuckled, and his whitened eye lost a little of its haze. 'People believed all sorts of things of the pearl. That it was born as a result of a flash of lightning. I rather like that one. And in years when there were very few pearls, that was because there were not very many storms.'

'That's stupid,' she pronounced.

'Stupid?' he said, his breath whistling through his moustache. 'You don't say that about people's beliefs. You say that it is magic. That's what we're talking about. I suppose because it is difficult to explain, isn't it, how a small, perfect, beautiful thing can be found in the slime at the bottom of the sea. The Persians believed that pearls came from the sun. The Indians believed they came from clouds. If you listened to the poets, you'd think that pearls were tears cried by the gods, or by angels.

'The natives in the Malay Archipelago and on the coast of Borneo are convinced that pearls themselves breed. They say –' and here he leaned toward Vera and adopted a stage whisper as if he were imparting a secret of the greatest importance '– if a few pearls are locked in a small box with some grains of rice and a little cotton wool for several months, that when the box is opened – abracadabra!' His eyes widened and his great fur-trimmed mouth gaped '– that there are several new pearls in the box! And,' he added, 'the ends have been nibbled off the grains of rice! Do you believe it?'

She did not know whether to answer yes or no, so she kept quiet.

Captain James Lowinger flat out laughed here, heartily and in a way not exactly mirthful. And as he laughed, water spurted from the corners of his eyes and he picked up the thin paper napkin that Roberta had dispensed with the cinnamon toast, and wiped the water from his cheeks.

'And there are a lot of men who wished that was true!'

He laughed down into his chest, and picked at the remaining crumbs of toast on his plate.

'Mind you,' he said again, settling back, 'these breeder pearls are just as tiny as a pinhead. So –' His hands fell flat on the tabletop '– what's the use of that? The Chinese grind them for medicine.'

They drank their coffee then. Roberta leaned on her cash register and stared gloomily out of the window into the Vancouver rain. But she was only pretending to stare; Vera could tell she was actually listening.

'Well, do you believe it?' he asked.

'No,' she said.

'So, you don't believe it?' He peered at her.

'Well,' she began to doubt herself. 'Maybe a little –'

'When Columbus came to America, you know, he found that the natives on this continent believed it too. They had pearls galore, so many pearls, do you know? Pearls were not just in the Orient. No, not at all. When Fernando de Soto got to Florida he found the dead embalmed in wooden coffins with baskets of pearls beside them. In Montezuma's temple, the walls were all laden with pearls. The Temple of Tolomecco had walls and roof of mother-of-pearl and strings of pearls hung from the walls.'

'Where did they come from?'

'Quite literally, they grew on trees. You didn't know that, did you, Vera?'

'No,' she said.

'Yes. In the Gulf of Paria, Columbus found oysters clinging to the branches of trees, their shells gaping open. Do you believe that?'

'No,' she breathed. This time she had to have guessed right.

'Wrong!' he roared. Roberta looked back at them, her reverie interrupted, and grinned to see the old man teasing his grand-daughter, and Vera's pale face heating up again to the roots of her nearly white hair.

'Oysters really did grow on trees.' He went all scientific on her then. 'The oyster in question is Dendrostrea, or Tree Oyster, a mollusc that is to be found upon roots or branches of mangrove trees overhanging the water.'

She was reduced to silence.

'There, I fooled you. But you got me going. What did you want to know? What were you asking about?'

'Ceylon. You went to Ceylon.'

'Oh, everyone went to Ceylon. My father too. Way back in the 1860s. That's a long time ago, you can't imagine how long, my dear.'

'Of course I can. Seventy years ago.' She was better at arithmetic now.

'Give or take a decade, that's how old your grandfather is. My father was away with the pearling ships when I was born.'

'Just like my father was away when I was born,' Vera offered this as a bond.

'But I came to see you, didn't I?'

'Yes, you did.'

29

Captain Lowinger banged his thick cup on the table. It bounced. The windowpanes seemed to rock in their frames. 'Consider yourself lucky. My father never came to see me. I am sure I remember being born. I looked around and he wasn't there. I had to wait years to see him, as far as I can remember. When he saw *me*, he was not really satisfied. Later, he took me along to make a man of me.'

He rubbed the tips of his forefinger and thumb together. The good eye steadily gazed into Vera's face. The other one saw her too, but she must have had a white cloud over her head. 'It's the way of men in our family. Seafaring men. Go off and leave the woman at home, minding things. It's a good deal if you're the man. Mind you, it never worked for me. I tried it with your grandmother, but she was not the type of woman who'd wait around. For that, I lost her and I lost your mother too.'

He looked sad. Roberta brought fresh coffee and he took a long slurp. 'But we were talking about fathers.'

*10 February 1860*

Night was falling as they landed at the British garrison in the Strait of Manaar. Before they left the deck of their little vessel, Papa Lowinger took the boy to one side, looking away from the streaky red of the setting sun. That was his first memory.

'Do you see that land there?' Papa said to James, pointing into the darkness. The white waving beach and dark hills above were two miles away. 'That is the island of Ceylon. The people here believe that it was Paradise, the Garden of Eden. Up in the hills lives the King of Candy.'

That impressed James, and he focused his sleepy eyes

30

on it. The small base they had come to was separated from Ceylon only by a shallow arm of the sea, full of sandbars. Candy looked remote. Paradise was closer.

'At low tide you can nearly walk there,' Papa said. 'There's a string of sandbars called Adam's Bridge. The people say it was the very spot Adam crossed over when he was expelled from Paradise.'

The bridge was a series of white sand circles and they gleamed under the moon as the water surrounding them went darker and darker. It glistened and seemed to beckon him. James knew that Papa was laying on an enchantment. He did that to people. His voice became like a swallow: it rose and dipped and winged its way into your heart, and then it took fright and flapped upwards and was gone.

The sand fleas were biting. Soldiers stood at the water's edge, swinging their storm lamps by the handle, luring their boat in. James was bundled up and put in to bed. Through the wall he heard one of those tight-lipped voices. He didn't know how men got them – at Sandhurst he supposed. His mother wanted him to go there when he grew up. But his father wanted to teach him the pearling business. He was still in the larval stage, white as a fish and squeaky-voiced.

The leader of the garrison talked on.

'Time and again Ceylon's conquerors have exhausted the great pearling grounds. First the Portuguese, then the Dutch. We've let the banks rest now for four years. Each year we've made a survey to see if the oysters were ready,' the barking voice went on. 'Some years they are invisible, some years too small. We can't wait much longer; at seven years of age, an oyster is too old: it will have vomited its pearl.'

Seven was James's age. Too old!

'We mean to auction off leases on the pearl fishery.' That was a different English voice, also clipped, but lower.

The roar of laughter came from his father. He was European in origin, Papa. You could hear a husky German or Austrian in there if you listened. He was a man who left country and religion behind to journey after the pearl. He spoke in his peculiar way, hearty and learned, but rough-edged until he wanted to persuade you; then he was smooth as satin 'The manner of getting pearls has always been a mad amalgam of religious rituals and native cunning. Now the British Army believes it can apply science to the problem?'

'This year the fishery will again be great,' continued the clipped voice in an unhurried way. 'This is why we have invited you. I tell you, everyone has come to see.'

In the morning they set out in a native boat, pulled by a government steamer. It was all sand, and difficult going; water sometimes disappeared altogether. When this happened, native men with long bare legs jumped into the surf and attached ropes to the boat, and pulled it. They had to be pulled a long way around to find deep water again. It was only twelve miles down to the Bay of Candatchey, but it took for ever, the boat running aground and being pushed off. The soldiers were flaming hot in their red coats, and got a lecture from their leader about how they shouldn't complain. But the man on the oars told James about the buffaloes that lived in the jungle beyond the beaches and frequented the roads like high-waymen; he said they were known to go quite mad at the sight of red. If a scrap of scarlet cloth flapped to the ground, the creature would run at it and trample it, then get down on its knees as if to pray, and gore it.

'But your jackets!' James cried, 'they're red as berries!'

The soldier rolled his eyes at James and went on to say there were elephants in this jungle, ('pests', he called them) and wild boars and even small tigers.

They made their slow way over the crystal sea toward the morning sun. They looked off to the Indian side and saw nothing but blue salt water divided into amusing little mazes. They looked to the Ceylon side and saw nothing but a huge reflecting collar of sand around a dim, green layer of trees. But something vertical stood out, wavering in the sun, a stick moving along the sand. It was a man running in a solitary manner along the beach. He had a most determined, yet peaceful expression, as if he were in a trance. Bearing in mind that they were passing through Adam's Bridge, James asked his father if it was the first man himself.

'Papa, is it Adam?'

'Where?' he said, absently. He was often that way.

'There, Papa. Running.' His image arrested James.

'Adam?' His father laughed. 'Well, son, perhaps it is,' he said.

And if it were, where was Eve? The boy wanted to know.

Now his father laughed long. 'I suppose Eve will be along soon. Isn't it for her sake he's running?'

James supposed Eve had got behind. He looked long and hard on that shore, but he never saw her.

Papa eventually took pity on James. He squeezed his hand and then he said, 'No, that man is called a peon. He is running from Colombo, Ceylon, to Madras, India, with the post,' his father said. 'It is five hundred miles and he will do it in ten days.'

James never forgot the sight of him.

How ridiculous he must have been, in the schoolboy grey flannels and blazer that his father had made him wear. His straw boater tried to lift off his head at every minute, so he was kept busy jamming it back down. His skin – so pink in contrast to the skin of every other human they met – prickled, stung with sweat, burned, and peeled until it bled. It took him many more years to supply himself with the bark he had as an old man, seasoned and lined and impervious to insult.

At last they drew in to the large, half-moon-shaped bay. There were hundreds of boats pulled up on the shore. The wind was blowing away from them: sand flew, and in amongst the gusts of it he could see figures swirling in purple and black and burned orange, green and indigo.

He was so short he had to stand on the thwart to jump down out of the boat. He landed, squinting despite the shade of his straw hat, in hard wet sand. This grew lighter in colour, and dried, as they walked inland. But it was still sand, hot, and slippery underfoot. So this was Paradise.

There was nothing built on it, only a few fragile open-sided sheds, straw roofed with skinny crooked poles at the sides to hold them up. And hundreds of tents, which flapped in the wind and hissed with the onslaught of sand that came on the gusts. Papa explained that the fleet had gone out with the land breeze at the firing of the guns at ten o'clock the evening before. It would have reached the banks at daybreak and the divers would set to work. At noon they would stop as the air began to stir to warn them to come back. They were due back, on the sea breeze, in a few hours.

James could see, emerging out of the sand clouds, people. People of every kind he could imagine, hundreds and hundreds of them. He and his Papa had arrived at a giant, seething fair which was all the more astonishing for having appeared on a sand spit, out of nowhere. There were black men, yellow and brown men too, men in long robes, men with pigtails and satin hats, nearly naked and squatting in loincloths, long-haired, turbaned, wrapped in shawls and crowned with fez. There were Malay soldiers with their curved blades called kreese; his father said to watch out. Once drawn, a kreese was bound to draw blood.

It was all impermanent, an encampment, and better than a circus. They passed men with rings through their lips, and women so freighted with jewellery and hardware they had to be supported as they walked. Others were shrouded so that they appeared as only a pair of large wary eyes, in a black triangle. The sun-burned laughing girls

34

who flipped their tambourines at him were sea-gypsies. And there were dancing boys with hips as narrow as a dog's, who insinuated themselves between the soldiers as they walked.

It was hot, huge and festive. Pigs squealed, donkeys brayed and people shouted in tongues. James stopped before a shy graceful animal like a small deer, in a cage. A gazelle, his Papa said, waiting to be sold. A worldly-looking monkey with a white beard made its way without touching ground, by climbing over the shoulders and heads of whole rows of people.

Papa kept him by the hand. Maybe he thought he'd be stolen. Maybe he would have been. He dragged behind, caught up by a snake charmer playing on a flageolet who coaxed his cobra halfway up out of the basket only to let him drop again. A scribe sat cross-legged on a straw mat on the sand with a little crowd waiting for him to put some message on paper. He crooked his finger at James, but Papa pulled him past. They ducked under the flaps of a tent draped with coloured carpets. An Arab with a long white headdress and a massive black beard greeted his father with open arms; he looked on James kindly and the boy shrank behind his father's leg. Papa prised James off and showed him the scales, and the tongs, with which the trader handled the pearls, and weighed them. There were big brass sieves for sizing, a whole set of them, each with a different sized hole for the pearls to slip through, and the corn tongs he knew well because his Papa used them himself.

The men in line had pearls to sell. As for buyers, the richest of the rich were there, his father said. James was very impressed by how many of these exotic individuals his father knew by name. This one bought for the Sultan of Sarawak and that one represented the rulers of an Indian province. This man bought for the markets of Paris and London, for opera singers, and famous French courtesans. All this Papa told James. He waited while his father spoke to them and watched a man at a spindle, making holes in pearls. He had a half coconut sitting beside him, full of water, in which he dipped each pearl before he set to work on it. The pearls gleamed in the dim tent.

When they went out again, Papa took the boy to where, under the open sheds, rows of half-naked men were prising open the scabrous shells of oysters. They had white cloth wrapped around their heads and sat cross-legged. Only their hands moved, and if one moved too quickly or too far, one of the Malay soldiers came down on him with knife drawn. In front of them were little trays. A man circled briskly around the openers, and as soon as a few pearls appeared in the tray, he carried it off.

'There's the second best job you can have in the pearling game,' said Papa. 'If you've got nimble fingers and luck you might get away with a pearl or two.'

'What is the best?' James asked. He was anxious to impress him, the Papa newly in his life.

'You'll see.'

As the afternoon grew hot the breeze died. Papa pointed at a group of naked men behind a fence. 'Those are divers who were caught swallowing pearls. They've been given a herb, and they'll sit there until they've emptied themselves out. Some lucky fellow will have the job of looking for the stolen merchandise.'

The boy stared at the men. They were sullen and defiant as if determined to hold the contents of their stomachs in for ever. He half hoped they would succeed. The place stank of shit.

'Who thinks of it?' Papa said. 'A pearl in a princess's tiara may have been regurgitated – or worse –' he said, rolling his eyes significantly '– under extreme pressure from that lot –'

James thought about that. It was ugly to contemplate, but not for Papa. He went on. 'Isn't it odd, isn't it marvellous? A pearl may go from sinking in the most foul-smelling mass of dead matter you can imagine, straight to the most beautiful neck in the world. It will wash clean and look as innocent as a newborn babe. That is the beauty of pearls. They come up fresh again and again.'

His father was educating him, you see, as they strode in that sand, and hard work it was. He was a feeble boy and he whined, a mother's boy, he had been until then. But Papa kept on, determined that the boy should know, and follow him in his way of life. James ate some roasted meat – goat, judging from the upset displayed by the goat's relatives who were tied up outside. He thought he might be sick. Sweet-smelling smoke came from certain tents along the side of the crowd; this was where the men were smoking 'bang', his father said.

The air was alive with hailing and haggling, and Papa was joyous. He pointed out a weird solitary figure at the fringe of the water, facing out in the direction of the pearl banks. They called him the shark binder. *Pullul Karras*. His job was to keep the sharks from eating the divers. He did this by casting spells. Papa said that the man was a charlatan, but the divers would not go near the sea if he were not there.

'His is the best job in pearling,' Papa grinned.

'Why?'

'Why don't you see? He has fantastic opportunities for snitching.'

Apparently everyone snitched.

The conjuror kept up a tranced dancing, his voice rising into a wail, and dropping to a polite appeasing manner, and his body curling and snapping up, arms flung high, repeatedly, like a whip. His eyes were glassy and his lips were black. Papa said that he was supposed to abstain from both food and drink. But, as they watched, he regularly hailed a young boy in a filmy fabric skirt, who had a brass tray with drinks on it. This was 'toddy' from the palm wine

37

tree. The shark binder drank one and ordered another. Then another. Now his song came and went without its former conviction, and his arms lost their former height.

'Papa,' James said, 'I don't think he's saying the chant right.'

'Never mind,' he said, 'I'm sure the sharks will get the point.'

There were fortune tellers and charm setters and religious fanatics. He watched an Indian with matted hair put hooks into the flesh of his breast. Then he was hoisted on ropes and swung around a post, his skin tearing.

'Don't look,' his father said when James screamed. 'He's doing penance.'

The hour stretched on and the sun inched its way over to the west, where India lay. The boy wanted to see the divers.

'The best are called Malawas and are from the Tutacoreen shore,' said his father, speaking of them as if they were dumb animals, although James was certain they understood. 'They're Roman Catholics. A long time ago St Francis Xavier went to the coast of India and baptised the people. Because they're Christian, they don't work on Sundays but they also observe any festival, Hindu or Mohammedan. They want protection of all the gods, and you would too if you had to earn your living under a ton of water.'

James wanted to see them go down, so his father contrived for them to go out in one of the diving boats. They set sail for the banks at ten that same evening with the landward breeze. James lay on a wooden seat under a robe with his head on Papa's lap. The sky overhead was a whirl of southern stars, brighter than any he had ever seen. The divers sat on the bottom of the boat, silent, dark, strangely passive shapes. There were ten of them, and several sailors on each boat. His mind went to where theirs was – he saw a shimmering heat, foul smells, salt, and wonderment. Then darkness. Tomorrow might bring their death.

He must have slept. The dawn was a miracle of gold and pink, with clouds shaped like a funnel through which the daylight poured. He watched the divers oil their bodies, and talk amongst themselves. Each had his set of equipment, ropes, and a large red stone shaped like a pyramid with a hole through the top. Each man picked up the rope and the stone with the toes of his right foot, and the net bag with the toes of his left. He held another rope with his right hand, and, keeping his nostrils shut with the left, jumped into the water and, riding on the stone, sank, rapidly toward the bottom.

James rushed to the edge of the boat. The water was so clear that, by hanging over the thwart, he could see to the bottom. Plunging, the divers became blurred black figures with wavy appendages. When the stones hit bottom they threw themselves flat on the sand and began to swim like insects. They were picking up oysters which lay on the sandy slope and thrusting them into the bags. After a minute, they pulled on the rope and the rowers, who now held the other ends, pulled hand over hand to raise them back to the surface.

And so it went, for hours. When they came to the surface, the divers spewed water from their mouths and nostrils. Sometimes their ears were bleeding. They unloaded, took deep breaths, and picked up their stones with their toes, then they threw them overboard again. They went down fifty times, and each time returned with a bag holding easily a hundred oysters. The boat was filling up with the thorny, grey shells; as they lay in the sun the two halves began to gape. James saw one man slip a wooden wedge in the gap. He watched without letting on as the man ran his finger inside the half opened shell, feeling for pearls. And once at least, James thought the man found what he was looking for.

He had few places to hide a pearl, this diver. He put his hand up and casually wiped his eye. James realised that the pearl was gone – into his eye. He did not tell Papa for fear the man would be punished. If sharks were near they were not biting. James sat in dread and fascination, watching the shining black men who shot in a stream of bubbles straight down into the crystal blue that extended to murk. They were down for what seemed like for ever, then they began to reappear, raised majestically like statues that had been buried.

This was his indoctrination to the pearl hunt. 'I would like to be a diver for pearls,' he said solemnly then. But his father said no. 'No white man could ever go to those depths.'

At noon, the wind changed to blow them back to Ceylon. They sailed in, slowly, and when they neared the beach the oars came out. The gun fired and all the trading and singing stopped. The tied elephants brayed. The tambourines rattled to a climax; the crowd began to run toward the shore. Everyone stared out to sea. Owners and investors, fakirs, traders all, in their eyes a look James was to see more than he ever imagined – a look that was avid and fearful. These men had gambled everything on the find of pearls.

He had listened to his papa well, and understood that no one knew how good the oyster fishery would be. Perhaps the starfish had wormed their way in and eaten the flesh, or the seaweed growing on the shells had killed the animal. The anticipation became a murmur. The murmur became a roar. The sea wind with its sting of salt and sand blew in the waiting faces. Finally the boats were within calling distance. Then everyone – jewellers and boat-owners and officials with sticks in their hands, entertainers with monkeys on their shoulders, with skirts flying and veils lifting, robes flapping against legs – began to move toward the shore.

First James and his father's boat landed, and then another and another. Amidst the shouting and embracing, the boy understood that there was a huge haul. A great cheer and a roaring began. The soldiers stamped about, excited for their chance to bid and make a fortune. The horses whinnied.

The divers sat, bent over at the chest as if all the air had been pushed out of them. They were shivering, even though it was very hot in the sun, cold inside their dark, oiled skin. Their thin extended ribs made their chests look like birdcages. They alone were silent. James could not take his eyes off them. These men consumed him; those who descend. He remembered a poem from school, Keats's 'Endymion': 'a moon-beam to the deep, deep water-world'. If they spoke and we listened, what would we learn, the boy wondered

But the divers were herded off to be searched.

James made his way in the pearling business, though not as his father would have had it. He was known neither for acuity nor gambler's instinct, or skill at selling. He'd be remembered as the one with the gift of the gab, a man of words, armed with a poem when a dirkin or a kreese might do better. Some thought they could get the better of him because of this tendency, but it rarely happened. John Keats and his fellow poets were good company, better, he judged, than his country folk, the English, with their lordly manner.

The next day James and his father stayed on shore with the traders. Late in the day there was a commotion as one of the boats came in. He thought at first they'd taken on a log and laid it out on the nets between the divers' feet. Then he understood that this burden was a man. He could see the black head and arms. It was a diver, his lower body wrapped in a sail. The sail was soaked in blood. The man had lost his leg to a shark.

The boy saw his face; his eyes were closed, his mouth open, as if he had looked on something of awe and had retreated inward. The leg was with him at the moment

41

although James understood it was discarded later. He and it were a strange colour of grey.

There was an outcry, then, about the shark binder. Right on the spot the military Poo-Bah brought him up to account. The Superintendent was high on his horse. He bellowed and the conjuror ought to have quaked, but he was consummate in his act of defiance.

'A man has been attacked by a shark? Shark binder, it is your task to keep the sharks away. How can you explain the failure of your charms?'

The man stood firm, if you could call his fantastical gesturing firm, undulating his torso and sniffing the breeze for a message, or an excuse. The whole affair was understood as theatre, amongst the Europeans, and the conjurors, too, but not amongst the divers. They stood wide-eyed with terror, but obdurate. It was in their power to shut down the entire fishery; they need merely refuse to sink. It was a lesson to James. The naked ones, because they risk death, had the power.

A crowd gathered around these two men. Papa and he moved in to hear. The shark binder defended himself, waving his arms weirdly and impressively and calling out explanations that surely made no sense even to him.

'What does he say, what does he say?' the English asked.

'He says that a very great witch issued a counter-conjuration,' explained the Superintendent disgustedly from his horse. 'That was why the shark bit. He says he will prove he is stronger than she is by issuing an even greater charm to bind the sharks for the rest of the season. I suppose I shall have to pay him double.'

'Do you see?' whispered Papa. 'He can't lose, that conjuror. He's got it covered either way.'

The conjuror began with further charms, more exaggerated and bizarre contortions, ululations, screechings and mumblings. Finally, his adherents appeared to be satisfied. Only then did the owners begin to unload the oysters. They lay in heaps to be sold in lots, unopened. When the auction began the bids were fast; each lot went to the highest bidder who then came and hauled away the bags.

It was on that day, in Ceylon, that James saw one more extraordinary sight. A small girl about his age. Proper, dressed for a garden party in flounces of white all dotted with yellow. Sashed and bonneted like Little Miss Muffet on her tuffet, in all that sand and wind she held, over her small self, casting a useless pale shadow in which she was careful to stay, a red, ruffled umbrella.

His eye was drawn to the red umbrella. Red spot in the centre, making the whole scene revolve around it. She was the eye of the storm, that's what she was. She was the heart of the matter.

'Who is that?' he asked his Papa.

'That?' his father replied, following his finger. 'Don't point!'

There were thousands of people on the beach. He had to point. 'The girl with the umbrella,' he said.

'*That*,' he said. 'You mean *she*. *She* is the daughter of a man from the garrison. I believe he is called Mr Avery McBean.'

They were getting closer. She was plump and she pouted. She had a magisterial air about her. He knew as soon as he saw this child that she would make planets revolve around her.

'Do you know her Papa?' he asked.

'I cannot say that I know her,' said his father, 'but I have been introduced. And so shall you be.'

And they set out across what seemed like the Sahara, this mile-wide expanse of dry sand. It grew softer underfoot the farther they went from the ocean's edge. James's feet sank into it, making each step a little harder than the previous had been, giving him the sense that even as he approached Miss McBean so also did he retreat from her, the sole of one foot moving backwards in the shifting sand

43

and digging itself a little hole as he stepped out on the other. Slowly, ever so slowly, face into the wind and clinging to his hat, he made progress toward her.

Thus men approach their fate.

It was not quick enough. As mentioned, there were, in that area of Ceylon at that time, in the untrimmed jungles that lay behind that godforsaken beach, all manner of wild beasts. Elephants that came steaming out at road crossings, tigers whose golden eyes could be seen in the dark, and buffalos. The buffalos did not like red.

Just then one of these bad-tempered buffalos appeared out of nowhere. He caught a glimpse of the plump, pouting Miss McBean, and took exception to her red umbrella. He put his head down. A charging buffalo is not amusing. It was wide of shoulder with a bony ridge down its back and a tail with a point on it like the devil. Its hoary head was low with shiny black horns at the ready.

'Papa!' James cried. His heart began to pound. Had no one told Miss McBean about the colour red? Probably she would have paid no attention if they had. Or did she wear it as the soldiers did, with a fated desire to draw attention to herself?

The buffalo did not stop to think. He headed for her with murder in his eyes.

Dawdling and oblivious, she swung her umbrella over her head, then lowered it to waist level and then, holding it in front of her body as if she were a vaudeville dancer, twirled it. The animal bellowed straight at her.

James did not recall his Papa answering. But in a minute they were running in dry sand. The more they hurried, the deeper they sank. Papa held on to James with one hand and waved his hat with the other, hallooing like mad, though his words were lost in the wind. The buffalo ploughed on. A few men in the crowd shouted warnings. A soldier on horseback wheeled around and cantered toward the rolling red frills. A man who must have been the girl's father appeared out of a tent and they suddenly were all, all – buffalo, horse and soldier, Papa and James, her doting dad – racing against sand and time toward the girl while she – surprised, but unflinching – got a whiff of danger, and lowered her lovely toy to the sand. She found herself staring down the nose of a charging buffalo.

And what did she do? She put one little fist on her hip and made as if to stamp a foot in a wee Scottish tantrum. But just as she lifted it off the sand, a long arm that might have belonged to a polo player grabbed her around the waist and scooped her up to hold her against a solid military thigh where she remained unbending and in full possession of her umbrella. The buffalo charged into empty space, looking foolish and disappointed.

Later that trip he must have met her. He must have heard her piercing little voice and seen her dimples and righteous blue eyes and pale protected skin. But the voice and the eyes desert him; he has no memory of them. He only remembers the untouched froth of her, the childish form of her, there on that mystic and desolate beach. He remembers her innocent and altogether misplaced lack of fear.

That was the charm. It was not the one his father meant to put on him, a bondage to the business of pearls. To pearls James became an ambivalent servant. To Miss McBean he became a slave, and remained so for many years to come.

The coffee was drained from their cups.

'It's all in the past,' said James Lowinger. 'You mustn't be so interested,' he chided, gently. 'And not you, Vera, for certain. And a good thing it is that there are no pearls left in the oceans and rivers of the world, my darling,' he said then with an

45

irresistible and roguish look of tenderness. 'You can be the first of our family to be free of it.'

Roberta fussed getting James Lowinger's coat. He shambled to the door, this big man, and pulled his umbrella from the corner where he'd propped it, and paused on the step to open it skyward and herded Vera under it on to the street. She walked him carefully back to the warehouse. Fifteen minutes later, Vera stood waiting for the streetcar in the rain. *The first in the family to be free of it.* That meant the others were not free. Her grandfather was a captive, she saw that. His father too, from the sound of it: pearls were his religion. *Her* father must be a captive as well. It must be that which kept him in the Far East and away from her all her life so far. Even her mother, dead now, must have been a slave. The Lowingers were all that way, set apart. And so would she be. Vera Lowinger Drew: the last of a line of men and women whose lives were governed by the pearl. It was sad but glorious. She got off the streetcar and began to walk home. And now the pearls were gone, as the family was almost gone; it had come down to the two of them.

Or three.

She entered the house by the front door, throwing it behind her so that it slammed. Keiko emerged from the kitchen, smiling.

'Vera.' Probably she practised the name half the day. Vera was filled with scorn. She let Keiko take her bag. She could see behind her in the kitchen the shells and bowls of water that betrayed the various weeds and molluscs that would be her dinner.

'Can't we have meatloaf like everyone else?'

Keiko set the book bag on the side table. In her halting English she offered to learn how to make it, if Vera would teach her. Vera said never mind, she would only eat the rice. Rice was white and so was she.

Then she took her bag and went into her little room to read. Within an hour, the front door opened again and her grandfather's step resounded in the little stucco house. Coming out to greet him, Vera was stopped by the vision of Keiko on her knees in front of him, pulling off his shoes. 'Oh for God's sake,' she began to mutter, but the old man's eyes, the one so bright and the other whitened, met hers and she subsided in shame.

And she went back to her room and did her schoolwork, biding her time, biding her time.

# 2

## *Ushiro*
### Attacking from behind

Two years passed this way. Vera, James, and Keiko. Now it was 1936.

Vera was thin, pale, and possessed of a ferocious will. Her features had sharpened, and her eye sockets were deeper. Her nose was longer, sharper, and had a bone. It was a patrician nose, her grandfather said, looking at it askance. 'God knows you didn't get it from me.'

Keiko tended to both her charges in the morning, seeing Vera off to school and bundling James to the streetcar to his warehouse. Then she washed every item that had been used since the night before; cutlery, dishes, towels, clothing. The fabrics she put out on bushes to dry, running out to collect them when it rained. Once her housework was done she too set out on foot, for the end of the street.

She went in the same direction as James Lowinger, but farther, down to the east end, to the shops in Japantown. Here she would learn the news about her country – never good, because of the war in China – and find the fish, radish, and seaweed she liked. She had a few friends there. One was a dressmaker who made tunics and jackets for Vera. The other was a fishmonger. She would return home before either Vera or James appeared. On the clothesline she pinned the squid to dry; it was transparent, at first, but slowly, as it hung, it turned brown. She cooked eels and little fish on a small charcoal burner on the back step.

She did not seem unhappy; she giggled often and ate heartily, smacking her lips. She smiled directly into the eyes of the neighbour ladies who had yet to think of one single thing to say to her other than, 'Lovely morning isn't it?' They didn't know what to call her; nobody had told them her name. So that when the first one, the most kindly, called her Mrs Lowinger and Keiko bowed in acknowledgement, that became her name. In this way Keiko was ensconced in the family and on the street. Days and weeks and months went by and Vera continued courting her grandfather and taunting his young wife, his not-wife. The word for Keiko, which Vera was to learn later, was *aisho*.

Vera was conscientious at school. She too had friends, ordinary girls in tunics and curled hair and rolled stockings; girls who were taking stenography courses and already had boyfriends. But like Keiko she did not like her friends to come to the house or perhaps they did not like to come to the house. Perhaps they had been told not to come. She was never certain. The girls didn't tease her, just as the neighbours didn't shun Keiko; that would be too obvious and they were all good Christians. They admired the old man they called Captain James. They were a little afraid of Vera: she was austere and thin. People did whisper that she had changed. It was *an irregular situation*, as her teachers said, in that house. They praised the girl for her English composition and her skill at volleyball. For being good to her grandfather. They did notice that she grew thinner and whiter (nothing but rice in that house!), and that she lost interest in her friends, and ran off to the warehouse every day when the bell rang. She'd taken it to heart they said, the death of a mother. What could be worse for a girl that age?

But Vera did not think of Belle. She did not, she believed, miss her mother. She could see past her mother now. Where once Belle had loomed, billowy and anxious-eyed, in the doorway between childhood and real life, now there was an absence, an exhilaration. The passageway was visible. Every day after school she parted from her schoolmates at the gate. She ran past the boys for the streetcar along Granville. On the boisterous streets of Gastown, still running, she neatly dodged little gangs of sailors and men with carpets braced over their shoulders and policemen who might ask her why she was at large. It was cold and the rain penetrated her coat; the sleeves were too short because she was growing so fast. The sky was glowering with low clouds; at the edge of the water in the reflected neon lights, red and green, bark and kelp floated on oily smears. She breathed in the air through her nostrils and felt free.

It would be twilight as she climbed the stairs on Homer Street. Through the fogged glass of the window in the upper half of the door she could see the green shade of Miss Hinchcliffe's desk lamp. She tossed down her bag of books on the chair with the curved wooden arms and bade an offhand hello to Miss Hinchcliffe. Miss Hinchcliffe might have been about to leave for the night, but now that Vera had arrived she'd stay on. And from down the hall came the dry roll of her grandfather's voice. 'Is that you, Vera?'

'It's me all right!' She shed the wet coat and hoisted it to the coat tree, and sitting in the captain's chair, prised off her Oxfords one by one. In her sock feet she slid on the green linoleum to his door and peeked in. Her grandfather's long narrow jaw seemed to hang a little nearer the blotter, as the curve in his spine deepened.

'Hello, dear.' He put his hands on the arms of his chair and pushed himself to his feet. He wavered halfway up, and then, with an extra push, stood.

She kissed his cheek. He smelled sweeter now. Like an old thing. It was death approaching, or maybe all the fish Keiko fed him. He smelled like a grandfather, not a sea captain. Of clean cotton and sweet tobacco and only a hint of the ocean.

'Just let me deal with Miss Hinchcliffe and I'll be back,' Vera said.

Her presence at Lowinger and McBean had changed from being that of a visitor and a child to that of a watcher, and a keeper. Vera had adopted a bustle, as if she actually had jobs to

50

do in the office. She stood in front of Hinchcliffe's desk. 'Did the shipment come in? Did he meet the man from Birks?' She wanted to make sure that these visitors conveyed their needs to him, and not to the secretary.

Miss Hinchcliffe faced Vera with an ironic twist to her mouth. She protected the old man, but he refused to be endangered. Her expression said that Vera was a child and childhood was a phase; it would end, and she would go on to another passion, while she, Hinchcliffe would remain permanently on guard at her desk.

While Vera stood wishing she could get rid of Hinchcliffe. The secretary was like a foreign power. Her grandfather would find this ridiculous, of course. If she complained he would only chuckle; he would never say a word against anyone. He said the office couldn't be run without her. Hinchcliffe sometimes complained of Vera as well.

'She doesn't need to come here day after day,' the older woman said. 'She's taking up a great deal of our time.'

And James chuckled over that, too.

'Did he have lunch?' Vera asked.

'He won't eat the sandwiches,' said Miss Hinchcliffe. The sandwiches came around every day from a man with a cart; they'd been coming to everyone in the block for years. 'That Japanese housekeeper has got him used to noodles. That's all he wants.'

Vera bridled. Keiko was Vera's to insult, not Miss Hinchcliffe's.

'She is not the housekeeper,' Vera said.

'What is she then?' said Miss Hinchcliffe daringly.

Vera ostentatiously let her jaw drop open. You dare to ask?

'Does she not cook the meals?' Implied was, such as they are. A long pointed stare at Vera's concave midriff.

'Yes,' said Vera. 'She doesn't actually cook much. Mostly we eat raw fish.' She said this to annoy.

Miss Hinchcliffe rolled her eyes. 'It isn't my place –' she began, but Vera could see that she did think it was her place.

'I don't think that –' Vera flipped her plank of long, thin, blonde hair.

No one finished what they began to say.

51

Vera retreated to the table where the woodcut prints were kept. Someone had put out a set of three. She wondered if her grandfather had been looking at them. Or if he had left them there for her to look at.

'Did you see those?' he said, appearing at the door of his office, poking his head in, his large sinking head with the handlebar moustaches still hoisted to the horizontal. 'Quite lovely. You can spend plenty of time lost in there.' Idly, as if it didn't really matter, he turned away.

The three prints had been enclosed in a folder, which lay beside them. On the front of the folder was written, in fading blue ink, in a hand that Vera did not recognise, *Three Views of Crystal Water*.

James disappeared back into his office, telling her they'd go for coffee in a few minutes, and she was left alone with the pictures.

The first view was of a seashore, seen from the top of a dune, as if an observer were crouched there unseen. Near the edge of the water was a circle of women, standing and sitting. They had built a small fire and it was this that drew them together, as if they were warming themselves. They did not huddle and shiver, but stood, tall, and elegant, revelling in their beauty. The women wore only a loose fabric draped over their hips, leaving belly and breasts bare. They were wet, hair dripping down their bare backs. Around their feet were baskets.

It was strange to name this a view of water, because the women were the interesting part, an even dozen of them, with their gently curved arms and their modesty, which she could feel, despite their nakedness. There was a child with them. The child had a small string bag of shells in her hand and a little three-pronged rake. The child's clothing matched the women's red underrobes. They had all covered their heads with a white kerchief with blue leaves. They had been in the water and had come out, and these baskets held their catch, perhaps seashells, or fish, although Vera could see no means of catching fish in the picture.

Yet, she realised, as she continued to look, more than half the picture was water. It was flat and turquoise close in, and, where rocks stood up from the surface, transparent: you could see through to the base of the rocks beneath. But out from this shore, the sea reached from one side of the paper to the other and up to a flat horizon. There were waves drawn on it, hard white lines marching relentlessly one after another. The sea was not easy for the small boats that dotted it.

She put the print aside. In the second print the crystal water was black and without waves. The sky was dark, but Vera guessed it was nearly dawn. There were stars, like pricks of white; the artist had copied these stars into asterisks of white in the water as well. Two people, their faces hidden in travelling robes that half covered kimonos of orange and peacock blue, were on a graceful, arched bridge that crossed a stream of water. Drawn together by equal forces from opposite sides to the highest point of the arch, they seemed to tremble there. They were not facing, but back to back: each had walked a few steps past the other, as if they had tried to pass by, but could not. There was danger in the air, and yearning. The woman reached back, a long tapered hand emerging from her robe; she handed the man a letter.

Vera gazed long and hard at this one. It was a very satisfying picture, with the deep black and the royal blue, and the orange patterns of both the kimonos, and the white letter changing hands. Whatever secret was here was successfully passed; she felt relief.

She lifted that print and put it to the side, revealing the last of the three.

In the third view, there had been a catastrophe. It was snowing and the ground was white. But on the horizon, far back in the picture, a pagoda was in flames, turning the sky orange. A road wound through skeletal trees from the gates of that pagoda down to the centre bottom of the picture, and on that road were two hooded women. One was on horseback; the other stood beside her. They wore black and white cloaks with pointed black hoods that draped over the sides of their faces, half concealing them. The mounted woman held a long spear with a curved blade. Vera understood that she would journey through danger, and must protect herself and her younger charge. Behind them, outside the pagoda gate, was a fearsome warrior in laced armour, brandishing his sword. He was their scourge, or their protector. His skirts flew up revealing thick legs in sandals, and the scabbard from his curved sword.

At first Vera didn't see the crystal water. But there, under the snow-laden branch of a tree was a stream. Unfrozen, the water bubbled over rocks. Aside from the roaring of the flames it would be the only sound. The women would follow its path to safety.

Vera wondered who had named these 'Three Views of Crystal Water'. The pictures belonged together, and therefore they must tell a story. But it was not clear where the story began.

She stared at the three prints, making up a story that would put them in order. Twelve women went to the seashore to fish and were seen by a stranger. The stranger fell in love with one of the women; but she was promised, or bound. Her trusted servant met him in the dead of night and gave him a letter telling him to go away, that all was lost. However, he would not go away. Instead he set fire to the pagoda and killed everyone in it except the woman and her servant, who escaped, while he watched over the destruction he had wrought.

'Ready!' called James.

That day, they made their way down the few steps, next door to the flatiron building where Roberta presided, the Captain stepping gallantly but perhaps a little more slowly than the season before. Vera could see Roberta turn to warn the waiting others. Because by now it was known on Homer Street that the old merchant would come in. And he had an audience. There was the hatter, and a printer with inky hands, and another few traders, in rugs and fabrics. There was Kemp who also traded with Japan, and sometimes his son. There was Malcolm the mailman, if he'd finished his run. Vera and James nodded to the gathered audience, and went to their booth. Roberta's fierce hand with her damp cloth swept across the table; they watched her midriff at eye level against the tabletop and heard her voice asking what they would have.

'The usual,' James said. And then exclaimed 'Wet!' with fresh surprise, as if it had never been wet before. 'Wet today, Roberta.' He surveyed the other coffee drinkers, now studying their napkins or gazing out of one window or the other to one street or the other. 'Quite a crowd here today! Afternoon, Kemp.'

'If it isn't Lowinger, of Lowinger and McBean,' said Kemp. 'Where's that son-in-law of yours? I heard he was in Madagascar. No, it was Marrakesh.'

They slid into their chairs. Vera was conscious that they made an odd pair, the old man and the girl.

'I don't know,' said her grandfather. 'He hasn't been home for some time. Since . . .' his voice trailed off. He always stopped talking when Belle or Hamilton Drew came to his mind. Soon after their marriage, they had moved here. Drew had been given the task of keeping the portside office open. The idea was to branch out from pearls. Canadian Pacific had plenty of steamships going to Japan and coming back with imported goods. Smart merchants bought them and divided them up and put them in new packages and sent them on. It was not easy to lose. But Hamilton . . .

Vera tried to picture her father. Was he part of her distant childhood? It seemed to her there had been a pram, and a sweet tooth for toffee. 'I turned around and he was absent.' That's what her grandfather said about his own father. She remembered her mother crying.

This time James kept talking. 'The trouble with my son-in-law,' he said dramatically. He knew he had an audience. 'The trouble is he was too late.'

'Too late for what?'

'Just too late. For everything. He's an imitator. Never had a thought of his own. Never could go his own way. Like the real people do.' He sputtered to a stand still. Then he started again. 'The trouble with your father was he was Scottish.'

Vera laughed at that one. Just one more reason her grandfather gave for not liking him.

He peered at Vera. 'You're thin, you're pale, too, young lady. Are you eating properly? You know Keiko makes very good meals.'

Vera smiled primly.

'You don't want to be sickly.'

Unspoken words to follow were 'like your mother'.

She was branching out too, from white food. She ate the cinnamon toast: the sugar and bread were white at least.

He laughed his pebbly laugh, the one she had come to love, the one of true mirth – as opposed to the other, hollow draining that was not a laugh but a view of the world.

He sipped his coffee. He had developed a tremor, and it spilled in the saucer. 'You're not going to try to get me to talk about pearls today.'

'Everybody's here and waiting.'

'Nonsense. They're here to have their coffee.'

James Lowinger liked to go out with the pearl divers, to see the stone go overboard and the men stand on it and let it carry them down to the bottom, like the lifts in the flat in London. They swarmed across the sea bed all arms and legs, as if they could stay down for ever. He wished he could do it. The rest of it he hated.

It was six years after his first visit, and the British had again announced that there would be a great harvest. His father got bidding for the rights to the oysters, and up went the price and down went the sun and suddenly it was his. He bought it all. The boats returned with hundreds of thousands of oysters, one in a thousand of which might have a pearl. The overseers slung the bags out of the boats and onto the sand.

Now, what to do? Papa Lowinger could hire the natives to open the shells. But then he still needed men to search for pearls. The larger pearls would be hidden in the hinge of the oyster. To remove such a pearl you've got to use bare hands and a special prising, cutting tool. So he had to trust some workers. And there were none he trusted. He could chain them and forbid them to chew their blasted betel nut because they would hide any pearls they found in their teeth, and punish them if they did. But he didn't want the bother, or the brutality of it.

Happily some pearls came loose by themselves and turned up in the silt that built up at the bottom of the tubs. The pearls he found he bottled and sent back to London. But he still had hundreds upon thousands of oysters. He found a place outside Condatchey Bay, where the natives lived. He dumped his oysters in open tubs and they did their part like the docile creatures that they were and began to rot.

There was just one problem. The stench. It grew. In the heat, the dead molluscs smelled absolutely vile. And the smell clung; it did not blow away or dissipate after dark. Day after day, a week, two weeks, there was still the stink of it and more oysters coming in on the boats every day. The village rose up in protest and demanded that the English take the oysters away. But they were poor people and the natives needed the pearling fleets, and the traders persuaded them to let them stay on until they finished.

To keep an eye on the locals, James and his father stayed in a hastily built hut on the beach. James walked on the sand at night, looking at the stars, but it was impossible to escape the smell. He was ashamed. Of the filth. Of the big English brutes with their whips. Of the smell of death. He sometimes wondered if he himself were rotting.

When the rotting was done, and the oysters nearly water,

they hired the women and children. They were the poorest of the poor – no one else would do it. Mostly naked they waded in to the mass of decomposing oyster flesh, and felt around on the bottom for pearls. They were up to their armpits in it, and kneeling, gagging at having their faces so close. His father's men patrolled the edges of the pit with whips. James's father himself was on a horse. From the height of his seat he saw an old crone slip a pearl into her mouth. He caught her before she swallowed and took her away and bound her to the mast in the hot sun and whipped her until she was nearly crippled.

At nights in their ramshackle house on the beach his papa swore about the greedy government that opened the fishery every year so that the pearls were getting smaller. James went out again to walk on the beach and saw the sun set over India. This is the family business, he thought to himself. This is how Mother got her fine hats and many schoolbooks.

The next day at dawn they woke to find a squad of local officials on the beach.

'Move on,' the men were shouting, 'Go! Away with you!'

They waved their arms. The workers scrambled out of their tents half awake. The officials kicked in their direction, and began to fling sticks at them. The workers began to collect their few small possessions.

Papa came out of the little house to remonstrate. He put on his best manners.

'Friends! Colleagues! What can I help you with?'

But he was confronted by a short, fat man, who had no small-talk. The Englishman had bought the right to hire the divers and bring up the oysters, he said, but he had not bought the right to let them rot there. He must move on.

'Impossible,' said Lowinger. 'I cannot move this operation, which brings prosperity to you as well as to me. As you see. We are in the midst –'

Ceylon had anticipated his dilemma, said the fat man. In

58

this case the government would help them out by taking two thirds of the oysters as a royalty.

By dark of night they moved on to another village, which had very few people. The oysters continued to appear, every day, on the boats from the pearl banks. James's papa hoped the government did not notice him this time. He built huts and disguised them with palm branches. They dug trenches and lay the oysters down in them and caused water to run through to clean them. But still they smelled. The police came, but he bribed the police: the oysters were almost decomposed. When the inhabitants began to complain of the stench, he bribed them too.

Dead matter does not give way easily. As the oysters rotted they were infested with larvae and these larvae gave a man strange diseases. While the cleaning went on they had to have a big bonfire burning. It helped with the smell. One man fell into the flames and was burned; he was bitten by flies then and died of oozing infections.

Men's lungs were damaged. The Chinese coolies seemed to manage the best. The old ladies who waded in the stuff, filtering all that dead flesh through their fingers, seemed indestructible but sometimes one would fall over and nearly drown.

There were flies everywhere. James could not breathe the air; it was oppression, and a plague upon the earth. They tried to clean it up. But more oysters kept coming out of the sea, every day. Lowinger had bought a share of the whole harvest, and the harvest was a good one. He moved from town to town but the locals refused to let him warehouse his putrefying little shellfish, pearls inside or no pearls inside.

At night in their house on the beach – once again, a shack made of boards thrown together, poles and a tin roof – James asked his father to pull up and leave. But no. Oh no, where pearls were concerned, Papa could always come up with a new idea.

When the next batch came ashore Papa produced four huge boxes lined with tin. They were like double-sized coffins. The tin was supposed to keep the smell in, and to stop any leakage when the flesh of the oysters started to go, as inevitably it would go, on the sea voyage to England. He had plans to ship the four large tin-lined boxes to England to be washed on the River Ouse at Buxted where there was running water. He had got a merchant ship to agree to take them. He sent the crates by ox cart to Colombo.

But there was some delay in the shipping. It could have been a storm; perhaps the ship needed repair or took another, better-paying load. The boxes sat sealed in the harbour. The oysters started to decompose and when they decomposed they set off the same disgusting smell, only this time it was enclosed.

James and his father went in to Colombo to pay the boxes a visit. James gave them a wary look. The smell was coming out through the hinges. He stared at the containers and thought he could hear popping sounds inside. There were chemical changes as oyster flesh decomposed, and those changes produced gas. He had an awful premonition.

The two entrepreneurs were not around when it happened. They were back at Condatchey Bay dragging more oysters out of the sea. But they heard about the explosions soon after. The gas blew open the tin-lined cases, and the explosion was heard all over Colombo. The air was fouled and the sky blackened for miles around. The smoke had not cleared when the government authorities were on the trail of the Lowingers, father and son.

They were little wiry men not far removed from the ones Lowinger hired to go down and shorten their lives under water. He scoffed at them all. But these authorities were impervious to insult. They responded by seizing the ruptured cases. They took them away and buried them; no one knew where, but James heard a report they'd gone by in bullock carts toward the jungle.

James's father sat and fumed in his beach house. He made his son's life hell, carping on about his schoolwork and having him write out algebraic equations. That made James anxious to go home to England, but his father wouldn't abandon his oysters.

Then they had a visitor. A man came riding along the beach on his horse, a military man who, like many of the soldiers in Ceylon, had taken an administrative post in the local government. Add to that he gambled a little in the pearl market. His name was Avery McBean.

They'd all met before. He hailed them and then he jumped down off his horse. And who was behind him in the saddle, but that overdressed girl with her pout. Except now she was fifteen and on the cusp of beauty and thought herself even grander than once she had. James hated her on sight. She did not move from the saddle; she was six feet up on the horse and probably couldn't. The conversation took place like that, with the girl watching from above.

'We've impounded the tin-lined cases,' said McBean. 'We had to build new lids, for which incidentally, we'll charge you. The exciting news is that we found pearls in there just as beautiful and just as big as you'd find elsewhere. However they are the property of the government. And you're in a deficit situation, Lowinger.'

After the ranting and raving settled down, McBean offered friendly advice. He had figured out the system. You'd not see him buying up lots of unopened oysters. The only smart thing was to buy from the small independent boatmen who will wash a small quantity of the oysters themselves.

'They'll do you every time,' said McBean, infuriatingly calm with his Scottish burr. 'They see that the English are greedy and their greed makes them desperate and a desperate man has little success outwitting molluscs or little wiry brown men.' *The English*, he said, as if he were somehow in a different category.

61

'Thank you very much,' said the senior Lowinger, 'but you are wrong.'

'Aye, if you say so,' said McBean easily. 'You'll find out the wisdom of my words, sooner or later.'

And the girl sat like a princess on her steed. She smirked down on James. Neither child nor woman, she was something alarmingly in between. He squirmed. He went pale under his hot red face. She parted her perfect lips and stuck out her tongue at him. Then she giggled and rolled her eyes at her father. James smiled, uncertainly.

McBean got on his horse and whirled around.

She looked back over her shoulder and blew James a kiss.

He would never be free of her.

Vera hated to see her grandfather in his bed. For years she had heard people reassuring Belle that since the old man had been all over the world, he'd come home safe and sound and end his days with her. It was what you were supposed to do when you led a life of great danger. 'He'll likely die in his bed.'

Therefore, Vera thought bed was the most dangerous place for him to be. She tried to drag him out of it, in the morning. Some days he would shake his head, and go limp, as if all the energy had drained away under the sheets. She would jump on top and rumple up the sheets, prodding him, until he roared for her to go away. He would not come out of his room before she left for school, and those days were not good days for algebra and geography. Vera would worry about him and race to the streetcar for Homer Street as soon as the bell rang for the end of classes. When she burst in the door, her eyes would go first to Hinchcliffe's face for any clue of mishap, and then to her grandfather's office door. He'd be in there, a little pale, perhaps, and sinking into his chin. On the way to coffee she would hold his arm at every step he took.

But on other mornings he gamely shook her off with the lion's roar she wanted, and said he'd be up just as soon as she left him alone. He would wash, and put on his white shirt for the office. Vera would pay a little better attention in school but still make haste for Homer Street immediately after.

On Sundays – most Sundays, if it wasn't raining – they walked. This particular Sunday the sun was shining. They started at English Bay. James wore a wide straw hat, and Keiko wore a headscarf, blue with white figures on it. People glanced at them, as they passed, no doubt thinking they were an odd group. But Keiko never seemed to notice. She loved the bleached, lost logs that rolled in on the tide and was forever marvelling.

'So big, so big,' she said. 'Where from are they?'

'They've been logged somewhere up north I suppose,' said James. 'And sent down in a log boom, and got loose from it.'

'Oh, oh,' said Keiko.

Vera liked the kelp with its beads of bright green, which she could squeeze between her fingers and pop. She wandered down to the water to pull up some kelp and back to her grandfather to walk beside him, and away again to walk along a log and hop over another tangle of them, teetering on a rock. No one told her not to now. Her mother had loved to walk on the beach too, and they would pick up shells, and sometimes sit in the lee of the sea wall, looking at what they'd found. But her mother had been nervous of the sea and especially of Vera on the beach, afraid she'd be swept away or fall off a log. They talked about her mother a little then. How she had gone to boarding school in England. How he had been out of touch for so long, until she came to Paris. 'We all lived together then,' said James Lowinger reflectively. 'Until she found Hamilton Drew. Or he found her.'

They reached the path through Stanley Park.

Keiko was different here from the woman she was at home.

She seemed to have known the water for a long time. She cast an expert eye on the rivulets and the bubbles in the sand and knew exactly what rock to pick up to find the crabs. She walked beside James, head inclined toward him, attentive to his words and to his step, if it faltered. But she was also listening to the wind on the water, and smelling the salt. Sometimes she stood and scanned the horizon.

'Weather changing,' she would say, or, 'tide changing.'

'Keiko knows all about the sea,' James would say, squeezing her elbow. 'All my life I have wanted a girl just like her. A deep diver,' he would say. Then he would laugh, that dry chuckle that wasn't really aimed at anyone. 'Has all my life come to this?' he said. 'Do I talk about it as if it was over? I suppose it will be, soon. I suppose I could begin to sum it up.'

They went as far as the benches at First Beach before he sat. Keiko had tea in a thermos. She poured some into the tiny china cup that she brought for him. And when he spoke his eyes looked far out to the east as if there might appear, on the horizon, one of the great sailing ships he'd been on as a boy.

'At weddings, the Indians used to bring up a pearl from the bottom of the sea and bore it through with a hole to symbolize the taking of a maidenhead. You wouldn't understand –'

'Of course I would. Do you think I'm an infant?'

'We did it when your mother married that man, my son-in-law.'

'You hate my father,' said Vera sadly.

'We saw through him, that's all. It wasn't difficult. We saw him for what he was. An opportunist. I saw that in him maybe even before he saw it. But your mother was determined. You couldn't stop her. Even her mother couldn't stop her. She said she'd give her a wedding and give her a pearl and give her away and that would be the end of it. Never speak to her again. And she never did.'

He shook his head and laughed again without humour, out of amazement, perhaps. 'Far as I knew. Of course she wasn't speaking to me either. When she stepped up to the priest Belle wore one rosee pearl in each ear, a perfect match they were. Your grandmother got them in Kuwait and had kept them all that time.' He looked very thoughtful then. 'She sold everything she could make a gain on. They were freshwater pearls from the bottom of the sea. It's a magical thing, that. We also took our pension pearls and made a necklace so close to the earrings you'd have sworn they came out of sister shells. They got married and that was that. Hamilton Drew took it all. He took my daughter. He took the pearls. He took –'

He stopped.

'What did he take?'

The old man thought about it for a while.

'He took my name, that's what he took. He took my good name and used it for his own ends.' He brooded and when he spoke again he was back on the Romans.

'You know Seneca had to chastise Roman women for wearing so many pearls. You can read about it, go look it up. Emperor Caligula's widow wore pearls in rows and lines all around her head, her bodice, her sleeves and her hem. She wore them hanging from her ears, around her neck, on her wrists, and on her fingers. When she went out into the streets people had to look away so as not to be blinded. And it became the fashion. Ladies began to wear them on their feet, on their shoe buckles, in the thongs between their toes and between their legs too, no doubt.

'Do you know why Rome invaded Britain? Your teachers probably told you something about Gauls and Caesar. But that's all hooey. The real reason was the Romans wanted British pearls. They were freshwater pearls, found in lakes and streams, small and of poor colour, some said. But the Romans were desperate. The rage for pearls consumed them. Finally they had to pass laws, prohibiting persons of lower rank and unmarried women from wearing them. This greatly increased the number of marriages, as you can imagine.

'But you see – and here's the rub, my dears – pearls have always been connected with wars and theft and ugliness. It's just the opposite of all that purity. Conquered people had to pay a tribute in pearls, just as they did in women, and in slaves. There was once a battle lost by an emperor called Pezores. I don't remember what country was his. But he wore an unrivalled pearl in his right ear. Just as he was about to be killed by his enemies, Pezores tore this pearl from his ear and threw it ahead of him into the pit. Emperor Anastasius, the victor, was furious. He promised five hundred gold pieces to anyone who would comb the pit, full of dead men and dead horses. And hundreds did, pawing through that gore. But no one found the pearl. It was lost for ever, with the dead.'

Here James Lowinger shook his head. Vera knew they were talking about her mother again. And Keiko screwed the lid of the thermos back on, and put the tiny china cup back in the cloth bag that she hung around her waist, and they stood up and turned back along the beach.

It was as if he had run into a wall.

What was the wall? Vera wondered. It was the wall of death, perhaps. Belle had gone into it. Her grandmother, the Captain's wife, must have gone into it, and now he himself was looking at it.

On Sundays when it rained, Keiko kept James at home. He coughed now, and when he coughed his whole body was wracked. Vera went out alone. She walked in the grey drizzle and thought about pearls, and slaves, and women. A fresh pearl white and perfect was beautiful. It had a value beyond price. But a marred pearl was worthless. A woman about to be married was 'bored' by a man; an eel could prise open the oyster shell and feed on the animal inside, swallowing the pearl as well.

James Lowinger could talk about pearls in literature, he could talk about pearls in history, pearls of the conquered and the conquerors. But any story hung subject to cancellation, as he rambled. Her grandfather said he did not want to tell. But he did want to tell. It was as if he had come home to tell her something. But the story began long ago; he could not tell it all at once.

'You know I don't want my stories falling on the wrong ears,' he said, teasing.

'Who do you mean?'

He put his finger alongside his nose. 'You know who I mean.'

'You don't mean Keiko?'

Of course he didn't. He held out his hand to her; his face was lit with the pleasure he felt in her nearness.

'You mean Miss Hinchcliffe?'

'Don't be ridiculous, Vera. She is no more than a functionary.'

'You mean my father then.'

'Oh, interesting suggestion. My son-in law,' he said. 'My *erstwhile* son-in-law.' James Lowinger took full responsibility for the error in judgement that had put Hamilton into the family: this weak link was his, not his beloved Belle's and certainly not Vera's. 'What an unnatural cruelty! Do I still have a son-in-law when I have no daughter?'

Some days he mentioned the book again. Some days he said he had already got it half written. But he certainly would not finish. The problem was, he said –

'I know, Grandfather. It puts you into an impossible struggle between truth and loyalty. You told me.'

'Good girl, you remember.'


When James was ill Keiko nursed him and Vera went to school in a rage and fought with her friends and went after school to Homer Street, even though he was not there, to stare at the *ukiyo-e*. A silent Miss Hinchcliffe sat over her typewriter.

'Where is Mr McBean?' Vera asked her.

'There is no Mr McBean.'

Vera did not believe this.

'But his name is on the door,' she said stubbornly. 'See? Lowinger and McBean.'

Miss Hinchcliffe smiled in a pinched way. 'I know it seems that way.'

'Is he in the Far East, the way my father is?'

'I told you there is no one called Mr McBean.'

'Wherever he is, it is time for him to come back,' said Vera.

'Aren't you going to go for coffee?' Hinchcliffe would say.

'Not by myself,'

One day when James was ill in bed, Kemp came down from the office above and took Vera to the coffee shop with him. When they burst in through the door shaking rain from their umbrellas, Roberta looked up with hope that the Captain would be with them. Malcolm the mailman was there, at the end of his rounds. The hatter was telling stories about the sailors and how one would come ashore and buy a smart hat, a Borsalino, say. Then he'd go on a big tear and lose it. The hatter could go around the bars and pick up lost hats in the morning if he felt like it. And the next day, before his leave was up, the sailor would come back and buy the same one again.

They murmured appreciatively at this homely story and then it was silent in the triangular café with its three booths.

Roberta said, 'How is he?'

And Vera burst into tears.

The men sat embarrassed while Roberta took Vera in her arms and patted her on the back.

'What are we going to do with her?' she said to the others.

James Lowinger lay in his bed. His veins stood out under the skin on his head. Vera had not imagined that a head could get thinner, but his had. His flesh was clinging to his skull. He lay with his eyes shut but his voice did not change and he could still laugh so that it sounded even more as if his voice were gurgling down a drain. Day by day he grew lighter, his face more luminous. It was as if he were getting younger, on a cosmic timescale that had nothing to do with the days and the months and the years they were living through.

He spoke to Vera in a valedictory way.

'A longing, almost like lust, to tell the tale as we have lived it, grows stronger the older we are. God knows that man's lust is a subject of which I have some experience. I mean only the lust for objects. I say "only", as if this were more manageable, more civilised than sexual lust: it is not, only an expression that has a more public acceptance.

'I have no greed for gems or gold, which may strike you as odd. Indifference is rare in my trade and the one aspect of my personality to which my survival can be attributed. My lust inclines to the private and the physical, far healthier if you ask me. And for much of my life I was unsatisfied. It made me a good observer of others mind you. That is the story – how their lust entwined with mine.'

There were good days and bad days. Keiko heard news in Japantown that made her cry, and she wrote letters home, letters to which she got no replies. She found one man in Japantown who was from Kobe, and every few days she went to hear his news. But the letters he received were vague, and in contradiction to the news she heard in Vancouver. In Japan the people said the war in China was going well. Papers came to call up men and boys, and this was an honour, to serve the Emperor. Here, the papers said the Japanese were going to lose the war in China, and that the soldiers themselves were poor and hungry, and the people in Japan were even hungrier.

One day, while visiting her friend in the tailor's shop, Keiko heard about the drowning of a fisherman. Although he was no one Keiko knew, and from a village many miles from her own, she was struck with dire premonitions and went home silent. While she was washing the dishes after dinner she told Vera about the sea near her home.

'It can be dangerous if you don't know. Every child is made to swim. The father throws –' here she demonstrated with her hands cupped at the level of her knees, as if she were pushing a large bag of laundry over a wall '– throws the child over the boat into the sea. And watches. The child will go down and breathe in the water. The child will nearly drown –' she mimed choking, dying, 'then the father will dive in and bring the child back. But as soon as the child has' – she acted out spitting out the water '– the father again –' she made the scooping motion with her arms '– into the sea. Second time, the child knows how to swim. Anyone who learn to swim that way – while going down to drown – is safe for ever.'

She did not bother James with her worries. He was very busy in his half-conscious world. At times he needed her care, calling out weakly, but good-naturedly, for tea. Sometimes he was sick on himself, and she came with a basin and towels to clean him. But he was often asleep. In his sleep he expended a great deal of energy. He thrashed and sometimes spoke, and even laughed, or scoffed, at imaginary companions in his dreams.

'He simply must eat more,' said the doctor.

'He eat what he want,' said Keiko.

But to Vera she explained. 'He is fighting demons. Meeting old friends. It is very much work. That's why he is so thin. He dreams away his food.' She backed away from the bedside when the doctor came to look at James but she did not take her eyes off him.

The doctor did not push further. 'He is old,' he said. 'He has come home to die, like an animal does.'

Keiko bowed and did not contradict the doctor. But when she and Vera were alone she spoke. 'An animal does not come home to die,' said Keiko. 'An animal crawls away by himself. He come home for other thing.'

'What other thing?' Vera hung by her grandfather's bedside and when he spoke she listened. Open, his eyes burned red at the rims and bright blue in the centre; his collarbones under the pyjama top stood up higher. Often she watched him sleep. Even then his eyes were busy under the lids.

'Are you going to the office today?' Vera asked, tearful, at the bedroom door.

'I don't think so, my dear. You'll have to go for me.'

She went, crying.


As James Lowinger lay dying, he knew he'd been wrong about what was important. He'd been wrong about pearls, and even wrong about the stories. They were in the past. Soon he too would be in the past, and join his stories there. They were on record and official; in them he was clearly in command. They were of the mind and, in the life of his body, they were utterly worthless.

He sank into his body.

He sang, he wrestled, he suckled, he grappled and he danced with the love of his life in those last few hours. He lived to the full reach of his senses without fear or guilt, because what was to be regretted, now? He knew that Keiko came and went from the room with her basin and her cool cloth; he knew that she knelt beside him. He supposed, even, that she understood he had descended into a realm of pure delight, or rather that the world had risen away from him. He no longer felt the pain of Belle's death, a pain he had tried hard to hide. He was loosed to his own flesh and every bliss it had to offer. That day, he lived one night, over and over. When it finally eased away he was ready, this time, to let go.

When Vera came home he was gone.

Keiko was quietly washing his body.

'He works so hard,' she said, 'to die. He –' and she acted out the thrashings and groans that had mysteriously accompanied his last hours. 'And he –' she closed her eyes and allowed a wide smile to cover her face.

Vera slapped her across the cheek.

Keiko stood with the red marks of Vera's fingers spreading sideways over her cheekbone, and a well of deeper crimson, rage perhaps, climbing from her chest to suffuse her face. She said nothing. Vera burst into tears and ran from the room.

*    *    *

What can happen after a girl has fallen in love with her grandfather and with the storied life of her grandfather and his father too? Only one thing. The grandfather can die.

And that is what he did.

He died.

Not very original of him.

He couldn't be blamed; he was old. All Vera knew was that here was the same thing all over again. Her mother, her grandfather. Her loved one, the one who took care of her, suddenly gone from his frame, leaving behind the waxy white flesh.

How did he die? She can't tell you. She forgot about his warnings, his readiness for it. It seemed to her that at one moment he was there, entertaining the regulars in the coffee shop, and the next – when he had tricked her, by asking her to go on without him, leaving him with Keiko – he let go of his life.

It was as if Vera had just come through a sickness herself; she had been asleep and now she was awake.

The neighbours came out of their houses to help. He had to have a Christian burial, they said to each other. There was just Keiko and Vera, and Keiko had no idea what to do. Besides, none of the officials they dealt with would give her any standing, would allow her to be in charge. It had to be Vera. But Vera was fifteen. They spoke of the embalming, the funeral home, the grave site, and the cost of it all. Hinchcliffe took the bills out of Vera's hands.

Keiko inclined her head at all these conversations, taking note of what was said although no one was sure she understood it. Her young face was unlined and patient and endlessly *correct*. Vera hated that. She gave herself licence to be awful to the woman, by behaving either with exquisite iciness or appalling rudeness, to keep her guessing.

A crowd of neighbours and Gastown merchants came to the funeral. *How sad*, they said, and *wonderful man*, as they came up to shake Vera's hand. She stood between Miss Hinchcliffe and Keiko at the door to the visiting room in the funeral parlour. She did not like the way Hinchcliffe had taken over, but then who was to do it? Her mind spun with the nursery rhymes her mother had read to her. Parlour, she thought, come into my parlour said the spider to the fly. Hark, hark, the dogs do bark. Wednesday's child is full of woe. The parlour was all burgundy and varnished wood and there was no air in it. There was no smell of the sea, not even in Grandfather's clothes, because Keiko had cleaned everything so well.

The minister came; he hugged Vera and said that it was very hard, so soon after her mother's death. The Captain did not go to the church the way her mother had. But he had lived a good life.

'A good life?' protested Vera. What could the insipid word 'good' mean in the days of James Lowinger? Did they mean he should have been content to die, as if he'd taken a large helping of life and ought not to be greedy? In fact his life was huge and sometimes horrible, but marvellous, and not to be taken away from her. She had asked for his stories but she could not piece it all together, or make a wholeness out of it.

'He saw a great deal of the world, I suppose,' said the minister dubiously.

Keiko knelt beside the coffin. Although they tried, no one could displace her. She sat on her heels and her face was on her hands, which were flat on the floor, folded up like a fan. She raised her body from time to time, and bowed, and then went back down, with no expression on her face. Like the women in the prints, Vera thought.

Vera's schoolteacher got down on his knees beside her, trying to shake her hand.

'Miss Tanaka?' he said. He alone had troubled to discover her name.

When she wouldn't raise her head he put his down on the

floor beside hers and said loudly, as if to wake a sleeper, 'Thank you so much for taking good care of Vera.'

He was the only one.

But it was because he thought that it was over, Keiko's taking care of Vera.

'I suppose her father will come,' said the neighbours.

No one had thought of Hamilton Drew.

'And your father? Will he be coming home?' asked the minister.

Vera looked at Hinchcliffe.

'We are attempting to locate him,' the secretary said with a firm smile. 'I have wired. I have also sent a letter. I am not certain where he is . . .'

And then they all went home.

And it was silent.

James Lowinger did not wake up and shake the house with his morning sneezes. And there was no bustle to get his morning tea or his shoes and no secret laughter coming from that room and no secret tears either, which was what Vera hoped for. She wanted Keiko to suffer. She wanted Keiko to show on her face the desolation of Vera's insides. Since she had the temerity to love the old man, she might as well pay the price. What did she expect, taking up with a man so much older? She had to know he would die, didn't she?

Vera's pathetic hymns of grief, her English nursery rhymes, swirled in her head. London Bridge is falling down falling down falling down. The North wind doth blow and we shall have snow, what shall we do then? He had died; old men do that, that was what they did. Maybe it was even Keiko's fault. There were many cruel things she planned to say to Keiko, but when she saw her, head bent over the little iron grill on the back step to cook fish, something moved inside of Vera and she could not.

She went to Lowinger and McBean after school. There was, temporarily, a sense of urgency in the warehouse. The captains came in their blue caps and Hinchcliffe talked to them tersely; they left again. There was no word from Hamilton Drew. Vera was curious, but not heartbroken. She did not remember the man, anyway. The business would have to keep on running, said Hinchcliffe; it could not close because they were always in the middle of a shipment, or an order, and there was no right time to stop. Vera nonetheless hoped that every day would be Miss Hinchcliffe's last. That she would stand up from her desk and put on her coat and hand over the key to Vera. But no. Hinchcliffe showed no signs of going away.

The flurry of visits soon ended. Vera planned to ransack her grandfather's office. But Hinchcliffe was there, letting nothing out in the open. She appeared to be very busy with filing and typing letters with two sheets of blue carbon paper behind them. Vera walked slowly across in front of her desk.

Was Miss Hinchcliffe sad?

Hadn't she too been in love with her grandfather?

Vera used to think that. But now she did not.

She wanted to ask her if she'd seen any signs of the book he was writing, or was going to write, the book that put him in the famous conflict between truth and loyalty, but on entering the door once more after school she thought better of it. She did not want to alert Miss Hinchcliffe. She thought of her grandfather's impish face, his long chin with the permanent dimple, his finger laid alongside his nose, and she wanted to cry, but she did not.

She wondered if the mythical Mr McBean would appear. She wondered if her father would come. Miss Hinchcliffe divulged nothing. Vera sped past her and disappeared into the back. The pictures lay where she'd left them.

*Three Views of Crystal Water*. She ran her fingers over the paper, the way he had the day she and her grandfather had looked at the pictures together. She told herself the story again. A stranger surprised the beautiful diving women taking their ease on the beach. A man and a woman crossed paths under cover of midnight on the arch of a bridge, and a letter changed hands. And then the third, conflagration: the pagoda in flames, the samurai at the gate, the women fleeing.

\*　　\*　　\*

One day Keiko came to the warehouse with Vera. She presented herself to Hinchcliffe, bowing. Hinchcliffe barely looked up.

'Honourable Miss Hinchcliffe,' Keiko began. She was still bowing.

There was no response. Hinchcliffe's neck tendons showed more definitely under her chin, that was all.

Keiko looked to Vera for guidance. 'We come to you,' she began.

Vera nudged her to stand up straight. Hinchcliffe was gazing intently at a letter she was typing.

'Hinchcliffe!' said Vera, like someone prompting a rude child.

Hinchcliffe blushed red.

'She's pretending we're not here,' said Vera to Keiko by way of explanation. Keiko understood Vera's English, but then so too did Hinchcliffe. This riled the secretary. She looked up.

'Yes, Miss Tanaka, what can I do for you?' she asked.

'We must talk about what James left for us,' said Keiko. 'He told me –'

'I have my instructions.' Hinchcliffe's face was elaborately innocent. Vera examined it closely enough however to be certain that the woman was struggling against tears.

'Instructions from who?' said Vera innocently.

'I really cannot discuss it.'

'What work are you doing now?' asked Vera with equal innocence, nodding at the typewriter.

Hinchcliffe whipped her head around. She let her jaw drop in imitation – conscious? Or not? – of the insolent way Vera had previously let her jaw drop in their altercations. The pink of her face powder stood out like crayon on her cheeks, as her complexion took on the chalky pallor of anger.

'How can you ask that? I have been keeping this business going for years, while the Captain . . .' She raised her eyebrows in the general direction of Keiko. 'Don't you know it would all be nothing if it weren't for me?'

Keiko was not giving up. She stood very firmly in front of the desk.

'We have come to you.'

'Yes?'

'We have come.'

Keiko stood smiling, intermittently nodding, pulling Vera into her orbit, willing Vera to copy her. Somehow all three adopted her manner.

'I see that you have come. But why?' asked Hinchcliffe. Vera could have sworn she bobbed her head, in an inadvertent bow. She had lost the struggle now, but she did not know it.

'I have to go shopping,' Keiko said. 'But –' she pulled out the cloth bag she kept tied to a band around her waist. 'Money is none.'

'He had it in his desk,' said Vera. She went into his office and tried to slide open the wide, shallow drawer under her grandfather's desk, but it was locked.

'Money is none?' said Hinchcliffe.

'He always kept the coffee money there.'

Hinchcliffe reached into her desk and pulled out ten dollars. 'Coffee money I have. There's coffee money.'

'Coffee money is good,' said Keiko, bowing again graciously. 'And now we like to have fish money. Rice money. Coal money.'

Hinchcliffe produced several hundred dollars. It was a small fortune. And Keiko rolled it carefully and placed it in her cloth bag. Enough for two more months.

Vera watched carefully where it came from. And she recognised in the quick, practised gesture a habit, and she understood with a cold feeling around her heart, that it was the same gesture with which Hinchcliffe had given money to her grandfather.

'Of course, I understand,' said Keiko, bowing.

'Maybe Mr McBean will come,' Vera said.

There was something there under all of this but she didn't understand it, not yet. Someday she would; it was a knot to untangle.

'McBean?' said Miss Hinchcliffe. 'What do you know of McBean? There is no Mr McBean, I have told you many times.'

And Vera thought perhaps this was true. There was no Mr McBean.

Hinchcliffe dusted her hands in a gesture that clearly meant, 'I am through with you'. Once, twice, three times, the palms together, passing each other, as if she were removing traces of a noxious substance.

Hinchcliffe was the picture of the fierce loyal retainer behind the desk, a figure all too familiar in the lore of Japan. Keiko stood up to her full five feet in height now; the bowing was over. And while Hinchcliffe was still sputtering, now Keiko the humble widow was fully in control of the situation.

'Understood. Understood. Thank you very much,' she said. 'Thank you. We are grateful. Vera and I so grateful.' She bowed again.

Watching Miss Hinchcliffe dispense with Keiko gave Vera her first inklings of a sorrow that was not entirely selfish. She saw the hands, dusted together; she saw the firm little knot of Hinchcliffe's lips, that oh so wasp Canadian, 'Well what did you expect? You had it coming', and she felt sorry for Keiko. She was her grandfather's wife, sort of, Vera supposed. Which made her a sort of grandmother. Except that she was younger than her mother had been. Vera hadn't thought much about Keiko's age before.

'How old are you, Keiko?' she asked.

'Two times as you,' said Keiko, smiling shyly.

Thirty.

That night she watched Keiko slowly, carefully cooking the dried fish that she had soaked all day. And she ate it, to please her. Keiko did not smile too broadly. But she looked into Vera's eyes and nodded, and gave a little bow. Then she got a haughty look on her face and dusted her hands. There was the soft sound of her palms brushing against each other, once, twice, three times. It was her first joke.

Vera burst out laughing. They laughed until tears got the better of them, and put their arms awkwardly over each other's shoulders and sat, heads down, over the kitchen table. They were stuck with each other.

'What we will do?' asked Keiko.

'I won't leave you,' Vera said. Her grandfather would want

her to stay with Keiko. 'All my life,' he had said. 'I wanted a deep diver.' That was a very long time to want.

'I won't leave you,' repeated Keiko.

Vera knew it was true.

The days crawled by, the weeks crawled by; she watched the size of Keiko's cloth bag shrink. She returned by herself to Hinchcliffe.

'We need to buy food. And pay for the bills,' Vera said. 'Where is the money for that?'

Hinchcliffe had not recovered from the fact that Keiko had got the better of her. 'She is not his wife.'

*Aisho.*

'He must have left money for her. And for me,' said Vera.

'It is better to wait until your father comes back,' said Hinchcliffe.

'And what if he doesn't?' asked Vera.

Miss Hinchcliffe said that since she first wrote about Captain Lowinger's death, her father had not answered the telegrams.

In retrospect, it seems preposterous that they did not press her more. That they did not ask for a will. That no adult other than Keiko inquired about provisions. That no one questioned the ownership of the company. That the unknown person who had given Miss Hinchcliffe instructions did not appear, or at least give more instructions. That Hamilton Drew did not answer the telegrams.

But many things were mysteries and they were not to be solved because James Lowinger had died. And no matter what the neighbours called her, Keiko was not Mrs Lowinger. She did not speak good English and she was Japanese.

And Vera was no longer a child, but not quite an adult.

'How will you live? Who will you live with?' her teacher asked her. 'Did Captain Lowinger provide for your schooling?'

'I will get a job,' said Vera.

The teacher mentioned the Depression. Men out of work everywhere.

'I do know it's a depression,' said Vera. 'I'm not an idiot.'

You couldn't tell her anything, the teacher remarked to his colleagues.

The doors of the neighbouring houses remained closed and few people expressed curiosity about how they were managing.

By mutual agreement, Vera and Keiko had arrived at the conclusion that it was beneath their dignity to go in front of Hinchcliffe again.

'I will find a job,' said Keiko. Her eyes were round and bright. Vera read the newspapers to see what was available. But there were no jobs. And men came to the door almost every day asking for work, asking for food.

Keiko went to the dry cleaners and offered her services: they were Chinese. No no no, they said. Chinese workers were dying of starvation. And China was the enemy of Japan.

In Japantown her friends told her to go to the fishing boats. So Vera and Keiko took a long bus ride to Horseshoe Bay. They stood on the docks there and sniffed the air. It smelled of gasoline and kelp. But it also smelled of ocean and timber and wilder places farther north and they were excited. Keiko waited for the boats to arrive and spoke to the men in Japanese. She said she could dive. She said she could clean fish, scrub boats, anything. She said she was *ama*. But the men who ran the ships laughed. If they had jobs they had to give them to a man, with a family.

By then even the kindliest neighbours said, 'But surely the girl's father will come?'

But Hamilton Drew did not come.

Vera went again to the warehouse, which now was like a tomb; entering the door there was like entering a place of pain. 'Where is my father?' she asked.

This time Miss Hinchcliffe said she had heard from him. The letter was postmarked in Kobe, Japan, she said, emphasising the capitals. He wished to return and settle matters. But he was unable to do so at this time. She had confidence that he would. In the meantime he had asked her to carry on.

'You are lying,' said Vera. She was certain of it; she could tell by the spots of red on the secretary's cheeks. She backed away from the desk. 'I will write to him myself.' Then she ran out of the door into the evening gloom, so that the secretary could not see her crying.

'What did she do before, in Japan?' the kindliest neighbour asked Vera, about Keiko, encountering the two on the street.

'I am a diver,' Keiko said, understanding.

'Oh,' said the neighbour, her eyes jumping from Vera to Keiko. A furrow developed in her brow. Perhaps she thought that Keiko was a performing diver, like in a circus. 'I don't suppose there is much call for a diver here.'

Vera's teacher advised Keiko to go to the aquarium; maybe Keiko could find a job cleaning tanks. This was a good idea, and they both went, but once again Keiko was refused. Men did that job.

They returned to Horseshoe Bay. 'I am a good diver,' said Keiko. 'What I love to do. Go to shore I do it. Pick up shellfish under the water,' she said.

They tried a strip of beach on Bowen Island. But even Keiko could not work underwater, not in Canada. It was too cold. One man told her to go to Australia, but she did not know how to get there. There was only one place she could dive. Japan.

And suddenly, more than anything, that was what Vera wanted. To go with Keiko to Japan. She was angry at Hamilton Drew. She did write to him, but all she could put for an address was Kobe, Japan. If her father came, if he at long last materialised, she wanted to be gone. To have disappeared somewhere, so that he would look for her, and mourn. Even better to have disappeared in the Far East, where he had disappeared himself.

She felt that she was a failure, a useless, unlovable girl. She had been insufficient to keep her mother alive, and no better at keeping her grandfather alive. Whatever it was they were fighting her father about, whatever it was the men were looking for, it was more important than she was: that was the message. She might as well go off to Japan, wherever that was: she was no good for anything else.

It happened quickly, after that.

Keiko's fishmonger in Japantown would let her work to earn the money to get home to Japan. Only for three months, he said, she could clean fish. But you cannot take that girl with you, he said. She is white, and she will not be safe.

'He must be crazy,' said Keiko to Vera. 'It is not so.'

'Japan will have war with all the white people of the world,' said the fishmonger. 'It is you who are crazy.'

Because they knew it would be for the last time, they returned to Homer Street. Hinchcliffe was positively rigid, Keiko strangely poised.

'Honourable Miss Hinchcliffe,' she said, bowing deeply. Hinchcliffe could not see the little smile around her mouth because Keiko's face was directed toward the green linoleum floor. 'We have much use of money you before given. And now we come to say that we like to go shopping more.'

'It is for me,' said Vera. 'Grandfather would not have wanted me to be hungry.'

'No,' said Miss Hinchcliffe. 'He would not. Whatever he left, it is for you. But he left nothing. I have looked.'

Vera felt as if she had lost him all over again.

'I don't believe it,' she whispered.

Perhaps that was why Hinchcliffe opened the desk drawer and pulled out another two hundred dollars.

Keiko and Vera were ecstatic. It would go toward their tickets.

Anger was not all that drove Vera to go to a strange country. There was something more grand and admirable, under the

82

rage of an abandoned child. Japan was a palace of marvels. She wanted to go there to find beauty and tranquillity and mystery. She had seen this in the pictures. This was the Japan of her grandfather's travels, of his life. She did not understand, or remember, that the pictures were ancient, that the world they described was one hundred and more years old. What difference did it make? The pictures spoke the language of dreams. She went to find the land where it was spoken.

But the language of dreams is loss. The love of beauty is elegy. Made of flesh, we see with the eyes of the past, over the shoulders of the living. The older Vera will tell this to her collectors, the ones who love the *ukiyo-e* but do not understand why. The 'here and now' that the *ukiyo-e* artists carved and coloured was already dying, even in its own time. It is useless to mourn or to fight it. We might as well celebrate. It is a kind of ecstasy.

But so dangerous, in the West. To give in is to give up ambitions. She will see this, in the prints she had examined so minutely, in her grandfather's elderly wisdom. To adopt an inspired idleness, an absorbing ritual. It was so foreign and alluring in the land of her upbringing, her Canadian, Protestant upbringing. Though sad, Belle was never idle, but earnestly found digging up the flower beds or mowing the grass, rattling the dishes in the drying rack or sighing over the wringer washer. Never so beautifully turned out as the Japanese in their riotously painted kimonos behind a screen with chopsticks in their hair, busy in occupations of the moment, blissfully turned away from, but patiently awaiting, eternity. Vera would not get it right herself, not for many years.

Now she had an ambition.

She would go to the place where he had been, this grandfather of hers.

She would go into the pictures.

Maybe that is what happens to people who have been abandoned.

They go to the place where their abandoners have gone.

She went to where her grandfather had been.

But her mother had also left her.

She could not go to where Belle had gone. She would not go.

Later, when life was very dark and when she was nearly the age Belle had been when she died, Vera did think of going where her mother had gone. Of taking the bus, paying the exact fare, making her way along between the rows of seats, as that young mother with the faraway husband had done, lurching because her balance had never been good and it was worse with the medicine. And then ringing the bell for a stop. The handbag carefully left by the side of the bank.

She did not go that way.

'*For that you may be proud of yourself,*' said the sword polisher.

'Do you think so? Some days I wonder.'

He offers neither condemnation nor praise.

'*You had another path to find.*'

# 3

## *Uke-nagashi*
### Warding off: take and give back

*Yokohama 27 February 1936*

High, light piles of snow sat on every flat surface – benches, roofs, even the narrow edges of the incomprehensible street signs. The sky was black and luminous; red beams of emergency lights criss-crossed in the sky above their heads. Trucks were parked across each end of the empty street. Apart from distant sirens, there was not a sound.

'This is not Japan,' whispered Vera. 'We got off the boat at the wrong place.'

Keiko stood on the portside walkway, one cloth satchel in each hand. She lifted her face to the night and sniffed the sea air, trying to sense her way back. She had been gone for nearly three years. She had told Vera so many times that she would cry tears of joy when she stepped off the boat onto Japanese soil. But her face showed confusion and doubt.

The street was nearly empty. Keiko swayed. There were always crowds, cars and streetcars, men stepping wide-legged in kimono or swiftly in black suits with round black bowler hats. There were always women with babies bundled on their backs. Now there was no one. Then into the emptiness came the sound of a snare drum. And footsteps, so many. Around the corner came a column of soldiers marching on the broad, empty street. The men's eyes did not look anywhere but straight ahead. On and on they came.

This was the Japanese Imperial Army. Keiko and Vera stood silent, in awe. The soldiers held their bayonets over their right shoulders; one man in front held the flag, that red ball of a sun with its radial spokes.

The column of soldiers turned a corner and was gone. The footsteps echoed for long minutes after.

When the army had passed, one bystander ran, ducking from doorway to doorway. Another, in an army uniform, trained a limp fire hose on the front of a building. No water came out of the nozzle. It was as if he were waiting for the building to burst into flames.

Keiko told Vera to stand against a wall. She darted across the street; surely the man with the hose would tell her what was happening.

Vera watched their terse exchange. Keiko walked back slowly toward her charge. Vera could tell she was shocked despite her composure. Her shaky English was not quite up to the task of explanation. There had been a 'fight' in the army. More than a thousand army soldiers had gone into the Diet, the government chambers. Certain important men were dead, killed by soldiers. Junior officers had killed their superiors. 'Savagely and without regard for the aged,' was what the soldier had said. They even tried to kill the Prime Minister. What would happen next? Keiko had gone pale. 'He said we should go home while the trains are still working. And stay inside.'

'But what home?' Vera asked. It was the first time she had thought about it: where would they live?

Keiko dug into her satchel for a headscarf. She wrapped it over Vera's head, tying it at the nape of her neck, as if in that way she could make the girl blend in. Then, carrying their luggage, they began to make their way through the city to the train station. It was not very far.

Vera gazed around her; overhead the searchlight beams slashed and slashed the darkness. A man stood silently in front of the newsstand reading a sandwich board. Keiko read it out loud. 'The Emperor has said the rebels will be caught and punished.'

Vera had not known until then that there was an emperor.

'The officers will be killed. And others are killing themselves,' Keiko said.

Vera did not understand why they would do that. Keiko spent some of their few yen to buy the newspaper. She was scanning the article for names.

'Is someone you know in the army?' Vera asked.

Keiko shook her head.

'Someone who came to our village used to be in the army. But I believe he is not any more.'

She did not find his name, and Vera could see that she was relieved.

More snow began to fall, silent, and pink where it crossed the hard white beams of searchlights.

It was morning when they got off the train in Toba. The station was on a platform, high above the ground. There was snow here also but the sky was blue; behind were mountain slopes. At least the peaks were white and high and reminded Vera of the pictures. Not far away, the town ran down to a beach; beyond it was a bay of small, tree-covered islands.

Keiko and Vera carried their wrapped bundles through narrow streets, their feet cold and wet. They came to a house and the door was opened to them. The woman who looked at them gave a little cry and covered her mouth, and then ran behind a screen. A man came out. He was grave and stern, but not very old. He looked at Vera, and embraced Keiko, but he did not smile. Vera stood with her head hanging down. She was so tired she could have slept leaning against the doorpost. The man took pity, and let them come in and gave them a place to sleep.

When they rose it was night again. Vera sat in absolute silence; she could not say one word to anyone, and no one would look her in the face. It was as if she did not exist. This invisibility gave her a curious freedom. She watched, and listened. What she observed was that, overnight, Keiko had grown. She was a tall woman here, and stood straight. Her glance was direct. Her voice was loud and her movements decisive. She was Mrs Lowinger: she had been away in Canada and she had come home. Vera could not understand her words, but she knew that Keiko explained her as James's granddaughter, now Keiko's charge.

Vera did understand that the people in the house said they could not stay longer than a few days. The children were afraid of her. They asked if she were a devil, and Vera understood the question, and blushed fiery red. Their mother told the children to be quiet, but she did not look at Vera any more.

Keiko agreed that they must leave: all she needed, she said, was a bicycle, a job, and a little house. She repeated these words in English to Vera.

'Come,' she said, after the evening meal.

They went out of the little slope-roofed house and walked down the slippery hill to the shops. Men passed them going up; they bowed and greeted Keiko, restrained, but respectful. In the centre of the town there was a tangle of narrow streets. Along the streets were little shops with cloth banners hanging beside the doors. Keiko pointed into the dark insides. Here was where the men drank. Here was a cinema, new since Keiko had left. Here was a noodle shop, run by an old aunt of hers, and there a stationer's.

There were few people out on the streets. The night air was raw with icy sleet, and on the pavements was a thick layer of slush. Vera begged to go back to the house. Once there, she slept again, hoping that she would wake up and find herself back in Vancouver.

But she did not.

On the second day, as soon as the household was awake, Keiko and Vera dressed and went outside. Again they walked down the hill into the town. This morning the sun was shining on the iced pavement and the women were abroad. One of them exclaimed in joy when she saw Keiko. She put down the bicycle she was pushing and embraced her. More women followed her example, and in a few moments Keiko and Vera were in the centre of a crowd of exclaiming, laughing women. They were all small, with rounded, strong bodies; under their old-fashioned bonnets with long brims were bright, curious eyes. Keiko proudly introduced Vera to each one. These were her friends, the *ama* divers, she told Vera.

These women stared frankly into Vera's face. Their eyes were laughing and they looked her curiously all over, making exclamations to themselves. They pointed at her hair. But they were delighted. And Keiko was so proud. If Vera could have felt anything but a seething self-pity she would have been ashamed, as she had never presented Keiko this way when they were in Vancouver.

Keiko took her to the temple and to the vegetable stalls and to the harbour where the fishing boats came in. They walked up the hillside to get a view of Ago Bay, and Keiko showed Vera the rafts that floated in the protected inlets. These belonged to Mikimoto, the pearl king. Keiko explained that there were baskets of oysters suspended in the water under these rafts, and each of these oysters had been seeded with a pearl. The oysters had to be protected from cold and seaweed and other enemies, so that the pearls could grow.

But even the pearls could not pacify Vera. She was cold and afraid. Where had Keiko brought her? This was not Japan. It was frigid, and poor, and there were soldiers in the streets. The State of Emergency because of the attempted coup in the army continued. At night Vera lay on her floor mat and heard raised voices, harsh cries, and the sounds of drunkenness from the street.

Inside the home it was not quiet either. Keiko asked her brother to lend them money. The sounds of their arguing passed through each paper partition. Vera could not understand. She asked Keiko: what does it mean. 'My brother does not have money,' said Keiko. 'He goes to borrow from a loan shark.' There was little money to be had anywhere: the war in China was draining them all.

'But then it is a bad war,' said Vera. It seemed obvious.

'You cannot say this. You do not speak against what the Emperor has asked of us. We must sacrifice.'

Then the brother relented and said that the country was

running out of oil, but that you could not say that either, because it was a military secret.

'If it is a secret, how do you know it?' Keiko asked, full of scorn. 'Do they tell you their mind, these lieutenants of the Emperor?'

'Be careful what you say,' the brother said, his face darkening. 'You went away. You do not understand what we've become.'

But he did one thing for her, perhaps because her presence with the white girl made him fearful. He came home to say that the charcoal man had received his call-up papers. He would leave immediately, probably even tonight. As he was a single man, and lived alone, his house would be empty. The brother had arranged that Keiko could live there. She could put the rent the charcoal man asked for in a special metal box and save it for when he came home from the war. Now the brother stood at his door with his feet apart and his hands on his hips. Vera and Keiko packed their bags without even seeing the little house. When they left, the brother's wife pressed some paper money into Keiko's hand.

'Perhaps the charcoal man will never come back from the war,' said Vera, as they trudged back down the hill.

'That is terrible to say,' said Keiko.

The house was high up on the other side of the town, near the forest. Black dust was on everything, as if the owner had slept with charcoal and eaten with charcoal and lived with charcoal piled around him. Keiko began to clean. Vera sulked, until she could not stand herself any more, and then she got up and helped to wash the floor. The good thing, Keiko said, was that the owner had left a small pile of charcoal behind the house, and they could use it to keep warm. When that ran out they would go up into the forest to collect firewood.

With the money from her brother's wife, Keiko bought a bicycle. They bought eggs and fish and a large bag of rice. It would last a few weeks, Keiko said.

'I begged before, from Miss Hinchcliffe. I not beg again,' said Keiko. 'I am *ama* diver and I will find work.'

She went to the inspectors' office and put her name on the list. But there would be no diving until May. In winter her fellow *ama* worked for Mikimoto cleaning oysters at the pearl farm. But even Mikimoto had fewer jobs now than before. All over the world the Depression had cut into the pearl business. Keiko spoke to her friends in the street. She heard that some *ama* had to go *dekasegi*, away from home. Some worked as farm labourers. There were no machines for this work, only women with long knives in the fields. Some went to Yokohama or even Tokyo, to do cleaning work. But in those strange places, there would be fewer jobs as well, Keiko reasoned. She was determined to remain in Toba. The Emperor's lieutenants, she said, would not change the sea.

Vera stayed inside, huddled on the futon. It was her job to keep the fire going in the hearth. Every hour she got up and raked the coals, and put on more charcoal, and when the charcoal was gone she put on some of the twisted roots she and Keiko found in the forest. She could not believe this was happening to her. It was as if she had descended into a fairy tale.

'Soon spring comes,' said Keiko. 'It is better.'

One day when Keiko was out, a man came to the door. Vera was afraid to answer. He tapped gently, and then he looked in through the window. Finally, Vera answered but she could not understand what he was saying. That evening, when Keiko was home, he came again. He was a friend with a message. A woman had slipped on the bamboo raft in Ago Bay where the *ama* worked cleaning the oyster shells. She had fallen into the icy water and her foot had been caught between the poles. She had broken her ankle.

Keiko met the others to take the ferry to work the next morning.

'Don't be afraid,' Keiko said to Vera when she left the house. 'I will come back.'

Vera did not feel afraid. She felt nothing, other than cold. She lay on the floor, under the layers of cotton cloths that were meant to keep her warm, and hated Japan. She was afraid to go outside because she looked different and people stared. No one spoke to her. If they had, she would not have understood. Finally, in the afternoon, hunger forced her out. In town, one man looked her in the eye. He wore a heavy sack of tools on his back, and he limped. He had a long, grey, thin beard. When he smiled at Vera she could see that most of his teeth were gone, and she was frightened of him. She had no strength; climbing the steep streets with a bucket of potatoes nearly made her faint. Once a man came out of a shop waving a bamboo stick and shouted at her.

'Why?' she asked Keiko later.

'Only because you are strange to him.'

She felt just as strange to herself. She wondered if she were still the same girl she had been. There was one tiny pane of mirror in the house, and it hung on the wall by the door in a small shrine. Vera looked into it over and over. What she saw was a ghost with lifeless, nearly white hair and a red nose that ran with the cold.

She thought of the pictures she'd pored over on Homer Street, and tried to find even one thing that looked like the Japan she had fallen in love with. There was wind, and rain, and snow, but the people were braced against it; they were not sensuous or graceful. There was no promise of cherry blossoms or teahouses around the bend in the stream, or after the shower had passed. Something frigid and hard had found its way into this tropical place. The snow was no genteel flurry of white to walk through in sandals. It beleaguered the people's walking, and weighted their every gesture. Like great white waves, it was water turned enemy, lying stiffly at their feet, in the frozen froth at the sea's edge, or crouching on the roofs and hills as if to kill.

When Keiko came home with her wages they went to the shops and bought coffee beans. Their biggest expenditure was for a hand grinder. Vera put the beans in the small wooden drawer and turned the handle, while the smell of coffee beans came out. It was the one thing that made her happy, because it reminded her of the café in the flatiron building on Homer Street. Keiko used the big iron pot that the charcoal man had left, to make broth and noodles.

One night when the sky was white with a freezing fog, Vera woke from her sleep on the floor mat to the sound of whistle blasts in the street. The blasts were shrill, and insistent. Footsteps pounded past the door. Keiko told Vera not to get up, but she herself stood by the window in the darkness, peering out. She could see down the hill to the rooftops of the main streets.

'They're chasing that man who everyone says is a Red,' she said.

'What is a Red?'

'A Communist.' Keiko sucked in her breath. 'I can see him. He is on the roof next door.'

The shouting and footsteps were right outside their house. Vera cowered under her blanket. 'Come inside, away from the window,' she hissed at Keiko.

But Keiko stood where she was.

'They are men in black. They have seen him. Now they're running over the roof. I fear they will catch him.'

There was a brief exchange of shouts, and then the shots of a gun.

'Did they kill him?'

'No. They take him away.'

'What did he do?' Vera asked.

Keiko said something in Japanese.

'What does it mean?'

'I cannot explain.'

'Please.'

'He has been taken for what is called "Dangerous Thoughts". There is a law against them. He will be in prison. Maybe if very many people know what he has said, the newspapers will publish that he has changed his mind,' Keiko said, and climbed silently into bed.

Vera lay awake pondering the idea of thoughts that were dangerous. Could the police here read people's thoughts?

'I think we should go home again,' said Vera in the morning.

She knew it would not be easy. 'Maybe Miss Hinchcliffe will send us the money. Maybe my father –'

'Be patient,' said Keiko. 'In a few months it will be spring.'

She got a calendar and hung it on the wall. She explained the way the Japanese counted the days: eighty-seven days after February 4th, which they call *risshun*, a change would come. On the eighty-eighth day, which would be the beginning of May, the fishing season would begin and they would sail for the summer island. They had always done this and would do it again.

Vera counted the days. Spring came, and the trees were in blossom, and there was warmth in the air that blew off the crusted remains of icy snow in the shadiest parts of the treed hillsides. With the ice went a stiffness and fear from the people.

When the eighty-eighth day came, the whole village set out together with ceremonial flags flying, nearly three hundred men, women and children, in small sailboats and a few motorboats. She and Keiko went in the boat of Keiko's old aunt and uncle, and their son. They had one of the few motorboats. The island was twelve miles from the main-land, a journey of six hours. At the end they stepped onto a low, bare volcanic rock and were welcomed by a posse of wild cats. There were dozens and dozens of them, arching from behind the rocks, meowing and stalking with tails swishing, giving no quarter. Vera had never seen a wild cat. To her a cat was a pampered pet, sleeping on a pillow. Keiko explained that the cats were left behind the year before, and the year before that, for as long as the people had been coming to the summer island for the fishing season. They lived on mice and snakes.

They unloaded their belongings onto the pebbly shore. They brought very little, just their sleeping bundles, a few *yakata* and baskets containing rice, diving gear and cooking pots. Keiko gestured to Vera to lift up the cloth-tied bundles that she had brought. The men went to put in place the wooden docks that had been stored away from the water and the winter storms.

Carrying their bundles, the people walked all together up the small winding street that ran up from the harbour. The procession was natural, and unhurried, passing one after another of the low, weathered wooden houses that, like the cats, had been left behind the year before and the year before that for as long as anyone could remember. Stones were set in rows on the roofs of the houses, which were grey and matched the rock. As each family reached its home, the members disengaged from the group, bowed, and disappeared inside.

That first night of the first summer on the island, Vera lay down on the floor mat, exhausted from the day's sail. She could hear nothing but the wind and the sound of the water, a hollow percussive sound as it broke somewhere over the rocks. Where had she come to now? This island was a farther place even than the village from her world. She wanted to cry, but Keiko was beside her. The old aunt and uncle and even a boy, near her age but a little older, could hear. She was determined not to make a sound. She went to sleep pretending she was dead.

But sunrise came even to the dead. Her spot on the floor was directly in line with the rising sun; a beam crept slowly over the windowsill, and made its way up from her feet to her face. Vera opened her eyes. She was awake in a wooden box. And it was as if she had woken up for the first time in a year. Every board and mat and corner and basket Vera could see was freshly cut and full of meaning.

The box had been constructed carefully, simply. Vera could

see each board as it lay next to the other, and the beams that were the straight trunks of thin trees that lay across them. Probably years ago, perhaps even one hundred years ago or more, when this box was built, the trees grew on this island. Perhaps that was why there were no trees here now. They had all gone for houses. The wood was grey and in some places russet, and in spots it showed the stains of water that had got through. There were knots and eyes in it and where there was a hard round eye, the surrounding log had been shaven. That meant that all along the planks Vera could see round hard grey places like pupils, each one in the centre of an oval like an iris, so that the whole made an eye. They did not feel like peering eyes, but like spirits that were friendlier now, less strange.

The box was perfect, square at each end, with thin paper screens dividing their sleeping section from their eating section, and a hearth in the middle. Vera liked the neatness of it and the sense she had of being small inside it, miniaturised by the house that was itself like a toy house in its simplicity.

She stumbled outside and saw that the sun was turning the sky pink and gold, highlighting the stray clouds that wandered across the great empty dome above this flat floating land. As the sun came up, birds began to fly in circles over the houses. Vera imagined them living all through the dark night on the bare rocks, or roosting in the cliff in this comfortless volcanic ruin without a safe leafy tree to be seen.

She wished she had been the first up, but greeting the day as it dawned was a custom here, and others had been up before her. The village was coming alive creakily and with good cheer. She went along the street; the doors were open. Vera heard screens sliding, and water buckets clanging. The men stood and scratched and looked out at the water.

Vera had to stare to recognise these people, although she had seen them in Toba and even sailed with them the day before. They had shed their stiffened look, and the wooden gestures that made them strange all winter. They might have been coming out of hibernation. They had the alert and avid look of hunters whose season had come. This was home, their faces said; the long sojourn on the mainland had been just a waiting.

And, Vera thought, there would be no whistles and men in black uniforms here. This was a safe place.

The water lay all around, everywhere you looked. Vera watched as men stretched their arms, barked directions and trotted down to the water. There was much groaning and heaving as they lifted the fishing boats down from the wooden stands where they had spent the winter. Their words, though still indecipherable, sounded exuberant. The men shouted to be heard over the surf. They looked bolder and bigger than they had in town, stripped down to the skin, like people who had been freed.

But the women, especially, were changed from the huddled souls Vera had seen on the mainland. Gathering around the well, they laughed together. They had removed their bonnets. Faces open, they filled their buckets, one after the other. They stripped to wash, and then went bare-breasted through the streets, old and young. It was a matter-of-fact and purposeful nakedness. They took no notice of themselves or each other in this state, but trundled back to their houses, each one nearly the same as the next.

The children were in the sea immediately. Mothers set down even the toddlers at the water's edge, where they began making curious, rocking steps outward.

As she looked at the easy working swing of the other women's bodies, Vera was envious. She imagined herself the object of stares and curiosity. One old woman with tiny wizened breasts stopped Vera in the path. She pointed overhead to the brightening sky and rows of narrow clouds. It was a good sunrise; it had fish scales in it, the woman seemed to be saying.

Vera was so astonished to be greeted that she could do nothing but stare. But the woman went away smiling. Vera resolved to do just what the others did. If she went around bare in the sun her pale skin would burn and peel and freckle. Then maybe – she hoped – she'd turn the same colour as they were.

She continued on the path through the village, past the harbour and along to the far end where there was a little height and she could look down on the water and see the shaded scrawling on its surface. Like the pattern on a huge tapestry, it was repeated as far as Vera could see. She wondered what those long lines of bubbles were, if they were foam that came with an overnight wind, now diminished.

Vera counted four different birds. There were terns, gulls, plovers, and cormorants. She paid special attention to the cormorants because they were the best divers. They had necks like black snakes: she could see one out on the water; his head went full circle around. His eye was like the eye of a needle. Their fellows flew low over the water in squadrons with serious intent. Vera saw just one goose, far overhead, and thought perhaps he was lost. Turning on the spot in her high place, she looked back into the heart of the village to see how far advanced the morning was. People were still emerging from their houses with water buckets. She saw the smoke of a cooking fire coming from the house she thought was hers. But she did not want to go back yet, she wanted to go on and explore.

She could see the mountains of the mainland, distant and small off the side where the harbour was. The other side faced away into the open sea. The island was not large, maybe four times as long as it was across, a distance Vera could walk in half an hour, and shaped like an elongated figure eight.

It had taller cones on each end, and a marshy place in the middle. It must have been two volcanoes once; the remains had been stretched as if someone had tried to pull the two sections apart. The narrow middle had nearly disappeared under water. A bridge of boards lay across it in several places. She stepped down on the boards and a white snake shot out from under, hissing. She stepped off the boards and waded through the water, which had eelgrass in it, and noticed tiny fish darting right up onto the land.

Butterflies and moths, the names of which Vera had not learned, some pale blue and some pink, stopped on the pale wild flowers that spotted the grass. There were orange butterflies too that she recognised from home; they were named Monarchs. Vera pulled out a clump of bamboo grass; it was as fine as green hair and it cut her. There were many kinds of moss: the thick velvety green, the red, dry, wiry moss, the moss that consisted of tiny stalks each with a minute yellow head.

She heard the great honking, almost barking sounds rise from the misty beds of bamboo grass.

She stopped, terrified.

Wild jungle animals – lions or rhinoceros?

She was suddenly blind. The flat lines of the rising sun had got entangled with the grass, and there was mist too, caught probably because the shallow water was warmer here than elsewhere. Vera squinted and shaded her eyes. She could see large brown-backed shapes in the tall grass of the marsh. Like great dogs or coyotes, barking. Then one of them unfolded its wings and flapped messily into the air. They were giant, unruly birds. When she approached the grasses where they waded, bending and snatching little fish for their breakfast, two more flew up and the rest stalked away, out of sight. They made her laugh with joy.

She turned back toward the house. At home, breakfast was ready. As she drank her morning soup, Vera told Keiko about the huge birds.

'You are lucky!' Keiko said. 'You have seen the cranes.'

She told the old people Vera had seen the cranes.

They smiled and nodded and looked very impressed.

Lucky, Keiko repeated. She told Vera they danced too but she had never seen them.

Suddenly, everyone was working. Keiko had taken her goggles and her lunch box and her fishing basket and had gone down to meet the other divers. The young boy, her nephew, with whom Vera had been steadily avoiding eye contact, followed Keiko. The old aunt had gone out to dig in the soil and the uncle to mending boats with the other older men. No one said anything about what Vera should do.

Vera walked along the path and stood and watched the *ama* boats go off. There was an oar in the back at the centre, pulled up so that the rudder didn't hit the sand. The women came splashing aboard, all exclaiming about the water, which Vera understood was cold. The men and boys ran alongside, pushing. Then they hopped aboard, and an *ama* woman took the oar. She began to sway, rowing the boat, and they were gone, without looking back. Vera was left alone.

She headed in the opposite direction she'd walked earlier. Here too, the ground rose a little, unevenly. The street petered out at some houses, which looked older and more dilapidated than the others. A few old women and men scratched at the dirt with hoes.

She came to the end of the village. There was a path that continued: it went to a shrine, probably. There were always shrines, with wooden arches painted red, with stones that were mossy and covered with lichen. Long tapes hung in these shrines, from the branches of trees, and papers were tied on them, or amulets or dolls. Vera did not understand these shrines; she had seen them in Toba and always turned away as if they contained something she should not see. She went onward from the path to the shrine, and discovered a square house, taller than the others. Its door was shut. She peeked in the cracks. But she could see only darkness. There was straw on the ground in front of it, and a horrendous chill around it. She thought it might be a tomb. But no, now that her eyes adjusted, she could see there were huge, square, straw-coloured, dirty blocks of ice inside, packed down in a hole. How had it got here? Some of the men must have come out in the winter, and cut the ice and saved it.

She explored behind the ice house and came to a depression in the sandy ground, where, deep in the centre, she saw a little lake, a lagoon. There were rocks around its edges and a few birds splashing in it. Vera climbed over the rocks and tasted the water. It was fresh water. She sat for a while and put her feet in.

It was all so strange:

She talked to herself, pityingly. I am so alone. I am a stranger who doesn't understand the language. I don't look like the island people. I have come so far from home. Everyone died on me: my mother and then my grandfather.

The minister, attempting to comfort her, had told her that deaths compound in their ravages on the living. This is only the beginning, he had said to her. As you get older there will be more deaths of people you love; it is part of life. You are experiencing this early, he had said. That means you must try especially hard to stay strong. Perhaps it will be the making of you.

To her mind came the lines of poetry her grandfather would recite: how the poor formless oyster 'shed this lovely lustre on his grief'.

It began with an intrusion. Something got into the shell by accident – a parasite, a grain of sand, or a small crab. If the oyster did not react it would die. Half pearls, which were simply bumps on the inside of the shell, were even called 'blister' pearls, as if to emphasise the hurt.

She thought perhaps she could do that. Make herself a pearl, to soften the hurt, a smooth round bud that she carried inside instead of this grating hurt.

She thought about real pearls then. Any mollusc could produce one. Their shell lining was silky. It formed in concentric circles, but there were radial spokes too. It had tiny ridges all through it. These took the light and refracted it. And that was what made the 'lustre'. Her grandfather had drawn diagrams, to explain the glow that men had been fascinated by since the time of first recorded history. She could hear his voice.

He had drawn pictures, too, of shellfish. They had beautiful names, like 'Black-winged Oyster' and 'Silver-lipped Oyster'. In Japan, he told her, there was the 'White Jewel Shiratama' and the 'Red Jewel Akadama.' Keiko said the Japanese paid almost no attention to pearls in the wild. The women dove for shellfish for food, in particular the abalone. Usually the divers did not open the abalone they brought to the surface. They were very careful not to damage the shell; awabi was expensive, more expensive than anything the divers could afford to eat. But on feast days they opened and ate awabi. Then you might find a pearl. The awabi pearls Keiko had seen were red in colour. When the people found them they gave them to the priest for the temple.

Perhaps Vera would find a pearl.

But how, and when? Vera had no idea how to behave in this place. And it appeared that no one was going to show her. Vera gave herself a moment to feel a little retrospective pity for Keiko, who had been so foreign in Vancouver. She decided that she would do what Keiko had done. She would watch, and that way she would learn.

She stood and ventured on. By going around the little lake and walking through the grass and low bushes, she made her way across the island to the outside. Here the edge was steep and high and the rocks were black. In some places they were jagged. In others the rock was smooth and lay in folds and curves, as if it had once been a thick liquid, poured down. There was an old hut there, battened down against the weather with rocks. She wanted to investigate it, but she was afraid someone might be living in it. When she looked out she knew she was looking straight onto the ocean that went clear across the globe to Vancouver.

It was nearly noon and suddenly the island felt hot and dusty. She turned away from the sea. She clambered over the rocks, planning to avoid the marshy centre and return to the village by circling the perimeter. But the rocks became higher and more difficult to climb. The bushes came right to the edge, and they were prickly and thick; she scratched her bare legs and arms getting through them. The weather, too, was different on this side. The wind was rising and there were large waves moving out from the shore. Her mood changed, as suddenly as the weather. It frightened her, this place, so poor, and low, and vulnerable to the sea and the wind.

At the very tip of the island, neither on the inland side nor the outside, she found a sheltered place above the rocky beach. She was not exactly hidden, but out of the way; no one would notice her. She tucked herself down out of the wind.

Vera sat that afternoon for hours, looking at each stone she found to see if it had anything interesting to offer. Most of them were bits of broken black lava, porous and harsh to the touch, with nothing pleasing in their shape. But a few were lighter grey or brown, rounded, and fitted in the palm of her hand; turning them over gave her fingers pleasure. These stones, she thought, must have come from somewhere else. She saved the smooth, round ones apart, and examined their strips of green, red and white, dull when dry but much brighter when wet.

In the late afternoon she saw the fishing boats returning. They were still far out from shore. She stood and worked her way along the harbour side, stopping before she was in view, but where she could see. She sat in a low place on the beach. Vera saw the boats come near, all in a row, behind the one that had a motor. She saw the girls jump out and run up the sand, and the boys and men push the boats up. Keiko's nephew performed his tasks with grave attention. Then the women set off home, calling out farewells to each other, with their baskets balanced on one hip. She saw Keiko, happy amongst her friends, saying goodbye for the day and heading toward the house. Vera stopped herself from running up to ask what she'd caught. The fish would be collected by the Headman and counted, Keiko had explained. There was a tally for every family. When the ferry came, the shellfish would go to the market. Awabi went to the market. Turban shell and eels the people could keep: the seaweed was dried and divided, some for sale and some to eat.

Now in the houses, the fires would start up; someone would heat the bath. But Vera did not go in. She stayed as the sun got lower and lower. Finally, she stood up. Hunger, and the fact that she had been alone all day, drove her out of her hiding place to Keiko's house.

She did this for days. Every afternoon she moved a little closer to the landing spot for the boats. Soon, she was close enough to be seen. But the girls of the summer village walked past her with their faces blank, as if she were a stone.

'Where do you go?' Keiko asked.

'Just around.' Long silence, and then, because although Vera was angry she was not really angry with Keiko, she tried to explain. 'It was windy on the other side.'

'So, you come to know the island, that's good,' said Keiko. 'And how the weather changes. If it is not good where you are then you go to the other side. If there is a big wind, now you are sheltered. If you were in shadow, now you are in sun.'

Vera tried to wake up before everyone else, and to slide out of the house at the first ray of sun, so that she could avoid the people. She ran across the marshy place, which now had a stronger plank for a bridge. She continued down the beach past all the boats to the raised flat spot at the very end of the island she called the High Place. No one came here. It was the perfect place to see the sun rise. Alone there she watched every second of this quick breaching. By eight o'clock, the *ama* women would gather on the beach. By then usually a skin had developed on the water, a little wind out of the east, accompanied by sharp little wavelets. Vera stood and put her face into it.

From the High Place, Vera could believe this island was a ship, that it was sailing bravely on and the water was lying still around it. It was taking her home, across the Pacific, back to Vancouver. Or, if the wind was the other way, to India, or Italy. Vera didn't mind where it was taking her, she just wanted to be going into the wind and leaving a wake behind.

One morning when she went to the High Place, the wind was already strong. It was blowing too hard for the *ama* to go out in their boats. They gathered on the beach, and spoke, and the men tied the boats firmly in place. The women turned and conferred. They tried to hold their hair from blowing across their faces, but she could not hear their voices. Vera thought for a moment they would not dive that day. But they only went to fetch some wide, flat baskets, which they hung on their arms. Then the women, without the men, set out to cross the island. It looked as if they went along the little lake: they disappeared into the low bushes and Vera could not see. She crept back along the outside of the island, over the steep and difficult rocks, through the scratchy bushes, and saw them emerge on the outside, midway along on the cliffs. They went into the little hut.

So it was the women's house!

Vera watched from the rocks. Smoke began to rise from the centre of the rounded roof. The women had lit a fire in there, to warm themselves. Soon, one by one, they emerged with their baskets and began to clamber down the rocks to the water. Once they reached the edge, without hesitating, they put goggles on their eyes and plunged in, and swam out, their tethered baskets floating behind them.

It appeared that in this wind the women were going to fish off the rocks. That meant Vera could watch them, and she did. They bobbed up and down from the surface, pulling up weed from the bottom, and placing it in their baskets. When their baskets were full, they swam back to shore, climbed out and, laughing together, disappeared into the hut.

Vera climbed down from the rocky point to the quiet, grassy spot beneath it. This place was out of sight of the sweep of tilty houses, and the harbour, and the outside fishing rocks, out of sight of everywhere and every one of these busy island people. She called it the Low Place.

Vera was startled, thinking she was alone, to see movement. She peered through the bushes. In the centre was a circle of grassy sand, quite hidden away. In it stood a man with a curved scabbard tied to his left hip. She recognised the shape of the weapon from the old prints she had memorised; the samurai carried two of them, sticking out behind them like a big X. This man had one and wore it casually, as if it were part of him. She stopped in fright, wondering if he was some sort of bandit, or perhaps a policeman who had come to the island to mete out old-fashioned justice.

He stood quite still. The wind was coming around the point at him. Grass grew up through the sand, waving around his feet. She could not tell if he was young or old. His hair was black, but a fierce white streak rode back on a thick wave from his widow's peak. He held the scabbard in his left hand, pressing it against his left hip. It was black and curved down toward his heels.

He faced the water, and seemed to be far away in his thoughts. Perhaps because the wind blew, he did not hear her approach. As Vera watched, he bent, brushing the split skirt from between his knees, and knelt. He placed the long,

curved scabbard, which had the handle of a sword pro-
truding from it, on the ground before him. He placed first
his right hand and then his left on the ground in front of
his knees, forming a triangle between his fingers. He bowed
reverently, for a long time, as Vera stood motionless.

It was not unusual to see a person on his knees in Japan,
and even sometimes, like this man, bent so low that his face
was to the ground, his two hands flat on the earth, forefingers and thumbs meeting at the tips. Before a person of
great importance, or a shrine, one bowed this way. Although
Vera saw nothing before him on the shore or in the water
she knew he was acknowledging some power. What was he
worshipping? Something private. She fell back, but not, she
sensed, before he became aware that she was there. He gave
no sign of this awareness, but she felt it.

He raised his head. Then he reached forward and lifted
the sword, and, holding it above his head, bowed again.
Then he turned the tip of the scabbard toward his belly, slid
it under his belt, and, without looking away from the fixed
point ahead of him, tied the scabbard to his waistband.

He sat back on his heels with his hands on his knees.
Vera was waiting for him to draw the sword, but she missed
it. He had instantly lunged forward; the blade had flown
like a silver bird out of its sheath and divided the air in
front of him, the edge flashing in the sun. It hovered at his
right side and then again, without warning and from complete stillness, flew over his left ear and cut downward de-
cisively.

The man kept his eyes on the imaginary beast he had
slain; with the swift, sure flight of a bird, the sword took
itself back into the black scabbard.

Stillness again. Vera held her breath. He watched intently
a place beyond, a place from where, it seemed to her, all
movement came, all threat. Although his eyes did not move,
his watchfulness was such that there would be no surprising
him, not from any angle.

She was afraid, childishly, that he would cut her down. The wise thing was to be still. She waited. And then, out of this stillness, he exploded upward from his heels, the sword braced above his head. He was fending off an opponent, but the opponent was not there. He was jousting with it and staying alive. There was a force, a pressure behind all his movements. He sliced, he braced, he thrust, he flicked his sword as if to remove the blood. Then he was back on his knees again.

It couldn't be long before he turned and stared at her. Probably he would be angry at being seen. Vera crept away.

She asked Keiko, 'Who is that man who dances with his sword when no one is looking?'

'What do you mean no one? I think you were looking.' Often Keiko spoke very solemnly and Vera didn't understand that she was teasing until she saw the tiny smile at the corners of her lips and her eyes.

'I was. But he didn't know.'

'Oh yes, he knew.'

'Did he tell you?'

'No, I just know he knew. That man is Ikkanshi Tadatsuna. The sword polisher. *Katanatogi*.'

'He was not polishing. He was cutting.'

'Perhaps he was practising his cuts. Testing a blade to see if it is true. He must be very careful because a sword brings life and death to the ones who use it.'

Keiko explained that the Ikkanshi were an ancient family that had polished swords for over two hundred years. 'He is a great artist. It is an important occupation; even emperors and samurai will polish swords, after battles.'

'Will they use his swords in battle? In China?'

'I don't think so.' Keiko smiled. 'It is not for that he practises.'

'Then for what?'

'To test the sword,' Keiko repeated. 'And to test himself.'

'Why does he come here?' Vera asked. 'The people don't need swords here.'

'He sharpens our knives and spears, and he makes fish hooks,' said Keiko. But she sounded a little defensive, and Vera could see that this was not a true answer.

After that Vera saw the *katanatogi* often. She discovered that he had a little shop off the main street, the only street, a footpath really, that ran along the spine of the island and off which they all had their dwelling places. Merchants, those who distributed back to the people the products of the sea that they harvested, and the few utensils, ropes, fuel and fabrics they needed on the summer island, had their one-room establishments here.

The *katanatogi*'s room was nearly empty. When he worked, he sat in the centre of it on a low stool in front of a stone altar. This stone was like a little bench with legs, and it was on this that he polished, oiled, dusted and sharpened the knife blades and tools that the people brought him. He was never dirty, as a blacksmith would have been at home. Sometimes while he worked he wore nothing on his upper body and Vera saw the way the pattern of the firm, braided muscles of his upper arms was repeated under his ribs. His chest hair was spiked with grey. He never acknowledged her presence. He was almost always fixed in deep concentration on a blade. When she passed him on the path, Vera imitated the deep bows made to him by others on the island, even by the Headman of the Fisherman's Union.

At first Vera had been proud to be alone and stubbornly revelled in it. But now she was lonely. The girls acted as if she was invisible. She sat at the rim of the High Place when the wind blew, crawled in and out of the pitted rocks. Keiko joked that she was becoming like the wild cats that lived off the mice.

One day she came again upon Ikkanshi-san at the Low Place. As soon as she saw him, she crouched and hid, although it was no use. He knew she was there. But he gave no sign. The *katanatogi* never looked at her. For long moments he kneeled as before in front of a long, flat, gleaming blade. Vera wondered as she watched if, coming from the ancient family of sword polishers, he had any choice when he became a *katanatogi*. How did he come to live on the summer island? Or was he under some compulsion, a prisoner here, like herself?

He knew she was there. He sensed her presence although she made not a sound.

He closed his eyes and strove for the mind like water. But on its surface he saw her reflected. Only the blind would have missed seeing her, the pale white skin and yellow hair. Also, she was sad and her sadness reached out for him.

There was a story in her life, a story that touched his.

He remembered her grandfather, James Lowinger. He was a big, bearded Englishman, who came to the summer island not so many years ago. They said he was a friend of Mikimoto Taisho and that he had visited these islands many times over his long life. This last time he brought his son-in-law: that was Hamilton Drew, the girl's father. The younger one came to him when he discovered the *katanatogi* had been to England and spoke his language. He wanted to see swords. He was a collector – of gems, of art, of anything other people valued. Of women, the sword polisher supposed, although perhaps he left that to the old man. He did not show any swords to Hamilton Drew. They are not made for one such as him. There was nothing else of value here, he told the collector: we are simple people and those treasures we have we do not bring to the summer island.

And Hamilton Drew said to him, 'But you are not one of them.'

He was perceptive, that was one thing.

'Perhaps I am not one of them, but I know them better than you do. I know that what you came for is not here,' he said.

What the old man had come for was not quite as obvious.

Ikkanshi can still see James Lowinger getting off the ferry with his great, waxed barbs of hair curling out from under his nose, like the Greek sea god who he had seen in the British Museum. He went directly down to the shore to meet the *ama* diving girls. That was his mistake: he did not present himself to the Headman. The sword polisher thought to himself: no one of his kind ever comes here. This is a poor island and foreign visitors visit the sophisticated centres.

He saw the Englishman walking by the harbour, back and forth, in the long coat that buttoned over his chest. The divers were far out from shore and he shielded his eyes to see them. He returned to the village and spoke to this man and that, found himself a place to sleep at the temple, and remained. He was clever. He made no requests, at first. In this way he could not be turned down.

He knew how to wait. Still that mistake cost him much time. Since he had been ignored, the Headman would not see him for many days. Lowinger would walk on the beach and meet the women when they came in from diving. But of course they would not talk to him. They had been told not to. They presented him with the face of *shiran kao*, he who knows nothing. If it was pearls he was after he would not be lucky. They were only diving for shellfish.

The day was hot. James Lowinger removed his long coat and met the returning boats in an open-necked shirt. The diving girls giggled into their hands as they came in, standing in the little boats, one of them wielding the handle of the single fixed oar that also served as rudder. They jumped out in thigh-high water as they always did and pulled the boats up. Keiko, he remembers, stood boldly beside him as she tied on her *yakata*. The old man looked older than ever beside her, older than her father would have been had he been alive. Keiko's father had been a fine, strong man who died too young.

Keiko was a pretty young diver then. In her twenties and not married yet, a rare circumstance. The *ama* girls choose their husbands, unlike other Japanese women. She had not chosen. Or more correctly she had chosen but her choice was not possible.

Ikkanshi saw her with him. He understood Keiko. If the rest would pretend they did not see him, because it was custom, or because they were told to do so, she would be compelled to do the opposite. He saw her point to where they had fished that day, this side of the island out beyond the harbour, toward the Watchers.

That was the first time. The next day, and every day for a week, Lowinger met the *ama* as they came in. The women carefully ignored him. That only made Keiko more friendly. He brought her small things, too small to see from a distance. He brought her new goggles. She tried them but preferred her own.

Even the sword polisher could see what was happening. She was falling in love with the old man. Well, of course. He was like a white god and she had never seen one before. Perhaps a diving girl was what the white-haired trader had come for. Ikkanshi feared she would go with him if he took her. It was not good. *Ama* girls do not fare well in the outside world. They are divers; that is what they are bred for. If they go to Australia or far away California, as some do, they are badly treated for their yellow skin. If they do not dive, they lose themselves. Keiko was not the first *ama* woman to mistake her longing to leave this place for love of one who could show her the way. The polisher could have told her. It is better to find your own way, if you must go. If you must follow another person it is not your true way. But he noticed that women rarely do this.

In the end Hamilton Drew made a proposal to the Fisherman's Union that when the season was right the *ama* should dive for akoya oysters, and sell to him. He offered a fair percentage. The polisher was present at these discussions, because he spoke

English. He assumed the younger man spoke for both visitors. The trader said he liked their ways; he did not wish to abuse the divers or even the sea. Nevertheless, the Headman spurned him. The people control their own harvest. Outside demand would lead to destruction of the sea creatures they depended on. It is the same reason they do not use fins or tanks; when people take too much, there will be none left.

And in any case, the Headman insisted, the women do not dive for oysters, and certainly not for pearls. They dive for awabi, turban shell and seaweed. Awabi they can sell for a good price. Fish they can eat. Akoya shells perhaps three days a year. But for their own market. And if by any long chance, a pearl was found, it would go to the shrine. None had been found in a long time, he said and he repeated.

Ikkanshi was not satisfied that pearl oysters was what the white men were after. He was not certain that the two men sought the same thing. The old man was married: not a surprise to the sword polisher, most men were. But his wife was dead. He was searching for a woman, but not for just any woman, not for just the usual purposes.

No doubt Lowinger had spent the years when his wife and children needed him running some errand, the way men do. His errand had been to find pearls, but it could have been to find greatness or power. Now he had lost faith in his dream. But he, being romantic, did not assume the consequences of those years lost. He had a vision of how he wished to have lived. Late in life he thought he could resume this ideal way.

And the son-in-law, Drew? What was he after? Ikkanshi had observed from his time amongst the English that the men often marry the father rather than the daughter, in all but point of fact. But perhaps Drew believed the old man was rich. It would not be the first such case of mistaken identity. He had read a little of their literature; he knew that much. Was Lowinger rich? He doubted it. Fair percentages do not make anyone rich. The pearl trade was for dreamers, not for builders of fortunes.

The two white men grew even more resentful of each other.

He could see that, even in their steps, side by side, even in the angles of their shoulders as they edged alongside each other on the narrow street here. In the end, Ikkanshi had blamed the younger man. But was he wrong? Perhaps. Had he unfairly judged Hamilton Drew? Was the young man trying to stop the old one from making a foolish mistake? This too happens in novels.

There was some kind of argument between them, perhaps about the diving woman. Ikkanshi witnessed it. He heard the old man say, coldly, 'You cannot tell me what to do. You value nothing and no one.'

Hamilton Drew left on the next ferry, gone to Nagasaki looking for other treasures, no doubt.

The old man stayed on.

And he got what he wanted.

Ikkanshi had a clear picture of Keiko's departure. It was three years ago on a cool evening at the end of the season. The day had been hot, and with the change of temperature a mist was blowing in. She was wrapped in her *kosode* and smiling bravely. All her friends lined up on the beach to bear witness. But she did not catch his eye. She had a bundle of her clothes and a look of triumph about her, although she tried to hide it. The old man tenderly put his hand behind the small of her waist as she walked. The watching sword polisher could tell by that gesture that she had confided in him her fears and that he would try to assuage them.

Then they were gone.

He stood and watched the ferry pulling away, the mist taking it. It was a shocking thing, and not just for Ikkanshi. The *ama* divers are the wealth of the people. Keiko was too innocent to know what she was heading into. He hoped for good luck for her, but he also hoped that he would one day see her again.

The wash came over the flimsy dock.

One more thing happened that evening as Keiko sailed away with her English god. The basket maker had arrived on the ferry that had taken her away. When the sword polisher awoke from

114

his reverie he saw the man. This basket maker had come back from the last war with a bad leg. He too had apprenticed for several years to learn his complex trade. He came once, at most twice, every summer to replace the eel baskets and rice caddies and backpack baskets that had worn out since his last appearance. He lived on the road as he worked; the people who needed his services would open their doors to him. That day the little boys asked him to make spinning tops out of his spare bamboo strips. He was kind enough to do that. Ikkanshi watched as he set down his pack and took out some bamboo to begin.

They greeted one another with a quiet bow. They were not acquainted.

The mist brought a chill with it. The basket maker knew everyone in the village; he recognised a stranger. The sword polisher moved amongst these simple fishing people peacefully enough. But when the basket maker saw him it was as if all that he stood for was written on his face. He was from an educated class, born in Kyoto. He had gone to officer school. He had been abroad. He had come home, and stepped away from the army, taken up the tools of the *katanatogi*, and come to this island. Why? said the basket maker's look.

But that was three years ago. Now Keiko was home and the old man dead and it appeared she had truly cared for him. The Englishman had been lucky after all on the summer island. And Keiko had this girl, the grandchild, with her. That Ikkanshi had not counted on.

One day the girl stayed a very long time in the doorway of his workshop. He happened to have a blade on the whetstone. He was beginning to reshape its natural lines. He had to be very careful, because if he removed too much metal, the sword would be mined. He was using a stone of coarsest grit, and water. He rocked on his heels, before the stone. She did not move, or go away. Finally he stopped what he was doing.

'I know you are there,' he said.

He was not blind. He had seen her slink about the town curling in and out of doorways, ashamed as a cat without a tail. She had in her the quiet of a feral creature.

He waved to her to come in and asked if she would like to sit at the hearth. She behaved with complete decorum, revealing nothing. He watched her sit. She took the teacup between her hands and sipped noisily from it. She was learning.

'What is your job?' she asked.

He explained to her, and showed her the blade. It was not a particularly good one, made in the modern period. He was simply practising.

'So you give it a sharp edge,' she said.

He chuckled. She had reduced his task in her practical western way. 'My goal is to bring out the spirit of the blade. It is a slow process and one I find soothing, like a meditation.'

'Did you make it?'

'The *katanakaji*, the swordsmith made it. I find its natural qualities and make them visible.'

'Oh, that's all?'

'It may sound as if it is not so difficult, but in fact it is. I can fail. I can destroy a good blade by trying to grind away a flaw. I can ruin the cut.'

She showed no feeling when he spoke English. The English believe their language is the normal form of human speech, and are mystified and a little pitying when they find places in the world where it is not common currency. But that was not the case with her. Her seeming lack of surprise was not incuriosity. It was that she had learned not to let anyone have the advantage over her. That seemed to him a sad thing in a child, or nearly a child. There must have been troubles for her, early in her life.

'What is your name?' he asked.

'My name is Vera.'

'It is a good name. Where did you get it?'

'From my mother. But I don't like it much. I think it is old fashioned.'

'But it is straight and true,' he said.

116

'She was going to call me Verity. The Verity is the movie theatre at Broadway and Granville. In Vancouver,' she added as an afterthought. 'That would have been even worse.'

He laughed. 'I've never met anyone named after a movie theatre. Why would she do that?'

'She was lonely and the movies made her happy.'

'You can be grateful,' he added gravely, 'that she did not call you Lux. Or Bijou,' he said, thinking back to cinemas he had known.

'Yes,' she said, 'or Palace. Or Showtime.'

They were surprised to be laughing together.

'At least she shortened it to Vera. My grandfather convinced her.'

'I see,' he said. 'And like the movies, you were meant to make her happy? Did you?'

'Not happy enough,' said Verity known as Vera, as if it were the most interesting thing about her. 'She died. I was at school. I came home and the police were there. She went on a bus. They found her body in the water.'

'Oh,' he said. This was new information to him. 'It is a hard thing. But not your fault.'

She said nothing.

'And what did you do then?'

'I had a funeral and buried her. What do you think I did?'

'Of course,' he said. It was as if they were talking fairy stories. Bravado, he supposed. 'Alone you did this?'

'No. There was a minister from the church, and the neighbours.'

'Your father?'

'He wasn't there.'

As he had imagined. Hamilton Drew was off somewhere looking for treasures. Some flicker must have crossed his face that the girl took to be criticism of her father.

'It wasn't his fault. He was somewhere in the Far East,' she said, emphasising the capitals. 'We sent him a telegram. I sent him a letter too. But he never got it. Otherwise he would have

117

come. Still, I knew what to do. I found a letter in my mother's purse from Grandfather. It said he was sailing for Vancouver, expected in two weeks. When the time came, I went to meet him at the docks.'

There it was, the other bookend to his picture of Keiko leaving their shore with her loved one. Greeted at the other end by this white-haired waif. Hard to say who got the bigger shock.

Vera watched him closely. He felt she could almost see what he was thinking, so he closed his mind to thoughts. There must have been a reason for this all to happen, for her to come to them. He liked her. He thought that he would watch over her.

Finally the question came. 'How come you know how to speak English?' she asked. 'Do they teach you that at sword school?'

He laughed. If only she knew what they taught them at sword school. 'A little,' he confessed. 'But mainly I learned English in England itself.'

'Why did you go to England?'

'I went there to work for my country.'

'Were you a spy?'

He laughed again. 'No. I was a diplomat. But some people think they are the same thing.'

'Your English is quite good. I never heard any other Japanese speak it so well.'

'Thank you,' he said. In fact he was proud of his English. He had spoken it better than anyone in his class. Better than his fellow officers at the Embassy in London. 'I learned excellent English because I loved to go to the theatre.'

'What did you see?' she asked.

'Anything by Shakespeare,' he said.

'Say something in Shakespeare,' she laughed.

'Othello after death of Desdemona,' he said, striking a grand pose. "Speak of me as I am; nothing extenuate,
Nor set down aught in malice. Then must you speak
Of one that lov'd not wisely, but too well;
Of one not easily jealous, but, being wrought,
Perplexed in the extreme; of one whose hand,

Like the base Indian, threw a pearl away
Richer than all his tribe."'

He looked away. Tears had come to her eyes and she was angry that he should see her feelings.

'My grandfather knew every poem there was about pearls,' she said, haughtily. 'Maybe you should stick to polishing swords.'

Ikkanshi bowed.

She went away.

He resumed his work.

Without really planning to, he began to teach her.

They talked about how the Japanese sword was different from the western sword, the sword she might have remembered from nursery tales, King Arthur's sword, and the knights that jousted.

'The western sword,' he said, 'is used to thrust.' He demonstrated the thrust. They were out on the point. The diving girls came by here on the way home from the day's work. That was one reason he could always find her there. She was waiting for them to recognise her, to accept that she could be one of them. But she did not show that she was waiting.

'Do you see, Vera?'

He stood with his right shoulder toward her and asked her to stand the same way toward him. They had sticks in their right hands.

'Westerners fight this way,' he said. He lunged forward on his right foot and poked the stick straight at her chest. 'They poke. They have a shield in their left hand, which they use to protect themselves if the other man's sword comes close to piercing them.'

He poked at her. She danced away. He moved in on her and parried her stick until she slashed at him and broke it. Then he thrust at her chest and pinned her.

'Because of the way it is used, the western sword is thin with a sharp point and a short handle with a large guard around it. The side of the blade is only a little sharp.

'But we Japanese fight this way.'

Now he faced her square on, his right foot a little ahead of his left. He put both hands on the stick that served as his sword, and held it in front of his *tan tien*, his midriff. 'The *katana* is used to cut. Therefore it is longer and heavier, and it is a little more stiff. Not so brittle that it will break when you use it to block, but much stiffer than the western sword. It is your shield. You hold it with two hands and when your opponent attacks, you block his sword with it.'

They played a little with their make-believe swords. He let her have the sun at her back. It was late in the afternoon when they did this and the sun was moving to the west. Drawing on her shadow as it fell toward him, he showed her the high, the low and the middle cuts, and the *kesa*, which goes from shoulder to hip.

'The draw must appear out of nowhere. It is like a shark in a deep sea. You float, you look all around, see nothing; there is a tiny gap, a greater silence and stillness. And then the shark is there, as if it flashed into being. So the sword materialises in the hand,' he said.

When he saw her nearly white hair he thought of her grandfather, the Englishman. And his merry old ways. Her mother, the Canadian, who had left her by dying. Her father, wherever he was. And he wondered what he was fighting with.

The women and girls were out diving and the boys, and often the young men, went with them, managing the boats. The older men fished. The old women scratched at their hopeless little gardens in the dry rocky soil, and the old men repaired the fishing nets. The naked children played in the water. The *katanatogi* was in his workshop, bent over the sharpening stone with a blade in his hand.

Alone, Vera circled the island, and circled it again.

It was not very big, but big enough that she could walk in three directions until the village disappeared. She could walk down to the High Place, up to the shrine, or across, to the outside. The marshy middle connected it all: the two old volcanic cones had stood side by side on the ocean floor for so long that they gradually wore down and joined forces: what remained was an island low in the centre but higher, with the remains of craters, at either end. In one of these was the shrine, the ice house, and beyond it, Dragon Lake. The lake had no source of water but rain, and sometimes it was very low and almost disappeared. On the other was the High Place, and the lighthouse. This was the first bit of the island that was visible when you approached from the sea and the last that remained when you sailed away. Made of wood, the lighthouse had once been red and white, but the paint had worn off. It had a small circular room with a door in its base, and a set of stairs that went up to the light. Recently a generator had been placed there, to run the beam. It was the only electricity on the island.

In the lowland centre was a spring-fed pond. This was called Lost Lake. It was not really a lake but a marsh, frequented by birds in the morning and deserted all day. The water was sweet and cold. Vera looked around for the source of the spring but she could not find it. At the edge of the water were narrow reeds and bamboo grass called *sasa*. In some places the bushes were impenetrable, covered with prickles. She stayed at the edge of the Lost Lake for hours at a time, throwing rocks. When she was tired of throwing them in the water, she threw them at the wild cats. When she was tired of that, she went into the bushes and lay down. She laid her cheek on the ground. She saw, out of the corner of her eye, snails in their shells. She heard a whisper and saw a small white snake slither between the sharp grasses, and it frightened her so much she jumped up, breathing hard. There were swallows and gulls; the

121

other birds made themselves scarce during the hours of sunlight.

When she walked back toward the harbour she could see the flat sea marked out with fishing nets and stakes, to guide the boats in and out, as if it were a farmer's field. At the water's edge, dozens of small children ran under the direction of a naked boy of about six who was their commander. They clambered over the rocks in bare feet and tumbled in and out of the fringes of the sea. Their skin was gilded with sand. Above the shore, gnome-like old women worked the soil, digging it and softening it and digging it again with fish remains to make it fertile.

At the end of the afternoon, Vera watched the boys pole up to the shore, and the girls and women jump over the side of the boat into the foaming small surf, and run it up on the beach. She tried to learn their economical movements as they bent and carried the loaded baskets. They did not look at her, and she imagined they could not see her, sitting amongst the rocks and bushes, picking up smooth stones. She made no effort to disguise her hungry, lonely look.

She singled out one girl of the group of younger diving girls with a special longing, thinking – she was just her age. And she looked kind, and also brave, even a little bold. Her legs were very straight, and her small round buttocks split by the thong that rode up between. Her back was strong and her middle thin. Her neck was longer than the others' necks, and her face oval.

Vera compared this girl to herself, taking the measure of face, legs and hands, knees, even the nape of her neck. She wondered if her breasts were as big or bigger than this girl's, and if people could see her vertebrae like that when she kneeled and bent. She wondered if the girl was a good diver. She wondered if she, Vera, would like her. She looked at the strange girl as she would hold a mirror to herself.

Vera judged that their torsos were nearly the same length,

122

although the *ama* girl's legs were shorter, making Vera inches taller. But the other girl made up for her lack of height in coordination. Her limbs pulled neatly together, arms and legs knowing exactly what to do and being well connected to her centre, whereas Vera felt she had no centre, only dangling limbs. The girl's hands were deft and sure and even her feet were knowing. Collecting her tools and her catch, she bent and straightened, and it was like dancing. Vera watched so intently in secret that she felt sure that any time, years later, in another country, were she to see this girl again, she would recognise the backs of her ankles, the touching angularity of her shoulder, the way her wrists swayed. Some things are imprinted, as on one of those smooth stones, and the stone never thrown away.

When they had finished, never glancing in Vera's direction, the divers and their boatmen began to walk up the path toward their weathered homes. This was *shiran kao*. The *katanatogi* had explained: to know nothing and see nothing of her was, to them, good manners. It was clear that even if Vera had stood, and smiled, and waved, they would have continued on as if she were not there.

But one day it changed.

The *ama* divers returned in the usual way, and with the usual chatter turned toward home. But halfway along the path, the girl Vera always watched stopped. She turned and looked directly into the bushes where Vera sat, picking up smooth stones, and said a few words, loudly; Vera recognised it as a greeting. She went still as if to hide herself further; she could not answer; she had no words. The girl walked toward her then and pressed the bushes apart with her bare arms. Vera could see her two small, sand-dusted feet.

'Hello,' Vera said. She continued to stare at her stones, rattling them in her hand. The sound they made was pleasing; it was as if she had coins, or beads to play with.

'Hello. I am Hanako.'

Hanako stepped through the row of bushes and came to the sandy place where Vera sat. She stood beside her for a few seconds and then let her knees buckle inward, easily, carelessly, as if someone had let go of a string that held her up, and the hinges that were her joints simply folded beneath her. She stayed upright when her knees hit the ground. With this characteristic, curious limpness that Vera would come to know, the *ama* girl joined her.

Wordlessly she too picked up a stone. Her face as she examined it was assessing, interested. She turned the stone in her hand, found that it did not meet her criteria, and discarded it. Then she picked up another. Vera could not look at her. She blushed and played with the stones in her palm. Hanako picked another rock from the sand, and examined it just as carefully as the first. But she found something amiss with that too, and tossed it aside. She tried ten stones before she found one she liked, to offer Vera for her pile.

Vera took the stone. It was smooth, flat, round, perfect. She accepted it.

It was a child's game, but they were no longer children. Still, it was all they could do together.

Vera had many questions, but she couldn't ask the girl. Who had declared that the period of *shiran kao* was magically over? Was it over for everyone? Or was this particular girl, the one Vera had been watching, Hanako, a rebel? Vera thought Hanako must be the boldest of the girls. And she liked that in her. Vera imagined she would have been the same, friendly and curious if a girl from another country dropped into her neighbourhood in Vancouver.

Hanako mimed her questions. What was her name? Where did she come from? What was her country called? Did people there all have long white hair and long legs? Keiko had been to this place called Vancouver, but no one else on the island had. Perhaps Hanako had grasped that although life here was perfect in its way, the summer island

124

was only a little blob of land barely holding its two heads above the sea. Not everyone who lived there knew the special melancholy of that. But maybe Vera interpreted too much. Maybe it was only that Hanako had been watching too, and liked the look of Vera and thought that they could be friends.

She tipped her face down to the serious task of sorting the stones. She picked up and discarded, picked up and discarded a series. Then she found another perfect one, smooth, dark, oval, flat. She showed it to Hanako, who nodded vigorously. Vera saved it in her pile.

And so their language began as the stones, and everything that appeared on the shore.

# 4

## *Tsuka-ate*
### Strike with the handle

On the summer island, the naked babies were set down in the tidepools to pull out crayfish. As they grew bigger they crawled to plunge their chubby hands in deeper pools for a shell that looked to be in reach. But the water had magnified it, and it wasn't in reach; perhaps, striving for it, they overbalanced and fell in. When their faces went under they pulled them out quickly, looking startled, and then simply closed their lips, and tried it again. After one mouthful or noseful of sea water, they learned to hold their breath. At two, they floated and bobbed under the surface. At five and six years, they dived for shells at depths over their heads.

Not so Vera. She had been taught to fear the water. It was frigid, overpowering, and probably dirty. At English Bay, where she walked with her mother, the surf was cold and there were big rocks. If she swam, her mother stood anxiously at the exact spot where Vera's footprints entered the water, willing her return to dry land. Here on the summer island, the water was warmer, but she was nervous, and she had confined her rock games to several yards back from where the waves broke.

Hanako's first wordless manoeuvre was to move their search for stones out of the Low Place to the tide fringe where the shells and pebbles were dumped by the waves. They sat on the bigger rocks and put their feet up to the ankles in the sea. Immediately the feet appeared to swell, which amused them.

126

They pulled them in and out, laughing at the way they grew fat and thin. They picked up pebbles with their toes. Little crabs, disturbed, flew up in clouds of sand. Minute fish jerked in straight lines this way and that, neon stripes on their sides. Tiny shellfish slumbered at the very rim of the water, but if you splashed them, they shot forward, pushing a cloud of sand up behind them. Hanako chased them, clutching her hands uselessly as they passed. She stumbled and fell into the water, clowning to get a real laugh out of Vera. There was no fooling her with a pretend laugh.

Then Hanako stood, and beckoned Vera to follow her on the path. She walked inland to the Lost Lake. She walked through the reeds and came to the spot where the spring came out of the ground. This was what Vera had not been able to find. There, Hanako rinsed off the salt water, and dried herself on her *yakata*, and waving goodbye, went home.

Most days after that, Hanako met Vera at the water's edge after her day of diving. They played their child's games, but quickly made them more complex. They got down on hands and knees and picked up the shells that were cast there in a fine line by the departing waves. She told Vera the names of the shells: there were the sun and moon shells she called *tsukihigai*, and the shells, named for the birds that darted along the water line, that she called *chidorigai*, and Vera called plovers. The sun and moon shells were called that because they were different on each side. The crabs were called *kani* and there was something mystical about them. Vera understood from Hanako's slashing movements and fierce posturing that the crabs were warriors who had come back to life.

They found a snail, and passed it from palm to palm. They tickled its little greasy foot until it retreated and stayed firmly hidden. And in the warm water at the very edge when there was low tide, and there were little pools, Hanako showed Vera the fry of the scallops. How they could skip nimbly through the water in a zigzag way. They made themselves shoot forward by suddenly opening and closing their shells.

Without seeming to notice, Hanako crawled back and forth equally through water and air. They walked on the stones, and ran on them, over and over, hardening the soles of Vera's feet. Hanako ran in the water and out of it, but Vera remained at the edge. She let the waves lap her, but never carry her off the sand.

After a week, Hanako brought Vera a pair of the goggles that the *ama* wore. They were simple, glass eyepieces that attached around the back of her head with a piece of rubber. When Hanako wore them, her eyes looked round and bulging. In the sea where the water was chest-deep, they stood staring into each other's magnified eyes, taking breaths, and staying under, blowing bubbles up to the surface and making faces through the bubble stream.

They dived from there, pressing their hands, and then their feet on the ocean floor and shooting up into the air. They floated on their stomachs in the tide pools over beds of seaweed, parting the green grasses and looking down to their roots to see what shellfish they could find. Vera learned to judge the depth of the water by its colour. The green stripes that came with the wind, the white lines of foam, the yellow places where the rocks were near the surface, the warmer spots where there was no current.

When they got cold in the water, they came onto the grassy sand. They collected two dozen half shells, and put coloured stones under them and played the memory game where they turned the halves upside down and had to find the match. There was another game called Waiting for the Snake, which they played in the eel grass at the edge of the marshy place. The little white snake had something to do with a goddess who lived on the island, that Vera understood, but no more. She had begun to know some words, and even to speak simple sentences.

All this happened in the late afternoons. The sun would still be bearing down hard, and the wind, if there had been a wind, died. The rocks were baking hot and the water still. It was the sweetest time of day. But eventually Hanako's skin began to pucker and goose-bumps to appear in the fine, nearly invisible hairs along her legs and arms. Vera would say 'cold', and hug herself and make burring noises with her lips. She would say, 'you must go home', and pick up the *yukata* and gesture for her friend to wrap herself in it. Hanako insisted she was not cold. But as the sun passed five o'clock and began its steady decline toward the water, they felt the faint stirrings of what might be an evening breeze. Hanako would say that she had to go home to help her mother.

'Mother,' she said, and smiled enquiringly. 'You, mother? Not Keiko.' She would giggle at the thought.

Here Vera was silent.

She did not have to go home.

She did not have a mother.

'No, no, no,' she said to Hanako. 'I'll stay outside.'

Surely there were some advantages to being motherless! Keiko could not make her help in the house. She could not make her do anything. Vera ran by herself on the summer island. She had made up her mind, those many hours when she lay with her cheek on the hard ground. She had given in to Keiko enough, in coming here, and the rest would be her way.

And Hanako accepted, although it seemed she did not understand.

There was a ritual to the way they said goodbye. First they walked a little way inland to the spring by the lake. They splashed – it was always cold, that water, colder than the salty lip of the sea where they'd been playing – and dunked their heads and scrubbed everywhere to get the prickly salt out of their skin. They mirrored each other the whole time: if Hanako scrubbed out her right ear, Vera scrubbed her left. If Hanako stood like a crane on her right leg and brushed sand off her left foot, Vera did the opposite. They laughed with great delight while they did this. Then, turning and spinning, in the spots of sun that remained, they dried themselves. Finally Hanako collected the stones or snails they had saved from their hours foraging, and, with only a look and a slight wave of her hand, turned toward home.

Vera watched her go and then walked in the other direction. She went over the bridge made of planks and up the incline to the broken edges of the crater, farther away from the village and above the rim of the beach, to the High Place. She imagined long ago this was a small volcano, that black lava and fiery rocks had flown out of it. The flat top was ringed by boulders poised as if about to slide down the slope. She climbed part way down. There were places you could sit amongst these boulders, and look out to the sea.

Out of sight and protected from the evening wind, she leaned back on a warm rock and pondered. In the lengthening light she was alone, more alone than she had been all day waiting for Hanako. She thought about her mother. She saw her standing there above the beach in her apron with her hands on her hips calling Vera in to dinner. It was strange for her to appear, here on the summer island, so far from Vancouver and from her life. It had been four years since Belle had taken her handbag and got on the bus, and Vera had come home from school to the empty house. But for those years, Vera had her grandfather. Now that James Lowinger was buried, and she had come to this alien island, Vera was face to face with it: her mother was dead and gone.

But even as Vera swallowed this hard lump in her throat, she looked up and there Belle was, transformed from a burning hurt to a shape flared with the lowering sun. She was standing in the centre of the High Place looking down on Vera. Her outline was clear and dark against the deep blue sky of evening. She wore a woollen skirt with box pleats behind the knee, and a pale pink blouse, everything fitting at the waist. She looked severe; her dress was formal, compared with the local style of dress, which was, basically, undress. Vera knew it was not possible for Belle to be here, and yet she could see her clearly, her arms folded across her waist, pacing a little while keeping an eye on Vera, just as she had long ago at English Bay. It gave Vera the shivers just sitting, so she got up and, with a stick in her hand, began to imitate the *katanatogi*'s movements with his sword, making sideways cuts and overhead blocks and swinging the stick as hard as she could, to see if she could hear a whistle.

'Who are you fighting?' Belle asked.

Vera looked up. There was a tremor in her mother's voice. Belle was always sad, but less sad when she was at the shore, pulling up ropes of kelp and popping its buttons between her thumb and forefinger. Maybe the water had made her feel she could get away.

'Water! I am fighting the water.'

'Water!' Belle said, hugging herself. 'Why pick a fight with water? It doesn't fight back.'

'Oh yes it does. It's hard and cold and slaps you. It goes everywhere.'

'I see.' She laughed a little, as she had at Vera's cleverness when she was very small.

'It's strong. Very strong!'

Vera clambered down through the boulders and crossed the narrow bit of sand to the water's edge where she smacked the surface of the sea with her stick. She did not make a dint. She smacked it again and a small wave formed.

'See? At first it just resists you, but eventually it will react, if you keep at it.'

'Ah! Remember that,' Belle said. Then she came down from the High Place and was beside Vera. It seemed at that moment as if Belle were happy. At least Vera's antics roused her from the doldrums.

'Look, it's transparent when it's still. But now –' Vera plunged the end of her stick in and stirred it '– it gets all boiled up and you can't see through it.' She pressed her stick deeper and then found she couldn't stir. 'It is heavy! It is bad.' She said this last word proudly in Japanese.

'Be careful what you say,' Belle retorted. 'You are born from water. It is like your mother. The womb is a small, enclosed sea, and it is salty, too.'

This made Vera angry. Belle had to play that trump card, didn't she? She smacked the water some more and walked off down the beach. But Belle followed, walking along the edge of the High Place. She had put on a cardigan, pulled close around her waist, and her brown hair was blowing out of the chignon she always wound, little bits of it coming across her cheeks like the age lines she never lived to get. She stopped above the place where Vera was and looked out to where the sea drew its thin straight line across the sky. She had to finish her lecture.

'But after you are born, water is fatal to you. You are a land creature.'

'You are. That doesn't mean I am.'

Her mother said nothing. She had ended her life in water, after all.

'Japan is your home country,' said Vera to her mother. 'Weren't you born here? Is that why you came back?'

'I was born in Yokohama. But I don't remember it. My mother took me to England and put me in school, when I was four. You know that.'

Vera tried to imagine a four-year-old in boarding school. She could not.

'Where did your mother go?'

'She came to see me,' said Belle, quietly. 'Just as I am coming to see you.'

'Was she dead?'

'No, she was not dead.'

'What was she like, my grandmother?' It just occurred to her now: her mother had never talked about her own mother.

'She had a good eye for a pearl, they said,' said Belle. And that was all.

'You never talk about her. She took you away from here.'

'My mother hated Japan,' said Belle.

'Why?' Vera asked.

Belle did not answer. 'It is not a good place for you. You made a mistake coming here.'

The two sat companionably enough side by side at the rim of the sea. Belle, thought Vera, was alone too much of her life. And now Vera was alone.

132

'Do you know that when you were born your father was away at sea?'

'Yes, I know, Mum. You told me.'

'And your grandfather came to see you? You know he came in from the South Seas, all that way, to be there for the birth. I was so proud when I held you in my arms, and showed you to him, and he bent down to look at your face.'

'I've heard this a hundred times, Mum.' For some reason Vera did not like the scene she conjured: Poseidon coming to claim his little pearl.

'And you screwed your face up in a big red ball and screamed at him!'

'You better believe I did!' She danced away with her stick.

Sometimes Vera hated the old man, her grandfather. There had to be some balance, between the two of them, and if her mother adored him that much Vera should go the other way. Besides, he was the one who got her here. If he was so great, Vera thought, where was he now? If it was a betrayal for her father to be out on the ocean, then why was it not the same for her grandfather?

'But that was his life! My father came from a seafaring family,' Belle said. 'It was always that way, when I grew up.'

Vera ran off to inspect a water-soaked log that had drifted in. It had green moss on one side and the ends were split. It was crusted with salt and full of insects. When she kicked one end, it exploded.

Belle was gone.

Then she began to cry. She always cried when she felt unfairly treated. This weakness maddened her. Just when she wanted to be defiant, she collapsed. Never when she was injured, or when other kids picked on her, when she could have been expected to cry. Only when the accusation was unfair.

After Hanako went home she cried, most evenings, when the sun finally sank off the end of the island, and, only after she had wiped her eyes, did she go home to Keiko's hearth.

*   *   *

133

Keiko was a single woman, a widow, as she was politely known in the village. But she did not live alone. No one lived alone on the summer island. The house, the paper box as Vera called it, did not belong to her, but to her family. Keiko had grown up coming to this simple house for the fishing season, and had memories of it filled with mother and father, aunts and uncles, cousins. But now there were only a few of them. Keiko's father had died, and her mother stayed on the mainland to care for his parents. Keiko's brothers, like her, wanted to escape: one lived in Tokyo now, another had gone to Australia with a fishing fleet. One had to stay at home, the one Keiko and Vera had gone to in Toba, but he no longer fished at the summer island. There were, this summer, five: Keiko and Vera, an old aunt, an uncle, and the boy. Vera hardly noticed the others, they were so small, and quiet, and focused on their curious tasks of scraping the earth and sewing the nets and preparing mysterious food. And then, too, she had not learned their language. In fact, except when she was with the *katanatogi* or Hanako, she felt a positive determination not to learn their language. Keiko spoke to her in English.

When Vera entered the shaded house with its small stone oil lamps, there was a rustle amongst the older folk. Perhaps they counselled Keiko to keep her inside, to make her help with the chores; Vera imagined they said unsympathetic things like, 'There she comes, the wild one, the foreign girl'. She was to discover later that their instincts were more protective. They did not want her out observing the sunset, which to them was an omen of death and decay. But Keiko's face showed nothing but an easy pleasure to have Vera back amongst them. She made a place for her around the square hearth with the few coals burning in the centre of a little plot of grey ash. The ash was raked to a fine smoothness, and stood in perfect rows like a field ready to be planted.

She motioned Vera to come to sit in the place she had made. Vera held out her hands for the customary bowl of miso, and drank it quickly.

'And your day, how was it?' Keiko asked.

Vera looked away and mumbled, 'My day was nothing.'

And suddenly the day, which had been in its way miraculous and full of challenge, wonder and tenderness, became, indeed, nothing. Vera held it to be Keiko's fault that she was here, on this lost little rock, when she could have been in Vancouver, at her school, shopping on Granville Street with her friends, going to films at her namesake theatre. And she was not ready to stop blaming her, so in her eyes she had to have had a miserable day.

Perhaps Keiko understood this. She did nothing but take in a quick, barely audible breath. Her eyes strained at the lids, just a little, with her effort to hide the hurt. Vera felt a thrill of pleasure, then a wash of regret which, again, made her angry.

But Keiko immediately inclined her head with an accepting smile. 'Oh, it was nothing, so?' she said, with that lilt at the end of the phrase. Then, in halting English, she talked about her own day, at sea, about the catch, which had been good, but not as good as it might have been. The old couple spoke together and soon, because it was dark, everyone prepared for sleep, bringing out their mosquito nets and draping them over the futons. Vera too, felt sleepy and lay down quite satisfied with her day although she would never admit it to Keiko.

The next morning as usual, Vera set out on her circuit of the island. She visited the old shrine. She saw the priest there, writing on paper, but she slunk away. She went past the ice house: the hole was covered with dried grass, but she could feel the chill of it. She went to the Lost Lake and threw stones, and then came back to the Low Place. She watched the babies on the shore, lolling and splashing, almost black now with suntan. They played in the wheeled wooden carts that their parents used to carry heavy items from the boats to the houses, lying down in them, rolling them over the stones, shouting. There was no one her age. She walked up the street toward the houses. She went

135

past the sword polisher's door and saw that he was seated on his tiny bench, immersed in his work.

'What are you doing?' he asked.

'Nothing.'

'Yes,' he said. 'In the village, people don't know what to do with you.'

She inched her way into his workshop. She bowed, and then she hesitated. He made a movement of his hand that told her she could sit. She dropped onto her knees, as she had learned to do from Hanako. He sat back from his work, lifting his eyes.

'Would you like some tea?'

She watched him take the iron teapot from the fire.

'Keiko says I can be a diver. Earn my way and learn a trade. But the Headman says no.'

'You are not *ama*.'

'Keiko says I am now that she has charge of me'

'*Ama* means born of the sea.'

'I am born of the sea,' she said. 'My mother said so. The womb is full of salt water.'

He laughed. 'You are clever, that's one thing.'

'Keiko says that what I become is for her to decide and that she has decided this much: I must be of use, and in this village that means I must dive.'

'But, you are English.'

'Not English. My mother was born in Yokohama, Japan. I am Canadian. And a little bit Japanese.'

'You look English,' said Ikkanshi-san. 'Your family would never allow a loved one, a granddaughter, to dive. It is dangerous, cold work, work for fishing people, for sea people, who understand sea gods. The Headman puts his views like stones on the ground. He cannot be moved.'

'Keiko will not move either,' Vera said.

'So. They are like warriors. They both wait. There is plenty of time. Neither one will fight the other; neither one wants a showdown.'

'But I have nothing to do,' she said.

136

'Keiko is wise,' said the *katanatogi*. 'In whatever way is possible she will see that you can learn what you need to meet your life.'

Vera drained her cup of tea, and looked again to see if there was any left in the bottom of the cup. She said nothing.

'Talk more,' he said. 'I like to hear your words. They bring back my English.'

'Where did you learn it again?' she asked casually, as if she had taken no real interest in his answer the first time. Since she could not talk to Keiko, he was the only person she could communicate with in English. She had to know how he came by this grace and how he had been given to her in her current predicament.

'At school here in Japan,' he said, 'but it improved when I went to England.'

Then she asked him what he did in England, and who he met.

'I played some tennis,' he said. 'At a club where the grass was under a roof and inside a house. The English built it this way, because it rained so much we could not play outside.'

'Were you a good tennis player?'

'Tennis was rather easy for me,' he confessed. 'Golf also. It is the swing. If you have been dividing in two with your sword pieces of fruit that have been tossed at you, for a dozen years, it gives you an advantage.'

This was meant to make her laugh, but the diversionary tactic did not work with Vera. She persisted in her line of questioning. Her mother had been in boarding school in England. Vera was curious about it. And here was a Japanese man who had gone there.

'Did you wear that in London?' she asked, nodding to his bare chest and wrapped skirt.

'No.' He told her what he remembered: he wore linen suits with creased and pleated pants, and the shaped felt hats that made him feel like a film star. 'I used to take the Tube,' he said, pronouncing it 'teeyoube', 'to Covent Garden. The Royal Opera

137

House.' He remembered how he used to stand at the top in the back of the theatre, and lean over the rail and count the hundreds of tiny red lampshades that were positioned on the curved wall. There were women in satin dresses that clung to their hips.

'Did you go alone?' she asked.

'No,' he said, and his face creased up as if he did not want to remember.

'Who did you go with?'

'There were others of us at the Japanese Consulate,' he said. 'My fellow students from officer school. Sometimes one of them would go with me.'

'What were their names?' she persisted.

'They had various names. You would only forget them,' said the *katanatogi* quietly.

'No, I wouldn't.'

'One was called Oshima, Hiroshi.' Now there was a formidable look on his face, so that even Vera did not dare ask more.

But Ikkanshi-san pushed himself forward.

'A friend would join me there, and he loved *Swan Lake* almost as much as I did. The theatre,' he said. 'We went to the theatre in Drury Lane. And saw *The Mikado*.' He laughed. She did not find this funny until he explained that it was about how ridiculous the English found the Japanese. This his friends did not find amusing.

His hands strayed back to the blade that he had been working on. 'But that was a long time ago.'

'How long ago?' she challenged.

'Not so very long,' he corrected. 'Not more than five years. It only feels like long ago.'

'Why did you come back to this place?'

'Because I am *katanatogi*. And my father was and his father before him and many many fathers disappearing into the centuries past.'

'But why to the summer island?'

'You ask a great many questions,' he said.

138

'And you answer them.'

'Sometimes to practise an art you must go away from nearly all the world, to a quiet place, and remain apart from what is happening. This is what *katanatogi* must do. Then, perhaps the world will come to him.'

She did not accept this answer. 'And you did not know this before?' Vera sniffed.

'I knew it, but I did not believe it,' he said, and returned to squat over the polishing stone until the girl bowed (learning, every day) and went silently away.

On some days a storm or wind prevented the fishing; other days the women stopped early to meet the ferry. One day, when the boat pulled up to the small dock, looking as always, as if it might simply plough the simple board structure under the sand, the basket maker came.

He stepped onto the land with his strong foot, his weaker one dragging a little. He carried on his back a large woven pack full of bamboo strips and tools and some small belongings. It was just the right time; the baskets he had made or repaired the year before had begun to need attention. The people saw him coming and waved, and went inside their houses to find the baskets that needed repair. He stopped by the well and took the pack off his back. He took the scoop and poured himself a cup of water, drank it noisily, and then poured himself another, which he overturned on top of his head. Then he shook his shaggy locks and looked around, pleased with himself.

Vera had seen him in the village on the mainland. He bowed and smiled to her as if he knew her, but she was frightened of him. She did not expect to see him here. She went back to her special haunts. When she returned later in the day, he was seated by the well, surrounded by baskets. The little children danced around him asking for toys. They did not seem afraid. He waved them off; he would make them something when he had finished for the day. He had too much work, it seemed, to return with the ferry. He would stay an entire week, then. That was the only way. For some reason this made Vera uneasy.

One afternoon, when Vera and Hanako went to the spring to rinse the sand and salt from their bodies, Hanako held up eight fingers.

'*Hatch*,' she said.

Vera repeated the word.

'*Ju-ich*,' said Hanako. Nine.

'*Ju-i*.' Ten.

At '*ju-i*' on the clock they would meet at the end of the street that ran through the centre of the village. Vera was neither allowed nor prevented from going out. When the others went to sleep, she simply rose from her futon, put on her *yakata*, and went out of the door.

The moment she left the protection of the doorway and entered the night she wondered why it had taken so long to do this. Here was night itself, dark, inky, soft. Night in the open, night above the whisper of the sea and under the flaring cape of the sky. The huts were reduced to grey shambles; only the angles of their roofs and the sharp edges of the shale that held the roof tiles in place showed. Studded into this cushion of delicious black were a few orangey pricks of the oil lamplight just visible through a window.

A sliver of new moon gave the weathered wooden walls a cool blue cast, and even made shadows at corners, which to Vera were entirely new. She had never seen a moon shadow in Vancouver, in fact it was rare to see stars. Nights at home were usually cloudy, the sky enclosed by square buildings and made darker by their lights. The streetlights, and the cars that striped the streets stole perspective. The air over the city had a close, artificial glow. But here was a serene blackness stretching out-wards, stabbed through by stars like the ones she'd first seen in the *ukiyo-e* on Homer Street.

*Here*, Vera thought. And where is that? An island somewhere off Japan. An island that barely has a name. But she knew more

140

about it already than she knew about anywhere else. That was it; she had never before been so aware of where she was on earth.

The air was cool, but underfoot the rocks were warm. It was high summer by now. She thought of the promised swim: the water would slip easily over her skin. Vera crept along the main path of the village, passing one door after the next. A glance through a half-open screen gave her a vision of people squatting around the stone hearth. The firelight flickered in the cracks between the wooden siding. It was all so thin, so temporary. Yet it was somehow safe, too, safe because everyone was there.

She went along to the far end of the village, the poor end. Even here, with the Fisherman's Union and so little in the way of material things, some people were poorer than others. Perhaps it had to do with drinking. The fishermen went to houses here to drink and take their baths. Women went there too, certain women that Keiko did not like. Vera heard the laughter, and she retreated.

At the Low Place, Vera sat on the warm rock and waited. In a minute the mosquitoes found her. She wrapped her blanket over her back and head. The mosquitoes swarmed but they could not find their way in to her skin. She wondered if Hana would come. She wondered how it was that Hanako ever did come out to be with her. No one else was allowed to speak to her. It did not occur to her that Hanako's mother and grandmother had told the girl to befriend her. She could not know that the *ama* women had discussed her predicament, and that they saw that this was the best way for her to become part of the summer island. They could not all disobey, but one girl could, and that girl was Hanako. Even if the Headman had not approved it, even though it had never happened before.

That first night, Hanako did not come. After listening a long time to the sea and the wind, and the insects, Vera went home. She did not really mind. Simply waiting for Hana had itself been an important mission. She would be happy to do it again and again. As she walked silently up the path she could see that

141

even this late, some people were awake. Always there was an adult world at night, but here it was tantalizingly close at hand, thinly screened. She turned into Keiko's doorway and made her way unnoticed across the floor to bed, and slept.

On the second night, Hanako did come, appearing in front of her, dancing, to avoid the mosquitoes. She laughed at Vera's blanket-hood. Gesturing for her friend to throw off the wraps, she told her to get up, they were going to the High Place.

There, under the moonlight, they could see far out over the water. Waves crested in broken lines perhaps a hundred feet from shore; a rail of moonlit foam raced, like a shooting star, from one end to the other, fading, then rising again at another spot and racing outward. They stood staring. Instantly it became a game, to guess where a white foam-bud would rise, and how long it would last, shooting slowly along the top of the breaking wave. They pointed and danced, slapping their legs to kill not the mosquitoes, but the sting they left, pointed and danced, four skinny legs, four skinny arms, mimicked by their moon shadows attached to their heels on the hard sand.

When they tired of this they climbed down the boulder slope to the shore and lifted rocks. Crabs – the old warriors in their awkward armour – cranked themselves up and fled, effortlessly, on lightning toes from one hiding place to another. When the girls lifted that rock, the crabs levered themselves up on their legs and challenged them.

Vera waded, first to her ankles, then to her knees. The water was silky, almost oily around her skin. She felt its touch now, at night, more than in the day; the darkness took away the distraction of sight. She stood with her feet apart, and fell to her knees, abased in the sand, splashing the sea water over her arms and chest. Hanako lay on her stomach, trusting her midriff to anything that might walk on this sloping verandah to the deeper water, and rolled like a log. Vera too fell over sideways and washed in the surf.

The water was soft. It was warm too, warmer than the air,

warmer than the sand. The water came all over and around her and, if she wasn't careful, into her, its sharp salt making her cough and her eyes blur so she could not see Hanako any more.

At the harbour the fishermen were working in the dark. In little wooden boats, they floated in the shallows, casting nets onto the water where their strands made cross-hatches on the silken surface before falling out of sight. At intervals along the length the men tethered the nets by making a tepee of three bamboo sticks leaning together. They tied the sticks together with a strip of cloth. These fragile markers were evenly spaced, standing in the shallows, extending perhaps three feet above the water. When the nets were all laid down, the fishermen con- tinued to cross over the place where they sank, swinging their oil lanterns. Hanako said that the fish would come to the light. When the nets were lifted near morning, they would be full of big shrimp, *isebi*.

The water in the sheltered curve of the harbour was utterly flat and calm, and the lights and the tied poles made it look like a mysterious field, not liquid at all. These poles made lines, fences, depending on where one stood behind them. If Vera stood in a certain place and looked through them, she saw a narrowing, a portal, a gateway to the sea. Here was a funnel, narrow at the middle and wide on either end. The sticks with their knotted cloths were like signs begging to be understood. Like letters painted on rice paper. But Vera could not read them.

On the third night, Hanako brought a small lantern from home. She led Vera away from the lights to the *ura*, the backside of the island, walking on the path that twisted across the inland.

It was dark on the backside. This was the steep, rough edge where there was no beach and no safe harbour, only the bizarre, worn out old rocks standing in tiers above the water, some high, some low enough to sit on with your feet in the sea. At the *ura* too, there were little spits of islands off the summer island, as if it had once extended farther into the sea, but had given up and sunk, leaving only these traces.

The girls found a rock without too many rough places and sat on it, looking out. One of the standing rocks was muffin-shaped, worn nearly through at the bottom and coiffed with a few trees. One looked like a shrunken head; and another must have been a shrine; it had a spindly torii arch on top. Because it was night, the colour was gone from everything, and there was only the alternating black and silver of the water, the island, more water, and the sky. Silver, black, silver, black, silver, black, in layers.

Vera shivered.

Hana pulled closer to her. Here they were unprotected from the small, steady salt wind that breathed into their faces. The moon was a little bigger than it had been the night before, with a blurred edge to show that it would be bigger tomorrow. Its glow fringed the wavelets silver.

'There are fish,' Hanako said, 'that come by night. Night fish.'

Vera shivered again.

'There are fish that blink like lanterns.' She pointed to her lantern. 'They are lantern fish.' She wanted Vera to go down to the edge with her and see. She coaxed her toward the water.

Vera said no. Dark, unknown water: what was down there?

'It's not dark,' Hanako promised, 'when you dive down.' She took her hand and pulled her off the rock. She showed her a shallower place. Indeed it was not so dark. The moon reflected back up off the sand at the bottom.

'No, no, no,' said Vera. 'Fish will touch me in the dark.'

'Nice fish,' Hana laughed. 'No bad fish. I promise.'

Vera had taught her these words. The sign language was universal; to make a cross on the heart. The rest she made Vera understand, without using words. There will be no sharks or anything bad. It is too close to the island. Look we are right on the best swimming rock. You can slip in easily and almost touch bottom. Come and lie in the water.

The following day, Vera stopped by to talk to the sword polisher.

'My friend has taught me to swim at night,' she told him.

144

'I saw that.'

'You watch us?'

'Not really,' he said. 'Everyone sees everything that happens on this island.'

She thought about that, and realised that he must be right. It was a good thing, in a way.

'Keiko says you are the best polisher in all Japan,' she said.

He bowed. 'Of course it is not so,' he said, composing a forbidding look. But Ikkanshi was inordinately pleased to hear that Keiko had spoken well of him.

He had a blade on the stone. Looking around his room with its bare walls which went straight to the stony ground, she asked him where he had got it.

'It came to me,' he said.

She could see that he wanted to stop there, but she would not let him.

'It came? How did it come? Must be on the ferry,' she said.

'From the *katanakaji*. The swordsmith.' He did not name him or say where he was.

'The *katanakaji* came here? I did not see him. Perhaps he sent a messenger.'

Ikkanshi kept his head down.

'I know who the messenger is,' she said. 'It is the basket maker. And I don't like him.'

He raised one eyebrow. 'You make up an opinion very quickly.'

'Is he a friend of yours?' she asked.

'Perhaps.'

But Vera could tell he wasn't. 'That's like your other friends, in London,' she said. 'You're not certain if they were friends either!'

He gave one of the warning looks; she had gone far enough. She changed tactics.

'So, the *katanakaji* made it?' she said with a look of disbelief. 'How did he make it?'

'He does it in a very hot fire,' he said. 'He must heat and fold over and hammer out the same piece of metal thousands of

145

times to eliminate impurities. He makes the blade by combining a soft inner core of steel with a hard outer skin. That way he will come up with a material that is hard enough to cut well, but soft enough to be flexible, so that it will not snap. It is no good to make a hard sword that will snap the moment it meets an enemy's armour.'

'I don't believe anyone can make a sword like that,' she said.

'Where do you think it comes from then?'

'I don't know. A factory, I suppose.'

'You westerners think everything is made by machines.' It made him laugh. 'There are blades that are made now very quickly and partly by machine,' he said. 'But they are very poor quality. To make a sword properly, there is only one way, and it is a long and a hard way.'

'Why are they making bad ones now?' Vera asked. And when he did not answer, she answered herself. 'It is for the war in China, isn't it?'

'Yes. The war is the cause of making all these bad swords.'

'How do you know about the war? We have no news here.'

He avoided the question. 'A sword is not just a thing of metal. It is a spirit. Each sword has its own mysterious quality. That makes it different from every other sword.'

'Will that be used in the war?' she asked. 'I thought you would not make a sword that would be used for killing. I thought you only made a sword for a work of art.'

He looked down at his whetstone, and ground the blade a little faster. He did not expect the sword to be used in battle; that was true. But he could not be sure. He did not want to mislead the girl. 'It is a ceremonial sword. But that does not mean it should be weak. There is no excuse for poor workmanship.'

She went on her way and he continued with his blade.

She reminded him of himself.

146

When he had first come to the island he was so used to shouting that his voice cracked in his voice-box when he tried to speak normally. He had come home from England and left the army behind, giving only the excuse that his old father was dying. So he was, and so he did. Ikkanshi had sat with him the last few times the master went to his whetstone. He told his father he could no longer be in the Emperor's service; he had become convinced, over his years in London, that the way of the new Japan would destroy them. It seemed his colleagues were against the whole world.

His father was silent and went on examining a blade.

'You must take great care to find the spirit of the blade,' he said. 'It will not be readily apparent. But if you hold it quietly and for a long time, it will come to you.'

Ikkanshi knew he understood.

After his father's death, Ikkanshi sent word: he would follow in his master's footsteps. To do that meant many more years. It was his calling.

The High Command could not complain.

Why he chose the summer island he was not certain. It was more than a place of hiding. He wanted to be by the sea for years at a time and to feel its rhythm. He imagined that the sea had something to tell him about how to be Japanese, and how to be human.

He took the ferry and held his face up to the wind. The salt air made tears in the corners of his eyes. He walked alone up the path from the ferry dock. This was no place to visit. There was no hotel for tourists, no restaurant. No one came here, no summer tourists, no foreigners, and no students. There were only *ama* here, like a tribe unto themselves. The Japanese feel a little of two things about the *ama*. The fisher people were primitive, and they were poor. They were what all Japanese must have been, at one time, and that made them ashamed. Yet they should honour their past, and therefore be proud.

He presented himself to the Headman. The Headman allowed him to sleep in the temple, and when he learned that he was a sword polisher, offered him a room to work in. But Ikkanshi was not ready to polish swords. He had not completed the apprenticeship he had begun with his father; he had instead gone away to go to officer school. That was the modern way. He could help, however, with the knives and tools the people used for fishing.

Keiko brought him her *tagane*, the knife she used to cut the foot of the awabi away from the rock. He was seated in front of his whetstones looking down, when she appeared, a pair of feet, two narrow ankles with bones that met at one eloquent point, from which small strong legs rose up invitingly. He did not look.

He took the knife from her hands. Her hands were light of touch, not padded or moistened with oil as were the hands of the girls his parents had presented to him. They were lean, wary hands, very strong and wilful, he could see. He took the knife, but he continued to look at her hands, and to his shame all he could imagine was the magic those powerful, pretty hands could work if they should touch him.

Aroused, he glanced quickly down, and commanded his body to cease and desist. This was not a very good sign for the future which he saw for himself, which was as a species of sword monk. He did not look up again when he promised her the knife by the next day. He had other work he should have put before it, but he wanted to finish quickly, so that she would come back soon.

He knew that men saw the *ama* women as erotic. It was

not their nakedness, near nakedness: that was a matter of no account, merely a sign of the type of work they did. It was something else, their muscularity of form and of personality. He watched the shore and saw them going out in the morning, then coming in, in the evening. They were loose and free in their laughter. Although they were of this place and no other, they had about them a curious air, a manner that no other Japanese women bore. It was the air of emancipation. They could survive alone, without men, and they knew it. The males were all on sufferance. Yet the community held the women close. This was a contradiction.

And it was exhilarating to Ikkanshi. He saw that Keiko, the one who had brought him her knife, was the most spirited of all. He imagined her under the sea, slipping like a fish between the rocks with the weeds drifting along her thighs.

He had not come here to satisfy his creature longings. That was possible in Tokyo any night. He had come to quash them. He had come to train himself to live in a place where they would have no expression.

Ikkanshi filed her knife to a dangerous sharpness and did not look into Keiko's eyes when she returned for it.

The heat, and the dryness that it brought, were exceptional that summer. The winds took the clouds that so often floated above the horizon, gradually enveloping the sun, and blew them away. The sky was left exposed, pure blue, scoured. And the sun poured out of it relentlessly, baffling the people's faces with blocks of pure light.

In the baking daylight he stayed inside, with his stones and sometimes his fire. He sharpened the hoes of the old women who scraped at their gardens in the tough soil. He made large needles that could be threaded to mend the nets. He fixed the thinning bottoms of cooking pots. In the late evening, when he was not mending or fixing, he went to the water and swam.

It was not common, to see people swim for pleasure there. The people had no need to do so; they were in the water and out of it all day long. But he was different. He was from the city. He was exercising. He was an officer, and he was of samurai class. This much was obvious even in this simple backdrop, although he had no possessions to show his difference. It was in his speech, his manners, his posture, and his silence. Why should it not be in his swimming?

The fishermen would gather on shore and watch him. He would begin, and not stop for an hour or more, as the sun was going down. He swam in a line along the shore, straight as a destroyer would steer. If there came a rock in his path, he veered carefully around it, without lifting his head. He did not go out deeper, or in shallower.

'Good thing he's not pointing out that way,' one of them might say, gesturing toward the open sea. 'You'd never know where he would stop.'

Ikkanshi would go around the High Point and then turn an exact one hundred and eighty degrees, which would bring him back to the same path along the beach, returning to the far end of the settled strip, near the baths. Then he would get out and go into the baths with the other men.

There, a space would open for him on the bench. At first, when he entered, the rowdy brown-skinned men with their lined faces and strong torsos would drop their voices and their eyes. He said little, but grunted when the wind, the rain, the blasting heat, the number of awabi caught this year as compared with last year, came up in the conversation. If the fishermen expected him to put himself above them, they were disappointed. He put himself in their midst, a mystery.

But even a mystery is absorbed in an incurious place, and the men appeared to forget that he was different. Island life took its usual shape around him, neither including nor excluding Ikkanshi. And that was what he wanted. That was what he should have insisted on. If the women talked about him, they whispered that he was old. He was not old. He was thoughtful. Maybe he was burdened. But even the women lost their curiosity after a time.

He had refused the wife his mother found for him. She was a young girl, very young, only eighteen, while he was thirty-two. He said that it was because he was going away and that he did not know how long he would be gone, practising his art, or even if he would come back. It was not fair to take a protected Japanese girl to the island, where she would be so different. Sometimes near sunset, as he walked along the beach, he would see Keiko at the well, or arm in arm with another woman. She was not married. This was strange because the *ama* girls married young. Very casually, in the baths, he asked about her. That one is fussy, the men said, laughing strangely. Or just, That one! And nothing more.

It was not difficult to find Keiko alone; it happened naturally that she was at her doorway as he climbed the path to the temple. He bowed to her the first time, and the second time he stopped.

'Your knife, is it sharpened to your satisfaction?' he asked.

'Yes, thank you very much, sword polisher,' she replied, and she giggled at his formality.

'If you have any other metal tools, I would like to fix them for you,' he said.

'You are a soldier, I believe,' she said. 'You must save your strength for battle.'

'I am resting now,' he said. 'For a long time.'

It seemed to him that her smile was a little warmer. Her voice was louder than any Japanese woman he had ever spoken to, and low pitched too. The sinews of her throat led down to a V between her small high breasts. Her expressive, active hands on their fine wrists swam before his eyes. She was so slender, one arm could pull her toward him.

151

He stepped away, for fear she could feel the pull that heated him.

After that he only bowed to her when they passed, and she bowed back. But then she appeared in the cool of the evening outside the temple. He understood that he was to follow her down to the shore by the rocks, out of sight of the village. Her boldness pleased him inordinately. He kissed her and could not stop.

That was the beginning.

From there it happened so quickly. They were lovers and there was, for him, no other moment in his day but the moment when he saw her and knew he was to follow. It was as he imagined, when he was in her arms. She took him with her strength and her subtlety. Only when she was satisfied and her eyes that had watched it all, unashamed, closed at last, did he assume control. And he was carried on passions he had never known before.

He imagined her in England, an England of which she knew nothing. He'd dress her in western clothes, and she would walk beside him on those crowded pavements he remembered, with big shop windows they could look into, and enormous tall stone churches with dark interiors full of tombstones. She would be brave, he knew: a woman who could harvest shellfish from the bottom of the sea would not be frightened of a double-decker bus.

Only when his thoughts came to the idea of the Japanese Embassy which would take them there, did his courage fail. She was only a local girl from a little fishing village, and would never be considered good enough. And anyway, he had withdrawn from the only service that could take him away from the island.

Not that night, but the next time the girls went out in the dark, Vera was finally tempted off the rock and into the immense salty arm of the sea. She lay on top of it, on her back, looking up. The moon had grown; it was half full. Then she rolled over and looked down. The sand was lighter than the air. She put her arms out sideways. She felt as if she were flying, that the sand was not ocean bottom, but ground she could walk on. She scooped her arms and went down into it, driving with her head to make a space. She felt the water take her weight and drew a big breath so that her lungs made her buoyant. When she was well below the surface, she blew bubbles out of her nose and rolled over to look up.

Long, fractured rays of moonlight broke their angle at the surface and plunged straight into the deep, passing her. The water was dark, lustrous blue. Hanako floated alongside, blurry, smiling, waving. Vera looked at Hanako's skin; it was a green, grey colour. She followed her friend, swimming a foot below the surface, looking up at the blurred stars, and down onto the sand bottom. They swam near the black rocks, which, under-water, in the dark, were splotched with light-giving green rocks or clinging creatures, Vera could not tell which. When they sur-faced, they trod water and whispered with their heads in the air and their shoulders underwater.

'Look,' Hanako kept saying, 'look.' She was looking over the surface of the sea. She took her lantern from the rock and swung it back and forth. Swarms of tiny glowing grains headed toward her in the water until Vera thought she would be speckled green like a frog.

'A fish like a bird,' she said, 'it will come. It will jump.'

And it did. A huge winged shining creature flew out of the water. It seemed as big as a blanket. It flapped its huge wavy fins, and flopped under the waves again. It was electric blue. Vera shrank back against the rock shelf, her skin puckering into goose-bumps.

'You promised!'

'Yes,' Hana said. 'Promised. No bad fish. Playing.'

Vera cowered, and Hanako swung the lantern, but the flying carpet fish did not rise up again.

'It is hiding. Come down,' said Hanako. She made a neat surface dive and languidly kicked in a circle around Vera's legs.

One big breath was all it needed. One big breath, and to bend at the waist and force her head down, like a wedge, into the heavy water. And then she was in it and tumbling down to touch the sand and crouch, looking back up to the sky beyond the surface, to the fuzzed moon. She could see the little halo of light from Hanako's lantern on the rocky ledge and it made her feel safe. She pushed herself back up and burst out toward the moon, exultant. She was not afraid.

They dived again, over and over.

Vera crouched on the bottom as long as she could, but Hanako could always stay down longer. Once, when they were down, Hanako touched Vera's arm and pointed, There. There. Lying in the sand, dotted with its wavy edges and long thin tail, was the big manta ray. Vera wanted to swim off in fear, but Hanako shook her head, No. It was peacefully grazing on the little green specks that were still swarming into the light source.

After that they came out into the water as many nights as they could, and they swam underwater and watched the fish in the dark. Some had glowing green stripes and others had great leonine manes that gave off a yellow light; they floated above the seaweed like so many coloured birds above a forest. And Vera adored the black silken beauty of it. She learned to recognise the creatures in their hideouts, to penetrate the disguise of the starfish that turns itself into a rock, and the tube worms that lay like dead twigs around the entrance to the octopus's cave. Hanako showed her how to spot an octopus's cave, by the pile of empty clamshells out in front. Sometimes they could see the octopus himself, just two eyes resting on a crooked arm, looking out through the mouth of the cave.

This creature was Vera's favourite. After the night swims, and after she'd slept in the morning past sunrise, lying inert in the house as Keiko got breakfast and then set off to go diving, Vera

154

went by herself into the water of the shallow harbour and searched out the octopus. She loved the way it took so many shapes. It could be, on the sand, a large, ornate button, each of its eight legs curled tightly in clockwise fashion, a purple-red colour. Or it could be seen swimming with great determination, its head leading, pressed by the water into a bulgy arrowhead shape, with its legs streaming out behind in a bundle. Or it could be a wizened and pimply set of limbs, when, half-buried in sand, it lay on the ocean floor, waiting for something edible to come by.

Hanako showed her its small mop of eggs lying unprotected on the ocean floor. Nearby, the octopus was a dead flower, the petals all furled and lying in one direction, or a cluster of twenty little fingers, slightly luminous, palest pink. The eyes were the funny parts, because try as he might, the octopus could not quite hide them. They stood out from his wizened face whether he hid in algae or coral or sand.

Octopuses were the disguise artists of the underwater world, she decided. An octopus was soft, but not always. It had a way of telling you it could be dangerous. That you should back off. It stiffened, and its arms made flaring cape-like swirls, pale blue, and when it was even angrier, white. The eyes stood out sideways at the two ends of a hammerhead. Very close up – and Vera only got very close up to it by accident – it looked like a human baby, with transparent, veined skin, all crumpled in the folds. But if you surprised it, it reared up, like a tripod, white with black lace edges. Or else it wrapped itself up and became a white-spotted turban, its eyes the jewel in front. You looked away for a second and you could not see it. But you knew it was not gone; it had simply become invisible.

One night, walking back home in the dark, very late, Vera passed by the workshop of Ikkanshi-san. She thought that if he was there she would tell him about the octopus. But she didn't see him in the workroom. The polishing stone sat by itself in the centre and it seemed to glow, although there was no moonlight there. It took her a few moments to notice him, in the windowless dark, by the back wall of the room. Then she heard a muffled sound. It was unmistakeable, the bang of a generator. She had heard the one at the lighthouse often enough. This one was smaller, and packed in dried grass. You would not hear it unless you came very close to the door and listened. She could see that it gave power to a radio.

He was kneeling in front of the set, watching as the tubes slowly lit. Then he sat back on his heels, hands on knees, attentive to the talking. The voices became shrill, then explosive. He reached out to grasp the set in both hands, as if to shake it. He pressed his ear to the swollen circle that was the speaker. He was not aware that Vera was there. She was shocked: it should not be possible to surprise Ikkanshi-san. But he had turned up the volume loud to hear over the din of the generator.

The sounds that came out of the radio were scratchy and angry, a rush of Japanese oratory. Even he could barely understand it, Vera thought. She did not want to interrupt him, bent over the radio, all his energy trained on the speaker. She backed away.

The basket maker had come again. That was twice in one summer, perhaps a little unusual. Ikkanshi stopped and watched as the pedlar limped up the stony street, little more than a path, from the docks. All the houses were lined along it, each one looking out over the harbour. None looked the other way, or turned its back to where the boats came in. Ikkanshi attempted to pass by the man. This time the basket maker frankly revealed that he was looking for him.

'I suppose your radio has given you the news,' he said.

'What news?' Ikkanshi asked. 'I live on an island; I do not think of news.' He made up a skeptical look for the

156

other's benefit. He had hoped his radio remained a secret.

'Someone you knew at officer school has gone now from England to Berlin. It is your friend Oshima Hiroshi. He is the senior attaché in Germany now. They say he will be the Ambassador.'

Ikkanshi was surprised. This he had not heard. But he only gave a small bow and continued on past. The assumption was in these parts that the basket maker knew everything. One did not stop to ask him how.

Oshima in Berlin! He was indeed one of Ikkanshi's friends from officer school. Of course Germany was important now, to the Japanese. The country had signed an anti-Soviet pact with the Nazis. He did not like it. But Hiroshi would. His father had been one of the architects of the new Japan. In fact Hiroshi had been in his mind the last weeks because the Canadian girl had been asking him about the others from Japan who were in London. Oshima was one of them. He had been quiet in England, and not particularly happy, Ikkanshi thought. He had not liked the British very much. He would do well in Germany, the sword polisher thought. He could speak German well.

Oshima was not, in fact, the most brilliant of students at the officers' school. He was a small boy and shy, at first. He had clung to Ikkanshi who was one year older. In the barracks where they stayed as boys, his bed was near to the older boy's. Ikkanshi used to watch out for Oshima at night, to see that he was safe and well when they went to sleep. The training was so difficult, and there was never enough to eat. He himself was used to it by then. He was one of the stronger boys, from the start, and his father had prepared him well for the rigours of the school. But Oshima's father was away from home his whole youth, because of his role in the government. The others called him a Mama's boy, while they had a chance. Ikkanshi sometimes kept a little rice ball that he could slip to Oshima at the end of the day. He knew the younger boy needed

157

that. In the silence, their eyes would meet, and say good-night wordlessly.

It was only when the Nationalist movement rose up at their university that Oshima began to shine. This shy boy whom the masters used to pick on became the leader in all that, the leader of the group who sought to raise Japan to become the star of the entire East. It turned out that although he was weak in his body, he was strong in his words. He had the power to impress the politicians and the power too to move large groups of people with his oratory. Ikkanshi had stood by and listened to him, feeling concerned that his lot was making progress with their leaders.

Ikkanshi wondered what it was like for Oshima in Berlin. What would he be doing? Making himself known to the Nazis and sending letters back to High Command in Tokyo, he supposed. Probably not attending the opera. He thought of his own time in London, longingly, as he had often done. He had had no military duties. He had been a mere translator. He had had time to meet beautiful ladies in tea shops and go to Covent Garden.

There was a spot in the Royal Opera House where he loved to stand. It was on the staircase, halfway to the mezzanine. He could see over the heads of all the people milling in the foyer. He felt invulnerable there, and inspired. When he would go into the theatre and hear the music and watch the dancers he would be seized with a melancholic joy. All this they were supposed to reject as British, and white, and not Japanese. But he adored it. When he left, he had to remind himself: life is not ballet. These beauties of gesture and sound were dreams.

Everything spoke of summer's coming end. The wind raised its voice; the waves came closer to the shore, harassing, hurrying the *ama* back to land with the day's catch. The sky was changing; the clouds came charging in from the east, as if on a track, like overloaded boxcars, their bottom edges flat and their tops bulging. The light was newly penetrating, coming from another angle across the sea. The water was so clear now that Vera could see through it down ten feet or even twenty, on calm bright days. The bottom of the sea jumped up so it seemed that if you put your hand in the water you could touch the rocks and the grasses. But they were thirty feet, forty feet down.

And then, suddenly, the summer that had been a seamless ribbon of transparent days broke up. It dissipated into wisps and ragtag ends. And in the confusion of rain gusts, erratic winds, a false return to perfection and then a plunge in temperature, another pageant began to play.

There were no more games on the beach in the late afternoon. After the day's fishing, the men carried larger stones for the roofs of the huts, and pulled up the docks onto the shore where the giant winter waves would not carry them away. The old women dried and mended and folded away the nets. Others dug up the potatoes from their little gardens. The *ama* tied their baskets together into the back corners of their houses, up high and out of reach of the mice. They piled the dried squid in baskets specially made for them. The boys carried all the bundles down to the shore. Even the island began to change, retreating into itself. The grass that had grown so tall it made a fine, green forest went brown and lay down. On the shortened evenings, the grey wooden houses under their weight of stones merged into the twilight.

Vera went to say goodbye to the sword polisher.

He sat in his black *gi* and *hakama* on the wooden stool that stood only eight inches above the floor. In front of him were his stone block, and the big wooden bucket of water, with the metal bands around it holding the staves in place. His polishing stones were to one side, stones of different shades, brown, and light grey and a dark bluish grey. He started with the most coarse, the *iyoto* stone. This day, on this blade, he had done the rough work and moved on to a finer stone. Vera could see that he was working with the *nagurado* stone, removing the marks left by the *iyoto*. The process would go on for seven or eight stages, with seven or eight different stones; he had told her that.

He did not look up, but she knew he saw her. His eyes remained fixed on the sword.

'What sword is that?'

He did not answer.

He put his right hand in the water and then ran it along the length of the blade, making it wet. With one hand near the tip and the other hand near the blunt end he began to rub the blade rhythmically against the stone, rocking it a little. It made a soft noise: k-cha, k-cha, k-cha. He moved the blade up and down the stone, and the soft noise became a little higher, then a little lower, as if the metal were the string of a musical instrument. And his stone was a strange bow.

As she watched, a fine grey paste began to develop on the metal. An equally fine sweat formed on his smooth upper lip.

Vera fell mesmerised by his concentration, and did not speak.

He lifted the blade, ran his fingers along it, and wiped it with a cloth. Then he held it to the light, the clear white sea light that came in through the open door, and looked along the length of it. He plucked the edge with his thumb.

'Do you see?' he said, 'the *hamon.*'

A wavy line was in the metal, like the grain in a piece of wood. Like a line of blue hills over water. She had not known that metal had these graces, like a living thing.

'I do,' said Vera.

'And the shadow above it? We call that *utsuri*. That is the sign of a good, old blade.'

He spoke with his head on the side. His wire-frame glasses reflected a white light that disguised his eyes. His black hair with its white stripe was slicked back today, while it most often stood up loosely. He had dressed up formally to sit before the blade.

He changed his position on the stool so that now one knee was up and to the side, the other tucked under him. He took a fine, soft brush and cleared the paste from the blade. Then he began to rub again, the blade against the stone. K-cha, k-cha, k-cha. This went on for a long time. At one point Ikkanshi-san pointed to a small pillow that sat at the side of the room and she brought it. He stopped his rubbing and put it on his wooden bench, then sat back on it.

Ah, he was human.

She watched as he leaned forward, using his body weight to bring pressure. He rocked the blade on the stone, and the grey paste built up. He was holding the blade in two fists. His fingers were clenched as he rubbed and the sweat gathered on his brow. He stopped, and put his hands in the water.

'Will you talk to me?' Vera asked.

He continued with his work. He did not say yes and he did not say no. She saw the small pile of boards he had saved. And the nails he made himself from any little bits of scrap he had.

'What are you doing? Are you becoming a carpenter?' she asked.

'As a matter of fact I am.'

'What for?' she said. 'What will you make?'

'Another room for my house,' he said.

'You don't need another room! What are you going to do? Have parties?' she teased.

She often mocked his sombreness. He laughed to humour her.

'Maybe,' he said. 'The new room will be beautiful and peaceful. Its purpose will reveal itself by and by.'

'They say you will stay here all winter.'

He did not deny it and so she knew that it was true.

'Is that the purpose of your new room? Will it be someplace for you to stay when it is cold? Nobody lives here all winter,' she said. 'This is the summer island. It always has been. You told me so yourself.'

She thought she saw his head incline toward the radio in the

161

corner, half sunk in the darkness. She seemed to hear, although it was not turned on, the shrill hectoring voices, the roaring of crowds.

'And your radio will be company?' she insisted. She laughed, a slightly mocking laugh. She was mocking herself and not him, for caring, for presuming that she could look after him.

He wet the blade again. He rubbed its sharp edge with his thumb, turning the blade, squinting along the edge of it. Now the waves of deepening blue flashed. She saw his perfect, short cut fingernails.

'If no one has stayed here over the winter before, I wonder why a person chooses to do it now,' she said, rhetorically. It was a way of talking to him because he did not respond, talking to herself about him as if he were someone else and that someone else were not there.

She was not certain that he heard. He held the blade straight out from his right eye and looked long and slowly along it, as if he were looking into the sights of a rifle. There were several nicks in the metal. With his thumbnail he scraped off a chip of the pale stone and, breaking it between his thumb and fore-finger, made it into small, thin pieces, like soap flakes. Then he dabbed these on the marks on the blade, and rubbed.

'The blade has seen battles,' he said, finally.

'Someone has sent it to you?' she asked. 'That someone wants you to make it like new?'

'It is a *meito*,' he said. 'Remember the word I told you? A sword of some importance. One with a name.'

'What is the name?' Vera asked.

'Sometimes we find a *Kamakura*, or a *Bizen*. There is also a fine blade called *Sagami*. This may be one. I do not know, yet. I have seen very few of them. There are not so many good old swords. So many were destroyed.'

'Who destroyed them?'

'Soldiers. In Meiji,' he said, 'some years after the Americans broke our isolation it was in March of your year 1876. There was a battle. The samurai fought as they had fought for cen-

162

turies, with *katana* and *naginata*. They were laden with heavy armour and weapons. Can you imagine, on the battlefield, each samurai had servants running after him to carry his baggage?'

He gave a little snort. 'They thought they could not lose. They fought against army that had been raised by conscription from the population of farmers who knew nothing of *bushido*. But they did not need to. Something which the samurai were too blind to see had replaced their swords. You can imagine what. The gun, of course. These peasants were armed with rifles from the outside, from America, and France, and Britain. They simply raised the rifles, and aimed, and the samurai fell. The days of fighting face to face, one against one, were over. You see, while Japan had been closed to the outside world, the samurai had become outdated. And more than that. From arrogance, from corruption, the rulers had lost their soul. There is a saying we learned in school. "A military man without poetry is a savage, not a samurai."'

'You have poetry,' Vera said. 'You have Shakespeare.'

He inclined his head. He had no quotation this time.

'So the great samurai and his sword with its *kami* was humiliated. Then Japan herself was humiliated by the likes of your kind.' He smiled. 'It was forbidden to wear a sword. By an edict from the Emperor. Hiro-rei. The soldiers of the Emperor went around the countryside finding and seizing all the old swords. They made huge fires and melted them back into iron. But this one –' he lifted it again and took another sighting along its edge '– this one was hidden in the ground.'

'Where?' Vera asked.

'You ask a question about what is unimportant,' he said. 'It does not matter where it was hidden. Only that it was hidden. And that it has come to light again. The spirit does not truly die. It is part of a cycle: death and rebirth.'

'It is not coming back to life by itself,' insisted Vera. 'You are bringing it back.' He put his hand in the water and began to rinse off the paste. She watched the gleam on the blade grow stronger.

'An old sword is good because it is both hard and soft. I

told you this: remember it. Hard so as to cut well, and soft so as not to break. A sword made today is not good. *Gendaito*. Modern. They are too hard. They have no ability to bend, no softness. They are not quenched in water, but in sand. Do you know what it is to quench?'

He knew more English than she did.

'It means to put out the flame. They are made for a bad purpose, without understanding, in a fever to make a war.'

He spoke with great intensity while looking at the blade in his hand. He had not seemed to be addressing Vera, and she listened without really understanding, to the ferocity in his voice as he continued. She was caught by surprise when he included her again.

'And Japan is once again descended to *kuro taniwa*. Do you know what that is? I believe you would call it military fascism. And I forbid you to say those words I have said to you.'

It made no sense to Vera. 'All right,' she said.

'Do you understand? I forbid you.'

'Yes.' There was a silence. She thought he was angry at her. 'Where did the sword come from?' she asked again, to break the quiet. If it was so unimportant perhaps he would say.

'It was buried in the back yard of a house in Kumamoto.'

'And why has it come out now? Who has sent it to you?'

He did not answer.

'I saw the basket maker come,' she said.

Not a muscle of Ikkanshi-san's face moved, but she knew she had guessed right.

He squatted barefoot over the stones. His feet were white and waxy. His hands too, were hard and smooth and hairless, like the hands of a marble statue. They kept about their business of the fine work as if no thought were needed to guide them. But he had said, 'your kind'. Why was he making them on opposite sides? She tried to imagine the smooth-faced Japanese man in a western suit attending the theatre in Covent Garden. The operas he had loved, that he still remembered, and sometimes still heard on his radio.

'Why do you have to do everything so many times over?' she asked. 'It must be very boring.'

At last he stopped the rocking.

'There it is, proof of how little you understand,' he said, smiling. 'Or perhaps you only want my attention.'

The light was still coming in through the doorway but it was at such an angle it was not useful to him. He got up to start his generator. He reached to pull the cord.

'Can I do it?'

He handed Vera the little handle at the end of the cord. She pulled hard. The starter did not catch. She pulled again. The handle came part way back and then slipped out of her hand, clattering back against the generator. Her arm felt as if it would come out of her shoulder socket. Ikkanshi-san laughed. She frowned, drawing her eyebrows together in an imitation of his. She concentrated all her efforts, and took a deep breath, grasped the handle more firmly and the third time the motor roared and shook. Then it settled into a rhythmic throb. Ikkanshi had a small electric light; slowly it began to glow, brighter and brighter. He trained the beam on his work. He put his face right up to the blade and peered along the length. The light came on it and it glowed like a sullen fire. He raised his face to hers, and bowed. Now his voice was different.

'It is not boring, I can assure you,' he said. 'Repetition is good. This is how it is done. It is a privilege for me to work on such a blade and teaches me a great deal.'

The people left, all together. One by one the little vessels leaped off the shore, forming a row first, and then

165

flaring out in a V formation, like silent ducks, sails flapping as they took to the wind. Hanako was in one of them, Vera in another with Keiko and the old aunt and the old uncle. Keiko's nephew manned the tiller-oar, not looking in Vera's face but blushing when he was forced to steer it across her. He stared outward to the invisible mainland, and the wind took his hair back from his forehead.

On the shore, Ikkanshi-san stood, his hands crossed at the wrist beneath his belly. He looked immoveable, like a standard, not a real man at all.

Vera looked back. She said goodbye to each part of the island in her mind: the rocks and the stretch of beach where she practised diving. The bushes, reeds and the bamboo grass they called *sasa*. Farther up toward the High Place, the prickly briar. The Dragon Lake where she sat when she was lonely, and the Lost Lake with all the marsh grasses. The swallows, the gulls, the snakes, even the snails with which she and Hana had played.

The island itself vanished first, so flat that as the waves rose it began to disappear. Then the rooftops went. Then he. The lighthouse was still visible. Her eyes clung to it.

'The island has been the same for many years,' said the aunt. 'And now it begins to be a little different.'

'What kind of person would build a winter house on the summer island,' the uncle asked. 'Such a person must be stupid.'

'A person staying all winter there,' said the aunt. 'Perhaps one who has reason to hide.'

They directed their remarks to Keiko, but did not look at her. Vera watched Keiko's face. A faint pressure built under her skin.

'You are right,' said the aunt evenly. 'One might think to hide on the summer island. But not in a big house. A big house, people will see.'

'Forgive me, aunt, but I disagree. Building a big house

is proof that the person has no reason to hide,' said Keiko.

'That is proof that the person is stupid,' said the aunt contentedly.

'Will the ferry come, in the winter?' Vera asked, thinking of the basket maker. Keiko did not look back.

'For a little while, and then, not.'

'Who will bring him food?'

'He will have enough.'

Vera thought about the potatoes the old women had grown, the seaweed and the dried octopus. There must be rice. And the cats would keep the mice from it. 'Won't he be lonely?'

'No,' said Keiko. 'I do not believe so. I believe he will be glad.' She showed her *shiran kao* face: she who knows nothing.

The next time she looked back, the summer island was gone, swallowed by the waves. The boats flew onward. Keiko's face was blank in the wind.

# VIEW 2

In the old Japanese prints, love is the driving force. When rain pelts, it is the rain of rejection; the moon behind Fuji's cone is the moon of longing. And that love is echoed not in any heaven but in the body. Daily I watch those ordinary Edo people thronging their gates and their shrines, waiting patiently for boats to take them across the river, climbing mountain paths under burdens of logs, and poling barges against the current. Every warrior, priest and common labourer is sinew-carved, and every woman, whether she is writing a letter or hazarding her way along a snowy path, has limbs softened and a face swollen by passion.

When as a child I pored over my grandfather's prints, I wondered about this thing called love. Such power to invest a landscape, a population! But perhaps it was merely 'wind', as the old sword masters say, a style, an affectation that was currently in fashion. This love for the body nevertheless had found itself a perfect expression in the *ukiyo-e*. The art was born, and it died, on the surface. It is a servant, not a master. It is beautiful, not because it was truthful, but because it was faithful.

I buy and sell the *ukiyo-e*, art that was, in its time, of the commoner and for the commoner. Those ordinary people who were rising out of feudal servitude to become free men and women, in thought if not in deed, could now enjoy the fruits of their labour. They left us a record of their time. I know how they wrapped their sumptuous fabrics around their bodies, and how the women did their hair. How they kneeled in *seiza*; on which side the weapons lay; what bird or animal adorned their over garments. I've come to understand that this elaboration was coding, a fantasy. These compelling images of life were dreams, even in their own time. In truth, the people of Edo were caked in mud, shivering, and more concerned about the next meal than about a

171

message from a lover. But they picked up the latest *ukiyo-e*, looked at the print, and saw themselves as resplendent.

There are messages buried in this code. I mentioned hair. Hair was an Edo obsession. Tied up above the neck, it signified a coy purity that may be for sale. 'A woman's neck is her soul and her life', was true for the courtesans: her living was made on it. In the *nijinga* – the portraits of beautiful women; my grandfather called them his 'Beauties' – loose hair at the nape of a woman's neck indicated that she had fallen in love. Long, loose hair meant wantonness – as in Utamaro's triptych of the abalone divers. This too was a fantasy. In fact the divers were sturdy, hard-working fisherwomen. But their legend lived in the pictures. Diving women have fascinated the Japanese for centuries, and when the Westerners saw them, they too were fascinated.

My grandfather's *Three Views of Crystal Water*: I still have it in my possession. Sometimes I take out the triptych and stare at it. I had originally put the seashore first, then the bridge, and finally the fire in the pagoda.

This story satisfied me for a while. But one afternoon, in that strange period where I lived with my grandfather, at the tail end of my short childhood, I flung open the folder and saw the three prints. I was suddenly convinced that they were in the wrong order. I had set them in order in my mind: first, the women on the beach; second, the letter passed at night; third, the flight from fire. But now I saw a different story. First, should be the fire at the pagoda. This was an unexplained calamity. The samurai stood at the gate, a guard or a scourge. He watched the two women escape, older and younger, or mistress and servant, one armed and on horseback, the other on foot. He could do nothing.

But the second picture showed an encounter at night. The women were out in the dark land and unprotected when, secretly, a stranger passed the maid a message. The message was an offer of shelter, the messenger, perhaps, in disguise, the samurai. He was an honourable man, and although he loved the highborn woman, he would not harm her.

Then the third picture would be the women by the seashore,

a happy ending. The refuge was to be amongst this group of women, hidden, and cloistered. Still, the tall woman, the one in the front whose curved back nearly hides her bare breasts, casts a longing look over her shoulder to where, in the dunes, the man who had saved her watches from afar.

Now this version of the story seemed true to me.

I gazed at the last picture. The women were seen from the top of a slight rise. They were *ama*; they'd clearly been diving. The observer – we – looked over a circle of women, standing and sitting near the edge of the water. They were wet; their hair was dripping down their bare backs. The small fire drew them together as they warmed themselves. Around their feet were baskets. These baskets held their catch of abalone, or turban shell perhaps. It would have been a good day. The water was flat and turquoise and, where rocks stand up from the surface, it was transparent: you could see the other halves of the rocks beneath.

The sea was large and reached from one side of the paper to the other. Its blue stretched high in the picture to a flat horizon, at the far reach of which were rocky islands and a few boats. Childishly drawn waves marched out from the land. Even so, it was strange to name this a view of waters because the women were the most interesting part of the picture, with their gently curved arms and breasts and their modesty, which could be felt despite their nakedness. The water was their habitat, I suppose, their salvation.

But the feeling of the picture was of privacy violated by an unseen watcher. I feel – I always felt when I looked at this print – my grandfather's fascination with the beautiful, aloof diving women. Their sensuality is perhaps idealised and yet not entirely, I know, because I was amongst them.

As I said this morning to a client, in the *ukiyo-e* we have not just a window but a grandstand on a time as distant and as vital as Shakespeare's. The 'window' has been dressed by a genius. It is full of everything we desire, characters in a dozen activities beguiled by material goods that make us want to reach in and take them. The people mingle with their idols; 'big faces', as we

173

call the portraits, show actors distorted by rage or remorse; demure courtesans reveal a bit of red underslip.

But it is art by subjects, for subjects. The celebrated geisha is a captive in her pleasure quarters, an object of commerce. Edo's charm under lantern light is illusory. The labourer staggers under his load; the foot soldier faces the lethal sword; the blind and the lepers, the open road. It is not a beautiful world, but something infinitely more moving: a cruel world seen as beautiful. The pictures are of longing and of hope. This is Edo as it wanted to be. Only love could make it that way.

It is not my way. I am a realist. Love has little place in my world. Oh, when I was young I experimented with it, the way children play with matches, or venture into deep water.

But if it is not my way, why do I adore the *ukiyo-e*?

I think it is the particulars of the dream. The detail, the application, the elaboration! I feel the exchange of energy for grief. That parade ripples by the grandstand, luminous, gaudy, deadly as the underwater world.

The word that many use to describe Edo and its night denizens, is of course, 'the floating world': life lived in the moment, sweetened by an awareness of death. I favour 'buoyant world', with its sense of a bubble. Think of a rising, of the dawning of power to an underclass. Of joy, bought and sold. And after, the flooding that will carry it all away. Fatalistic, this pleasure. Did an uprising ever sweep away the powerful and fulfil its promise of earthly reward for the underclass? My time on the summer island coincided with the tragic crushing in war, war waged and war lost, of all that Edo raised up. And the knowledge of that end was present from the beginning. It is as if these artists furiously carving daily impressions into their blocks of wood knew that it was not to last. You can feel that in the pictures: they are full of reportage, but also suffused with fantasy, exactly the combination that I love.

Buddha says that sorrow results from trying to hold on to that which must disappear. The water in which we are immersed moves constantly on its tides and storms, and we must move with it. A tragedy, if we hang on; an entertainment, if we let go. The flux tosses such exquisite creatures our way! The artists' adherence then to 'real' things, material things, the faithful replication of fleshly pleasures is a futile kind of faith, clutching an anchor, a foothold as the stream carries us away.

Do you know, I said to my customer this morning as she left with her woodcut print, that Hokusai, one of the great artists of the *ukiyo-e*, lived in ninety-three houses, never cleaning up, and leaving when the rent became due? He said that he had come into the world without much and he would leave that way. How delicious, and ironic then, to be a collector of his works.

In the absence of any better guide, I took my world view from the *ukiyo-e*. As I saw it, lovers were tossed and bent by life, rather than the opposite. Love is what might have been, if not prevented by duty, or by what schoolteachers used to call a 'current event'.

Current events: that was a subject when I went to school in Vancouver. I liked the phrase: it meant electricity. Something sparked, in an instant, in a place you'd never heard of, for a reason you couldn't have guessed, and the shock went out all over the world. We tried to keep up: we memorised the names and leaders of a dozen countries, and dutifully wrote down the dates of the assassinations that led to wars: Archduke Ferdinand, for instance, I never forgot him. But current events shocked little people too, not famous, not rulers. Certain lives were struck by the lightning of history as it happened, pierced, lifted out of the ordinary.

Mine was, in its small way. Recently I saw a photograph in a book. It showed a long column of Japanese Imperial Army soldiers marching on a broad, empty street, soldiers with bayonets over their right shoulders, headed by a man in front with the flag, that sun with its spokes. I had seen such a parade, such a column, when I first arrived in Japan, so many years ago. But in this book, now, in our anti-military times, beside the phalanx, on the deserted pavement, a lone man crouched with a microphone, from which a black wire ran out of the picture. He was recording the sound of their footsteps. And that sound went around the world. That was all: empty street, marching soldiers, man with microphone.

How simple, how minimal, the soundtrack to mobilise a country! And how huge it became.

I came into this world amongst people who love objects. Pearls were the star and the beacons of my young life. I learned enough to know that pearls were the making and unmaking of my father and grandfather, my mother and stepmother. Is it any wonder that I do not deal in pearls?

*What thou lovest well is thy true heritage; the rest is dross.*

The pictures came to me. The pearls did not. More of that to come.

# 5

## *Kesa-giri*
### Diagonal cuts

The next time James Lowinger saw Miss McBean it was half a world away and he had grown into manhood. Or thought he had. It was in Panama City. His papa had sent him to assess the prospects of doing business there.

He sat at a bar in the centre of the square, the palm trees over him, the grand, white-painted and columned government buildings of the little republic eerily aglow in the setting sun. At a distance little children ran along the sea wall and women hung laundry on iron balconies. On the street, bicycles dodged men carrying bushel weights of provisions down the narrow, poor streets. Beside him was the national theatre, cheek by jowl with the armoury, and the official residence of the President, making a complete set for a new country all within a few minutes' walk.

James had just returned from the Pearl Islands in the Gulf of Papagayo. In his mind he prepared his report.

The waters were so clear that the Panama divers could distinguish an oyster from the surface at sixty feet. The season ran from June to October. The divers went out in canoes, four to a boat. They dived from one hour before low water, to one hour after and if there were many oysters they sank a basket between them. One diver could get ten dozen oysters a day. They claimed to go down twelve fathoms and be under for one minute, and even as long as one and a half minutes.

Or so they told him. The men were fugitive Mexicans, pursued at home for some crime. You could see them on their days off, in silk shirts and Panama hats, strutting barefoot, with brand new shoes hanging around their shoulders, a sign of their upward mobility. They were paid $250 for a season, but lost whatever they earned by drinking cane sugar alcohol. And why save it? They did not have long to live. The climate was deadly. There was no fresh water. Yellow fever, or sun stroke would kill them. Many of them were only boys, younger than James himself.

James was hardened to it now. He had walked the length of the coral islands until he found a diver who had a house, and a family who looked well fed. He asked him how he managed. The man said he worked for no master, and opened his own oysters. James had the depressing thought that Avery McBean had been right in his unwelcome advice back in Ceylon, his father should deal with individual divers, contracting with them to retrieve and to open the shells, and to dispose of the oysters.

He was to sail the following morning. Appearing at a table were several gentlemen from New York, one of them an engineer. Mr Hartley was thin with a tropical suit made of linen that crumpled around him. Coupled with his heat flush, it gave him a look of distress. Mr Tiffany, his partner, was a jeweller. On they sat, in the tropical evening. They were most elegant and well-spoken men. They bought quantities of drink. The three had a sumptuous dinner and saw native women dance, and were offered services James might have been tempted to accept, except that the conversation was so stimulating.

These men proposed to revolutionise the pearl fishery. They would dispense with the divers altogether.

'How could the divers be replaced?' James asked, 'with what? A dredge?'

'No, nothing so plebian.'

They proposed a water-tight vehicle that could go down to sit on the ocean floor allowing the men to exit, walk around on the ocean bed, and pick up the oysters. A submersible. Never mind how the men would walk; they'd have lead boots of course, and metal helmets. Hartley laughed at the general lack of imagination that had led all involved in this business until now to overlook this fine option.

James laughed in turn. 'I think you've been reading too much Jules Verne.'

'But how could you be so heartless?' said Hartley. 'Do you not see the suffering of the divers? Do you not know that the *tintero*, the shark, is constantly circling?'

'Well, even if you are heartless, which I don't for a minute believe,' said Tiffany, 'think of the practical savings, Mr Lowinger. The economies involved. A diver may make twelve or even twenty-four descents in a day. What if we could eliminate their taxing plunges and again their resurfacing? Take six men down in a submarine boat. They could work ten hours a day, from the fixed container full of air, on the bottom. In the submarine boat six men could do ten hours a day. Therefore six men would do the work of three hundred.'

'Yes, but,' said James, 'the shark would still be there if the men were taken by ship to the bottom, and elevated again in a ship. And not be deterred by any metal hats.'

They had an answer for everything.

'But, young man, I'm surprised you're not aware: it is the rapid flight of the divers upward that incenses the shark and causes it to bite – did you not know that?'

No, he didn't know. He was green, green, green. In their suit jackets and white trousers the Americans loomed large, futuristic. They were offering James his fortune. He was lucky to be here. James found himself thinking again of McBean.

I could best him, he thought, swelling a little. And wouldn't Papa be delighted? Wouldn't McBean have loved to be part of this? But no, the opportunity had come to him, young James Lowinger, and there was no chance on earth he would share the good fortune with old McBean. It was time the old Scot got paid back for his scheming in Ceylon, for the catch of pearls he'd stolen from his father.

Hartley and Tiffany were leaning on the table; they were asking for his word.

But perhaps he was being hasty.

He really ought to think it over, sleep on it, he told Hartley. To avoid their pressing eyes, he glanced away from his companions.

And then he saw her.

Recognised her, perhaps, because her father had been in his mind.

The plump, pouting Miss McBean.

She stood in the light on the columned staircase in front of the National Theatre. They were white columns and it was a marble staircase and behind it was a carved wooden door, very tall. She too was with a group, Europeans in evening dress. Men and women together, chattering, with a sense of their separate, foreign glamour in the setting. They were the kind of men and women who intimidated James. He'd spent most of his youth on ships and beaches. He was not glib then – though he would be, later – or self-assured. And he took a dislike to anyone who was. He would not have got on with her friends, he was certain. They were, he imagined, smug, rich, glittering, and indifferent to the natives, altogether superior in their imperial grandeur.

And she was with them. No less redoubtable at twenty than she had been at ten. A face had developed out of that childish set of cheeks, lips and liquid eyes. Her lips were long, firm and had a high, pointed bow. Her eyes were wide apart, deep set and calm, but no less righteous. Her forehead was also wide and judicious. She was pale, as if that red umbrella, now invisible, had been over her head against the sun for the past ten years. She was not so much tall as erect: her back, in the tightly-buttoned evening jacket, appearing to soar out of the same full frothy kind of skirt – he had no words for fashion – she'd worn as a child.

James excused himself from his entrepreneurial cohorts and took the marble steps at a run.

'How do you do, Miss McBean,' he said, and introduced himself. 'Our fathers are both in the business of pearls. I last met you on the beach at Condatchey Bay.' All this tumbled out of his mouth. He could see a mild sort of amusement in her eyes as she replied.

'Of course, you are James Lowinger,' she said. 'I'd have known you anywhere. You rescued me from that buffalo.'

'I did not,' he said. 'Although I tried to.'

The other men laughed and one of them said, 'You're too honest, my young friend. Say you did; it will go better for you.'

Which threw him back and made him wonder if he was ridiculous and what it was about his face and person that was so indelible from that day in the bright sun. She stood smiling, without surprise. She had a coolness about her on that tropical night. The girl who did not run from a charging buffalo was not about to wink an eyelash at him, James could see. But she took pity on his confusion and they talked a little.

She was in Panama with her father; he was up at the Pearl Islands. James was surprised that he had not met up with McBean in the islands. In his heart he was dashed: how did this Scot manage to turn up in front of him, just when James thought he had left him behind? But chagrin was mixed with the pleasure of meeting this beautiful young woman who felt, absurdly, like a dear friend. He asked her if she often travelled with her father and she said yes, that he relied on her, and her mother could not be spared.

Relied on her for what? he was rude enough to ask, and she threw him a haughty glance but said only that she had 'much experience of matters to do with the business'.

The friends were set to move on and so he bade her goodbye and returned to his North American partners, because that is what they had become in the few moments he'd turned his back on them. They had lost a little of their lustre.

'So you are acquainted with Miss McBean, the pearling queen,' Hartley said, with narrowed eyes. 'We've heard it said she has an eye for a good pearl.'

James knew that McBean's strongest suit was appraisal. He had a genius for choosing a beauty that was disguised by dirt or blemish, and having it skinned or doctored so that it was perfect. An unerring eye, they said, to see what was within.

He watched Miss McBean glide across the shining stones of the square as if on a small set of wheels – like a dancer in a Chinese opera, feet invisible and no distinguishable step. She turned as the group stepped into a horse carriage – turned back to smile at him and raised her hand as if it were a signal.

Three! She seemed to be saying. That's three times we've met in faraway lands. Where next?

And she was gone.

He realised he did not even know her first name.

All the more reason for investing in the Pacific Pearl Company with W. B. Hartley, President, and William Henry Tiffany, as secretary. Business was to be 'prosecuted' by means of a submarine boat allowing six men to do the work of three hundred. It was Pie in the Sky. Or rather, Pie in the Sea. The worst of it was they weren't even pulling his leg. Lowinger was the only investor. The submersible was never launched.

Hanako and Keiko's nephew Tamio took Vera to school, that first winter.

They had to wear black uniforms, skirts with a sailor top with white trim for the girls, and trousers for the boys. It was a child's uniform, and Vera felt foolish in hers. The others submitted without complaint.

At the school gate they separated. Vera was to stay with younger children who were learning to read. By now she could understand much of what was said. She wanted to write; the characters were so beautiful. She was not taught to write. The first morning and every morning after, the schoolmaster read from *The Cardinal Principles of Japanese Life*. The children followed along in a copy on their desks.

One story was 'All the World Under Japan's Roof'.

People in all countries of Asia would be happier and better off with Japan as their ruler. In order to rule Asia, Japan would need many soldiers. Every child should strive to develop his body and mind so that he could pass the examinations and join the army or the navy so that he could defend his country. What about the girls? Vera wanted to ask. But she was afraid she could not say it properly. Still it must have showed in her eyes. But it soon became clear. The girls were to be strong to support the men and raise the new generation. The most important lesson each child had to learn was to be obedient to his superior. The teacher looked with contempt at Vera who loomed over her desk, her knees knocking up against its underside.

In the afternoon all the students went outside and stood in rows. They had to do military drills. The girls wore a white apron over their black, and waved their arms. Vera felt like a scarecrow. The older boys had weapons; Vera saw them, skinny bodies struggling with heavy bayonets.

'I don't like school,' Vera said to Keiko. 'It isn't really school. It's a cross between church and cadets. I don't like what we have to learn. The teacher doesn't want me there anyway.'

'Just ignore what he says and learn your characters,' said Keiko without conviction.

'He stares at me in a funny way.'

Keiko laughed. 'Maybe he does,' she said. 'But you must be quiet. If you say anything bad, the military police will threaten you, or point a gun. They will think I said it and take my job away.'

But in the evening, after dinner, Vera begged. 'I can go to work with you. I want to be an *ama*.'

Outside the village was dark because the streets were not lit now. No one walked abroad after the early dark.

'Why did you bring me here?'

183

'There was nowhere else to go. I needed to work and this was the only place I could. Remember? There was no one else.'

In Vera's mind she saw the letters from her father. On the envelope was the return address, 'Kobe, Japan'. She had left the letters to Miss Hinchcliffe. But he did not write again. He must not have got her reply, she thought, for the hundredth time.

'My father wanted to come but couldn't,' she said.

'It doesn't make a difference,' said Keiko.

'It makes a difference,' Vera shouted. 'If he knew I needed him, wouldn't he have come?'

She had put her reply into Miss Hinchcliffe's hands. Those white, beringed hands had closed over the envelopes. Vera tried to think of what had happened next. In her mind, the letters disappeared, from that moment. Did Hinchcliffe put on stamps; did she run off to the post box? No, she did not. Now it seemed very obvious. There was no further addressing, no mailbox, no search. Miss Hinchcliffe had not sent Vera's letter. But why?

Could she have hated Hamilton Drew that much? Or hated Vera? Perhaps she was acting on instructions from that mysterious authority to which she sometimes referred.

And where and who was McBean?

Keiko lowered her eyes but not without Vera seeing something there. What did Keiko think? That they had been tricked? Or that Vera just wanted to believe her father would have come for her, when really, Keiko knew better? It made Vera furious. 'And anyway, where is Kobe, Japan?' she shouted. 'Maybe I can go there and find him.'

Keiko didn't refuse Vera, but neither did she say yes. They were two women, both young, but one no more than a girl, in their little house, dark timbered, dark with smoke, on the far side of Japan. Now it seemed audacious, what they'd done. Then it had only seemed necessary.

'Your grandfather never talk about what happen if he

dies,' Keiko said mildly. It was the nearest she came to criticising him.

'Why didn't you leave me in Vancouver by myself?'

'You are only fifteen. Besides you begged to come.'

'To the island, yes,' said Vera. 'But I didn't know . . .'

'You were determined,' said Keiko.

And so on, round and round the arguments would go, always ending with the schoolmaster, and Vera's stubborn assertion. 'He doesn't want me there. I know it.'

After that, silence. Keiko would not argue any more. There were two more days, days when Vera dragged her feet to school and sat, sulky and oversized in the desk, with the children. She shut her ears.

Keiko tried to explain, after dinner. 'We Japanese are different,' she began. 'We do not think about being one person, but about being a part of our country. The State has decided it must have a war. We do not know why, but we cannot disagree. We need a war, so we need an army.'

'I don't want to be in Japan's army!'

'The army begins with children and home life. We must support and we must believe,' said Keiko.

'You don't think that for a minute,' said Vera. 'You're just scared.'

The very next day the teacher began to read the book aloud. He moved from his position at the front of the room and came to stand near Vera. The students were all kneeling in *seiza* on the floor, which was cold. She could feel the heat of his agitated body although he was two feet away. If a child closed his eyes and drifted, the teacher came over and rapped him on the temple.

'Do you know who owns the clothes you wear?' He looked directly into her eyes. He was full of gleeful hatred. 'They are owned by his Royal Highness the Emperor of Japan.'

Vera scowled. She wanted to argue, but it was not possible, she could see that; arguing would have set him off.

185

He reached down to her shoulder and grasped the cloth of the jacket made for her by the tailor in Vancouver. He yanked it upward, looked with a smirk into her frightened eyes, and then let the cloth fall out of his fingers. Vera kept her eyes down. 'A meal you eat,' he said, his voice over her shoulder, 'does not belong to you. Nothing is your own, not when you play and not when you sleep. Your food and your toys and your clothing belong to the State. In the same way, your lives belong to the Emperor.'

He moved away. Vera wanted to jump up and run. But her legs, bent at the knees, were cramped and full of pins and needles. Her head was below the teacher's. When she raised her eyes he yelled, 'Bow!' When she bowed she could feel him, watching. Her neck felt naked, white. She decided that if he hit her, she would hit him back.

After dinner that evening she lay on the *tatami* mat and did not get up.

'I'm not going to school tomorrow,' she said to Keiko. 'The teacher hates me. I will go to work with you at the pearl farm.'

Keiko said nothing.

At dawn Keiko stood at the door, tying the blue triangle of cloth over her head. It was marked with the two *ama* good luck symbols, a five point star drawn by a single line, and a sign like a tick-tack-toe grid, only larger, made with five lines going up and down, and five lines going across. Vera had a pair of Keiko's overalls in her hands. She struggled to put them on.

'I will come,' said Vera.

'No, you will not. The work is too cold,' said Keiko. 'Mikimoto Taisho will not hire you.'

'I am an *ama*, so I will.'

'You are only a beginning *ama*,' Keiko said kindly. 'You do not know how cold it is and how difficult. You could fall into the water and drown.' She explained to Vera how they would walk out onto the rafts that lay on the surface of Ago Bay. They had to balance on the slippery bamboo poles that were lashed together to make the surface of the rafts. Their work was to pull up the metal cages of oysters that hung below in the sea. In the autumn rain, in the winter snow and wind. The women scrubbed the shells to rid them of barnacles and sea squirt.

'I can work inside, then,' said Vera.

But at the pearl farm only a few of the local women had inside work. And they were not divers. The inside women were like little surgeons, using sharp razors to slit open the gonad of the oyster, and to place inside it the bead of nacre that would form the nucleus of the pearl.

'I don't have to ask you anyway. I can go and ask Mikimoto-san if I can work at the pearl factory. He was a friend of my grandfather.'

Keiko set her jaw. 'Mikimoto Taisho knows nothing of you.'

Mikimoto Taisho was king of life in Toba and Vera was defeated.

'All right. I won't come with you today, but I will not go to school either,' said Vera, 'and you cannot make me.'

'No,' said Keiko. 'I cannot make you do anything at all,' she said. 'But if you will not be in school, then you must do something else.'

She began retying her kerchief. 'Too strong, too strong,' she said, shaking her head at Vera with a smile on her lips that told her she did not think there was such a thing as too strong at all. 'I don't know what to do with you. You would be a fine *ama*, but if you go back to Vancouver, where will be the man who will want to marry you?'

Her final thrust only made Vera scoff. To marry was the last thing she would ever want.

Vera sat on the *tatami* mat by the hearth. It was dark inside, although outside, she knew because she could see through the cracks around the window blinds, the sun was rising. She heard voices in the street, the high-pitched, childish voices of Japanese women, and the huskier voices of men, and then the hard, humourless voices of the monitors who stood on the corners and commanded the children to form lines to march to school. She was far away from home.

It would be evening in Vancouver, and she would be coming home from school. There would be a soft wet smell of cedar trees and ocean, a different ocean smell than this one, somehow younger, less rank, more innocent, emptier. A coaxing radio announcer whose purpose was to amuse the housewives, not to harass them. Women would walk with their babies in prams and stand in clusters talking; men would stride home from the streetcar stop. Vera could walk in her mind every step of the few blocks home, turning the first corner at the bus stop at Granville, heading down past the big old Douglas firs in front of the grocery store and the post office, turning again beside the park with the swings, and heading straight, parallel to the beach and two streets above it, to the house.

But probably nothing was left in the house that had been her mother's. Maybe it was sold in an auction, the neighbours coming in to view their chairs and their tables and their woodstove and coal bucket. Maybe, now, the house stood empty, and the neighbours walked past and shook their heads and said to each other, 'They have gone; gone to Japan.'

She moved herself over to the window, and lifted the blind so that she could just see out, but not be seen. She leaned back against the timber post of the window frame, and cried scant, angry tears. She stepped into her house slippers that stood by the door.

The fire cooled. She raked the coals and put in more charcoal.

'A fine shaped pearl is an accident that is impossible to account for,' her grandfather used to say. And she wondered about the other accident that it is impossible to account for, which is death, and before death, life itself. She wondered why she was born if everyone who was meant to love her had to die before she even grew up. She wondered if her father was dead too. Probably he was. She hugged these self-pitying thoughts to herself and went to the small glass that hung by the door beside the shrine. She looked at her face, and took a perverse pleasure in the way her mouth had tightened and turned down at the corners. She thought of her grandfather.

James Lowinger, the boy in the straw boater who had clung to his father's hand on the beach in Ceylon, was lonely too. At fifteen, Vera's age, he had begun working with his father. His book education ended when he went to sea. What did he dream of? The son of a wealthy man, he had a fortune already. He always hinted darkly about the bad that a fortune could do to a family. He never seemed like a merchant, or a man seeking to make his fortune. He thought about a great many things, and the pearl was always at the centre. 'The bone of the gods,' he called it, 'the tears wept by angels.'

When James was older than the innocent who had travelled in Panama, but still young, he went to Kuwait. 'The oysters I met with there,' he had said to Vera, his eyes twinkling, 'were of good quality. Most of the pearls of a distinct, yellow hue. But a few were a soft rosee.'

Kuwait was a romantic place, a city entirely dependent on the sea, where men of the sea swept through the narrow alleys in their white gowns as if carried by waves. It was a city of hundreds

189

of thousands, with a Palace and an inner souk where the mullah lived. In the port you'd see one hundred pearling vessels. When the diving season began, in May, the city would be emptied of men. But James had gone in August.

He did not like the town, but he could not leave. For one thing, he could not imagine what he would say to his father, coming home empty-handed. Or with no hands at all, as the case might be. They had nasty tempers, those Arabs; he did not wish to do business with them. It was a turning point in his life, he felt it. Walking the beach and looking down, he saw small jelly-fish the size of his palm, sticking to stones. There were many others stuck to the sea wall, he noticed, where they dried when the tide was out. It was a black jellyfish, with a red underside. On examining it he realised it was what they call ambergris. When it dried hard the children held it up to the sun; they believed they could see the future in it.

'What do they say?' he asked an English-speaker.

'They say, ambergris, ambergris, where are the divers?'

He met a merchant called Ahmad al-Farhan, an amusing fellow, a philosopher of a kind. Al-Farhan showed him some fine pearls of the creamy colour they favoured there, large, and perfectly round. He had others that were gargantuan, misshapen, and charcoal grey – fascinating in their ugliness.

Al-Farhan had been wealthy once, and had travelled to Paris to sell pearls. The King used to come to see his barques go in and out of the port. But that changed when he lost his money. His decline had begun on a sail to Bombay. A servant shook out his rug into the sea, when on the rug were spread his finest pearls. From this accident he had rapidly lost his money. His friends deserted him. He did not blame them. He said the rich were correct to shun him: after all, he might want to borrow money. But he minded that the poor had deserted him as well, because he was one of them, his house was open to them, and he would give them coffee.

Now he had only one ship left. He was going out at the very end of the season, and allowed James to accompany him.

He boarded in the evening in time for prayers. From the hillside mosque came the wolfish howl of the muezzins. The sailors were casting poison on the water to catch king mackerel. At dusk the divers rolled out their carpets, made of ropes bound together, in rows, on which they would sleep until dawn and the call to prayer. They preferred to sleep on oyster shells, but that would come when they'd made a catch.

At dawn the sun rose above the blistering white line of the sea. The divers donned black pyjama-like trousers, and shirts to protect them from the jellyfish. Then each one pulled out his own tortoiseshell noseclip and his leather finger covers, which gave him a sinister look. There were some, with longer hair, who also wore a black hood.

James sat beside a diver who was, strange to say, Bedu, from the desert, and had a little English. This Bedu, whose name was Hizam, was forced by need to come to the coast to dive for pearls in the summer season. He missed his camel, and his sheep, and his life of roaming. But as a diver he made good wages. He was allowed to sleep in the stern away from the damp. But more importantly, back on shore, women had to veil their faces before him. If, as with most Bedu, the women did not, this would indicate that he was not really a man.

Al-Farhan explained that the Bedu had courage as well as excellent eyesight, honed on their long rides through a landscape of sand, searching for the tiny dots on the horizon that might be friend or foe.

Each diver, before going into the sea, hung his peg on a string near the mast of the boat. This string of pegs was told like a rosary: the pegs were each made from the bones in a fish spine. The shipmaster counted the numbers of divers, shifting a peg along the thread for each one. When a diver had done ten dives, he rested. During their rest periods the divers shared puffs on the hubble-bubble to 'wake up the head' after being in water. Another took his place.

No sooner were the divers poised with their feet on the stones, or *hajar*, on which they would descend, than the chanter began.

Al-Farhan had hired him at considerable expense. It was his job to sing to keep the workers' spirits up and even to put a sort of spell on them, so that they would work beyond the fatigue which would otherwise have stopped them. 'He is like the man who leads a caravan, seated on camelback. If he has a good voice, the camels will walk almost mesmerised, sometimes until they drop dead,' he said.

This bearded giant, with his long white robes, tipped his flat face skyward and let forth howls, bellows, and moans. His poetry apparently allowed for a choral response, and in their turn, the sailors murmured along like adherents to a religion.

This was the part of the pearling life that James adored and he was happy. The full sails pulled them onward under the blistering sun, while the dark heads of the divers popped in and out of the foam, and the netted bags full of shells clattered to the deck, and the operatic exhortations of the chanter worked on them all.

'The men do not live so long. Diving is not healthy,' al-Farhan said, 'but neither is living in any particular way, unless, of course you are born a woman. In that case you may stay at home and not know the world at all and die when your baby is stuck in the birth canal.' His contempt was exquisite.

The divers dreaded the saw-fish with his flat snout with spines on it. Divers had been cut in two. But the greater risk of death came from mutinies. If the divers rose up against a ship owner, the fighting was to the death. An honest and even a lenient ship owner had no hesitation in cutting off a hand or even throwing a miscreant overboard if a pearl were stolen.

By evening of the first day, the deck was covered with oysters. Next morning the shells were to be opened. With some ceremony and at the crack of dawn, the opener set to work, but it soon became clear that he could not get through the catch although his hands flew, and the shells flew, and the poor flabby creatures inside were tossed into wooden containers from which they would be thrown away.

Al-Farhan guarded the catch. When it was finished he was in

a thoughtful mood. He explained why he thought that pearls fascinated men even more than gold.

'Beauty,' he said. 'But not the beauty that you see. It's the beauty of sadness and loss. The beauty of chance, and all those who die finding her.'

Seated with a pipe and a plate of dates, he expounded on his ideas of perfection in the pearl.

He also said something that James had never heard before. 'There are some freshwater pearls found in the ocean, where the springs gush out. These are of the very highest quality and are especially lucky.'

Perhaps these were the pearls that he could bring back to please his father.

On James's fifth day on board, there was a crisis with the drinking water. Stored in barrels, it had become very ugly, infected with rust from the iron nails, and alive with cockroaches. Once, having a late-night pipe on deck, he saw two divers creep out to the water barrel and scoop water to run over their various wounds, and septic sores. From then on he tried not to drink it, but in the heat, thirst drove him. He would rather drink and die of disease later, than die of thirst in the present, he decided.

It was decided that the ship must make a visit to the freshwater spring under the sea. It was called the Ighmisa Well and it was off the shore of Hasa.

No sooner had they turned to head for Hasa than the winds died; they sat, becalmed for a day and a half, the water becoming fouler as the supply dwindled. Al-Farhan was less perturbed by this than by the cool that was creeping over the sea. It was now necessary to keep the stove alight on ship all day. The divers hung a sheet of canvas they called a *barbar* behind it to keep the warmth of the flames near their bodies. As a result, the crew encouraged the divers to take more of the hubble-bubble. James watched the Bedu, who he had observed to be the strongest of all the divers, emerge from the water, and even he was staggering and heaving.

But the wind finally began to blow and it carried them swiftly in the direction of the underground spring. They arrived at what appeared to be a markless spot on the sea.

'This is it!' announced al-Farhan triumphantly.

James could see nothing, although the water was clear. Twelve fathoms down, the ship owner said, was a spring, and the water ran out from beneath a ledge of rock. There was a little bit of green growth around it. The sun streamed right through the deep water.

The divers were to be sent down once again on their stones with great bladders. But they did not want to go.

There was an argument.

Hizam, no doubt realising that he was the best, and had the best chance of fulfilling the dangerous task, offered himself. He went to the side. He put up his hand for his fellows to bring him his diving hood, and he put it on. It all had the air of an execution. There began a hue and cry among the other divers: James understood that they did not want him to go: he was too tired, it was too cold, and he was bleeding, which they thought would attract a shark.

But he was determined. James watched over the side of the boat as Hizam dived in the clear water, approaching the ledge with the water skin and held the mouth of it in place. The skin grew and grew and must have become very heavy, because Hizam pulled on the rope for help to lift it up: the sailors pulled from the deck. The other divers went overboard. But in the excitement one was struck on the head by the stone of another, and emerged from the sea with blood running down his face. Now the others were frightened that sharks would come. Two ropes tangled under the hull of the boat and the sailors began to fight. Meanwhile Hizam the Bedu swam around the rock ledge. He appeared to be putting shells in his hood. And once again, as he had done when he was a child in Ceylon, James remained silent.

The other divers created a commotion, and the sailors shouted to calm them, and al-Farhan was forced to intervene with his whip. Unnoticed, Hizam surfaced. He stumbled to the stove to warm himself; there he sat, with the fire in front of him and the shadow of the *barbar* behind him, keeping the wind off. He coughed and blood began to come up from his lungs, but no one paid any attention. It was normal, and would be considered normal, until one day he succumbed.

Al-Farhan withdrew to his pipe and his carpet in a corner of the deck.

It was then that Hizam took the shells out of his hood, and threw them in the heap of other oysters, but not without giving a slightly gaping shell a quick investigation with a fingertip. If James was not mistaken, he saw a flicker of surprise on the Bedu's face.

Al-Farhan's face had gone slack: he did not move an inch, nor express the slightest emotion.

It was hours later when he spoke. 'The divers have tricked me. I believe they have scoured the bottom.'

'Are you certain?' James asked. 'There was much confusion at the time.'

'No, I am not certain. But I have suspicion. That is enough.' Al-Farhan stepped back and pulled his whip from his holster.

The sailors cried out a warning.

With a roar al-Farhan leaped to his feet and over to the fire, where he fell upon Hizam with a fury, beating him on the shoulders and shouting in words the meaning of which James could only imagine. Hizam sat unmoving, withstanding the blows.

The other divers moved as one to the water barrel which was freshly full, and made as if to tip it. Al-Farhan bared his teeth and snarled, his features twisted in their nesting of black hair, but in the end he went still, and let his hands fall to his sides, after delivering Hizam one last cruel blow to the cheek.

Hizam still did not move, but sat wiping the blood from his mouth.

Now Ahmad invited James to sit on his carpet. He was morose, but calm. He snapped his fingers for tea, and in a few minutes, a sailor brought them each a cup.

'Do you understand what happened? It came to me. I saw it

in an instant, the way the Bedu offered to dive, and the others created a diversion, the fighting and shouting that occupied my attention. The whole ship is against me. They have stolen the most valuable pearl. Someone has eaten it, or hidden it. I will not know. But they will go to port and before too long, in not too many days, I will hear tell of a priceless freshwater pearl that was taken out of the water near Hasa.'

And he sank down into a gloom from which he did not rise during the entire return trip.

They came back to the port of Kuwait in time for the end of season, or *quffal*, as it was called. It was celebrated with a gun salute fired from shore. At the salute, the ships all ran up their flags and sails, the divers dived into the water, and the crew began to dance on deck, stepping like large mating birds around each other in circles, clapping their hands and watching their feet while the chanter crooned.

James could see mothers and wives scurrying back and forth from the souk in preparation for the return of their beloved men. As their boat came in on a swell, the crowds rushed into the shallow water of the sea to meet them. James stepped onto dry land into a throng of townsfolk. Beduin women plucked at his arms offering dates and rice. Traders in pearls had pitched their tents along the sand.

He decided to stay on. He did not really know why. The accommodations were horrid. The sun was monstrous. He slept on the roof of the house. His body poached in his own sweat, and he woke feeling exhausted at three in the morning. He bathed in sea water, as did everyone else. Fresh water could be bought for a price. But the price was steep. The reason for this, he was told, was that the freshwater was found under the sea, and had to be fished for by divers with skins made from the bellies of goats. He found this bizarre, yet reassuring: presumably he had not been dreaming. Almost everyone else was abroad in the souk at five in the morning. He went out again in the evening, from five to eight o'clock.

One evening, Hizam the Bedu appeared on the beach. The Englishman approached him. He mentioned that he was in the market for pearls, freshwater pearls from under the sea. But Hizam seemed not to understand. They spoke a few words: he had bought a camel and was going back to the desert. He smiled.

James decided to visit his friend once again. It was not difficult to find him: he merely went to his corner of the souk in the pre-dawn darkness, and stood, speaking his name to passersby. Soon a courtier appeared and led him through the maze.

Al-Farhan was seated on his carpet, his robes spread out around him. He rose to embrace James, full of warmth, and then, holding his shoulders in his enormous hands, held his friend at arms' length, looked into his face. 'You do not look well. It could have been you, not me, who lost a pearl of great value,' said al-Farhan.

'I am always losing,' said James.

'What is keeping you in my country?'

James confessed that he did not know. A strange lassitude had overtaken him.

'A curious coincidence,' said Ahmad, 'perhaps you are aware. There is a European woman who stays here. She has a servant with her as well. Three months they are living on a little fishing barque where men with guns protect them. She too is in search of pearls, but I believe no one will sell to her.'

James called on her in the evening. She came to the rail of her vessel with hair attractively dishevelled, cheeks flushed, and eyes enormous. Positive as he was of her spotless character, he could have sworn she was smoking the hubble-bubble herself.

'Miss McBean,' he said, from the shore.

'Mr Lowinger,' she replied, mockingly. At first she refused to let him on board but eyed him askance, as if he were the buffalo she'd seen years ago and she had latterly realised what was coming at her. It was desperately alluring, and had he known how rare a reckless mood was in this woman, he would have tried harder to get on board. As it was they spoke with several yards of filthy water between them. She called the barque her house and professed to adore it. She was to leave in several days. She implied that she had found many wonderful pearls. He implied the same. She asked him to call her Sophia.

At length, she invited him in. Her maid beat a speedy retreat to her couch on the roof of the boat, and they to the pillows within. It was so hot they were slick with sweat. And there passion unlike anything James had known before, or was to know since, overtook them.

She was an Englishwoman and so the outpouring shocked and reduced him. But she was not an ordinary Englishwoman; she had lived her life, in exotic circumstances, all over the world. She must have been, then, in her middle thirties. Was she drugged? Was he? Questions that tormented James for years later became, in the end, academic. What did it matter? They flew at each other like warriors. But at the first taste, and smell, he fell her victim. She ravished him, to be truthful. He lost all the words to speak, and even those to tell the tale. She bewitched him. He made only fits and starts of sentences; he had been reduced to basic components, of which grammar was not one.

'Who would have dreamed one so upright could be so supple?' had lasted as a complete thought.

But the rest were fragments.

'So many ways,' was a kind of sigh. Later, phrases returned to him: downy skin, soft breasts, thighs with a hollow between them, dainty deep cleft, soft fur, a well of sweet water.

It was over too soon, but not over. The maid appeared with cool liquor.

They lay naked together and it felt as if this was the reason they had met, over and over, in strange locations. Fate was willing them to come down to this, bare skin, yeasty odours, delicate fingertips on satin skin, whispered praises.

'May I tell you one secret,' she said, after the second, or perhaps the third time.

'Of course, my dear.'

'And will it be secret for ever?'

'It will indeed.'

'I have bought the most exquisite pair of pink rosées. Quite unexpectedly, from a Bedu man. They are fine, large, and perfectly round. I am told they came from the freshwater spring in the depths of the ocean.'

He begrudged her none of it. If only she would share with him that space between her breasts where he could lay his head, and let him hold her delicious hips one in each hand, and plunge into her, dividing her like a ripe fruit, she could have every pearl in the world. She was every pearl in the world.

As three a.m. came, and four, and the world was making its presence known on the harbour, Sophia said that he should go. They went through it all again – the tears, the clinging, the insane joy of discovering such beauty in each other, the equally insane grief of parting, even for a day. Sophia said that he should come back after dark and they would plan a future. Clutching that promise to his heart, he stumbled away and went to lie, dazed and beyond delight, on his roof until dawn arrived with its hideous red sun. Then, he went inside and slept like the dead.

The next evening when he returned to her houseboat, it was gone.

# 6

## *Morote-suki*
### Two-handed thrust

Between the hillsides and the edge of the sea, winds huffed, arriving and departing. Wet snow muffled the town and weighed on the houses. There was never enough wood for the fires.

The *ama* were in winter disguise. They hid under the funnel-like brims of their sun-bonnets. They pushed their bicycles, and when the snow was too much for the bicycle wheels they pulled small sledges behind them. The cheap sandals, called *zouri*, they made at home to sell were tied on the sledges.

'You may go to my aunt and uncle's *udon* shop,' Keiko instructed when she left for work. 'You can at least learn some more Japanese. The town is as good as the school for learning.'

But Vera was shy. The town was completely different from the summer island. She stayed at home all morning. But by noon, hunger would drive her to the noodle shop. She hung her head low because when she entered the talk amongst the men would cease. The aunt made her welcome.

'It's good, she comes. People come to look at her, brings business.'

She took her to a seat at the end of the counter; the aunt gave her soup. The talk began again. She could understand some things the people said now.

When Vera looked into the street she would sometimes see faces looking back at her with unfriendly curiosity. When school closed, Hana would go by with her friends. She waved gaily to Vera but she did not come in.

One day she saw the basket maker.

She remembered him from last winter; he was the first man in the village to speak to her. But she had been afraid of him. Then he had appeared on the summer island. Now it was winter and like the others he came to the village, to the mainland, and wandered, as restless as they all were.

He saw her in the window, and beckoned.

She held back.

He smiled. He had black teeth with one jagged point on the left. She thought he was old, very old. It was impossible to tell how old.

Vera stood up at her seat and went out through the door. She was taller than he was. He had a limp. Still he was always walking. They said he had fought in the war. 'Did you hurt your leg in the war before this one or was it already like that?' she asked him rudely, in English. To her surprise, he answered.

'It was not already like that, or I could not have fought in the war.'

'Is that why you make baskets, because you can't do other work?' Vera said.

'I make baskets because it keeps my mind from getting strange ideas.'

'Oh,' said Vera. 'What are the strange ideas?'

He laughed very hard.

'What is your name?'

'My name is Bamboo.'

'It is not your name,' said Vera. 'It is the name of the stuff you work with.'

He laughed again. 'It is not my real name but the name I chose.'

'Where do you live?'

'I live in my parents' home.' He named a village. 'But two times a year I go around to the villages. Autumn is the season to go up the mountain. The others cut wood to burn as charcoal.

They ask me to use up the bamboo they clear at the same time. I leave the stalks to dry and use them next spring.'

'You came to the island. Where else do you go?'

'I go everywhere,' he said.

'Do you go to Kobe?'

'No,' he said. 'That is too far.'

She was disappointed. But she did not tell him why.

'What do you want?' she said. He had beckoned her after all.

'You do not go to school because there is war,' he said, not asking, just knowing.

'Yes,' she said. 'No.' She did not know what to say.

'And you stay home, or come to *udon* shop,' he said.

He stopped talking and went into a little dance. It involved placing his feet as far apart as the width of his shoulders and twisting and turning and placing his hands on his shoulders, then lifting. He removed the backpack that contained his tools and set it down. '*Katanatogi* knows you are not in school.'

'How does he know?'

'Perhaps Keiko told him, I don't know,' said the basket maker, with a wide smile.

'But how does Keiko tell him?' Vera asked.

'People who write letters that they don't want anyone to see can send them by me. I carry letters wherever I go.'

Vera thought of the pleased smile the sword polisher tried to hide when she had told him, 'Keiko says you are the best polisher in Japan.' She had a strange sensation. She drew back to go inside again.

'You are the pearl girl, that is what we call you,' the basket maker said. He laughed and showed the jagged teeth.

'I know many things about pearls and much else too,' he said. 'You can ask me. I knew Lowinger-san as well. I saw your grandfather when he came here first, with his wife. Long time ago.'

Vera showed nothing on her face to let the basket maker know he knew something she did not know.

'Your grandfather's wife, that is your grandmother.'

'I know,' she said testily.

He rolled his eyes. 'That woman made everyone afraid.' Then he laughed.

So she was very fierce. That was fine; Vera could be fierce, too.

'I am a big friend of Mikimoto Taisho,' said the basket maker. 'I help him. Long time ago, early very early when he began with just a few oysters. Every oyster was in a basket. Now they are in metal cages. Then, every one, I made.'

Vera shrank from the man. She thought of him as sinister. He was armed with sharp things. He had knives, blades, pliers, and cutters. He came without being asked; he moved without apparent schedule between homes and was taken in without question, as if people knew they were fated to open their doors to him.

'Do you want to see where I work?' he asked. 'Come with me.'

She agreed to follow him. She wanted to know what else he could tell her. But when they reached the hut by the side of the road, Vera would not go inside. It smelled of *shochu* and by the smile on the basket maker's face she imagined he was going to drink some now.

He made a gesture of raising a small cup to his lips.

'This is how I do my best work,' he laughed. 'Your grandfather liked to join me.'

She shook her head.

'No,' she said.

'Nothing to fear,' he said. 'I tell my best stories with this too,' he said, lifting the cloth door and pointing to his bottles. 'Your grandfather, he had many stories too.'

He turned his back to her, concluding the conversation. He opened the tool basket at his feet and removed a small cross made of two pieces of wood, fitted a stalk of bamboo over it and stood its end on the ground. Then he found a hammer and banged the end of the stalk so that it split the bamboo into four. Vera watched for a minute, but he seemed to have forgotten her.

Vera kicked the snowdrifts all the way home. She did not like the basket maker but she was now connected to him.

'Why do people think bad things about the basket maker?' she asked Keiko later.

'I do not know what people think,' said Keiko, 'especially now.' She was silent for a minute.

Then Keiko lifted her hands and brushed her two palms together, swish swish swish. I am through with that, the gesture said. It had belonged to Miss Hinchcliffe but she had made it hers. They laughed a little too long, out of relief perhaps. Keiko gestured with the bottle and limped some more, but Vera said, 'Is it true he helped Mikimoto Taisho?'

'He made many baskets for the oysters to hang in the water. So many hundreds. He had to get helpers and train them. Mikimoto Taisho made work for most of the town, and others from the peninsula.'

'Did the basket maker truly know my grandfather?'

'Did he tell you that?' said Keiko. 'He knows many things.' She went very still.


Vera thought of what the *katanatogi* said. In this village people knew things. The old men and the old women saw everything. It was both good and bad.

Every day, at the *udon* shop, Vera sat at the counter, slumping, trying to fit in with the walls, hoping that the people would forget about her and talk. Again Vera saw the basket maker in the street. It did not take long to catch up with him because of his limp.

'If you wait a moment I will give you something.'

She stopped, and waited. He brought three strips of pliant bamboo out of his backpack and swiftly wrapped one around his finger, bent it backward, tucked the end in; then he made another figure – because that was what they were, figures – and attached it to the first. On one he made a tongue, or a finger that stuck out. On the other he made a hole. He put the stick from the male figure – because that was what it was, a man – into the hole of the female figure.

'*Katanatogi* and Keiko make like this.' He made a circle with the thumb and forefinger of one hand. With the other forefinger he poked through the hole.

She threw the figures back at him.

He laughed and showed the black hole in his mouth.


For New Year, Vera and Keiko made a *shimekazari* to put over their door. It was a clutch of rice straw tied up with jute. Its purpose was to ward off evil. In olden times, Keiko said, a dirty beggar had come asking for shelter. He went from door to door, in the whole town, and was turned away everywhere he went. But there was one family who took him in. They let him bathe. They gave him a meal. When he had eaten, the dirty beggar revealed himself to be a god.

By the time they had hung the decoration, and admired it there over the doorway, night had fallen. A boy was there in the gloom, across the narrow street. Vera saw him through the window. It was Tamio. She ran out toward him; he stopped. But he did not come near her. He looked straight ahead down the road.

'How are you?' Vera asked.

He scowled. 'My feet are cold and wet.' He made it seem as if it were Vera's fault.

She did not know what to say. He was so unlike his summer self. Keiko came out through the door.

'Come inside,' said Keiko. 'Can you visit us?'

He sat with his teacup in front of his heart, held in both hands. His hands were black. He had been taken out of school to work on the charcoal. He explained that he had to watch the fire all day. If the fire got too hot, the wood turned to ash and that was useless and he would be beaten. If it was not hot enough, then the wood did not burn. Gradually he softened, and his face softened; he was not angry at her, just angry.

'Are you hungry?' he asked Vera.

'Not so much,' she said. It was true. Somehow Keiko managed to feed them both well.

'Why are we talking like this, secretly?'

'It seems there is a rule that no one is to know we're friends.'
'Where did this rule come from?'
'I don't know,' said Tamio, 'where did they all come from?'
That was a joke, and they laughed together.

Winter deepened, and darkened, and the snow outside built up
to the window ledges, and the narrow walkways became nar-
rower between piles of snow, and everyone waited for the thaw.
If Vera saw the bent-over shape of the basket maker with his
large backpack, she turned and went up an alley until he was
gone. Vera's life had no luxuries, unless you counted the warmth
of the bed under its pile of cotton blankets, or the pearls; imaginary, white, smooth, lustrous, warming under her fingers, that
now appeared before her eyes when she closed them at night,
rolling out of the corners of the dark sky. So many pearls: she
was dreaming pearls there in the dark room, with the smoke-
stained timbers. Outside, the blazing white blinded her eyes, but
when she looked inside, it was as if the corners of the rooms
were adrift in pearls.

It was dark when Keiko came home, tired from work. Keiko
and Vera went to *o-furo*, the bath. The women waited outside
the little hut under the stars.

First went the men, who by right were treated to the water
at its cleanest and hottest. Some took their bottles of sake in with
them. Some, who had been loading and unloading charcoal from
the carts they pulled from the forest hillside, were black when
they entered, on their hands and feet and necks, even their faces.

That was the way it was done. By tradition, as well, the women
were not privy to men's conversation in the bath. Except that
the voices were loud and the night was silent. The women stood
outside the door waiting for the men to dress. So it was the case
that everyone knew how, in the bath, the schoolteacher said that
soldiers of the Emperor must overcome the Chinese. Once in
control, Japan would help the Chinese by driving out the white
men from China. Then with the help of China's vast riches they
could drive out the white men from all of Asia. This was the

goal. We have no fuel, he said. We have no resources. But we must reach the rich countries and instruct them in the right way.

'Hitler is sincere,' said the schoolteacher. 'Nothing he does is vulgar. He is a hero sent to achieve a new world order.'

Once or twice a voice was raised in disagreement.

'Where do you get these ideas?' said an old man. The old ones were safe, and could say what they wanted: no one would take them away. 'Not from the newspapers I hope. The newspapers are lying to us. They are not telling us what is happening in the world.'

Vera stood waiting under the stars. Even they were foreign to her. Everything looked strange to her now.

After the men had dried themselves, they filed past, important, some drunken. The women stepped off the path to give way. When the boys emerged, pink and scrubbed, steaming a little in the frigid air, the older *ama* laughed at them. The shy young women like Hanako cast down their eyes while the boisterous elders shouted names and ribald comments that Vera did not understand.

When the last man had passed out of the doorway, the women stepped forward. Setsu, the eldest, went first, with the next eldest on her heel.

Once inside, they pulled off their numerous wraps, and holding a thin washcloth over their pubis, went to the wooden buckets to wash with soap before stepping into the water. They squatted on their heels and without affectation busied themselves with great energy soaping and scrubbing under each arm and in the crevice under their bodies. Politics was gone, for the time. The youngest ones giggled. Vera and Hana shouted too; it was fun. Not until the last one sank herself below the surface of the water, in the steamy, condensation-dappled wooden shed, did the conversation become serious.

The women did not read the newspapers; they did not listen to the high-pitched voices on the radio. They listened to their husbands, but they spoke to each other.

'My husband says we must conquer others because we have so little space.'

'The men are mistaken when they said that Japan is poor. We are never poor because we have the sea.'

'We are not exactly poor. But we are small.'

'Yes, small is different from poor. We are only poor now because the country is preparing this war. It takes all our wealth to make war.'

'Whatever happens we will still have the sea. The sea is very rich.'

But even the sea now was not as it had been. The catch had been lower this year than last, and lower the last year than the one before. Some *ama* had found work making *zouri*; others were weaving at village shops. It happened this year again that some *ama* went to work in Kishu, to fish for agar-agar.

'Probably this war will not touch us, it will leave our simple lives as they are.'

'But it will take our men and even our boys. Then we can not be as we are,' said Keiko.

'Our men and our boys are good subjects and go to the war,' came a voice out of the steam. 'At the same time one of our best warriors hides on the summer island.'

'He spent years in the Emperor's service,' said Keiko without looking at the one who spoke. 'Now he has another task.'

'What task is that. Is it to be Keiko's lover?'

Some women laughed.

'Too late for that! If he had married Keiko she would not have left with the Englishman,' said another voice.

The women laughed again.

The water was too hot. Vera had to get out – when she stepped onto the stones she saw her skin: boiled red. She rubbed it as the others did and took the wooden half-bucket to throw cold water over her head, again and again.

Winter dragged toward spring. Still the nights were dark and closed-in, in the little town. No one came to Keiko's door, not even the old aunt and uncle. One day Vera saw Hana alone on the street in front of the *udon* shop. She jumped off her seat and ran outside.

208

'What are you doing?' she said to her friend. It was the middle of the day.

'I left school because a job came up at the pearl farm. My mother needs the money.'

Hana's father was away in the army.

'You are lucky,' said Vera. Even jobs at the pearl farm were few.

'It is necessary that I have a wage for my family. But I feel sad that I cannot finish school.'

At last it was *risshun* and the countdown until the day they left for the summer island.

Vera sat in the boat anxiously staring at the horizon.

'What is the matter, are you afraid it won't be there this time?' asked Keiko.

But Vera noticed that Keiko was just as anxious. As the boats pulled in they saw Ikkanshi-san on the shore with his arms folded in front, waiting for them.

So, he had survived.

Through the winter the sword polisher had only such feral friends as existed on the island – the cats, the mice, the snakes – the snails, the crabs. He had begun to build his new room. He had put all of his scavenged boards to work in the structure, and all of the nails he had made, but he did not have enough material to finish it. He had spent hours coming to understand the *meito*, the excellent old blade that his father had given him. He had to be very careful, not to damage it. Slowly he felt its *kami* and with great care he took the coarser grit stones to it. As spring returned he waited for Keiko and Vera. He had hoped to begin the sword lessons again. There was so much that he could teach her. When she came back Vera was shy of him. Perhaps she was more interested in becoming a woman.

These changes in Vera had the inevitability of the larva spinning its cocoon. That white, formless creature she had been the year before was no longer. She was secretive, weaving her threads, making herself a fine cocoon. He could no longer tell what she was thinking. He was fond of her, strangely fond of her, pale shapeless worm that she had been before she disappeared inside herself. But he remained alone.

In late afternoons he went out to the shore to swim. The boys hunted for octopus with their clumsy spear guns. Sometimes they found small lazy ones in the shallow warm water near the harbour. They shot them, and brought them ashore. The old women put them on drying lines to hang. The trailing, mop-like creatures were transparent for a few hours while they shrivelled, and then they became thick and opaque. The women soaked them in soy sauce and grilled them over the fire.

But sometimes the boys found big lazy ones near shore. They had games they played with the creatures, letting them wrap their tentacles over their backs. The boys sank down under the water. The octopus would stick to them. Then the boys rose bringing the creatures up to the surface. Everyone, even Ikkanshi, came and stood on the wooden boat ramp and watched and laughed. The octopuses were like long flopping balloons, or Swiss rolls. The strong boys could easily unwrap the arms and hold the creatures above their heads.

It was here that he saw Vera watching Tamio.

The boy was running in waist-deep water. He was laughing and then he lunged forward onto his chest, straining to keep his face above the foam. His chin jutted forward, and his arms were braided with fine long muscles, like the ropes that hung in the shrine. His skin sparkled with salt and foam in the sunlight. He fell, and disappeared under the surface. In a few seconds he rose out of the water, shedding glistening spray in all directions.

He saw that Tamio could have been the leader. The other boys and young men looked at him for reactions, for ideas, but he seldom gave more than an offhand shrug – or pointed to another: That one! Follow him! Yet he was expert in everything he had to do.

He also noticed that Vera could not stop looking. Tamio was unconscious of his beauty, and moved with absolute confidence that the spear he threw would hit the target, that his foot would fall on pure smooth sand and the spring of his step carry him clear out of the water. He went down and rose with an octopus. He managed to get it over his back, so that he had one of its eight legs in each hand, and several trailing down his legs. He shouted to the other boys, and began to run. Then he dived still running, under the water. Frightened, the octopus did what it was supposed to do: it suctioned onto him with its feet, and then shot out its liquid behind to propel itself forward. Tamio got his ride, flying under the octopus along the water.

His friends cheered and clapped.

Vera didn't know that anyone saw her watching, so she continued. The boy swam and strutted, with the weight of the waist-deep water holding him back. She kept watching him with the other boys until Hanako, giggling, elbowed her in the ribs.

'Tamio?' she said, smiling and rolling her eyes. 'You like him?'

'I don't! I don't even know who he is.'

'You're looking at him.'

'I am not. I never look at him.'

But she did watch Tamio, and so did Ikkanshi. The boy seemed to be intelligent. He was not silly and he didn't boast or shove like the other boys. He had a gravity to him, not just his weight, which gave a sureness to his movements, but in his demeanour. As if he were older than eighteen, the age Keiko said he was, and older than his friends too, older than the girls who clustered on the beach watching.

Now Vera had a language of English and Japanese mixed. But Tamio was different. He did not have the gift of languages or, probably, of friendship. He likely did not read well or analyse the grammar of his own language. Ikkanshi noticed that Vera did not smile at Tamio when he passed her on the path, which must have been morning and night: the rest of the day he was out with the diving women.

Keiko too seemed reluctant to see Ikkanshi. He stopped her one day on the path.

'Are you afraid to be with me?' he asked her, outright.

'I am not afraid,' she said.

'Then why do you not come to see me?' he asked.

'It is dangerous enough with the girl,' she replied.

'Dangerous because I am a man marked by my disagreement with the war?'

'For that, too,' she said.

'People know.'

'People know, what?'

'The basket maker,' she said.

'The basket maker!' said Ikkanshi, with anger. 'He is just a man who carries messages. That is what he does. Any message he gets, he will carry, anywhere. If there were anything to tell he would already have done so.'

Ikkanshi asked himself if he was fair to Keiko; if he should give up this friendship, which was more than a friendship, out of fear – no, he did not use the word fear, even to himself – out of concern that the High Command was watching him, that he was under suspicion, or could be imprisoned. He did not believe they could do anything to him, because of the regard in which he was held, and his father, especially, had been held, because of the regard with

212

which the sword was held. But Keiko was a simple diving woman. His crimes, whatever they might be, were not hers.

But he missed her visits very much.

Vera did not want to stay at Keiko's house on the summer island. She said she did not like Tamio.

'He stares at me.'

'Do you stare at him?' asked Keiko.

But she went to the well, and spoke to Maiko, and it was arranged that Vera could live at Hana's house that summer.

She went to the boats with Hana every morning, and watched the *ama* pole away from shore. It was still very early and the water was cold. She went to the beach, to practise.

That second summer on the island it had been decided that Vera would apprentice, to dive. The younger children threw the stones for her, and she went down, over and over, wearing the goggles Hana had given her. Every day, she went deeper, pulling up shells from the deeper and deeper places.

It was unclear whether Keiko had won her battle with the Headman. He wasn't saying that he was beaten, but there it was, Vera with the children getting used to the water. She would be a maiden diver, working from shore with a basket floating beside her.

Then came the day when all the *ama* would dive *kachido*, from the shore on the side of the island. And they said that Vera could go. Over the path they went, past the Lost Lake, in a silent row, baskets resting on their hips, to the *ura*, the backside of the island.

The women spoke and pointed and conferred. They clambered across and down the cliffs, their feet tender, yet uncalloused, over the sharp rocks. They spread over the cliffs, the divers and apprentice divers, women of eighty and girls of fifteen.

They stood on the edge of the rocks, like a row of cor-morants. Vera was on the very brink of the black rock, her toes curled over the edge of it. The rock repelled her. It was black and settled in frozen lips, as if once an evil sauce had been poured carefully from above, so that it lapped over and over itself, and set that way. There were scratchy grains within it that sparkled. Seen from underwater it was even more frightening; it absorbed all the daylight and gave it back in sparks and splinters like eyes, and fish scales, fright-ening things. In places, against the undersea flanks of the island, the rock breathed, Vera knew. She and Hana had gone down to look, and had seen the bubbles.

She put her foot in the water; her skin shrank and the hair on the back of her neck stood up. She removed her foot. The wind was blowing onshore, straight at her, raising goose bumps all over her legs and arms. That would mean good diving. The *ama* were happy. But the oldest ones deter-mined the rules: they would dive for only one hour now, then warm up and then one more hour.

Some jumped off right away and made a splash, laughing. They bobbed around in the green-grey element, getting used to the cold.

Vera dipped her foot. She dipped the other foot. She bent over and splashed her upper arms, and heart. She found her goggles and placed them on her head. Her fingers fum-bled tying the knot around her waist to hold the knife. She uncurled her toes from where they clutched the edge of the rock.

She did not jump.

'One, two, three,' she said. 'Now.'

The cold swallowed her and she was under. A trans-parent lid closed over her head, taking away everything that had been her strength above. Her arms lifted out from her shoulders, her legs scissored, and her feet, suddenly light, touched nothing. Even the hair that normally hid her neck lifted up, chilling her vulnerable nape. There was this helpless moment. That girl who stood hesitating on the cliff was gone.

And then. She felt it happen, the exchange. Land life flew off her, upward in a sweep of bubbles. The water assumed her weight. All parts of her were equal now. She was a fisher, a hunter. She would live by her skill, inside the instant, the sixty seconds underwater. She was, for a moment, at home in the sea.

She opened her eyes: her arm was white-green-yellow, and trails of white bubbles rose from her shoulders, her thighs. The hand in front of her eyes was larger than her own, swollen by the lens of her goggles. She stopped sinking and began to rise. Breaking the surface she gave the slow *ama-bui* like the others, and thrust herself onto her back and kicked to get warm, building a froth on the water. Yelping and ducking and surfacing, the *ama* made their way to the diving place, the strange black pillar with its escort of little underwater peaks that marked their spot.

It was not so deep there, only a few yards. They dived for seaweed, *wakame*. Vera began to go down, each time a little farther, each time trying to stay down a little longer. She watched Maiko, trying to learn the tricks of quick descent, of finding and cutting. They wouldn't teach her, not really. They wouldn't give her the secrets of diving until she could find them out herself. Once she had discovered the secrets, then Maiko and Setsu would recognise her as one of them.

She was only halfway down when her air started to break out of her. She came to the surface. Tried again. Breathed, bent, kicked. Farther this time, but not far enough. She needed more breath. She came up and steadied herself against the pillar of black rough stone. The women bobbed to the surface, putting their handfuls of seaweed in the baskets that floated behind, tethered to them. As they broke the surface they expelled the air, let out the whistle: it was low, and sweet, and a little mournful, like the sounds of birds over their nests.

Vera dived, and stretched out her arm, and slashed a little seaweed. She only succeeded in moving it around, like a curtain. Hanging upside down amongst the dark green fronds, Vera thought of her mother's Bible stories. Job wrestled with Satan who had no body. The weed was as evasive as hair, and the water gave her no hold. She thrashed to find a place from which to exert her pull. She remembered her grandfather's eyes, an old man's eyes on her, his sea-worn, one bright, one clouded, eyes over the white whiskers. He didn't hold with her mother's Bible. Fire and brimstone he called it. This rock must be brimstone.

The others swam back and forth to shore in a busy little platoon, sleek wet heads poking above the surface, towing their baskets of seaweed. Soon they'd all get out and go to the *amagoya* to warm up.

She gulped in the air, and folded herself at the waist and this time her feet recovered their scant expertise and she went down. Her arms found their position diagonally out from her shoulders and she found herself cruising the ocean floor, her eyes on a patch of seaweed. Time stopped until she was at the surface tugging a load. She swam to her basket, and tugged the seaweed over the side. It made a small wet dark spot on the bottom, hardly anything.

She returned to the spot she'd found, and went down again. Each time felt a little better. A little easier. She didn't notice the frightening eyes in the rocks and she didn't think about the fish that might brush up against her. She saw an octopus. A friend! It dangled there, looking at her no doubt with its hidden eyes. She pointed at it with her knife and the pinkish coils with darker suction cups boiled in front of her eyes.

The next time she surfaced, the *ama* were all heading back to the hut. Although her catch was still pitiful, she towed it in, and climbed on the hated lips of black rock, gouging her shins because her arms were not strong enough to boost herself up. As she walked she felt every coarse pore of lava under her feet. She picked her way carefully, her basket propped on her hip. She could taste the salt on her lips. She was very cold.

The *amagoya* was lashed to the rock to withstand winter storms. These storms were legendary in their power, but the summer fishermen did not see them. Now all was peaceful on this sheltered side. The little house was the *ama* women's refuge, a world apart, and by tradition men could not enter.

It was a simple, rounded hut, with an earth floor, a hearth and a pile of dried roots and charcoal that they burned for warmth, a door that shut to keep out the wind and keep in the heat. They made it comfortable. There was one *tatami* mat on the earth and a place to the side where the women set their baskets and their tools. Some hooks on the wall held their discarded *yakata*.

The fire in the hearth was alive. Setsu took the small rake and stirred up the ash so that the red coals underneath came into contact with the bit of twisted root she put on it. She heated the water that they had carried from the spring.

As each woman came in she dried herself on her *yakata*. They touched each other, as grateful greeting; you were alone in water, even if you could see others. They took tea and began to open the lunch boxes they had brought this morning. Setsu counted their number: twelve, today. And put twelve eggs in a pot.

Vera watched the eggs boil, holding the warm tea bowl in both hands. There was a knowledge in the weight and simplicity of objects. This work was old. It was done this way year after year, expressly by women. There was strength in that; they trusted this place and they were equal to it. There was respect for the oldest: she spoke first.

'She's getting breasts now, that one.'

'The better for Tamio to get hold of her.'

Loud guffaws.

217

She would blush, if she could, but she was blue with cold.

'If he hasn't yet, it's not for lack of trying.'

The round faces were like little beacons around the fire, reflecting its light. They were at home in the water and here drying themselves in front of the fire. They sipped their tea with gusto. They laughed so easily. Even at her. She used to think they hated her. But that was before she became a diving girl.

Outside the wind gusted and subsided. It wheeled around as if it might decide to blow offshore, and then it returned to where it had come from, teasing. The sun broke through, a blaze that promised summer; the grey water became blue and the rocks took up the sun too.

'Time to get back in the water,' Setsu said.

Down Vera went, braver this time. And right away, the first time, happened on a rich bed of the seaweed they called soft lace. She managed to cut some and, holding it in front of her waist in both hands, kicked to the surface. She dumped the seaweed in her tethered basket, and turned in a circle trying to locate the spot by way of landmarks on the shore and at sea. That particularly high peak of rock formed a straight line to the *amagoya*, and if she went from the farthest visible height of the shore out to – but there was nothing out there to give her a measure. She tried simply to sense it, to keep in her mind the distance she was out from shore, the distance she'd gone along the shore from the path.

Then she turned back and tried to locate the place again. But the sun had gone in. The featureless waves slid across the surface. The craggy bit of rock on land that she had measured by seemed to be gone. That line she thought she could draw, from her spot to the *amagoya*, did not mark the spot. She had never been any good at geometry at school. She dived and could not find the bed. She dived again, and this time she saw it, the dark waving clump, maybe twelve

218

feet away. She hesitated an instant: was it too far? In that way she lost a few seconds. She spurted over to the bed, and waved her knife into the green waving mass. She had almost no breath left. She tried to slash across the roots. Go, go, she silently cursed the seaweed, go! I am stronger than you, I am bigger than you and I want to live more than you want to live.

The patch of seaweed let out a bubble of water and a huge *tai* swam out. Vera opened her mouth to scream but no voice came out. Instead, water came in. She coughed it out, her throat stinging. Her head flared with the bitter smell like smoke from her nostrils. The fish turned at a right angle and, flapping its tail, swam coolly away. She thought her head was going to break open. She kicked and yearned upward; she seemed to be moving so slowly. She was begging the surface to appear, forcing her body to rise through the silky prison.

On the surface she coughed and spat and cried a bit. Then she found another spot and hoped for luck. But she dived once, twice, three times and came up with nothing. Stealthily she watched where the old women went. Nearer the cliff, she thought, and in deeper water. She swam in their direction. They could move so quickly, and disguise their direction as they went down. She tried to follow one of them but lost her in the dark where the sun did not reach.

Below, she cast one look back up. Above her was only greenish grey water. That shining line between water and air had vanished. It was a fear she had, that the surface would disappear. That she would push herself off the bottom, and shoot up and up, her breath cracking her chest, ready to explode, but the surface would never come, there was no air; water had risen to the sky.

At the well the women poured buckets of water over each other. Then they took their catch and their baskets and walked up the path, calling out loud farewells to their fellow divers as they stopped, each at her own cabin. But Vera and Hana had private things to say.

'Come – get warm.'

They ran along the path to the sand beach.

Last summer they'd collected clam shells. They painted the insides in matched pairs: two with a flower, two with an octopus, two with a basket. They had a dozen pairs. They set them in rows face down in the sand. The game was, you turned over one, and then tried to find its match. If you found the match, you could remove both shells. If you didn't, you turned them back over, giving up your turn, and tried to memorise where it was for the next turn. It was a child's game, but one they had loved to play.

Hana found the shells wrapped in cloth, hidden under a log. She was normally brilliant at the shell game. But today she turned up half a dozen – cat, moon, fish, flower – and did not get any pairs. She shook her head as if she'd never seen such a thing before. Her hand would hover over the three rows of shells. Was it here? Was it there? She knew there was another cat in there; she'd seen it. But she couldn't remember. She reached out and turned over a fish.

On Vera's turn it was easy picking. Hana had left so many opportunities. She knew where the cat was. She turned up the first one, and then found the second, clearing them off. She found the fish. Then she turned over a half moon. She didn't know where the other half moon was and she even tried not to get it, reaching up to the farthest left-hand corner of their rows and turning up an entirely new shell, one that had not been turned before. But there it was: a half moon. Vera cleared off the two half moons. Now she was three ahead. She turned up a shell that was painted with a bird, a clumsy bird she'd painted. She hoped that she wouldn't find another, and she didn't. Her turn was over.

Hana didn't move.

'It's your turn,' said Vera.

'Oh, OK,' said Hana. She was thinking of something else. She did not seem to care that Vera was winning. It made Vera cross. And so did the tall figure that hovered on the other side of the low bushes.

'Why doesn't he go away?' she said. 'He's bothering me.'

'Oh no, he's fine,' said Hana.

'As if you knew how he was! As if you had ever even spoken!' Vera exclaimed.

Hana stared mildly at the field of clam shells and said nothing.

'Well, have you?' Vera asked. Had Hana given the boy called Teru permission to stand there and spy on them? And why was she talking about him as if he were her property?

'I don't like him,' Vera whispered, this time boldly looking over her shoulder. The look was lost on Teru, who was gazing into the distance in a way that might be mistaken for boredom. But it was not. He stood with the kind of alertness you expected from a soldier. If anything moved within his peripheral vision, he'd pounce.

'How can you say you don't like him?' said Hana calmly, and not in a whisper at all. 'You don't even know him.'

'Neither do you!' said Vera.

Hana hadn't taken her turn. Vera nudged her.

'I don't think I want to play any more,' said Hana. She was not angry, but final.

'Is it because I'm winning?'

'No it is not because you're winning. You can win, it's all right.'

'I can't win if you won't play.'

Hana collected the shells, one by one and put them in her net bag. She and Vera walked up the path together. Neither of them looked at Teru. But he walked slowly behind them, right to the door of the house. Before the two girls went inside, Hana looked back at him and smiled her brilliant, slashing smile.

221

'Goodbye,' she said.

So he had permission. Hana had given it to him. Vera was shocked.

'Maiko, did you know Hanako has a boyfriend?'

Hana's mother smiled, unconcerned. 'Do you mean Teru?'

From then on he was part of everything.

Teru was older, already twenty-one. He stood waiting for Hana formally, as if he had been appointed bodyguard, his feet a little apart, and his hands folded in front of his body. This was his way of courtship, to appear, wordless, and to take up his position, and to stand there unsmiling. He appeared to have no further ambition but to be there, near Hanako.

'Oh no,' Vera would say. 'Here he comes.' She would giggle behind her hand when Teru hove into view. He walked purposefully as he approached the girls, as if he were going to work. He did not speak but would nod, curtly, when they caught sight of him. Then he would find a spot, separate his feet a little, toes pointing outward a little comically, shift his weight several times to get comfortable, catch one wrist in one hand in front of his body, or, sometimes, for variety, catch one wrist in the other hand behind his body, and stand.

Vera would roll her eyes. Both girls would turn their backs on him. He probably loved that, because Hana's back was so pretty. This gesture did not make him go, in fact it may have deepened his resolve to stay. He did not stare; he looked almost everywhere but at Hana. His eyes swept the area around her like a beacon, emptying the space around her. The boys her age retreated. Only Vera, scowling, remained close to her friend. They'd put their heads close together as they sat on the beach rolling snail shells between their fingers.

'Is he still there?' Hana would whisper.

Vera, who had eyes in the back of her head, or so the sword polisher always said, would grimace and hiss, 'Yes.'

But gradually even she became used to Teru's sombre, kindly presence. He was always there, after work, to wait for the girls. He did not make Vera feel crowded out, in fact he seemed to include her in his field of property, although it was very clear that Hana was his lord and master. Gradually, the distance between the girls' steps and his decreased. And then one day he was walking with them.

He had little in the way of conversation. But it was clear an understanding had been reached. Sometimes, in the evening, he came to the door and Hana went to talk to him just outside, standing so close to the walls that she might have been on a leash. These visits lasted perhaps fifteen minutes, and then Teru withdrew.

'What does he want?' Vera asked, late at night, in the dark in a voice so small that only a best friend could hear.

'Nothing,' said Hana.

'What do you talk about?' said Vera.

Hana did not answer.

That was the cruellest thing, that Hana wouldn't tell.

Now Vera was alone again. A space opened up beside her. When Hana wasn't right beside her, Vera could feel the cold wind on the right side of her body, where Hana usually walked. It was as if she'd lost something, a warm, extra bit of her body.

Sometimes she saw the sword polisher on the Low Place practising, and in the evenings, she could often see him in the water, swimming.

One night she was waiting for him when he stepped out of the water. She held up the large cotton cloth which was his towel and his wrap. He took it wordlessly, and wound the cloth around himself, thanking her. He turned as if to walk to the bath.

'Can we still practise the *kata*?' she said.

They began the next day, early, before the women left for fishing.

223

They began as they had the last year with the one-handed opening – *nukisuki* and the *noto*. It was important not to go too fast. Ikkanshi told her that in his old school, the students had to do the draw and *noto*- the sheathing-for one full year before moving on. He reviewed with her the vertical cut, making certain that she used the left hand to guide the sword. He tried to make her very familiar with the first cut- *mei*- and after that, the first four cuts, which are from sitting.

She was stronger than before and more used to the sitting position. She was firm too in her movements, and quick when she had to be. But he could not praise her. 'Again,' he said, and 'again.' 'Ten more times.'

Some days Vera concentrated very hard on her work. It was beautiful to be up at sunrise and before the people were on the harbour front. Sometimes they heard the cranes who had come again to the marshy place. Often they did not speak. But he would finish each *kata*, resheathe the sword, and wait, until he was certain she was ready to begin again. Then he would brush the fabric of his *hakama* from between his knees, bend his knees, and sit again.

'Again?' she complained one day.

'One thousand times and one thousand times again. After many years you may find enlightenment,' he teased. But it was not really teasing. He was so much quicker than Vera on the drawing he only needed to see her reach for her scabbard, and his sword was blocking her.

He taught her the names. The scabbard was *saya*. *Uchi* meant inside; she already knew that. *Kachi* meant victory. *Saya no uchi no kachi saya*. 'The sword in the saya, winning without drawing.'

They moved on to *ushiro*, from the back, and *ukenagashi*, warding off, from seated and to the side. *Tuske-ate* came next and then she had a set of four seated *kata* that she could practise. This was very painful to Vera's knees. But it was even more painful to Ikkanshi's, which he was careful to disguise from her.

Vera worked quickly, memorising, if not mastering the movements. He wanted to give her something that she could take away with her. He spoke about the wisdom of the way of the sword. *Katsukin ken*, he said, not *satsujin ken*. 'The sword that gives life, not the sword that takes life.'

'How can it give life?' Vera said. 'I am pretending to cut off the head of my imaginary opponent.'

'Exactly,' said the sword polisher. 'He is imaginary. You are cutting the ropes that tie you to his anger. You are making the separation from anything you must leave behind you in life.'

Some mornings she did not come to practise. Ikkanshi stayed on and did his own *kata*, seemingly indifferent to Vera's presence, or absence.

But then she returned, and they worked together. It was companionable. Then her absences became more frequent.

'It is not helping your progress,' said Ikkanshi mildly, 'that you have not been here three times this week.'

'I don't know why I should learn sword cutting,' she said, sulkily.

'Ah,' said Ikkanshi. 'We should all learn *budo*.'

'What is that?'

'*Kokoro*.'

'I don't know what *kokoro* means.'

'It is not an easy word to explain. It means many things. It is something like heart and something like spirit. It brings together the mind and the personality. To explain *kokoro* –'

He reached for her hair. It was long, bleached by sun and sea and it lay on her back. 'It is like trying to tie up a girl's loose hair.' He took it in his fist and held it tight. Some of the side hairs escaped his grip and he loosed his fingers to catch them. Then the main swatch of hair broke free. He took both hands and tried to put it all together. She stood in front of him quite still with her chin bowed. There was an awkward moment when he was still gathering the hair and he had realised that it was a mistake to touch her that way.

'Sorry,' he said, stepping back. He had forgotten that she was growing up. 'Some people say, I meant to demonstrate, that trying to explain *kokoro* was like trying to tie up a girl's loose hair.'

Vera stepped back from him then. 'So if I have *kokoro*,' she said, 'where does it live? In my neck? In my arm? Or only in my imagination?'

'It lives in your whole person. Shall we begin?' He wanted to get back to the *kata* quickly.

She had progressed, by mid summer, to the first ten, with only two more to teach her of the primary set.

But Vera showed her reluctance to come. Often she was late. Several times each week she slept in and was only woken by the other fisherwomen going out. It was as if she wanted him to chide her, and he refused to. Finally Vera said, 'I have missed three mornings. You are my teacher. Are you not angry with me?'

'I am not angry with you, Vera,' he said simply. 'A good *sensei* is never angry with the student. As student and *sensei* we are walking along together, that is all.'

Working on the standing *kata* was good. He taught her the footwork, going over the basics many times so that, later she would not develop bad habit.

'It is useful to imagine that there is a doorway here,' he would say, 'and your opponent is on the other side. You approach as if you will walk by the opening and let him jump out at you, but then, instantly and without warning, you put your hand on the *saya* and turn, ninety degrees, drawing on him.'

It was fun, prowling in the tall grass, hearing the first morning voices in the village, the women at the well, the men with the boats. And gradually these voices would become louder and begin to intrude on the practice.

'We will do *mei*, *ushiro*, *ukenagashi*, *tsuke-ate* and *kesa giri* one more time and then we will finish for this morning,' Ikkanshi would say.

And then they would perform the etiquette, which was very important, to kneel before the sword, to remove the ties from the waistband that held it in place, wind the ties around the *saya* and tuck the ends away, to bow to each other, and to retreat.

The girls no longer played the shell game. Hana and Vera walked along the beach, and Teru walked behind them. Along the way, Hana dropped behind Vera, and Teru moved up, so that he was beside her. Alone, Vera looked out into the crowd of younger boys in the water.

'What are they doing?' She spoke loudly, so that her voice would carry three feet behind.

'They're catching octopus. Mikimoto put a bounty on them,' Hana said.

'Why?'

'They get into his pearl oysters. You can get one *sen* for each octopus arm you catch. You can keep the octopus, too.'

This seemed a melancholy boon to Vera, and she kicked the sand and walked on. She was looking at the ground when Tamio burst out of the water and blocked her passage. He was streaming with water and laughing; he had an octopus in his hand, its tentacles hanging down to his knees.

'Look!'

'What are you doing with that?' she asked.

'I caught it.'

He meant to please her but she scowled.

'You can keep it.'

'No.' She turned away.

'Don't go.'

She stopped.

227

He looked at her, and then back at Teru and Hana, who were close together. Tamio was probably just trying to get her away from Hana. Helping out his friend Teru. Although she didn't think they were friends. Teru was old and serious, but Tamio was still racing around with the kids, cutting the arms off the octopuses.

'I walk with you?'

'Why?'

'You look *at* me,' he said. 'Every time.'

He stood between her and Hana, who was moving a little farther away, with Teru. He put his leg out to stop her passing.

'I do not!'

She had never looked at his eyes before. They were not black, but brown, flecked with gold. She was determined not to look away first. But there was no way of holding his eyes and not smiling. He was not going to look away either.

They could not walk or even move for fear of disconnecting their eyes. The smiles widened.

'Vera,' called Hana.

'Wait.'

'Vera, I'm going back.'

Vera could not speak for fear of blinking. She was annoyed that Tamio wasn't giving in. Most people gave in. Her eyes, although fiercely fixed on his, also took in the fine bone high in his cheek and the pale copper of his skin. He had long lashes too.

'Stop,' she said.

'Why?'

She thought he would reach for her and touch her. She wanted him to. Staring at him, not backing down, she stood there wanting him to reach out with both arms and put her head against his chest. She wondered if Hana was turning back. Her eyes wavered off to the side.

Then Tamio did step forward. He put his hands on her

228

shoulders. He pulled her lightly toward him. They were exactly the same height. He seemed about to kiss her lips but he, too, faltered. A small sound of regret came out of her mouth. He sprang away from her.

'Your friend is going,' he said, because now Vera was looking at Hana's retreating back.

Hana's walking away seemed much larger than just a one hundred and eighty degree turn while walking on the beach.

Vera must have looked desolate.

'No,' he said, and touched her arm. 'Don't be sad. Teru is good.'

After that the two boys, or rather, the man and the boy, were always on the beach after dinner. Hana was loyal, and stayed with Vera, but Vera could feel her waiting.

'Here they come.'

'I know.' Hana sighed, lazy, indolent, and confident.

'Are you going to talk to him tonight?'

'I might.'

'I'm not.'

'Not what?'

'Going to talk to Tamio.'

'Don't you like him?'

'I do like him, but . . .' Was he the only boy in the world? Vera looked out to the blank horizon – a line in a notebook that had not been written on. She knew where she was. She was on a little island, a speck of nowhere. There were other boys, other girls, in Vancouver, in London, every-where, and they – surely they didn't just choose each other by sight out of a crowd, and circle each other on the beach, and then go off together. She did not know what was next. At home she would have been able to tell. She would have read about it in books. The other girls would have told her. Here, nothing was said. It was as if this was all there was. And so she did not want it to happen.

229

'Are you going to?' she asked Hana.

'Going to what?'

'You know.' She did not even know the words in Japanese.

Hana laughed.

The boys were closer behind them. They were throwing something back and forth between them. Their voices and the sound of their efforts, reaching, running for the thing – it was a fishing buoy, Vera could see out of the corner of her eye – were closer.

'I will,' said Hana. 'Some day.'

'Soon?' said Vera.

Not slowly, but quickly, in a week, it changed. She came to like having the boys around. Walking out together, Hana and Vera were met by first one, then by the other. They exchanged secret smiles and branched off, Hana and Teru going to Dragon Lake, Vera and Tamio to the High Place. Vera didn't know what Hana and Teru did together. She soon ceased to care.

There were only a few hours before the girls had to go in. The sky darkened and the wind rustled the water, the tiny house fires went on, and a few oil lamps too. The whole village was tired from being in the sun and wind. The setting sun made everyone quiet, gentle. Vera and Tamio put their heads together.

By now Tamio had declared himself her boyfriend. And so he was that: Vera's boyfriend. She didn't resist. He was of the island, but perhaps – by being in Keiko's family – he had made himself apart from it. His eyes did not stop at the edge of the water: they looked to the horizon. He was curious, a little, and when he got over his shyness, he asked Vera questions about Vancouver, about Canada, about London. What were the streets like there? He had seen pictures and he knew there were a lot of cars. Did ordinary people truly get to meet the Queen, another shocking fact that he had heard.

'Don't ask me. I've never been in London!' she said.

'But you – English.'

'My mother was English.'

'Your English mother where is she?'

'She's gone,' said Vera. 'She died.'

'She come back *O-Bon*?'

*O-Bon* was the Festival of the Dead, and it happened near the end of the summer.

'She wouldn't come. She hated it here.'

Tamio bowed his head. He reached for her. She moved inside the circle of his arms but kept a little away from his chest. Not so close that they touched. Touching was too much. With his arms stretching around her shoulders and meeting behind her back he made a hoop. She turned around inside it. She could feel the heat of his body. They were almost the same height. But he was wide, in the shoulders. She liked the way his waist came in to a narrow V, and his hips, which were lower than hers, stayed that same width. She turned inside the hoop, her arms up, making a game of seeing how much room she had to move in there. She turned her back to him to see the water. It was nearly dark and little white rills of foam appeared here and there on the surface.

He moved the hoop down, around her waist. She turned again this time, but his arms were closer to her. She bumped into him, and said, 'Oh, sorry.' His arms tightened and pulled her in. She arched back to keep her face away from his. He placed the palms of his hands on the middle of her back.

'Why are you shy?' he said. His word was unfamiliar in Japanese but she understood his meaning.

She put her back to him again. His hands were near her heart and she was afraid he would discover how hard it was beating. She leaned over his arms, as if she were leaning over the rail of a ship. She thought of how, last summer – was it only last summer? – she had stood on these very

231

rocks and imagined the whole island steaming away like a passenger ship to take her home. To take her anywhere, in fact.

Tamio pressed his face against the back of her neck. A gust of wind caught her face. Here amongst the islands the winds were confusing. They came and went in the channels, intermittent, and unreliable in direction, brought on by a gust somewhere out at sea, a storm pulling air and water one way or another. Sometimes there was a rush of cold, and sometimes of warm. This one was warm. She felt Tamio's lips on the back of her neck. She imagined the ship sailing out of port. She would be on deck, waving, just as her grandfather and Keiko had when their ship had pulled in to Vancouver. That was long ago. And all because of that she was here.

She turned to face Tamio. She put her arms around his neck. His face was just at the level of hers, his eyes too close to see. She closed hers. His lips were all that was there.

His body smelled sweet, oddly sweet, and clean. His skin was very smooth, and stretched tight over his frame. There was the sense of braiding ropes under the surface. He seemed to be made of ropes that pulled her this way and that, supported her, bound her. She liked to explore the way they moved against her.

They found a rock to sit on. The same rocks where she had sat alone when she first came. She took her mind off herself, then.

Tamio put his arm over Vera's shoulders. She let him touch her breasts and that was enough. They looked into the water and wondered what was down there. She told him about the manta ray and how it came to the light. The next time, he promised, he would bring his lantern.

In the dark his warmth was more palpable. She leaned into it. His arms flexed around her. He felt like a man, sure of himself. He was right there and intent on her, his mouth at her ear, his arms long around her back. He did not feel like Tamio and she did not feel exactly like herself. She seemed to watch as, in the dark, another, bold girl came out of her skin. A girl who knew exactly what to do. Vera kept apart from this girl a little. The girl was under her control, but just barely.

When darkness came it was complete, amongst the bushes and the stones of the island. Only when the moon was full and the sky clear, when the water gave back its light, could they see. So then, whether in darkness, or in light, there was no refuge. The life of night existed inside the huts at the far end, where the rougher characters drank.

The last light drained out of the sky. It was too dark. Maiko would be looking for them. Tamio loosened his arms. As he withdrew she could feel the cold night. She was suddenly tired.

Most days, after dinner, in darkness, the girls slipped out of the hut. Maiko said nothing. They had been doing it for the past two years, together, night diving and just walking.

But it was different now. They looked for the boys. There was no agreement to meet. But if they hadn't appeared, the girls would have been insulted. And they did appear, first Teru, who never smiled, and then Tamio, who did. Sometimes all four of them stood sheepishly in a circle, but there was nothing to say. A few voices came from the harbour, and little wavery lines of light. The men had their oil lamps. They were putting out the night nets. The girls gave each other one final smile as Teru and Tamio pulled on their hands. Vera and Tamio always went to the High Place. Hana and Teru always took the path to the other side of the island.

Sometimes Vera could imagine her mother's admonitions – Come away from him! Where do you think you're going? But her mother was dead and it was different here. And Keiko, living in her family house, seeing Vera only by day, said nothing. No one said anything. It seemed that in this country she had a right to go off in the darkness with Tamio.

That was when the bold girl came from inside Vera. She could do things that made Vera feel so good, that made her feel as if she could not stop. When that happened it was as if Tamio was not Tamio anymore. And she was not Vera. Vera was a girl from another country. She was not going to stay here on this island. That meant she should stop. And she did stop.

But sometimes she thought the other way. If she did things she could not control, even if that bold girl took over her bones and went into the unknown with this boy, it would not really count, because she didn't live here.

Sitting on the rock facing the black water, with Tamio's arm behind her, bracing her so that she could lean back, she wondered what Hana was doing. She had no hint from her friend. A curtain had fallen between them. They mentioned the boys by name as if they were talismans, not people. 'Teru', Vera notified, in one word, when he hove into view. 'Has Teru gone yet?' or, 'you were with Teru' was permissible. But not, 'What did you and Teru do?' He was a fact, the details of which could not be discussed; he was an expected event. Nothing individual about him would be debated, not his wide nose, nor his jaw, which looked too firm to Vera. Not his deep solemn eyes, which did not match with the upturned lips, smiling at Vera as he moved to Hana's side as if he could steer her with a shoulder, nor his officious manner. He had been accepted.

The boys had come, and the girls would not talk about why they had let them in. Vera missed Hana, missed the simplicity of their play, and the way Hana had trained her. When she kissed Tamio she wondered if Hana kissed the sombre Teru as easily. If Teru were as easy to explore as Tamio was. She wondered where she and Tamio were going. She had no roadmap. No one spoke to her about it.

Except that during the day, in the *amagoya*, around the

234

fire, the *ama* teased her. Most of them had married at sixteen or seventeen. Marriage was altogether a comical thing.
Hana and Vera afforded amusement to the whole cluster
around the fire.

'What are the lovers doing when they walk on the shore
every night?' they said to Hana.

'Getting married,' said Setsu.

'Getting a baby!'

Gales of laughter. Hana simply continued to eat her rice
with a serene expression.

'You can dive with your stomach very very big.'

'Have baby in water, at work.'

'No!'

'Some do, some do. Setsu's mother did.'

Setsu nodded. 'Yes she did. And the baby is born swimming.'

More peals of laughter.

Only when they were in the water was Hana Vera's
again. They would sink a foot below the blue gel line that
was the ocean's top edge, and face one another. With arms
and legs akimbo, they'd press the water sideways, main-
taining themselves level. They'd look into each other's faces
and try to keep eye contact. Hana's hair would float sideways all around her. Vera's hair seemed to disappear into
threads of light lying in the water. They sculled, and smiled,
and sometimes circled around each other in a strange dance,
staying down, staying on the level, staying hooked together
by their eyes.

That was the way Vera wanted it.

Once, the *ama* let Vera go out in the boats to watch them
dive *funado*, in the deep. She hung over the side, and peered
down, ten, fifteen yards of water was below. She saw them
bob and descend, and come up. She heard the weird sweet
whistle of their breathing out, that announced the return
to air. She jumped in the sea to swim.

In the water, Hana was perfect to Vera still. In the water,

235

she would not leave her, or betray her. In the water, there was no Teru. The girls went under together.

The boats were above, on the surface, dark ellipses. In the shimmer of the surface were the *tomahi*'s dark, square heads. Sometimes she saw the dark square head of Tamio, leaning over, looking for them.

But outside, as the diving day ended, Hana's attention slipped away. She was the one who leaned on the handle that was the rudder, and also the paddle. She made a smooth, curving pull and then pushed it away. It was an easy, rocking motion and the boat slipped gently over little wavelets that were going the same way they were, toward shore. The *ama* were silent, mostly, seated two by two, tired and, despite the hot sun, chilled: after eight hours no amount of glow from sun or flame could warm their insides. That would only come when they reached land.

As the boats came in, all, from babies to ten-year-olds, were on the beach, rolling in and out of the water, finding shells and stones, shouting over games. The *ama*'s eyes turned from each other to find their own children in the group. Hana's eyes lifted from the rudder to the beach. Vera could see how she scanned it for tall men, and then how she looked farther up the diagonal path that led away. Perhaps Teru was out fishing; perhaps they'd come in already and he was at home, or repairing the bath, or at the temple with the other men, where they discussed the development of China.

Vera saw this but she did not know what Hana thought. She was more like a plant than a person at this time, simply bursting. Vera was hurt, and a little afraid. It seemed too soon, too simple to take the first one who offered himself.

The next morning she went to practise with Ikkanshi. But for once he lost patience with her. 'Are you practising seriously or not?' he said after she had forgotten three times in a row.

'Probably I am not good enough,' she said. 'Most people aren't.' For you she meant.

'Most people are not serious,' he said. 'If you are not practising seriously, don't get up in the morning, just stay in bed.'

For weeks the people prepared for the festival of *O-Bon*, laying out the tools and the clothing of their loved ones and preparing to welcome them in their homes. This was the time when the dead, who had gone to live in the sea, returned. It would be in the middle of August. Every family had someone to expect. The priest prepared special banners and polished the icons that were normally locked away. On the days of the festival the women would dress in white. Drums would beat for three days, and the green night would be lit by rows of torches. Keiko put out James Lowinger's cap and his cape, that he had worn when he had first come there. She put out the book of pearls she had brought with her from Vancouver.

In the festival, the boys and men had to carry a big wooden palanquin that was covered in gold, from the new shrine at the low end of the island to the harbour, and back again. They practised with one of the longer boats, getting in line one behind the other, and hoisting it to their shoulders. When the day came, they would perform this task dressed as women. No one seemed to know why this was, but it had always been so.

When the day came, the boys carried the long box down the length of the island to the shrine. Tamio shouldered the burden along with his friends, and laughed with them, and staggered, too, when he'd had too many sake breaks. But he was, or seemed to be, elsewhere. Perhaps he was not simple enough to be wholly present in these rituals. But his perfect face and body and his nearly perfect presence, marred only by this diffidence, were irresistible to Vera. She followed Hanako to the festival and began laughing loudly and joining arms with the other girls as if she were truly one of them. And acting this way, she became this way.

She was rewarded then by a public look from Tamio, straight into her eyes. His own were direct, as if a screen had slid away, he seemed to see her, completely, for the first time. She felt a deep blush begin at the roots of her hair. And she glanced away, looking for a place to hide her eyes. She tried not to smile but she could not stop herself.

Again, summer ended and the boats sailed for Toba.

# 7

## *San-po-giri*
### Three direction cuts

The second winter came swiftly, with snow as early as November, and a cruel wind.

Hana went back to work at the pearl factory. The boys had disappeared: Keiko said that they might go to war. Vera was allowed to help in the *udon* shop.

Despite all the privations of war, the uncle was full of an optimism that his wife could not share. He bought a neon sign for the *udon* shop, to bring in more business. It was red and black and was to hang beside the door, lengthwise, like a banner. He went up on a ladder in the street to attach it to the front of the shop, while Vera held the bottom. The aunt stood beside, inviting passersby to agree that her husband was foolish.

'He's making a celebration,' she said. 'He is mad. Or he is stupid. One of them.'

But when the sign was plugged in, it shone bright red in the gloomy street under the dark winter sky. It made them all smile. But it did not bring in more customers.

'You bring in customers, Vera,' laughed the uncle. 'They come to see you.'

Why would they come to see Vera? Because she was white. She could not have been more white.

'They come to see her, or they do not come, because she is here. They go by and,' the aunt made a gesture of flattening her face against the glass.

A new law was passed, called the National Mobilisation Law. It gave the government the special powers it needed because of the war. The people were all asked to make small sacrifices for the country. The sign had been up only a few weeks when the law pronounced that everyone had to turn off all electric signs because they used too much electricity. So it hung, dark with its white tube blank and empty of light. Rice was rationed, along with salt, sugar, and matches. Then it became illegal to polish rice. Polishing rice was not economical; it made waste. But unpolished rice was unpalatable; it made every meal a small humiliation. Thus the war ate its way into their lives. Some rules were not even about saving money at all. Women were forbidden to perm their hair, for instance. Curls were un-Japanese.

One day at the end of the afternoon, when she was returning home, Vera saw Tamio. He was bundled in a thick black coat that Vera recognised as belonging to the old uncle. His trousers were short and his ankles were bare. He was walking slowly and staring as if he might not see her, or if he did see her, as if he were angry. She stopped and held out her hand. When you are cold in the street sometimes you don't see anyone.

'Tamio,' she said.

He stopped obediently as if she had summoned him.

'Where have you been?'

He gestured up the hill. 'We are all there,' he said. 'All day long.'

'Where?' Vera knew the others in the town didn't trust her, by the way they kept information from her.

'In the mountains, in the trees. We go to the kilns,' he said. He relented.

'Are you still burning wood to make charcoal?'

It was green wood now, he explained. They were running out of wood that had been cut in years before.

'It must be warm by the fire,' said Vera.

'Yes,' he said, 'but not for the feet.'

He came into Keiko's house for tea. And she saw that he walked like an old man, because his feet were frozen and blistered.

240

'Still, all the news from China is good,' he said. 'Soon the war will be won.'

'Which war?' asked Vera, because now Ikkanshi had told her, there was fighting in Russia too.

'The grand "Holy War in Asia" to get rid of the white colonists, and to enshrine Japan at its head. We should be proud that we can give up certain things.'

Vera asked, 'What can we give? We have so little already. There is not enough wood to burn. The roads are full of holes so that the bicycles fall in. The schoolhouse is shabby and there were no notebooks to write in last year; now what will the students do?'

The other two looked at her silently.

She dared say it but they could not.


Every morning Keiko and Vera had their coffee. It was a habit they both had from James. They loved to make and to drink it. Keiko boiled the water in the kettle on the *irori*, and Vera ground the beans. They sat together, solemnly, and drank the hot, thick black liquid. It made them believe that there was still a world where there was no war, and that sometime that world would return.

'Vera,' whispered Keiko one morning after she had put her cup down, and was about to step out of the door to go to work, 'when did it happen that the street corner had four observers on it, one for each direction? Look –'

Vera came to the door and looked. They stood shivering in the damp. They knew these observers. They were friends and neighbours. And Vera remembered the words Ikkanshi-san had told her never to repeat: *kuro taniwa*.

In the darkest and coldest days of January, families were asked to set aside one day a month on which they would not eat. But even that was not as bad as the day that Keiko came home from her day on the rafts without her coffee. 'Coffee is no longer allowed,' she said.

It was the first, and only time Vera saw her cry.

\* \* \*

One day Vera saw Bamboo-san, the basket maker, as he limped down the street, bent under his backpack of tools, which was dusted all over with powdery snow.

'What do you know about my grandfather?' she asked. 'Or my father?'

'I know nothing special,' he said. 'Only what people know.'

'What do people know then?'

'What do you want to know about what people know?' he asked. His old teeth poked out from under his drawn-back lip. His skin was brown, like a beetle's hard back.

'There are stories,' he said. 'Stories that are told and told. They belong to the people who tell them, not the people who are in them. The one who is the storyteller is the one who collects. Maybe he is lame. Maybe he lives alone and has no one to talk to. Then he will remember them, go over them in his mind, so the stories are not lost. This is an old tradition. Now not so many will follow. When the storyteller is ready, he will tell the story. You may be in the story. It is not finished. You may be part of the story of James Lowinger the Englishman who came here.'

'I don't understand,' Vera said.

She walked away.

The ferry depended on the weather. In snow or storms it did not appear. Sometimes for weeks at a time Ikkanshi did not see it. He ate the fish he caught, and the potatoes the old women gardeners had discarded as being too small. He worked on his carpentry, noting how much of his new room had been completed since his last supply of materials – the boards which he had collected a little at a time, the nails which he had fashioned out of bits of iron. This summer one man had replaced a wall in his hut and Ikkanshi took its refuse. It pleased him to do that. And so he became a carpenter and it was pleasurable to cut the boards to exact length, and fit them together. He planed and sanded each piece to look like the others. To choose a board for its merits and place it where its strengths would be maximised, its weakness minimised.

As he worked he reminded himself why he wanted a bigger house. It would only take more charcoal to heat it. It had to be to show that he was not afraid. That he was not in shame and that he was not hiding. Sometimes, now, he had a feeling of immense change. He might even call it hope. Perhaps the new room would be home to it.

In the evenings he listened to his radio. He longed to know, and he could get no truthful news from the government stations. However, his shortwave in which he had a little skill was of more use. On the twenty-fifth of November he made contact with an operator in Britain. He was able to convince him of his sympathies because of his good English. From him he heard that the civilians were being evacuated from Nanking, that Chiang Kai Shek had gone up the Yangtze to safety. And he was fearful of what might happen. But he had never in his worst dreams imagined how bad it was to be.

He spent the days from the tenth of December talking on the radio and alternately working on the *meito* he had put aside in the days of the early autumn.

When he heard that the inhabitants of Nanking could not escape across the Yangtze, that they were caught in a pack at the gates in the north wall, and then that the Japanese were shelling them, he was seized with fear. He had to disguise his emotions when he spoke to the radio operator in Surrey.

The man in Surrey told him that the men of Nanking were roped together in groups of hundreds and then, with petrol thrown over them, they were burned alive. Women were raped and raped again and after the rapes, taken away by the soldiers to be raped at leisure wherever they found themselves domiciled.

How was it his fellow officers in training allowed the rape and murder of civilians? Had they nothing but bayonets for brains? 'That is very terrible,' Ikkanshi said to the radio operator. 'These are things we do not know in Japan. Even the others, on the mainland, who listen to the news and talk at the newsstands, they do not know. I am sure of it.'

But he could tell the British man did not really believe him. Ikkanshi had become overnight a member of a monster race and that meant he was a monster too.

One incident he heard was that a Japanese soldier approached three old women sitting on a bench, asked for younger women, and when no younger women were produced, he shot all three dead. The officers could not or did not stop the soldiers from killing whoever guarded a gate or sat on a bench they might like to sit on. They had not a shred of authority to defend an order not to kill, not to steal, not to rape.

And the British were there to see. The Red Cross was there to see. The churches were there to see. They called the Japanese barbarians and they were not wrong. The firing squad, the eyes gouged out, the men doused in petrol and burned alive. Even the Germans appealed to Hitler to stop the Japanese in their killing.

Ikkanshi prayed, although he did not know to whom. Hope drained away. He was seized by the most terrible anger, his intestines coiling and knotting like a poisonous snake. He sat opposite his radio with its persistent static, its excited voices filling his head with images of brutality that he had, somehow, to acknowledge as part of what he loved. The Japanese Imperial Army was feasting on the bodies of the conquered. And all the world was watching.

Those days went on for ever, it seemed to him: he would sleep, and wake in the morning, and turn on the transmitter like a wretched addict seeking more of the drug that would destroy him. German, British, American voices expressed outrage at the Japanese barbarians who burned up the streets of the towns, and stabbed the children to stop their cries while they raped their mothers. Up and up went the estimates of civilian deaths. Thousands, tens of thousands. He too began to feel that the Japanese were a race not quite human. Who were these soldiers and what empire did they seek to establish? Not that of Ikkanshi.

On one of the last days of autumn there was a milky blue sky and sun, and the morning's snow turned to dark stains on the stones. On that day the ferry appeared. The basket maker was on it. He could have come for no other reason than to see the sword polisher, for he was the only one there.

Bamboo – that was the name Ikkanshi borrowed from Vera for him – had his backpack. He sat down in the sun in a protected place, and worked with his bamboo and his hands on some creation. The sword polisher bowed to the man as he went by this way and that way later in the day, but neither of them broke the silence. When it was dark, Ikkanshi went inside. He did not wish to invite him to stay.

The basket maker must have slept in the temple, because the sword polisher saw a fire up there. He wondered if Bamboo had been sent to watch him.

In the morning Ikkanshi looked out and saw the ferry approach: the basket maker must have arranged for it to take him back. Bent over with his backpack, Bamboo limped to the dock. At that moment Ikkanshi envied him his freedom, the freedom to go back to the people.

Suddenly, he found himself running to catch up with him.

'I can't imagine you would find many baskets to mend,' he said.

The basket maker showed his unattractive teeth. 'I had another task.'

Ikkanshi did not ask him what it was. Instead he said, 'On the island news passes you by, Ikkanshi-san. Or does it?'

He knew about the shortwave too, then.

'I have the desire to know,' Ikkanshi replied. 'We must understand where we are being led.'

'Down a fearsome path,' the basket maker said, 'a fearsome one. But it is not for the little man to disagree, not in his words. Of course, in your heart you can believe anything.' He gave a toothless, unpleasant smile.

And therefore Ikkanshi knew he was not a bad man, but perhaps misled. He wanted to ask him who had sent him, but he was not certain he'd answer.

'I must go to Toba for provisions,' he said. 'What better time than now?'

On the ferry they talked in a small way of village people and affairs. They discussed the girl Vera and what she would do for the winter, her safety. The basket maker said he would watch for her. Ikkanshi wasn't sure whether this was good or bad. When he got to Toba, he waited for the basket maker to disappear up one of the winding streets, and then he went straight to find Keiko.

He came to her dark door when the fires were being lit for dinner. All up and down the streets the pathetic thin smoke columns rose. And the town was quiet, subdued. As if people knew: but surely they did not. The papers had said only they celebrated a great victory at Nanking. The children had been given a day off, and had made a parade.

Keiko received Ikkanshi only with a look and a bow; behind them was a long summer when she had avoided him. But between them the feelings had grown stronger.

Vera's hair was like smoke too, in the dimness of the little house. It was cold there, colder than at his place.

Ikkanshi took Keiko's hands and rubbed them between his own. Then he took Vera's and rubbed them too.

'We must talk,' he said to the girl. 'It is not for your ears.'

And she understood and because there was only the one room, she had either to go to bed, or go out. She took her towel and went: he presumed to the bath.

And he sat and poured his story out for Keiko.

'Where were the officers, my old classmates?' he said. 'Had the soldiers, perhaps, killed their superior officers?'

She had no answers, but her attention was comforting. He told her that he assumed official orders had been to take no prisoners. Horrific as that was, there was a certain logic to it. The army was nearly destitute itself; they could not afford prisoners, having nowhere to put them and nothing to feed them, so it became necessary to kill prisoners. But how is this accomplished? Sheer numbers make it a hell on earth.

'But did they teach you this, at officer school?' Keiko asked. 'Did they teach you how to make so many thousands of people die?'

'No,' he said. 'They did not. I believe it is accomplished by means of hunger.'

Hunger was something she understood.

First, the soldiers would confiscate the Chinese forces' food supplies. They would eat that food themselves, and the Chinese soldiers would be easier to kill because they were weak. The Chinese forces would be in disarray from the lack of food, and they would be undisciplined, which would help the Japanese. In this confusion the rest of it would happen.

Ikkanshi tried to explain to Keiko, and in doing so, he tried to explain it to himself. Officers would order soldiers to kill every Chinese who might be a soldier, rather than capture him. The soldiers would also have to kill every man who might become a soldier.

And orders must be carried out. It is strange to say, he

told Keiko, but the work of killing people all day long, or slicing off heads and stabbing through hearts, will build up a fearful appetite.

Keiko placed her hand on his knee and they sat for a moment, both rocking for comfort, as a mother would rock a baby.

The soldiers loot every store and pillage every home. These soldiers were poor men and subject to a brutal training and what had become a senseless ordeal. Did the soldiers steal out of a sense of duty to bring home something for their suffering families? This much he understood. But the rest of it he could not. And he spoke of it to Keiko, this gentle, strong, but simple woman. He spoke of it to her as if she would be able to offer him some consolation.

How did the soldiers come to think that every woman must be used? Was this how the soldiers treated their own wives? Were women animals to be mastered? Did they at first take them as reprisals? Did they feel they were about to die and that this was a reward, to rape another man's daughter? Could it possibly be for enjoyment? It could not. There was nothing of glory or of any impulse he could see as human.

Ikkanshi told Keiko then, much that he had never told her. It was out of her experience, the training he had in officer school. Until she met him she had never met one of the samurai class. He had excelled in sword class. He described their training; how they'd all been taught they were superior to the others. Bodies they would find impaled on the end of their bayonets, bodies that briefly resisted their blades, were not animate, not spirit and flesh. They practised on straw bundles. The bundles were soaked in water to most resemble human flesh. They cut and cut, dissecting the bundle into smaller and smaller pieces.

Ikkanshi broke down, that evening. He mourned his beautiful training, the cuts themselves, the prayer that went into strengthening oneself in the spirit of the old masters. He returned in his mind to his teachings. His beautiful *kata* – the economy of their movement, the spirit, the honour they had believed would be theirs when they raised the sword. All lost, and gone, and something dreadful in its place.

Vera came back and sat with them. When he looked at her face he wondered if she had gone away at all, if she had heard him.

'Do you remember that you told me the name of your friend. It was Oshima Hiroshi. I said I would not forget it.'

'I am impressed.'

'I heard the men talking about him in the *udon* shop. He has come back to Japan.'

'Truly,' said Ikkanshi, inclining his head.

If, in fact, he was back home in Japan, Oshima must not have become Ambassador, as the basket maker had predicted. There must have been a flaw in his plan. He would be disappointed. But he would continue to work hard, whatever he was asked to do.

Oshima was touring the country, Vera said, and wherever he went crowds came to hear him speak. The people talked about him in the *udon* shop where she worked. Strange that Ikkanshi knew him so well and now he was a distant force in the wind of the times, a measurable influence on this larger destiny toward which they all rushed. For a few brief moments he felt sad, that the whirl of power had far overtaken him.

Ikkanshi thought he would like to find Oshima. He would watch, and listen, and one day he would hear where he was, and he would go there.

It was so dark. He lay down and slept there. In the morning he crept away, but of course he was seen. It would not help Keiko to have the whole town know he had visited her, Ikkanshi-san the sword polisher, once an officer, now a man with dangerous thoughts.

*　　*　　*

The third summer on the island, it was decided that Vera could dive *funado*, in the deep. And Tamio was to be her *tomahi*.

'Why do only the women dive?' Vera asked Keiko. The divers she knew about were kept in chains by snarling merchants; they had no freedom and were likely to die young. But here on the summer island, the women plumbed the depths and grew old in perfect health, providing for their families.

'The men used to dive, before,' Keiko said vaguely. 'But everyone knows it was not as good. We do not have as much success with the fishing when the men are diving.'

'Why?' asked Vera.

Keiko laughed, her mouth open, her face split like a tropical fruit. She was brown from the sun. 'Some say it is because the men are only skin and bone and muscle, no fat to keep them warm.'

'So it is only that women are fat? I don't believe it.'

'The old men say it is because the women are more graceful and move more easily in the water.'

'What do you think?'

'The Headman says that it is women who dive because we can withstand the sea's cold; cold does not hurt us so much as it does the men.'

But Vera had seen Keiko suffer after standing on the icy rafts in winter storms, pulling up the oyster cages from below and scrubbing the shells. Cold does not hurt women! How convenient for them to believe that! Is this not what we like to think about any person or animal that we put to our selfish use? The fish bleeds but does not burn, the bird merely winks at the loss of its egg, the beef cow is too dull to feel the blade at its throat. But Vera wondered: how can you measure another creature's

250

pain? Even a woman's? To withstand pain is not the same as not to feel it.

'But what do you think, Keiko?'

'I think the difference is not so big between what a woman can do and what a man can do. But we see it once in a long time, when there is danger.'

'What do you mean?'

'There is the danger of coming up too fast. The danger of the rope getting caught under a rock. All of these are dangers. I say the women dive better because we are calmer. When we are under, a sharp or panicky move would kill us, and so we learn to be absolutely calm.'

Vera was far from calm when she jumped off the boat. She gasped, sank, and found herself flailing. She thought she would die, swallowed by the cold foreign element that had every inch of her covered.

I am not from this place, she screamed in her head. Seconds ago she had been dominant in her element; heavier than air, she moved easily through it. But now she was helpless, weaker than the water. She tried to stabilise herself, but her limbs, green and yellow to her submerged eyes, were slow to obey. She watched as a stream of white bubbles came off her shoulders and thighs, like wings. She fought sinking, fought to go up for the air.

At last, her plunge reversed, she broke the surface. She thanked God as she had before that water had a surface, a line where it ended, just like that, and you were out of it, at least your head was, and you could breathe. Air had no such line, or if it did she had never reached it.

She grabbed the side of her boat, coughing, spitting. I will get used to it, she told herself. Hanako and Maiko and Setsu were lined up, each with one hand over the side of their own boats, laughing, they with their dark heads and she with her yellow one. She tried to shake the water off, like a dog. But they were resting in it, sleek, restored, like fish that had been held in hands and were now released. They let go of the boat then, rising and falling, ducking and surfacing with the waves around their ears. They had shed their men and their houses and gravity too.

'Tie on your weights,' said Maiko. She was Hanako's mother but she might well be Vera's in water. Tamio handed down the weights with an impersonal, careful touch.

She tied them on, two iron bars, one at either side of her waist. She needed them to make her sink. She felt them drag her down, changing her. She was so heavy that she did not recognise herself. She could barely kick herself back to the surface and it frightened her.

She remembered that in Ceylon the divers had a stone on a rope. They held the rope between their toes. The diver stood on it, the rope was loosened and both plunged to the bottom. The stone made a lift shaft, pushing the heavy water out of the way, for a fast ride to the bottom. She was not going to get a free ride down on a stone. Here the women dived from the surface duck-style, bending at the waist, thrusting themselves down arms over heads to break a path through the resistant sea, legs firmly together.

She adjusted her goggles. She checked that her knife was tucked under the rope at the small of her back. She watched Setsu give one powerful kick and disappear without a splash. One by one the divers folded, kicked, and disappeared. Maiko waited for Hanako. She went, with a huge gulp of air and a lot of kicking. Vera went an instant later and as she descended she saw, by looking back under her arm, Hanako descend, a streak of lighter green, a little barbed arrow with her arms straight out in a V, her narrow waist, the bulb of her hips, and her tiny, clamped legs.

Down and down and down.

At first she didn't feel the air in her lungs, but then it made itself known, a pressure. It was too soon to feel this pressure. She knew she had not taken a big enough breath.

As she went deeper, the water became colder. It was clouded today, murky, filled with tiny dots of yellow-green, something stripped from the weeds far off, or driven off the ocean floor by pounding waves. But she could see the dark stain of the bottom, ahead of her. She tried to find a crevice, a cranny, a valley between rocks, or a shelf, something of interest, where the awabi might be attached. But she was too inexperienced to judge: would it grow in that direction of the big shelf, or that? She could not see any of her diving friends now. She was in a green cloud.

Now the rocks in their fearsome shapes heaved up below her. They had been worn smooth or perhaps they were not made from the same fire as those near the island: instead of being black and frothy, they were brown, pink, gold, humped up and alive-looking, like animals at rest. There was one like a rhinoceros over which she skimmed; one with a fierce point that could have been the nose of a shark. They came at her suddenly as if she was falling down a tunnel, as if she were Alice falling, falling, down the rabbit hole, tugged by her weights. She dropped past the waving yellow leaves that topped some underwater lily; the luminous weeds like a long expiring doodle curled up toward the light, tickling her leg. But she couldn't open her mouth and the scream was contained, swallowed, in her bursting lungs.

She saw a crevice between two rocks, a bit of lighter bottom that might be sand, and she wondered if the awabi would hide in there. Meiko would gesture to her if she were near, but some swell must have moved both her and Hanako away, because Vera combed this bit of bottom alone. She reached out to put her hand into the crevice, and felt the rough horny shell. Now she fought to right herself, to bring her feet down and her head up; but it was too hard, and there wasn't time; she reached behind her back and brought out her knife and kicked to keep herself within range to slash at the muscle that attached the shellfish to its rocky home. She got half of it, but she couldn't stand another second under there. She gave the bottom of the hateful shell one more slash – a slowed-down, artless, weak slash it was, and missed it altogether, except that her leg bumped up against the rough shell and suddenly bloomed with red. She was cut.

She thought she would explode, and pictured her blood as a bloom that would draw the sharks. Already she imagined the approach of the thirty-foot sawfish the Arabs feared, the one that would cut you in two. Her mouth burbled, about to open.

She had only to tug very hard on the rope at her back and Tamio would start the rapid hand-over-hand that would pull her up to air. She should try one more cut but no. She could not. She yanked the rope, hard. She felt him tug back and the rope lifted her off the bottom and out of the shadows of the rocks, past the strangling lilies, up, up to that overhead glow she was about to crack, up to where she could release this burden in her lungs. She flew through the barrier splashing and blasting out her staleness and she was free.

All of this took less than a minute.

Tamio smiled, into her eyes this time, while she clung to the edge of the boat. And as she expelled her air she made the sound that she had heard so often, the mournful whistle they called the *ama-bui*. And with her chin under water and her eyes steady across the surface, she looked at Tamio.

Meiko surfaced smoothly, unhurried, bearing an awabi. She turned and smiled at Vera but only for a second did her eyes rest on her face. They both looked to the space between them. And Hanako surfaced, face lifted to the sky, neck outstretched, her hands cradling another huge awabi.

Tamio pulled her out of the water. She saw herself in the green reflections on the surface, a wavering white-haired figure, mostly octopus legs and arms. When the surface moved, she was bent and swayed by it. Then Tamio lifted her into the boat. The water streamed off her. Vera had something of her own at last.

Keiko walked up the path beside Vera. Her step was sympathetic, in time with Vera's, but tired, and perhaps sad.

'Will you come to us for your meal?' she said this day. 'The aunt and the uncle miss seeing you.'

'And Tamio? Will he be there?' Vera asked. It would not be possible to contain all she knew and all that was happening between the two of them and to visit in the house where she had been a child, only two years ago.

Keiko spoke without inflection, 'No, Tamio will be at the temple preparing for the *O-Bon*.'

'Yes, I'll come,' she said.

The little hut was cool and dark, as always, darker than the hut of Hanako's family, Vera realised as she stepped inside. It was because of the angle of the door, which was into the slope rather than away from it: the sun did not cross the floor as it did at Hana's. On a hot day this was a relief, but after a day of diving into the twilight water, it felt like a small deprivation to enter it. Vera hadn't quite understood before, how Keiko and her family were a little apart from the others. Keiko had been, on her return from Vancouver, momentarily triumphant: she had come as a respected widow: her old white man had not left her, in fact he had given her this child of his. But now the novelty of that was over; Keiko was different, she had broken the rules. She had come back if not defeated, at least alone, and although the exact details of her transgression would not be mentioned, she would face an imposed penance. Now it was obvious too that whatever linked Keiko to Ikkanshi-san before did so again.

Vera sat by the fire. She took her soup, silently. Keiko lifted her grilled fish off the coals and passed it to her. The aunt and uncle watched her eat and smiled.

'Taller,' they said, nodding.

'Stronger,' they said.

'A diver now, an *ama*.'

'Yes,' said Vera. She hung her head over her soup bowl and did not know anything else to answer. She felt the kindness and pride of these old people. And she was grateful. She looked to Keiko, under the fringe of hair that hung over her eyes, using it as a curtain, beseechingly. Help me out of this. Keiko sat calmly dishing out food.

'You have learned much,' she said. 'Since you came here.'

Vera smiled and continued to look at her bowl.

'But there is more.'

'Always more,' said the aunt.

'It takes many years to become an *ama*. And the best are still the oldest ones. Maiko, and the others. Seventy-five and eighty years old. There is a reason. They have much experience.'

'I know.'

'I mean about the boy,' said Keiko.

The aunt and uncle looked dumb, as if nothing had been said. Vera was glad for the dimness, which she hoped, was hiding her blush.

'But we will talk about the diving.'

'Yes?'

'You know how deep you can go. You know it yourself. You test it every day. A little more. A little more. And you are so excited to find that you can do it and get back up to the surface. There are shells down there that you want. Each one is a little farther down, a little farther from the air, a little farther from the boat.'

'Yes.' That was the way it went, every day.

'And so you try to go there. And when you come back with the awabi you are proud. The boy is in the boat, and he takes it from you. But you are the one who takes the risk. You are the one who might not get back safely, am I right?'

'The *ama* always come back.'

'Once in a long while an *ama* dies.'

'How?'

'The rope. It is the rope,' said the aunt, clearly. She had caught on to the conversation for that minute, and then was gone again into wherever they go, those old women with faces like walnut shells and no teeth.

As Vera was leaving, Keiko spoke to her softly.

'I was one who did not take the first man my village offered,' she said. 'I too fell in love with a stranger. He belongs but you do not. Not truly. Be careful. There may be damage.' And Keiko said, 'When a girl wants love she polishes the man she must have it with, until he shines.'

'I don't understand,' said Vera.

256

'He does not read books, he cannot talk, but you see possibilities. You think that he will come out of himself, your love for him will make him strong. You think that only you know, no one else. Be careful.'

And Vera was ashamed that Keiko saw it, so she grew sullen.

# 8

## *Ganmen-ate*
### Strike to face

When Vera gave in to Tamio she heard only the sea in her ears. She was beyond the rocks at the far side of the island. She swam on her back and Tamio swam over her. Her arms and legs mirrored his, and together, with eight limbs, they were on octopus. They were both light, buoyed up by salt water.

When Vera gave in to Tamio there were no voices calling her back. Everyone had forgotten her. When she did give in it was because she had to have someone of her own. This would seal him to her. There was that thought and then there were no other thoughts. Here was a dive she understood and an act she knew already, from a space within, how to perform.

She dove inward. Physical hunger drove her on, and the heart of her wrestled away. Had wrestled away, even as his arms pinned her and his legs pinned her. Was it the words? The skin? The war? Was it only Vera: would she have done this, no matter where she fell in love? She stood beside herself with the safety rope, comforting: let go, it will be safe, if it is too dangerous, he will be there to pull you back.

She had gone to him. No one could bring her back. Keiko could not call her back although she could see through her and see into her future. Ikkanshi-san could not call her back although he watched them go down the path. Her dead mother stood on the High Rocks on the other side of the island. Her father did not answer letters. Tamio erased him, was erasing him daily.

Despite, or because of, her duplicity, she watched. There was the mirror of her own awareness. She wondered, who was this bold girl?

When Vera gave in to Tamio, she became a concave, glittering thing, a cup to his pouring, a vine to wrap around him. During the day when they went diving she tried to ignore him. When she and Hana walked out at night, her eyes scanned the ground, the low dry bushes, the forms of the fishermen on the beach, stretching dry nets, folding them, putting squid on the racks, running their fingers over the hulls of boats to see if there was a crack opening. Each of these men was not Tamio. She knew this by the shape of them, by the angle of their backs as they bent, by the length and shape of a calf or thigh.

And there was Tamio emerging from the street, or coming around the door of the temple wiping his hand across his mouth: had he been drinking? She could feel him approach and she veered away from Hana without so much as a goodbye. Then the High Place was not far enough. They were gone across the island as soon as they could retreat, into the high grass, over the mound of rocks, around the curve of the path that passed behind Ikkanshi's hut, and along the narrowing footpath that went straight past Dragon Lake and into the western edge of the world where the sun was declining. When they got to the edge of the island it would begin. And it would not stop until the stars came out and glittered on the still black surface of the sea.

Ikkanshi saw her go. He saw them both go, Vera leading the way.

The grass was up over Tamio's head, and even almost up to Vera's. But she was grass-like herself, and golden on top.

259

They stepped into it and vanished. The grass swayed aside to let them in, and closed again behind their backs.

He was so taken with the beauty of their exit that he tried it himself. He went around early one morning behind his new room and walked into the grass, parting it ahead of him with his hands.

He stepped in and felt the narrow, sharp edges of the stems along his legs and hips. He put his hands in front of his face to prevent their cutting his skin; they felt like tiny razors against his cheeks. And he enjoyed the secrecy as the grasses enveloped him, front and back, swallowing him as a snake might, absorbing him so that only his dark shadow would have revealed that there was a body within.

He was not following Tamio and Vera. He knew what they were doing. He had done it himself. He had been in love with someone who was not the same. He was not following, but remembering.

When he first came to the island, and Keiko had been his lover, they too believed that no one saw them, or knew what they were doing. They met in the grass, this way. They walked to the other side of the island.

They tasted each other and the salt water too. There was nothing more wonderful. He thought so, and he believed she thought so too. It was not easy to stop. It was not easy to control. Night after night they pushed each other away and went back to their homes alone. He laughed at himself: he was not a very good monk. Still, he was not a man to marry, either. She was understood in the village to be a single woman. She was asked for, by the young men. But she said no. And then he was there, and she was taken. Everyone knew, but no one said. He knew he could not keep her that way. He said to her, you will not stand for this much longer. And she said no. Finally he was the one who ended it. He told her no, not anymore. I do not love you. Her face seemed to crumble, and she ran from him. It was what he intended, but not what he meant. He meant,

I cannot make the promise to you that would take me from my class. That was why, when the Englishman came, Ikkanshi watched her. He had no right to stop her going. Her going was his fault.

When the grass was tall he could nearly become lost in it.

He stopped by the Lost Lake, and sat on a rock. He began to think about his years in London. Friday nights he would rush by Tube to Covent Garden for the ballet. He walked along a street called Long Acre and gazed in at bookshops, button shops, the shops selling socks in thirty-five lengths. The specificity of it all had warmed his Japanese heart; the foreignness of it, the freedom, the way each person was different from each other person and proud to be so. He climbed up the steps between the white columns and through to the bright foyer of the Royal Opera House, while the British were alighting from their black taxis with the yellow lights on the roof, noisy with the excitement of being there. He would stand on the top rank of seats, looking down into the amphitheatre. On the walls were rows and rows of lamps, each with its own red shade. They were so small and intimate, strange to be in such a large public place. They were of the size you might have at your bedside, and there were so many of them, not one big light. How English that was, how it warmed him!

He knew people found it amusing that a Japanese military man would enjoy *Swan Lake*, and *Coppelia*. But he was entranced, like a child in one of their stories, taken away to the land of the fairies. At the Embassy the Japanese said the British would be easy to defeat because they were children themselves, with their predilection for sweets, and their silly rhymes, and the way they thought they could rule the world, especially Asia, simply because they were white. But he did not agree with that or any call to war. He knew that the British understood the darkness too. He watched *The Rites of Spring*, once, in that theatre. He knew

261

it was choreographed by a Frenchman, to music by a Russian, but it was the British who staged it, danced it, and plugged the doorways of the theatre. And after the dance, after the staged frenzy of mating and killing, those 'childish' people were shocked into silence and then, after the silence, shaken to find themselves on their feet roaring approval, ladies throwing their corsages and men stamping their feet. That was a vision, was it not, of the untamed impulses in humankind? It was no more strange to them than it was to him.

And on a Saturday, you could window-shop on Jermyn Street for tailored shirts and hairbrushes made of natural bristle, fat newspapers by the armful. Then you could sit in the tearooms in the late afternoon as it grew dark. He liked the waitresses at Fortnum's in their starched white caps and ruffled white aprons over a grey frock. They were almost Japanese in the exactitude of their place-ment of the teacup, the napkin, the plate of scones. They did not like him or Hiroshi, who would leave the table early, tipping his hat in silence. Perhaps they did not approve of the slim woman who, eventually, joined him. She would tap on the screen of his open newspaper. He would lower it and there she would be, in her dove-grey straight silk suit, the one with the shoulder pads that were tiny replicas of military epaulettes, her hat pulled down over one ear to nearly cover the short-cropped chestnut hair. And he would be moved to near tears at her beauty, at her bravery.

There it is, you see, the heart of it. He had adored two women. The first betrayed her husband by falling in love with him. She went back to her husband but was not for-given. The second he betrayed in the service of his warrior class, his artistry. And so she left this island, and went away herself. They were both, are both, brave. Bravery was for him the fatal quality, irresistible in a woman. It is rare, but no more so in a woman than in a man. Perhaps, one might say, women were more frequently brave. Or is it only that the small slim frame, the resolute shoulder set above a delicate torso, a narrowed back to a small waist, seems incongruous to contain the heart of a lion?

It is why he loved the *ama*. He loved them for the dangers they faced daily with such calm humility. He loved them for what they knew after plunging down into the murky and cold water, always so close to death, but always swimming away and up bringing life with them. When he saw Keiko for the first time it was this way. He saw her heart-shaped face break open and the laughter splash out as she walked up the rocky bank. And he was breathless as if he himself had just dived to the bottom of the sea.

But he was not brave enough to be her lover then. He was born to marry another kind of woman, a soft, protected girl from some family known to his own. Not a rural girl from a fishing village, not an *ama*, the people of the sea. They speak a strange simple even coarse language! The women laugh and talk too loudly! They are like men, his mother said. But she had not seen them sitting on rocks by the shore around the fire, for all the world like the mermaids in those English fairy tales, who call mortal men away to their deaths.

Keiko was brave and he was not brave enough, and for his punishment spent years alone when she went to Canada. He imagined what it would be like for her. In London he had been the primitive, who talked the wrong way, under whose oriental appeal his lover was ultimately ashamed to have fallen. He had learned what it was to bring a blush to the cheek of the one in whose arms he had only hours before been lying.

Perhaps they were all betrayers, they who crossed borders for the sake of love.

And Vera and Tamio, how would that end?

\*      \*      \*

263

What happened in high summer they did not foresee. The grass died. It bent under the heat, and under its own enormous growth that had been brought on by the sun. And as it bent it lay down on itself, the lower part of the stems curving and lying on the ground, so that these entirely vertical stands became curved, sickle-shaped clumps that were not nearly so high nor so thick a screen. And there was the path their feet had beaten. And there the two children, on an adult's errand, headed across the island, heedless that their screen had collapsed. Ikkanshi would wish them well and smile and then turn away to give them the privacy they wanted. But others felt differently. What had been hidden was acceptable, when it was hidden. When it was revealed, it was not the same.

The third summer ended, and the people left. Ikkanshi remained on the island alone. Now it was established and the others did not speak of it.

Listening to his radio, Ikkanshi was kept informed of what they called the development of China. What the radio operator in Surrey told him: that the Imperial Army in Manchuko was collapsing under the strain. That the soldiers had killed their officers and that rape continued, by soldiers who knew that they themselves were without hope of going home alive. That it had become clear to the officers themselves that China was immense and could never be brought under Japanese control. And at the same time, there were hostilities on the Russian borders. On August the second, he learned that their soldiers were under a barrage of shells and bombs at Chankufeng. The hills were aflame and the ground had become mud, and one unit actually dug into the mountainside for shelter where they stayed until the diplomats arranged a ceasefire that no one believed would last.

Only a few days after the people had gone that autumn

he knew his chance had come. He heard on his radio that Oshima was coming to speak in Kobe. The ferry still came, once a week. Ikkanshi had a travelling cloak. It was black and hid everything, even his face. Even his thoughts, if he wanted it to.

He took the train from Toba. Nowadays few men, only monks, scholars and old-fashioned people, rode the trains wrapped in a cloak. Ikkanshi could be taken for one of their kind. No one paid him any attention. No one could really afford to pay attention to a stranger in their midst. He might be someone who was sympathetic to enemy aliens. He might have dangerous thoughts. Or he might be, as he hoped to be mistaken for, an artist or a professor of some ancient Japanese art, in which case the secret police would respect him.

On the way to Kobe the train track went along the sea. He looked out of the window and saw battleships in the water. Everyone else in the carriage looked the other way. They were not allowed to stare out of the window, in case they encountered military secrets.

In Kobe he found himself an inn and waited there for two days. It was good to walk the streets of a town. This was a place where he could have lived, if he had a normal life. There were many foreigners there, traders and people of all types. He wore his cloak in the streets and looked at the doorways of the traders. He saw a tailor who made western suits. He went inside just to see if he could make him a suit with pleated trousers and a three-button jacket.

'At one time,' he told this silent, small man, 'I lived in London.'

'You'd best be careful then,' the tailor said in a low voice. 'Many of my foreign clients have left the country,' he said. 'And some others will be taken as enemy aliens. They will go to the camp up the mountain.' He gestured but did not look in the direction of his hand, as if even looking there might raise suspicion.

'Did you know of a man called Hamilton Drew?' Ikkanshi asked, hoping to be casual. 'He is a man I knew once. From Scotland I believe. He was buying and selling pearls.'

'No,' said the tailor. 'I don't know this man. But you might ask elsewhere,' and he told him a place a few streets away. And then he took several steps around Ikkanshi's waist at the back as if he had never spoken. 'My apprentice has gone,' he said. 'He was called up into the army.'

'And what about you?' Ikkanshi asked.

'I do not expect to go. I got a C in my physical,' the tailor replied. He was not very strong, Ikkanshi could see. Probably that was why he was a tailor in the first place. 'Still,' he said. 'I must find another trade to practise. There is very little call for men's suits at the moment.'

He finished the measurements in silence.

'I will come back for my suit,' Ikkanshi said. 'It may be some time, but I will come back. Will you remember me?' And he gave him his real name.

'I will keep it for you, Ikkanshi-san,' the tailor said, with a solemn bow.

In the street, Ikkanshi went without hurrying in the direction the tailor had told him. There were many small shops and some bigger ones. In the windows were pearls and necklaces and dolls and lacquer boxes, for foreign consumption. It was the sort of place he might see Hamilton Drew. But he did not. Finally he went into a shop that was cluttered, and busy with a few foreigners at the counters. He looked at pearls in their cases. Pretty, round and white shining objects they were, but nothing more, to him. He did not understand their allure. Finally he asked one of the older men serving. He knew he would recognise the way he spoke.

'I beg your attention for a moment,' he said in his most formal Japanese. 'I have a very great favour to ask you. I am looking for an excellent old sword.'

'I do not carry such things in my shop', the man said

simply. It was impossible to interpret this statement.

Ikkanshi bowed. 'Of course you do not.' He could see that. 'Would there be anyone else in Kobe who would have old swords? I am Ikkanshi-san, *katanatogi*.'

The name was famous among a certain group of people. Knowing fine things and old things, he would be in such a group. The owner bowed to Ikkanshi and gave him directions to some establishment in the city.

Ikkanshi made as if to go.

'You are very kind. If I could trouble you,' he said before leaving. 'There was a Scottish man who was here several years ago. His name was Hamilton Drew. He came to me once looking for swords to sell. I wonder if you ever heard of him?'

'*Sensei*,' he said to the sword polisher. 'There were many such men a few years ago. Now there are only a few of them.'

'I understand,' he said. 'I thank you very much.'

'*Sensei*,' the shopkeeper said, 'this man did come into my shop from time to time. But I have not seen him for one year now, and perhaps more.'

The following day, Oshima was giving his talk in a middle-school auditorium. There was a big crowd to hear him. Ikkanshi sat at the back of the hall, but not too far back. He did not want to be conspicuous. Most of the crowd were men, and young boys, but there were some women there too, a few.

His friend was changed, he saw when Oshima came on stage. He had been a thin boy; now he was stocky. His face was flat, and drawn in to itself, as if he had walked up too often to face a hard wall, and his features had stepped back and were held to attention. His chin, on the other hand, held its ground. The result was a face that was scooped out as if with a shovel, hard staring eyes, and a chin which preceded all. He wore his uniform and saluted, while the men who came in with him saluted and all the boys and men in the hall who wore their cadet uniforms saluted too. He was surrounded by a small forest of salutes. Ikkanshi resisted the impulse, bred into him for all the years of his youth, to salute back.

Oshima's voice, when he spoke, had lost all its soft modulation. Ikkanshi remembered that; it was the way he himself had spoken once rattling like a piece of galvanised tin being shaken. He told the audience about how the Germans were their natural friends, a small country but very powerful, one that needed to expand its boundaries. He told them about the great army the Germans had. He boasted a little about his nearness to the higher-ups in the German cause, Ribbentrop and Hitler himself. He talked of course about ridding Asia of foreigners and he talked about the British and Americans as enemies, while the Italians and the Germans were apparently friends. Japan was the rightful and natural leader of all Asian nations, he said; the Soviet Union, which was Communist, must be taken under Japan's wing and the Germans, on the other side of the Soviets, were to be their natural allies.

At the end of his speech, Oshima was roundly applauded and saluted, and he stood and quickly escaped the crowd. Ikkanshi hoped to encounter him in the back halls of the school. Luckily almost all schools in Japan were made the same way, and he knew exactly where he would be. Having the advantage of surprise, Ikkanshi turned a corner and was suddenly before him. He pulled off his cloak.

'Hiroshi,' he said. 'It is I, Tadatsune.'

Oshima's men stepped forward instantly: perhaps they were on the alert for an attack on his person. But the sword polisher had thought of that. His training did not let him down. Before they had even moved he had anticipated each one and disarmed the first with a simple block. A gun clattered to the floor. Then he held his hands out to the side to show that he was harmless. The minute Hiroshi's eyes connected with Ikkanshi's, he signalled the guards away. Then he laughed. It was a strange, mixed laugh – harsh, mocking, and yet, buried within it he could hear rue and even the old needy respect.

'Good one,' he said. 'They told me about you.'

Although Ikkanshi wondered what 'they' had said about the officer who had resigned to become a sword polisher, he resisted the urge to ask. This was not a meeting that had anything to do with him.

'I trust you are well,' he replied. He surprised himself that he cared to ask. Hiroshi, in Ikkanshi's mind, had gone mad, but in person, especially now that his face was in motion, he was the same old young man of his memories and he felt the same old affection and concern.

'Exceptionally well,' Oshima said, with a glowing face. He had holidayed, he told Ikkanshi, the previous summer in the company of his good friend Ribbentrop. Ikkanshi recalled how miserably he had spent his own, and then quashed the feelings. He could in no way envy Oshima his central place in these hearts of darkness that had formed around the globe. Of course that was what Oshima wanted.

He tried and he failed to engage him. Meanwhile Oshima told him many wonderful things about Hitler and the German cause. He then surprised him by asking how the polisher occupied his time.

'I continue my father's work,' he said. 'I have several fine old blades and when I can spare the time from sharpening the tools and implements for the fisher people I live among, I work on restoring them. I have much to learn. In the meantime I have come to speak with you on the basis of our long friendship. You will not be surprised by my message,' he said.

'Ah Tadatsune,' said his old friend. 'You were always such a good student. Of course you have much to learn. But not from work at the polishing stone.'

Ikkanshi said he disagreed, then smiled and prepared to listen. Oshima did nothing, for which, he supposed, he should have been grateful. They could have taken him off to jail right then. Oshima spoke with the assumption of authority that he had grown up with and now, grown into.

Ikkanshi told Oshima what he wanted him to know: that he was mistaken, that Japan was already far overextended in China, that the world, and especially the British and their allies, regarded the Japanese as monstrous, and that he was taking a dangerous path. He told him that he understood what those in power in Tokyo now wanted to hear, and that Oshima would be under pressure to say it. But he said his was a position of great influence and he hoped that he would remember the better aspects of his training and would, instead, tell the truth. He indicated that he understood that now, as a civilian, he too was in his power.

'Soon I hope to return to Germany,' Oshima said. 'It is what I want, and what the Germans want.'

'Congratulations,' Ikkanshi said.

'It is always good to see an old friend.' Oshima's people were impatient nearby. 'Thank you for coming.' And he took hold of the sword polisher's shoulders, for one minute. Then he saluted. He bowed. It was over.

Fortunately for Ikkanshi, the train ran that day. From Toba he took the ferry back to the island, with more potatoes.

It was dark for two months and he was glad of the dark. He sat cross-legged in *zazen* and meditated as monks did; he drew his sword and practised the *kata* with grief in his heart. But gradually life returned. He longed for light as if it could somehow stop the spread of evil. The days grew a little longer and the sun returned to the land.

# 9

## *Soete-tsuki*

### Companion hand-thrust; turning to surprise one on your left

The cold was terrible during Vera's third full winter in Toba. There was not enough rice. In the village, Vera did not see Tamio. Many of the boys were not in school because their fathers had gone to war. They had jobs delivering or selling. Others, like Tamio, had gone farther up the side of the mountain making charcoal, and did not come home at night.

Teru was old enough to be in uniform. He did not wish to fight, but it was more and more difficult for him to stay out. Only because he was the only son was he allowed to remain at home. Of the soldiers who went away it was said 'they come home as bones'.

Keiko went every day by boat with the other *ama* to Tatoku Island to scrub the oyster shells. They had one day off every two weeks. Mikimoto carried on: apparently somewhere, women wore pearls. But the mother-of-pearl to seed the oysters that came from China was hard to find.

'He knows you are here,' Keiko said to Vera one day.

'Who knows?'

'Mikimoto Taisho.'

'He knows nothing about me.'

'He knows you are the granddaughter of his old friend. He talks to all the diving women. He asked me about you.'

'Then can I work at Tatoku Island?'

Keiko ducked her head. 'He says you may not work. Not in the water.'

Vera scowled.

'He says one day you may come to the island. Next Sunday. He is having a birthday party for one of his grandchildren.'

There was a crowd at the dock to meet her, Mikimoto aunts and brothers and nephews, she didn't know how many. They led her, smiling and cooing over her hair, long now, and silver white, touched with green from the sea. Ooh, the women said, and stroked it.

'Coming to the party?'

When she was young she hated birthday parties. Her mother had had to drag her to them and wait to make sure she didn't bolt. She felt like bolting on this day. The Japanese children were in a circle far down along by the sea walk, which was built of squared timbers over the stones. She could hear their laughing cries.

'Come,' said a kind woman, 'come with me.' And the two of them set out, walking to the children.

I wonder if she knows I am not a child? She must; I tower over them, thought Vera.

But the woman cooed on as if she expected Vera to join the game. She did not understand until she came closer to the knot of children. They were gathered around something, someone was making them scream and laugh. But she couldn't see who.

'Here, here,' said her guide. 'Stand, stay, you will see him.'

Looking over the children's heads, Vera did see him.

There was a thin, grey-haired man with enormous ears lying on his back on the path. His feet were in the air and on his feet was a ball. He was making the ball twirl, then throwing it, catching it. Each time the ball went in the air the children laughed more.

Of course it was Mikimoto Taisho. She knew that he did this. And still. 'But he must be very old,' she said.

'Eighty-two years. It is not so old, for him,' the woman replied.

The old man jumped up lightly, while the ball was in the air. He caught it in one hand and whisked it behind his back. He took out a coin, put his head back, and set the coin spinning on the tip of his nose. It flashed in the sun. The children screamed and jumped around. He took out another coin.

Head back, he shouted in Japanese, 'Do you think I can do it?'

'Yes,' shouted the children. 'Yes, you can do it!'

'I think I can do it,' he said.

'You can, you can!'

He took the other coin between thumb and forefinger. He rubbed it lightly, as if he were polishing a lens. He twirled it in his palm. The other coin was still spinning on his nose.

Vera began to laugh. If she were not looking at this she could not believe it was happening.

He tossed the second coin and caught it with the coin on his nose. It teetered there for a minute. Then it fell, and took with it the coin that was spinning. But Mikimoto caught them both. Then he reached into the folds of his *hakama*, somewhere in there, there must have been a bag, and he pulled out a handful of coins. He walked into the mass of children, giving them away.

Vera stepped back.

But he was coming toward her.

'How do you do?' he said, formally, bowing first and then extending his hand. She did the same.

'You are the girl from Canada. The daughter of the daughter of James Lowinger. He was my friend. Why are you here?'

'He left me with Keiko.'

'Yes I know. They tell me this strange thing. Then you are here because of the Pearl King. I brought James Lowinger here. He loved the *ama* you see.'

'I am an *ama*. I want a job. Please,' she said.

But he turned away. The children were calling, 'Grandpa.' Someone brought him an umbrella. He began to twirl it and once again he was on his back with his feet in the air, the sharp tip and curved handle of the umbrella spinning. The crowd closed in around him.

Later, when Vera was about to get in the boat, a man came.

'Mikimoto Taisho says you can work at Pearl Island, but not here.'

'Why not here?'

'You are too thin,' he said. 'The water is too cold. You can work at Pearl Island. You can speak English to the visitors.'

This at least felt to Vera as if she were closer to her grandfather, to his Japan.

Coming down from the Bund, a stone buttress that was intended to keep the foreigners from the Japanese, James Lowinger passed the rickshaw men with their bent backs and braying cries, their foreheads grooved by the strap they used when pulling a particularly heavy load. He'd been to the customs sheds, cavernous enclosures that seemed to have been there for centuries, but were in fact not much older than he was. The wood-beamed ceilings were thirty feet high; inside, men wearing *hachimangi* across their foreheads pulled two-wheeled carts loaded with crates. They strained, and they shouted to get people out of the way. Uniformed officials scanned the goods and made intricate markings on fine, nearly transparent paper. Old men sat in small, enclosed boxes amidst the fray, with brush and ink writing the exquisite *kangi*. This went on day and night.

He felt alive there amongst the goods, all wrapped and dedicated to this address and that, over the seas and far away. These items were world travellers, as he was. Coming from one place and destined for another, they kept their privacy, boarded up, with nails through, bolstered with straw stuffing against breakage.

His feet made a hollow sound on the wooden bridge over

the canal to Homura. The year was 1900. Not so long ago it was guarded; foreigners were not allowed to cross. But now the government of Japan had given up trying to keep the peoples apart. Sailors, merchants, and westerners who studied Japanese ways were drawn over this pretty arch to the other side.

In Homura, the houses were low and the doors were silent panels that slid away, to leave one wall open, and the interior visible to the world. He jostled along amidst women in high clogs, and samurai in straw sandals. Their swords may have been banned, but their wide-legged swagger gave them away. Message boys ran between them all. He went to the street where the tradesmen worked, the artisans. Looking in at the doors he saw the unmistakeable sway-backed shape of the Singer sewing machine, the bent head of a woman, the whir of the treadle. Then he found what he was looking for: the Yokohama printmakers. He always came here when he was in town, and he had become something of an expert on their work.

They were carving their wooden blocks to impress on the rice paper. James looked at the fresh prints, still damp from the ink. He was not sure he liked them. They were different than the older *ukiyo-e*. The lines had changed since the coming of the Americans. They were not so fluid, or so sensual. The landscape had retreated under the foreign influx.

He picked one up. Here was Mr Audubon, the American painter of birds, in a scene from his life. How had this story, this anecdote of despair, come to live in Japan, come to rest in a Yokohama print shop? The story was that the great artist had left his work for safekeeping with a friend. The friend kept it in a wooden box. The artist, who was poor, travelled all the year in the wilderness looking for birds. When he returned to collect the three hundred prints, his entire early work, he opened the box to find – nothing! sawdust! A rat leaped out, fat and resentful.

'Now you tell our stories,' James said in awkward Japanese.

The printmaker grinned. 'We are like the rats,' he said. 'As you have eaten ours, now we eat yours.' He laughed uproariously.

These shops had the easy bustle of newspaper offices; they were pressed with events of the moment. People came in to gossip; up and down the street stories were relayed like military dispatches. James lingered. Today the men talked about Mikimoto. How he won first prize in the sea products competition. How the Dowager Empress had ordered some of his pearls for her own collection. James knew Mikimoto; he had met him years ago, at the sea products exhibition. People had called him crazy, before, when he said he could coax the oysters to work for him.

At night the quarter was dotted with the paper lanterns that gave it a faintly macabre, ephemeral feel. The lanterns swung in the wind, and occasionally a flame went out, showing that all light was provisional. It might vanish, leaving him alone between strange doorways. But there was a place where he would be welcome, and that was where he was going. The *Miyosaki*, the pleasure district.

In his favourite house he was welcomed; he unbuttoned. Under the skilled hard hot fingertips of these small strong women he felt the muscles at the back of his neck and his thighs, even his jaw, and even his teeth, loosen. He travelled too much. He was always at sea and no land was home and now he was nearly forty, and he knew it. He breathed the salt sweet, sour plum air of Japan, and he thought that this place at least welcomed him.

He did not stay the night. He excused himself, bowing, backing out of the room. He had matters to attend to. At the Grand Hotel he slept for one hour. He rose, got hot water, and washed. He did not shave; already he had adopted the moustache and beard he would wear until his death.

He had oatmeal for breakfast: Japanese food was for later in the day. He had two places to go. The first was the Marine Products Exhibition. The second was the small Anglican church.

Amongst the displays of turban shells and dried octopus, the aquaria where wall-eyed fish circled the glass walls to show off their colours, the bins and bins of seaweed under its many names, James searched for him. He was not difficult to find.

A thickening of the crowd, a knot of people, grew, blocking the aisles. Their necks bent this way and that to get a look. He knew before he saw. Inside this circle would be a diminutive figure in his long black skirt, the *hakata*, with his cotton *haori* over his shoulders. You couldn't actually see him. What you could see was, every few seconds, an oar flying into the air, twirling and then dropping. James wedged his way in. The man he was looking for held his oar in front of his stomach, and spun it with both hands, as if it were a propeller. He passed it to the small of his back. He passed it over his head. He tipped back his head and placed the oar flat on his forehead and it spun there.

The crowd sighed and murmured.

James decided to wait out the flying things – the man had now replaced the oar with an umbrella and started spinning again. In a few moments the juggler ended with a flourish, bowed, and waved away the cheers. He picked up a bowler hat with a bamboo staff. The hat was a sign of a Western-thinking Japanese. He was smaller even than most, and as thick in the calf as a peasant. He had large ears that the Japanese considered lucky.

'Ah, Mikimoto, there you are,' James said. 'Ever the showman.' He clapped him on the back.

Mikimoto understood English but did not speak it. James understood a fraction of the Japanese he heard, but was able to intuit meanings, practised as he was in foreign languages.

Bowing and then raising his head, the little man extended his right hand. Any and all forms of greeting! his smile indicated. James reached to shake it but as he did a ball rolled out of Mikimoto's *haori* sleeve into his palm. His hand inadvertently retreated.

Mikimoto laughed uproariously. He removed the ball. He extended his hand again. As James reached to shake it, another ball appeared. Mikimoto was laughing very hard and two bystanders were laughing too. He took a third ball from somewhere in the folds of his *haori* and began to juggle.

They had met three years before, in this very building, both looking into a display case with a disappointing array of seed pearls offered at too high prices.

'Too many people want pearls,' the Japanese had said. 'Soon – five years, ten years – there will be no oysters left in the sea.'

They were pleased to have found a common concern. They had moved away from the shop and into the street. A young man materialised at Mikimoto's side. He led them to a teashop.

'We must –' Mikimoto said. He could not find the words in his limited arsenal '– We must –' He put up his hands. In a curious gesture he scooped his arms as if he were trying to hold water.

The other man explained then, that Mikimoto had a dream. In his dream he saw many thousands of oysters and abalone nesting along the ocean floor. Pearl banks tucked into the narrow channels were protected and harvested by the fishermen of Ago Bay, to give beautiful pearls for the necks of beautiful women.

'He has made a part of his dream come true. You know, Mikimoto *compels*' – that was the strange word he used – 'the oyster to make a pearl.'

James listened, his breath slowly coming in. He had been looking, during his long pearl pilgrimage, for some way to make this beauty come to light without the attendant ugliness, and some way to put the oysters back in the sea, to save something for the future.

Two years ago, the serious young Japanese explained, Mikimoto had convinced the people of Jinmyo Mura to give up fishing so that they could work with him on farming oysters. But he was not having so much luck. The oysters suffered from enemies: the starfish, the octopus, the red tide, the cold currents. 'You know about the oyster because you travel the world over. There is a question Mikimoto-san would like to ask you.'

'I am no expert on the mollusc,' James said. 'Mostly I see them in huge piles, rotting, and smelling vile. But by all means, ask.'

'What he would like to know is how the pearls get into the oyster.'

James was amused. 'He wonders about that?'

'Yes.'

'Then your boss is not alone. You and everyone else since time began. If I knew the answer to that I would be a wealthy man.'

The Japanese looked at him with complete seriousness. 'I am sorry but I do not understand.'

'I can give you theories going back to the Greeks. Great minds have studied this question and they do not know either. It is probably just an accident.'

The acolyte translated this to Mikimoto who answered back with a few terse words and a brilliant, wide smile.

'Thank you very much for your answer.'

'I have not given you an answer, my friend.'

'Yes you have. If it is an accident, he says, then we learn how to make it happen on purpose. We will sow pearls and make them grow like rice, like turnips.'

James looked into his little white porcelain cup and into the cups of these other two men.

'How much schooling?' he said to the interpreter, indicating the fierce, small silent figure at the table.

'Nothing past eight years when still a child. Mikimoto-san must go to work to support the family, noodle shop and selling vegetables.'

'Tell him science. What he is talking about is science. In Japan there are men who study the oysters in universities, who do research. That is who Mikimoto must ask if he wants to grow oysters like a crop.'

'Mikimoto-san knows everything about oysters. He studies them every day, watching. He opens thousand on thousands of oysters.'

'Yes I can believe that. Mikimoto knows the practical side of sea life, but a scientist will know other things that will help you.'

James could see the young man was already thinking of the next place to ask, and hardly noticed when they shook hands to say goodbye.

That was three years ago. Today, Mikimoto was haggard, thin, and grey in the face. But he smiled hugely, from ear to ear. 'Good luck or bad, my friend?' he asked.

'Some of each,' said James. 'How is it going, your grand concern?'

The same translator appeared from behind the booth. 'Magic continues. Mikimoto made pearls are the most beautiful. Thanks to you.'

'To me? No, I'm sure I have done nothing.'

'You explain that Mikimoto-san must see a scientist. He went to see a scientist, and stayed at his research station. He asked the scientist, what should I put in the shell? We had tried already many things: broken glass, clay, but the oyster spat it out. He tried wood, but it rotted. He has found an answer now.'

'And what is it?'

He did not answer. Instead the man continued.

'We had troubles. We had red tide. All along the beaches shells are pink and oysters are dying. We use the diving girls to move them, even so we only save one fifth of the crop. The seaweed called *mirumo* will kill them also. We employ women to remove seaweed and kill octopus. But good luck followed: we established pearl banks on the shore of Tatoku Island. Mikimoto settled there with his family. He has water all around on lease to within fifteen miles of the banks.'

James was impressed.

'You must come to Toba to see,' said Mikimoto.

That same day James went to church. He rarely went to church. But this day had felt portentous, since morning. Perhaps it was because he had run into Mikimoto: perhaps because he sensed that the event that was going to distinguish his life from other lives, whether – as Mikimoto said – good luck or bad, was coming.

It was an English church – made of wood, painted white, with a steeple, so out of place there. He stopped outside to look at it, and impulse propelled him to enter the building, so English in that alien land. Perhaps inspired by Mikimoto's 'godly' role in making nature do his bidding, he thought he could better his fate. Perhaps he went as penance for *Miyasato*.

And there, standing by the apse, was the woman he would have known anywhere.

She was not tall, only seemed tall because of her military posture. Her posture was erect, yet her drooping head said that although she was proud, and used to having her way, today she was beaten. She was tightly bound in around the waist, in the English style, in brown silk. Her hair was piled up on top of her head, exposing the vulnerable nape of her neck. On her cheek, the side of which he could just see, was a tear.

He was breathless. Astonished to find her, but then, not astonished: after all, he found her wherever he went. She was a talisman, and a memory that sent a rush through his nerves. He had dreamt of Kuwait for years.

281

'Miss McBean.'

And she turned to look at him with no less astonishment than he felt.

'It is you?' she said. 'Mr Lowinger.' She extended her hand. '*Sophia* McBean.'

'Yes, we meet again.' Sophia. Pronounced with a Fie! in it. So-*fie*!-a. So, fie on you.

He repeated his own name, no doubt idiotically, while taking her hand and pressing it to his lips. 'James Lowinger. How incredible that we should meet once again, in a foreign land.'

But he'd known always, that they would, perhaps even had known it when he woke up this morning. He went where all the pearl merchants went and she did too. His father by this time was dead; he had no idea about hers.

She cast her eyes down. 'It was Panama, wasn't it? Mr Lowinger.'

'It was Kuwait.'

It appeared the memory caused her pain. There were lines down the centre of both cheeks, wet lines, as tears had taken a course over her pale skin. He felt – unkind but true – a small elation at the sight. She had been invulnerable every other time he saw her. Now she was in despair. Perhaps he could help, and win her favour.

'I hope you will not mind my saying this, but you appear distressed.'

The very word caused her face to lose its shape.

Again he felt a small thrill, of vindication – she had been so composed in childhood, so clearly superior to him in maturity when they had met at twenty; at thirty, she had gained the upper hand; at forty – well he had improved his chances by arriving at a time of crisis for her. But he disguised – he hoped – his smallness with a look of grave concern.

'Is there anything I can do to help you?'

It was the sort of thing a person of his upbringing did in that circumstance, of course, appear in a moment of difficulty to an old family friend, as if by order of the King, as if the English knew the world so well that they could appear at will in any land that caught their interest, and take charge. Oh! Easy! A spot of difficulty in Japan, have we? I'll just nip down and take care of it . . .

But he did not know Sophia McBean: he had the illusion of knowing her that comes from having chanced upon a person in foreign climes, not once, not twice, but three times over the years. He was fated. It was written. He felt as if all the previous years since he'd clapped eyes on that pouting girl with her red umbrella had been leading him, inexorably, to this moment. He saw, or thought he saw, which is as good as the same thing, that their lives were destined not just to bounce off each other like lost croquet balls, but to take shape from each other. It was as if he'd found his home again after a long absence.

She burst into a sob then and stepped toward him. He held up his arms. She stepped into them and dropped her head so that her crown pressed lightly on his collar bone.

Her hair smelled like butterscotch. That copious, golden brown hair that he had seen before, gleaming in sunlight and moonlight, let down in long tresses when she was a child, and coiled in bright knobs when she was a young lady: now it was lifted and wrapped in knots and pushed forward over her crown. It made her look like a missionary. She felt chaste in his arms.

'We came here,' she said, brokenly, stepping back and wiping her tears, 'for the pearls.'

'Of course.'

'Father and Mother and I, and some of my brothers.'

'Yes,' he said. Other English merchants had done the same.

'We were living in Kobe.'

Where the pearls were sold.

'Our shop was burgled. Robbers came and – they stabbed my father. His arm. It's quite useless.'

283

'When did this happen?' he asked.

'Some months ago,' she said.

It crossed his mind to wonder why she was crying on that particular day, but it would have been callous to ask.

'They have left to go back to England. He cannot manage. I am to stay here and run the business.'

'Alone?'

She flashed him an unbudging look and he bit his tongue.

'It is tragic.'

He took her for a walk along the Bund. He took her to the teashop. They went to the gem dealers and he watched the way she placed a pearl in the very centre of her palm, cupped there, and looked at it quizzically as if expecting it to speak. The way she lifted it between thumb and fore-finger, and rolled it just lightly with the tips of her finger and thumb. She placed it on a flat surface, not the velvet pad the jeweller presented her, but the wooden table or stone stool, even if she had to sit on the floor as the Japanese did. She put the pearl down and nudged it gently, then nudged it again, to see the roll. She might do this for five full minutes, pushing it this way and that to see the freedom of its movement. Then she would pick it up again and hold it in the light, the half light and the darkness, to see what happened to it then. And then she would say,

'One hundred fifty yen.'

Or perhaps, 'One thousand yen.'

Or more likely, 'Fifteen yen.'

Or even, with a small flick of her nail, send it back to the shopkeeper. 'Cuckoo pearls in the mix,' she'd say. 'They all promise that the manufactured ones are kept out but they are not always.'

He was entranced by her manner, which was arrogant, coquettish, and deadly serious. He was a little afraid of her too. But she had only to laugh a little, over her shoulder, and raise an eyebrow at him, and he would dissolve. He was carried away. It was the beginning of an adventure, the end of the old him, and the start of a new James Lowinger. He was suddenly the sum total of his resumé – an aficionado, a world traveller, a lover, a trader – when throughout his stumblings from port to port he had never actually felt he added up to much at all.

Her mouth was the colour of cinnamon. She tasted of some fruit that was unfamiliar and perhaps still green, its fragrance held in but about to be released. Her lips were hard but would soften, under repeated kisses. He asked her to marry him in three days' time, and to his astonishment, she said yes.


They went to Toba for their honeymoon.

In the narrow streets, the fishermen and their wives went by face down, not wanting to meet their eyes. One who knew a little English made a giggling face and circles around his right ear. Mikimoto-san? He is crazy; he is *kichigai*. They sent them to the noodle shop. There the people said Mikimoto spent all day at the waterfront.

'What does he do there?'

'He plays with baby oysters. Mikimoto is mad for oysters. He prays to them and not to Buddha.'

They went to the seafront.

And there was Mikimoto. No bowler hat this time. Barefoot, standing in the water. A fleet of little boats was coming in. It was like something out of myth. A scene from Paradise. Standing in the boats laughing, smiling, nearly naked, were women. Their bodies were perfect, gilded and strong. Without fear, they moved like young animals with joy in their limbs.

It was how women ought to be; why had he not known? Unencumbered by heavy skirts and binding clothes, loose, breasts free, narrow midriffs and waists each one different, but each the same – the curve to wider hips, the apple shape of their cheeks with the black strap that held their modesty in place.

And James was blinded. Like Odysseus with those sirens. And amazed. These were the divers who went down to lift the oysters when they were threatened by the red tide? The ones Mikimoto hired to dive in March, when the water was so cold, to move the oysters near warmer currents? These beauties were the nursemaids to his mollusc children. These little goddesses were Mikimoto's secret weapon.

They rowed their little boats standing, one girl at the tiller, twisting it, gracefully. It was a dance, an enticement, but she did not intend it to be. As they beached their craft, they jumped over the sides and their feet scuffed the unfurling foaming waves. They took the ropes and pulled their boats up the sand, the muscles of their thighs and waists straining, their faces full of exuberance – not like other women of Japan or even women of England. Never in the world had he seen anything like the *ama* divers.

Slaves in the Red Sea, manacled; young boys, flogged when they rose to the surface without an oyster until their blood ran red, and then pushed back over the side of the dhows so that the salt got in their wounds. Grey corpses of divers who got caught underneath brought back to port in Broome. Malays with distended lungs and concave trunks; furtive alcoholic Mexicans with their knives. All of them were gone. The only couriers for pearls should be the *ama* girls.

'Good day, Mikimoto,' he said. 'You are the luckiest man in the world.'

He smiled. 'And they are loyal, too,' he said.

Sophia McBean stood by him, wedded wife in her English mourning, or that was what it looked like – the long skirt getting salt and sand in it. Poor woman, what did her many accomplishments matter then? She was eclipsed by the girls' beauty, and speechless for the second time that day. The first had been earlier that morning when the fact of marriage and the job required of her was impressed upon her. Missionary position indeed!

Mikimoto showed James his pearl banks. He showed him how the oysters spawned, creating a scum of bubbles on the surface in the sheltered coves, how the fisherman collected the spat in cones and let them grow, how many years it took. But the secret of how he coaxed those oysters to grow pearls, Mikimoto did not quite tell.

Vera sat in the entrance hall of the Pearl Museum. From here she could see the women inside working with bent heads and tweezers, moving perfect white balls across bands of black velvet. Many times she heard the guide explain how Mikimoto had developed the cultured pearl. Her job was to speak English to the English visitors, but there were no English visitors. There was the war.

Very occasionally foreigners came from Tokyo. Once a man in a fedora and overcoat appeared on the ramp leading up to the museum. He was big and wore glasses, and he looked like an American. When Vera saw his silhouette, she wondered for a fraction of a second if he were her father. But no, she did not expect Hamilton Drew. The man asked for a tour in English. But he was not truly listening as she made her explanation of how the nucleus was inserted into the gonad.

'What brought you here?' this man said. He said it quietly, in a different voice to the voice he'd used to ask her other questions. It was as if he thought she might be a prisoner.

'I brought myself,' said Vera.

'But you are only – what – sixteen?'

She was older but she said nothing. It was beneath her dignity to be asked her age.

'Where were you born?' he asked.

'Vancouver, Canada.'

She wished she hadn't answered. She wondered if this were a trick, if she should have papers that said she could live here.

'My grandfather was a pearl merchant,' she said. 'My mother was born here.'

He blew out his breath in a whistle.

'I don't think it's safe for you here. Go home to Canada while you can,' he said. 'There is a war –'

'I know there is a war,' she said. 'It is in China, and it is going very well.'

'Not that war,' he said. 'There is going to be a war in Europe and perhaps around the whole world.'

He gave her his card. She kept it at her desk. It said: Horace Calder, *Chicago Sun*.


The snow began to sag and dimple and melt from the stones. It ran away down the slopes of the mountains, and white mounds were isolated in shady places where they softened in the day, and turned crisp overnight. At last it was *risshun*, and time to leave, and once more the boats set sail for the summer island. Vera stood looking straight ahead over the water until she saw the flat low top of the island just distinguishing itself from the waves. She put her fists over her head and cheered.

'Were you afraid it was lost, that it would not be there this year?' Keiko asked.


The day the sails appeared on the horizon on that fourth *risshun*, he was surprised that he could feel such anticipation.

Keiko signalled her happiness to see him. But Vera did not look his way. She was even taller now and streaks of a soft brown had infiltrated her white-grass hair, as if with the coming adulthood she would be obliged to dim her light. She was no longer like a strip of cloth or a board. She had become wide in certain places and narrow in others. Her shoulders were broad and she had long arms and legs. She tripped walking up the beach. She and her friend leaned their sharp, thin

288

shoulders together and giggled. She was clumsy, he saw; there was too much length in her bones for her thin muscles to manage. Probably, like the rest of them, she had not had enough to eat.

She did not come near Ikkanshi.

He busied himself with the old blade, holding to his belief in its life-giving properties. He had reached the stage to use the *uchigimori*, which is the finest of all. He did not have one, and so had to ask the ferryman to bring it. He explained carefully: less than an eighth of an inch thick, it must be reinforced with paper backing. For this he would use not water as the lubricant, but *nugui*, an oil, with fine particles in it. This would darken and highlight the grain, which he could see was going to be very fine.

He knew the basket maker would arrive now that the ferries were running, and he was not wrong. There came a day when Bamboo stepped off the boat as jovial as ever and the children and women flocked to him. Ikkanshi saw this from the High Place where he was practising the cuts. He stopped the *kata* and folded the bag over his weapons and made his way back to his workshop. He had just sat on his stool when he sensed the man in the doorway.

'Ikkanshi-san,' he heard.

He sat very still.

'Good afternoon,' the basket maker said. '*Konichi-wa.*'

'*Konichi-wa,*' the sword polisher replied, and turned his upper body and head to see him bow deeply. He stood to return the bow, and then wordlessly set his back to him and once more squatted on his stool.

'How has your winter been?' the basket maker asked.

'Very productive. I have now progressed to the very finest stone and oil.'

'Then you are near the end?'

'Perhaps, perhaps not.'

There was a soft laugh at the end of this, which annoyed him. It was as if this simple man with his powerful masters were laughing at the notion of Ikkanshi's free will. The sword polisher ventured on. 'Forgive my wandering, however. You did not come to chat about my shopping list.'

The man moved further into the room. He sighed as he lifted his wicker pack off his back, the heavy sigh of the man who works by hand. Ikkanshi rose to get him tea. They understood each other. It was only that the peddlar was forced to bring these messages, and was too proud to admit that he was forced. He pretended to be as important as those who sent them.

'I have letters for you,' he said, gratefully taking the tea from his cupped hands. 'It is good news, I believe. You will be given a great opportunity.' He gave an eager grin, nodding. To him, Ikkanshi was the man who had been drummed out of the Imperial Army for his sympathies with the British, and now he had a chance to redeem himself. 'And I am requested to bring a written response to these letters.'

Ikkanshi sank onto the cushion. He took the rake to the coals and put on another piece of the wood he had painstakingly collected in the bushes, throughout the winter. The basket maker's strategy was clever, because it made it necessary for Ikkanshi to acknowledge that he'd received the letters, or else to reveal to the basket maker that he did not want to give a response.

Ikkanshi took the envelopes from his hands.

'It may take me rather a long time,' he cautioned.

'Never fear,' the basket maker said. 'I have two hours to pass before the ferry leaves this evening. And the children have asked for so many toys. If I could sit with you I will use my time profitably, as you do, and make them.'

Ikkanshi sat too, with his tea. The basket maker asked for water, which Ikkanshi gladly dipped for him out of the bucket. He used to fashion little whirligigs out of bamboo. They were made from a piece of hollow bamboo the boys could roll between their palms and a propeller shape that fited inside, that would take off and fly a few feet. Now they wanted bomber planes.

'More difficult!' said Bamboo. And there they were, two men in the prime of life, as they say, sitting quietly together as old friends might, with cups of tea and a banner of light lying on the earthen floor. Neither was exactly military and neither was exactly a prisoner. But one appeared to be the guard of the other.

The first letter was from the *katanakaji*. He inquired after the *katanatogi*'s health and then after the blade, in that order, so that Ikkanshi understood at least his universe was in working order.

The second was from Hiroshi.

He had no idea how Hiroshi had discovered his whereabouts. Yet, he realised, as he looked at the familiar blocky black *kanji* – familiar because they had sat together through so many classes, desk beside desk, as boys and then as young men – he had been expecting it.

He wasted no time in pleasantries, but said that Ikkanshi-san must know Oshima had been sent back to Germany. That the society was superb and he would have enjoyed the music. When they had met in Kobe he had been in Japan for nearly one year, but now, with changes in the government policy, he was summoned again to Berlin. He was Ambassador and the rulers in Germany were pleased. Together they would lead their countries to a great victory and the world to a great new order.

He had, he wrote, a very special honour for his friend. He recalled his saying that he had several fine old blades in his possession and that he was working on restoring them. He had the highest respect for Ikkanshi's position, and understood his desire to stand back from politics, that perhaps it was fitting for one who was a great artisan. But he also trusted that an officer such as he had been could never truly abandon the cause of his country and his Emperor.

He was now in a position where he wished for a special blade to present to the German commander, the Führer himself, to honour the alliance of Japan and Hitler's countries and in recognition of their great personal friendship.

291

He left no question here, but assumed that Ikkanshi would provide a good blade.

He would arrange to pick it up once Ikkanshi had finished with it.

And it was signed, 'Your friend, Hiroshi'.

Ikkanshi sat, stunned, as the basket maker wove his magic. He watched the other man's clever fingers and envied the peace of his concentration. The basket maker's eyes never left the flying strips of bamboo, yet he hardly saw them: his gaze was that of a man who has memorised every step of his task, and committed it to a place inside his body where the essentials, like breathing, swallowing, hunger and thirst, live. He did not have to think; thinking would have made him falter.

Ikkanshi felt a second flush of envy, this one hotter and more lasting than the first, about society in Berlin. This, Hiroshi had wanted him to feel. Friend? That was the second use of the word. Was he his friend? They had together been subjected to an arduous, spirit-breaking training. They had been beside one another. One of them – in fact Ikkanshi – had been stronger than the other, and had been a better student. But who had the other been? And had Oshima any idea what had been inside of his protector during that time? Yet he called upon this old loyalty, and made an extraordinary request.

But Ikkanshi himself had called upon that same old loyalty.

The difference was that Ikkanshi petitioned: he knew his power was negligible, or nonexistent. Whereas Oshima, the younger one, now commanded. Or imagined he did.

Bamboo work was done by people disdained by society: handicapped people, ill people. But it was beautiful, in a secondary way, which was the best way. Its beauty was due to the fact that the product was made to be useful.

What was the use of the sword?

As he watched the bamboo bend and curl, the polisher wondered why he had not chosen for the object of his contemplation something as harmonious, as humble, and as delicately strong, as the basket. The bamboo of its construction was supple and light. It allowed itself to be bent to any purpose. It waited, as did the basket maker, for a human need to be evident: carrying home shells that have been harvested from the sea, for instance, fitting against the *ama*'s hip. Then it complied with the weaver's invention. A thousand other uses for baskets came to mind. A thousand different expressions of the strength, the lightness and ingenuity of the bamboo.

The sword was so unforgiving, so harsh, so demanding of its maker. But it was of the highest stature. And it was in his family, his history, his clan. He began to see this as eerie. This is what had separated him from Keiko those years before, or had at least made him feel superior, apart from her. The sword divided. But not always for loss. *Katsukin ken*; the sword that brings life, not takes it.

Ikkanshi's father and his father's father and tens of fathers before them had been sword polishers. He had been raised in reverence of the blade. Always since his apprenticeship, his eyes had been fixed on the sharp edge of steel, the way the light flared on its hard surface. When the decision had been made that he should go, at seventeen, to the Officer's Training School in Tokyo, he thought he had put his sword polishing behind him. The grinding day-long classes, the physical training at dawn and dusk, the foreign languages (not English – that was for middle school), the long hours of drill, swimming, kendo, musketry. And they ate so little. He remembered a constant gnawing hunger. The school at Ichigaya had been harsh. Hiroshi and he had counted themselves lucky to have been finished with their training before the rebellion; they had been in the service, abroad. How lucky, too, he had been to be born an Ikkanshi, with the mantle of *katanatogi*. How timely had been his father's death; it was as if he had deliberately provided a way for Tadatsune to withdraw from the military. To come to the summer island; he had thought himself safe there.

Very well, if he were not safe, then he was in danger and would behave accordingly. He would be cunning and finally, of necessary, he would make a sacrifice of himself. That would be preferable to polishing a sword for Hitler.

He contemplated this and felt at ease with it. But then he realised that his actions had bearing on other lives.

There was Keiko, for instance.

There was Vera.

Could they keep her safely with them, on this island, if the police came?

There was Hamilton Drew, her father. When would he come? Because he had to come, he too would be flushed out of Asia with all the other white people.

All of this he thought while the basket maker sat before him, and he held Hiroshi's letter in his folded hands. It was a long journey Ikkanshi's mind made during that hour, and one that brought him right back to where he was. Hiroshi had asked for an acknowledgement.

'You must tell him that Ikkanshi has received the letter,' he said.

The basket maker bowed and replied, 'Perhaps I have not made myself clear, I have been asked to bring a written response.'

'Very well,' Ikkanshi said, sighing. 'I will write that down.'

As he rose to fetch his writing box, the basket maker spoke again to his back.

'Is that the response you will write?'

'It is.'

'But,' persisted the man, 'I have been asked to bring a response, not an acknowledgement.'

Ikkanshi supposed his masters had expected a completion date.

Had he not known him better, he'd have said the basket maker was insolent. As it was, he realised the basket maker felt powerful toward him, powerful because he served masters who had absolute power. Ikkanshi felt a slight chill. But he was more than a match for the basket maker, and well acquainted with his masters.

'I appreciate that that is what you have been asked for,' Ikkanshi said.

The basket maker sat for a moment; his gaze on the floor. He tried humility next. 'It will not be well for me if I bring this acknowledgement, without response.'

Ah yes, Ikkanshi did remember this. All through the High Command such pressure was brought to bear. It will not go well for you if you warn Tokyo that their ideas are false, that their hopes will be in vain, that the grand scheme of the Imperial Forces would lead all Japan to ruin. The instructions were given out from the upper echelons to their men around Europe: do not tell us what we don't want to know. Tell us only what we want to know. And so Japan's forces ground on in their innocence and barbarity.

Would he be the one?

'Very well,' he said, because of course he did not want to bring ruin on the poor basket maker. He took out pen and paper. He scratched out a response, and folded it inside another paper. It would not truly satisfy them, but perhaps it was sufficiently ambivalent to avoid disaster.

He presented it to the basket maker with a bow.

'It is nearly time for the ferry to depart.'

The basket maker was gentle now, as if he hadn't brought Ikkanshi nearer a doom that he had felt approaching for some years. Perhaps the doom had nothing to do with this simple man who was only trying to survive.

Or perhaps there were no simple men any more.

He had written only to Hiroshi. 'Message received. I am well and working on a sword of the Shinto style made by Nagasone Kotetsu. My father left it to me, the last of his works uncompleted. It must be for a great man. I am not certain any of the present intended would deserve it.'

And he had signed it only, 'Ikkanshi'.

The rest would happen in whatever way it had to happen.

Ikkanshi watched the basket maker as he took his leave. The boys ran to him asking for aeroplanes. And he answered them kindly and so they ran along beside him. He set down the backpack that carried his tools near the well. And although he had been called to make creels and to repair the colanders and the fishing baskets, he produced a plane with a propeller that had a pocket to hold stones. The children fed the plane stones, made it fly and watched it drop them.

# 10

## *Shi-ho-giri*
### Four direction cuts

That fourth summer on the island, Tamio was there amongst the boys, thinner, and darker, somehow, for his winter in the outdoors. His skin seemed almost to have been burned. Vera wanted to run her fingers over it from her first sight of him. She knew, and he knew, that they would begin again. It had marked them, and left a thirst.

If it was a good day for deep diving, they worked together. They did not speak, then. But they watched each other, and felt pleasure in what they saw, Tamio from the boat, and she from the water. At the end of the day they were salty and sun-parched. They trudged from the boats to the well and turned homeward without a word. But they knew when and where they would meet. At night they crossed the island with the express purpose of making love. Vera would part from Hana, touching her hand gently, and go down to the beach, in the dark, to sit beside Tamio's boat, at the far end of the path. He would always be there, cleaning it, or folding his ropes. Small lights would turn the air a greenish black along the water. They would go back away from the light, on the path past the Lost Lake, to the other side.

He was that much closer to being a man and she to being a woman. He was urgent and cried out at first, but after that he made no sound. They had lost what words they had found.

Hana met Teru and walked with him also, but there was a decorum in their manner, a space between their bodies when they met that Vera marked, without thinking about it, almost smugly; it could not be with them as it was with her and Tamio. She was more free and she was different. He took more pleasure, and more licence, because she was not from there. It did not matter. Nothing mattered but this.

It was a kind of food, soothing, and necessary. But it was also a hunger. First was the comfort and then the seizing that had them breathless and slick. Sometimes they bruised her on a rock; always she came home with sand in her hair, scrapes on her knees, various betrayals of this activity. No one spoke of it. Maiko kept her eyes down and Hana just giggled and put her hand over her mouth. She did not seem to want what Vera had, but rather to fear it.

Keiko had ceased warning Vera about the young man she loved. She appeared to have her own love affair in her mind. Vera saw her go to Ikkanshi's house; she did not see her return. Sometimes, when she, Vera and Tamio went to the far side of the island, she looked over her shoulder into the blank window of Ikkanshi's 'new' room, which was not new so much any more, and wondered if it were still unoccupied.

And so, in the summer of 1939, the island surrounded Vera and she thought very little about the outside world.

Vera saw the sword polisher from a distance, bending over the tiny stream that came from the spring at the Lost Lake. As if she suddenly remembered that they were friends, she came up behind. He knew she was there but gave no sign. He was holding the blade in the current, tip down. Patiently. He held it still, the sharp edge into the current. She could see how the water divided around it.

298

'What are you doing?'

'I am testing the blade.'

'How can it be tested in the water?'

'It is a good question. We need leaves to come along, and we will see if the blade cuts the leaves. But there are no leaves in this water.'

'I'll get grass,' she said. She scrambled up the rocky ground beside the little stream and pulled out a handful of the dry *sasa* grass. She went upstream ten steps or so and dropped the grasses in the water. They began to float, turning as they went, toward him.

Gravely he watched the grass advance. The long strands bumped against stones and stopped. Then they separated, as the current tugged. Several strands twirled off and began to advance toward the sharpened blade. But they went by. He did not move the sword to meet them.

'Why didn't you catch them?' Vera asked.

'They were going past.'

'Here comes one.'

But this too went past.

'You are missing them all,' she said in disappointment.

'That means it is a good blade.'

Now a piece of straw came along floating sideways across the current, directly in the centre of the stream.

'You cannot miss this one!'

'No,' he said.

They waited. It slowed, in an eddy. But it did not turn. It made its way directly into the line of the blade. Vera held her breath. And the blade sliced it neatly in half. One length of straw floated briskly along the right side of the blade, the other floated along the left side.

'It is good. It is very sharp,' she said.

'The test is not done. I want to see what happens when a straw comes along lengthwise.'

They waited for a long time. Vera pulled more grass and dropped it bit by bit. This strand and that escaped the others and floated past the blade. Some were caught on rocks and bent in the current, wrapping themselves around the stones' contours. But none came up against the blade, to be cut.

'I do not think it is possible,' said Vera. 'You'll never get a piece of straw that comes exactly in the middle of the blade.'

'See what you can do,' the sword polisher said.

Vera began to experiment. On one side of the stream the water moved more quickly into the eddy. On the other, the grass would immediately spin and most likely get caught on rocks, although, if it escaped, it was carried in a direct line to the blade. She decided to try the riskier route. She began dropping two bits of grass at once. Then three or four. All of this took a long time. They did not speak. He did not move the sword. It was Vera who changed the way she dropped the straw, learning how best to offer the strands of grass to the stream, which would in turn offer them to the sword. After a long time one strand sailed directly, clearly, into the blade.

'Here it comes.' She hardly dared breathe. She crouched on the stones at the edge of the water. The straw advanced quickly, offering no resistance. When it reached the blade its front end was deflected, by a fraction of an inch, and it passed along the right edge of the blade.

'Oh, no,' she cried.

'Yes, it is good,' he said.

'But it did not cut.'

'It is better that it did not cut. The straw should pass by. If it cuts it means the blade is not sharp enough.'

And it was like the summer before and the summer before that as they played their games near the little stream, to see if the leaf would be cut in half, or if it would be turned away, and only grazed as it passed by in the current. She was a girl for that hour, not a tomboy strangely become a woman, and he was an artist and they focused only on the task itself, and not its meaning.

Afterwards he gave her tea. She was upset by something. Everyone was upset. It was the war. The summer was taking longer than usual to work its magic of soothing and easing the people.

'How is Keiko?'

She drew a circle in the packed earth with her toe.

'And how is Tamio?'

She dug the toe deeper into the hard earth.

'That is my floor,' he protested. 'What are you doing?'

She looked startled and stopped digging. He had to laugh. There had been a meal once, in England, when he had had much on his mind. He had taken the tines of his fork and pressed them between the threads of the crocheted table-cloth and had he not been stopped by a firm pressure on his knee he'd have dug a hole in the wooden tabletop.

'You are nervous,' he said.

'I hate her,' she said.

'You hate Keiko? I am astonished. May I ask what is the reason?'

'She speaks to me as if I am a child. She keeps secrets from me.'

'Keiko cares only for your wellbeing.' It was the opening she wanted.

'You love Keiko,' she said. Her eyes filled with tears. 'No one told me,' she said. 'You made a fool of me.'

'No,' he said. 'No one could do that.'

She smiled and the tears ran down her cheeks. 'I don't like your secrets,' she said.

He pitied her. Their lives were a mystery, and appeared to be heading for a disaster. No wonder she buried herself in this love affair. Yet she was lucky, apart from it all, and a white person; she would come out of this free from harm.

'It is not a secret. It is only that no one knows,' he said.

She understood what he was telling her.

301

'Everyone knows. Why do you act as if no one knows?'

It was a good question. What could he say? Because there was a history, that he had left Keiko once, that now she was a widow in the eyes of the village and that was a protection for her. Even if the old social inequality were gone, the match would not be popular. He was, he believed, doomed. Therefore he was a danger to her. He tried to do what he could to keep Keiko safe by keeping her apart from him. But not always apart.

He said nothing.

And she said nothing, only sat for a while. She would have made an excellent Japanese headman. Finally she spoke.

'How is your friend, Oshima, wasn't that his name?' asked Vera casually. 'Did you go to see him?'

'I have no such friend,' he said.

'That's funny, because you used to have one.'

'That is true; I used to have one.'

She got up and paced around the hut. 'He has probably gone back to London. He is going to parties and the theatre. Meeting beautiful ladies in teashops and writing secret messages back to Tokyo. You must be bored,' she said, 'just being here on this little island in the middle of nowhere, polishing your blades.'

'I can assure you I am not jealous. And this man Oshima of whom you speak did not go back to London. He has been once again posted to Germany.'

'So you did go and see him! What did you tell him?'

The sword polisher merely bowed, as if to conclude their conversation.

'So if you bow does that mean you feel insulted? I don't see why you don't just say so,' she said.

'I bow to your cleverness,' he said. 'You have tripped me into saying what I do not wish to say. You do that by being unforgivably impertinent. But nonetheless, to speak was my mistake.'

Tears came to her eyes and she turned away so that he would not see them.

'I saw the basket maker come,' she said. 'And go away again. Did he bring something, or did he want something from you?'

He spoke from the dimness of the corner.

'Why would I be bored? Why would I have to go to London for entertainment?' he said. 'When you come in to visit me and entertain me with your beginner's mind?'

She knew what that was. The mind of ignorance. But also the mind that saw clearly, before all the learning confused it.

He walked with her to the doorway. The daylight was flat and frank, after the windowless room.

'Will you give me lessons again?' she asked.

He did not answer her question, but spoke, looking far out across the water.

'In my school, we had to recite every day. It was such an important document we learned it by heart, and the teachers knew it by heart. If we made a mistake, there would be great shame on them. I will tell you a small part of what we learned. I would like you to remember this, whatever else you may learn of me and my people.'

Vera understood that this was a farewell of sorts. She looked angry again. Perhaps that was why she did not listen very well.

'If you affect valour and act with violence, the world will in the end detest you and look upon you as wild beasts. Of this you should take heed.'

His work was done for the day. He began to put away his tools, the fine brush, the cloths, the wet one and the several dry ones, the stones, covered with cloth and set in the corner, the stool. Finally he lifted the bucket of water. He carried it to the door and poured it out; it ran down the path toward the sea.

\*　　\*　　\*

Vera sat in the boat with Tamio, on the seat looking straight ahead, her kerchief tied over her hair, feeling the mixture of sun and breeze on her skin. Hana was in a boat two ahead of her. Teru was not Hana's *tomahi*: Teru fished with the men on the surface. Hana's *tomahi* was a young boy from the village, a cousin of her mother's.

It is almost as difficult to be a *tomahi* as it is to be a diver. The *tomahi* works all day from early morning until late at night. The *tomahi* must care for the rope, making certain that it is coiled exactly and without tangles. He is also responsible for the *konachi*, the boat, to keep it in good condition, without leaks, and the sail mended. It is his job to push the boat off the shore and into the water, also to draw it back up at night. If they are going to the deep fishing grounds, which are a mile off shore, he will row while the women rest to conserve their energy.

It is understood that the *tomahi* serves the diver. He serves her, but she serves no one. The *tomahi* should know where the best places are, although he must pay attention to the women, who point their hands here, farther over, and there, closer. Some *ama* will only dive with husband or family; they believe that their tug on the rope from below may be felt, above, so slightly that a more casual acquaintance might not feel it.

The diving women put on their goggles, raising their elbows to the level of their shoulders, all at once, unconscious of their unison. They latch the lead belts and take the sharp iron *teganes* and tuck them behind their waists. The *tomahi* remain silent as they place the goggles over their eyes and squeeze the two rubber bulbs, one on each side of their head, that equalise the pressure inside and out. The women sit on the gunwhales and swing their legs over, so that their feet are in the water. They slide off the wooden sides of the *konachi* and into the water, dropping under the surface, then emerging with a hard kick, and their lips come together as they breathe out the mournful whistle they call the *ama-bui*.

When the diver is ready she flips nose down and feet up to dive. The *tomahi* watches sixty feet of rope spring off the boat's bottom to follow her. Once she has disappeared he is blind on the surface. He can't see her, but he can feel her. It is his connection to her that keeps her alive.

She propels herself down to the sea bed, fifty feet below, another plain with rocks and patches of bright green seaweed. Underneath where he sits in daylight in the boat, she streaks back and forth under the blue in shadow. He will keep watch for the *fuka*, the shark, watch that the boat does not drift or the rope catch on any other rope, protecting while he cannot protect her at all, ready to spring at her slightest tug.

That day, the sea was calm and shot with prisms and columns of sunlight. Still Vera was afraid. She was not used to diving *funado*. They would fish at the Watchers, the little group of rocky islands far to the east. They went out, twelve little boats together. The divers went overboard and the sea bobbed with black *ama* heads. They dived, and resurfaced, and there was the soft mourning dove sound of the *ama-bui*.

Vera made her dive, with Hana beside her, and did it well.

On surfacing, Vera held the gunwhale of the little boat. She looked beside her, at the place where Hana had gone down. At the same time Hana's mother and grandmother looked too.

'Hanako?'

Maiko looked. The rope was taut. She issued a short question, then spoke sharply to her younger cousin.

'Can you feel her?'

'The rope has not moved.'

What was she doing? Was she cutting a big shell?

He could not tell; the rope felt tight.

'Pull her up!'

He pulled. He could not make the rope come up.

Had Hanako found an awabi worthy of cracking her lungs to haul it off the ocean floor? Was she out at the far extension of her rope? Was she lingering, ashamed at having nothing?

There was no time. The longest dive was one minute and a half and that was only the oldest divers.

There was no time. Instantly and without words Maiko and Setsu took a breath, scooped water, and vanished, their feet marking the small incision in the water as they went.

Vera trod water with her face planted straight down. It would be easy to find her: the rope was clearly visible stretched down into the blue-green, into the murk. Hanako's *tomahi* pulled and pulled on her rope, but it thrummed like a harp string. He began to scream for the others. He was not calm. But he was a man, and his place was in the boat. It was the women who had gone to get her.

What made Vera dive after them? She was afraid. She had already made one dive. She had brought up a shell. She had passed the test. And she was useless to help.

But she dived, praying for her weights to carry her faster than the first time, straight and sure, alongside Hanako's rope. She passed the tops of the doodle weeds, entered the looming shadows of a menagerie of rocks. She entered the gold zone of the sandy bottom, saw where the dark rocks were, and the blackness between them. And she saw Hanako.

She was standing, upright on the bottom, her arms gently adrift on the current, her hair lifted over her ears. She stood, graceful and apparently unharmed, and Vera was relieved until she realised that it was impossible to stand like that on the bottom. The water wouldn't let you. And then she saw Hana's rope, snagged under a cornice, keeping her down, tethered like a goat.

Even then Vera did not quite understand.

It looked as if the accident had been a gentle one, as if death had come and the girl had not struggled. It must have taken only two or three breaths. She might have tried to loosen or cut the rope around her waist; maybe too she had reached for it where it was caught in the crevice, but if so, the water had laughed at her efforts, and erased them. It had taken all the force from her, all the resistance. She was like one of the many enchanted helpless plants Vera saw daily, waving to the sea's sway, mesmerised by the music that was no music at all, but silence.

She reached for Hana's hand.

It floated away.

Setsu swooped down between them. Vera saw her withered hindquarters, the frog kick of her feet, the masterful thrust of her sinewy right arm. She slashed at the rope over and over, finally cutting it. Maiko caught Hanako in her arms, trapping her so that she would not waver off in the company of the currents. Even then Hanako did not rise. Like Vera, she was weighted to make her stay down. They had to tie her again to a rope, to be hauled to the surface. The *tomahi* hoisted her into her boat and laid her across one of the struts that served as seats. Maiko turned her on her stomach and pressed on the strong muscles that crossed her back, what they called the wing bones. Water gushed from her mouth but no air rushed back in.

All twelve boats returned early that terrible morning, towed in lines by the ones with motors, with white flags instead of the many jubilantly coloured ones that would show they had caught many awabi. Those who were left in the village, mostly old women and little children, came down to the harbour. And the cry went up that there had been an accident. The men came running, with a door on their backs. Quickly they took Hana's small light body and laid it on the door. Then they ran to the bath. The fire had been lit already. They poured hot water on her body, in attempts to revive her.

But the hot water did not bring her back. As they lifted her body out of the bath, no one spoke. There were no words for the sorrow of that day. Vera stayed near her friend. But she knew that Hana was gone. If she, Vera, had been with her on the bottom, she could have freed the rope. If she, Vera, had taken that second dive more quickly, she would have seen her friend standing on the ocean floor, exactly as she stood outside her door in the wind, her hair lifting off her shoulders and her arms so graceful. Vera would see that over and over, throughout her life. Hana was smiling sadly, but her eyes were closed and tears were running down her face.

Vera could not have seen the tears. Hana was wearing her goggles.

When they carried Hana to the temple the following day, her body was wrapped in a white kimono, a *kyokatabira*. It was tied right over left, which was the opposite to the way she would have tied it in life. The priest had spent hours the night before writing on it with a black brush and ink. Vera did not know what he had written.

'A prayer,' said Keiko, 'a message for the gods who will welcome her to paradise.'

She had with her a small bag containing coins for her to pay for her passage over the bridge to the land of the dead. She was buried near the old shrine, where there were other graves, each with a small stone.

Maiko was calm. She did not cry. She stood and was supported by the *ama* women, who made their soft whistle, the *ama-bui*, the same soft whistle that they made when they came up for air.

Teru was not calm. He appeared to be broken. He could not stand up like the policeman he wanted to be. He could not watch. He had never been tender, until now. He tried to speak, and his hands rose helplessly from his sides and sank again. He could only raise his eyes pitifully skyward, and then drop his chin again.

Tamio held Vera's head in his lap for a long time, when they went to the rocks on the back of the island. He looked out to sea and he stroked her hair.

But the season was short and so the diving began again, only two days later. In the *amagoya* the soup was heating. The eggs, soft-boiled, were ready. Silence prevailed because they all thought of Hana.

Maiko knelt up near the fire. Her head was bowed.

'It was a freak accident.'

'One in a million dives, it happens.'

'It could have happened to any of us.'

'But it didn't! It was Hanako.'

'So young,' said Setsu.

The silence became heavier.

'It is a terrible thing.'

She had been down only two and a half minutes; that's how quickly the women reached her. But there was finality in her pose, as if she'd accepted that brutal, short statement: her dive was her last. The *ama* could see it, instantly. She had changed from a living body to a body adrift, caught on a rock. They'd seen others, the dead things that the water disposed of.

Maiko and the grandmother cried, something they had not been seen to do in the village. The women listened to them. The soup began to boil and someone pulled it off the fire. Someone else poured it into the little bowls they'd brought in their baskets. They waited another minute while Maiko and her mother composed themselves. Then they passed the warm round bowls hand-to-hand around the circle.

Maiko looked at Vera.

'You lost your friend,' she said.

Vera could say nothing, so she looked down at her lap. She knew her loss was small compared to Hana's mother's. But it felt huge.

'But you will go on to become a brave diver. I am very proud of you,' Maiko said.

Vera was a part of the world, down there and up here too; that too was because of Hanako.

Years later Vera learned how it is possible to revive a person who had been underwater even for an hour. Then, it was not, or they did not know it was. The wind peaked as they drank their soup in the *amagoya* and ate their eggs. The women talked that day: if there might have been a better way.

'If you put your hand into their mouth and try to open their throat they'll breathe again,' offered Setsu.

'Who told you that?' grumbled an older woman. 'Someone who has never tried! The jaws are locked.'

'The' jaws, and 'are' locked. She could not say 'her' jaws, and 'were' locked.

'If you press your fingers here –' the woman reached around behind Vera's neck and pushed her two index fingers into the joint that opened and shut her mouth '– it unlocks.'

'There was nothing,' said Maiko. 'It was decided. It was determined. The gods had spoken.'

Vera wiggled her jaw and the two probing fingers disappeared.

'I understand what happened to Hanako,' Maiko said to Vera. 'She was trying to please Grandmother and me by getting the biggest awabi. She was trying so hard that when she went under the rock arch she forgot that she had a rope tied to her waist and that she couldn't rise without going back the way she came. And by the time she realised, she could not return the way she came, she had stayed too long.'

And Vera understood. The important thing was not to think of the result, of the praise you will win, and how your family's share of the catch will be bigger. The important thing was to simply be there, an instrument without pride. It was what Ikkanshi taught. To think of action done through you, not of yourself doing it. Maiko was saying the same thing that Ikkanshi-san said. Observing oneself doing well is the error. Trying to please is the error. Trying to prove is the danger.

It is not the dive; it is the rope. Keiko told her. The *ama* told her. They were not afraid, until there was the rope.

Vera went back in the water that day. She dived and rested and dived again. She was inside herself and watching. After the evening meal with Maiko it was too sad to stay with the family. She felt she was a stranger now, in their grief.

'I will go home to Keiko,' she said, and Maiko said she understood.

But Tamio was there, in the house. And Keiko was not always there, but gone.

The feeling was too strong inside the four wooden walls. She could not sleep. She felt that what they did together was palpable in the air, between the old aunt and uncle, who still said nothing.

Keiko went to the sword polisher. Vera followed her.

'Perhaps you have made that new room for Vera,' Keiko said.

And he said that it was very likely he had done so.

Vera moved her sleeping mat to the empty room. And when she was inside it, she stood, and looked out of the little window, and saw the path through the grass. And it was her first move, away from the village. She did not see it then.

She went to meet Tamio at night because she was tired, and finished with being alone. The day in the cold water and the dim blue light of the undersea brought her so close to death that she wanted the life of him, the breath under his ribcage, and out of his mouth, the quick grapple of his eyes when she fitted herself against him.

No one spoke of it. Maiko kept her eyes down. Perhaps she understood; perhaps she did not understand. Teru walked with his head down as if he did not see her.

Now, again, it was as if she had just come, and she had no Hana. Vera thought about her escape. To get away she needed money. She had saved a little – only a few hundred yen – from her winter work at the Pearl Museum. But on the summer island there was no money; everything went to the Headman and the Fisherman's Union. Each family was given its allotment. She still looked in every shell, for pearls. She even looked in the eels they ate, in case she might find a pearl.

Every day she saw the sword polisher already at work over his whetstones when she rose to go diving.

'You are very quiet,' he said to her one day.

'*Sabishi*,' she said.

Lonely.

He continued the smooth movements over the blade.

'I thought you were finished.'

'I have tested its sharpness, but there is still work to do,' he said.

311

'What else?'

'I will work on the handle, where there is an engraving, called the *horimono.*'

It was an engraving of the god Fudo. It was a strange portrait of him; his wrathful face was buffoon-like and he had a swirling tail. Ikkanshi had cleaned this, to bring out its worn lines, thinking he might learn who had made the sword, four hundred years before.

'Do you see? He carries the rope to bind the emotions and the sword to cut down evil.'

They peered at it together: this Fudo, despite his great size, and his weapon, and the threatening way he stood ready to attack, with a strange grimace on his face, might almost be comic.

'It is a valuable old blade. I tell myself its *kami* is not destructive but life-giving. Do you see? He is laughing.'

Vera did not see.

He explained how he had taken an iron bar and polished the blade itself, to bring out the wavy *jihada* that makes it look like a living thing. Finally he would oil it, because rust is always an enemy. The oil was there to prevent rusting. The polishing stone exposed new spaces between the crystals of iron and steel, and that allowed damp to come in. The oil would stop that. He showed her the clove oil. It smelled sweet.

'How long will it be before you are finished?'

'If I work it in twice or three times a week for two or three months, all the water that has come inside the blade will have been replaced by good oil, no rust.'

'Then what will you do with it?'

'I have thought about this a great deal,' said the sword polisher. 'And I have decided it is not in my power to say what will become of the sword. It may stay here with me. Or someone will come to collect it.' He spoke of the sword as if it had a mind of its own. He looked down the blade, squinting over its gleam with one eye. It was as if he had had no business with it; it had been sharpened, it had been polished; it would be oiled; it would carry on: nothing to do with him.

'I thought you were going to keep it hidden,' she frowned. 'Because it is a very good sword, and now they are using very bad swords.'

She was accustomed to the times when he did not answer. But this time he looked angry, and she was frightened.

It was near the end of summer: September the fourth, to be exact. The sword polisher had been listening to his radio. The very day before, Britain had declared war on Germany.

He saw two men come off the ferry.

One was the basket maker. He had been expecting him.

The other was the white man.

Ikkanshi knew him.

It was the girl's father.

Hamilton Drew was changed; still Ikkanshi could tell it was he. He was older, heavier, a little soiled. He was a man who had been searching and had not found what he had been looking for, so he had made do with what he found. He had cheapened himself in the process.

He stepped off the boat. No one came to greet him. Perhaps no one knew who he was.

He had arrived at the time of the festival. Most of the village people were in front of their houses, watching the men practising to carry the palanquin to the shrine. It would begin in only four days. Vera was somewhere in the crowd. She was subdued, the way all the women were, because of Hana's death. He thought that he should find her, and warn her. They never spoke of her father and had not since the very beginning when she had told him how she had tried to find him, when her mother had died, and that he had not answered her letters. That was a long time ago now. Ikkanshi supposed he had always known that Hamilton Drew would find her. A lost father would be returned to his daughter; lost fathers always are. But he had hoped that it would be at her choice, not his.

He found her amongst the girls. She was watching the parade. He followed her eyes and saw her lover. Tamio could not make his limbs function. He must have been drunk; he was staggering but she was not laughing at him. She was watching him as if she did not know him, coolly, incuriously.

'A man has arrived on the ferry,' he told her.

'Is it your basket maker?' she asked.

'No. It is Hamilton Drew.'

The sword polisher startled her. More likely he shocked her. But Vera did not take her eyes off the cavorting boys with their burden, the idol on their shoulders. Her own shoulders were rigid.

'Your father,' he said.

'I know that's who he is,' she said, and for the space of time it took her to say it she was the old Vera. But he saw the change. She went hard at that moment. Ikkanshi saw in her who she would be twenty years hence, and he did not like it. She gave a raucous laugh. He wondered for a moment if she too were drunk.

'And so another man steps off a boat and thinks he will change my life?'

He supposed that she referred to her grandfather. That she was thinking back, years ago, to when she needed this man who went by the name of her father.

Ikkanshi wanted to caution her. 'We don't know what he is thinking.'

She gave him her headstrong stare, taking it as a reprimand.

'You will have a little time before he finds you. I believe he will go to the Headman first.' Hamilton would have learned his lesson, from his last visit; to bypass the Headman might save some hours at the beginning, but it would only make your errand longer in the end, if not impossible.

'Prepare yourself,' he told Vera.

She ran.

And he watched the back of her go into the grass.

There was no question of her running open-armed to her long lost father. She was running away. She would have run to Hana, but Hana stood in her mind's eye tied to a stone in the sea-forest. And she could not run to Tamio because he was one of the bearers. Even had he been there, what could he do? In that instant her young lover became a stranger. It was in the grief of Hana's death, it was in the age-old village ceremony, it was in the arrival of her father, all at once. They all became strangers to her, then. They became like people in a dream, familiar of face but opaque of motive and meaning. When the true stranger transformed himself into her nearest relation, her young lover and the rest of the people were transformed into creatures she did not know.

She ran and he watched her go.

The tide lifted the boats during the night, leaving meandering veins in the muddy places, and no marks at all on the sand. Then it let them settle back again. Early the next day, the *ama* went out to fish. Vera was with them.

Outside of the lee of the island, the winds took the surface of the sea and played with it. But that was only on the surface. Underneath, the water was as always. The blue light came from only one source: above. The currents went around the world.

Perhaps they left here and made their way by those arrows she had seen in geography books, arrows that went under the tips of continents and encircled islands, completely around the globe.

Diving down was like stripping off layers of herself.

It was an ecstasy. She felt skinned, completely alert. She could have snapped off her rope. She was connected to no one and nothing. She was not sinking; the world was drifting off. It was going away. She would have only herself.

'Be careful,' said Keiko. 'Go slowly. You want to do something very daring and very dangerous to prove that you deserve to live.' *Now that Hana is dead* was understood.

But that was not it: she wanted to become so exhausted that she expected nothing. She wanted to feel nothing, and to erase all that she loved here. She had longed to escape and now that escape was at hand – her father had come! – she hid from it.

Diving down, she saw that even fifteen yards was not far. The sea was so much deeper than that. When you swim over a hole in the sea the hole is so much darker. Creatures you cannot imagine live in those holes. What you are is only a cut, a scratch on the sea. There is a whole population, underneath, the white fingers of coral, the scabby fish, the octopus steaming along at its steady pace like a locomotive, its tentacles flowing out at the back. What she engaged in was a kind of courtship and she had fallen in love, fallen in love with the sea.

# VIEW 3

I sometimes think I see Hana in the street. She is not at all the simple diving girl. She has got away from the island, and has become sophisticated, sitting at a café in Vancouver with rumpled morning hair and a small dog on a leash. Or, she stands in the line-up for a film, arm-in-arm with a man. Today, she was window-shopping. I saw her from behind, the nape of her neck, the shape of her ankles unforgettable and bringing back those days on the beach fifteen, twenty years ago. I could also see her face in the glass, imposed on a pink satin music box that she seemed to like. There were fine, beautiful wrinkles at the corners of her eyes, crow's feet we call them in English – but the Japanese would have another name. I realise it is not Hana at the same moment that I realise that, all these years and on the other side of the Pacific, I have been looking for her.

'After the first death there is no other.' A famous saying, but it is wrong. First was my mother's. Then my grandfather's. The deaths begin to accumulate. Each one is a little less shocking than the one before – we know this blow. It has come down on us before – but now it is heavier. The deaths form a phalanx, a wall. This wall runs alongside the living, dividing our sightlines; it alters perspective. It is like the blinkers the old milk horse wore as he walked the alley behind the house on Ivy Street. You may see something of these blinkers in the *ukiyo-e*. The artist seems to be lurking, peering out from between two timbers, or alongside the eaves of a house, or even the back end of a horse. The obstruction looms so large in the foreground that the rest of the view is dwarfed. It is what you must look past, and it defines the life beyond.

On Homer Street, after Grandfather's death but before Keiko and I left for Japan, I went for weeks without looking at the *Three Views of Crystal Water*. But then I'd be curious, and return to it. Was there more? And there was.

The third time, I saw the pictures in a different order. They told another story. It was so obvious I wondered why I hadn't seen it before.

This time the story, like so many stories, began with the letter. A man and a woman passed by night on the arch of a bridge. They were both wrapped and unrecognisable in travelling cloaks. The woman extended a hand holding the paper; the man took it. The woman was a servant of a woman held captive in the pagoda behind, in the distance. It was her task to pass the message to this man, in the dark hour before dawn, hoping that he could help her mistress escape.

The bridge fascinated me. It was a short, rounded arch, an arc, a dream bridge. A bridge is a connector, a link, a way of crossing the water. People go over it, to exile, or freedom. There were so many bridges in my life: my grandfather and Keiko came down one toward me. My mother jumped or fell off one. There was Adam's Bridge, that my grandfather told me about, from the island of Paradise to the real world, the attached, mainland world that does not float. Later on, I crossed that bridge, or tried to.

The second print, in this third version of the story, was the one of the seashore. When the stranger had read the letter, he went to the secluded spot above the beach, and hid himself. He spied on the women in their secret nakedness drying around a fire after diving in the sea. They had children with them. They seemed at peace and happy. But in fact they were poor fisherwomen, and almost slaves, forced to remain that way by the rulers in the pagoda.

Amongst them, the onlooker saw the woman who had sent the missive. She was the most beautiful and he fell in love with her. Yes, he would help her escape.

But this could only lead to tragedy.

The last picture explained the tragedy. The lovestruck traveller was determined that the beautiful captive *ama* would be his. He had been, under his disguise, a powerful samurai. He attacked the rulers, entered and set fire to the pagoda and then stood outside to ensure that his adored one and her younger charge escaped. We see the two leaving, one on horseback, one armed with the long pole – *a naginata* – as a weapon. Too late they realised that freedom was banishment from the sea. This is a terrible vengeance, the greatest punishment, to be forced to leave. But there, small, in the foreground was the stream: crystal water. They would follow it up to its source, in the mountains far away. Their protector, their liberator, stood, armed, in front of his conflagration, unable to follow.

As a child, I placed *The Three Views* in the province of romance, of nostalgia, the poetry of secret meetings and forced separations, of one-must-go and one-must-stay, in a turbulent world. Now, as an adult, I place them in the province of prophecy. The pictures told the story of my life, and the people in it were or became those I have met, and those I loved.

On the subject of lovers, then. Unsatisfied longing was my romance. All my life, I would be drawn to a discontented man. Yes, it was what Keiko said about polishing a stone. Girls do find a young man who attracts them, and then, to justify that wanting, they apply to that hapless character all the wonderful qualities they think they ought to love. All they really want is him, simple and lusty and whole. But girls do not like to believe that of themselves. He has to be finer, purer; he has to be different, misunderstood, tormented, and vulnerable only to them.

I would place on his sullen, innocent head the mantle of deep thought, strong feeling, of a tragedy perhaps. And this mantle had one purpose: it allowed me to fall in love with him. It was as if his longing might be for me, his intellectual restlessness (of which

I had only the eyes for proof) created by need of a companion like myself. I could meet him in some unknown space, and be known by him, and he by me. His diffidence would be gone. I would save him, in other words. I would make him whole, make him come alive, become more than he was when I came upon him.

Tamio was distant from the island people, I thought. He deserved more, and if I promised more, he would come to me. I wonder who I really was saving – Tamio, myself, or possibly, layers down under the water, my disappointed father, or my far-away, so often sad, mother.

I took charge because I hated to be abandoned; I, Vera, could not tolerate being left. I went out to meet the man who would change my life, my father, because of that other time when I had stood at the port of Vancouver and waited, an abandoned child. I, Vera, went to meet my father not because I needed him – perhaps by then I did not need him – but because I did not want to be waiting for him.

I wonder what happened to Vera.

*How can you wonder*, Ikkanshi-san laughs to me, *because you are Vera. That girl was you.*

And she was me, I do admit. I do more than admit it; I strive to believe it. This entire exercise is, in a way, a means of my coming to know in my heart, in my gut, that Vera and I are the same. But the more I enter that young mind and body the more of a stranger I find her.

I mean, what happened to that brave girl, that nervy girl who took what she wanted and kept going back for more, who knew she would escape from it and not be drowned?

*She went on a journey of many years*, offers my samurai teacher.

That's not it.

*She forgot herself.*

But she did not entirely forget because all of it lived in her body, and her body remembered.

# 11

## *So-giri*

### Many cuts; running cutting through a crowd

Vera discovered her father in the Headman's house. The little house was a cave, despite the glow of the late afternoon, smelling of charcoal, smoky timbers, fish, wet rope and seaweed, of salty things left to dry in the sun. Inside the hut, she was temporarily confused by the darkness, which was punctured by two squares that glowed like fires, but were not fires, only small windows. In the hearth there were ashes with a faintly discernible pink glow. She hovered tall in the doorway before she bowed and then sank to her knees.

The Headman's daughter gave a small nodding bow in return. She served tea in small bowls and withdrew to the edge of the *tatami*. The Headman's sons, thickset men with sun-reddened skin, were seated behind their father, away from the hearth. Sitting on the *tatami* mat at the *irori* were two discernible figures, opposite in shape. The visitor had his bowl of tea in his hands and was balanced awkwardly on the side of one hip, with his long legs only half folded against the side of his body, and his opposite arm propping him up. He appeared to have been knocked over, and was straining to get back erect.

The Headman sat solidly on his heels, knees folded like knuckles. He could sit that way for ever. He appeared tall but he was not; like his sons, he was a short strong man, all of his height being above his hips.

Vera could tell by the smile on the visitor's face that he was attempting to charm the Headman and believed that he had succeeded. Vera knew better.

Her father was white-skinned with a lantern jaw and gangling stick-legs that normally launched him above the crowd but were in this context useless. He was ill at ease but not as ill at ease as he should have been, because he had not fully appreciated the solidity of the world he had entered. In this same way he underestimated all that he came up against, assuming a world as provisional, as up for grabs, as he was. Vera saw instantly what she would come to call his arrogance, but did not name it. He was unaffected, not bothered. That he could come and reclaim her after years of neglect, as if she were a piece of luggage forgotten on a platform, was stunning, but not to him. It was all in a day's work: Today I'll go and find that daughter of mine, tomorrow I'll open a business. She seemed to know all this as she looked at him before he had even recognised her. And maybe she did. But she would not know she knew it until later, much later.

She knelt in the doorway. He saw her and struggled from his seated position, unfolding his legs eagerly. Too eagerly. She knew that his legs would feel as if they had been broken. Depending on how long he had been sitting there, they might have had the circulation blocked, and be all pins and needles. There were cases when foreigners in Japan fell down when they meant to rise up from *seiza*, and broke a leg. But this did not happen to Hamilton Drew. Standing, he staggered, but caught his balance. He attempted to replace the pain in his face with joy at the vision of his grown-up daughter. No, she is not grown-up. She looks like her mother. She is not grown-up, in his eyes: but she is in her own.

All advantage to Vera, then. He was thunderstruck by her appearance; she barely recognised him. Would not have known him in a crowd. In the months to come she would revise this notion: she did know him instantly; she remembered more than she thought from her childhood; she shared his height, his skin tone. But now, he was simply a strange man who had come to her island claiming her.

His words of endearment, being in English, sounded unfamiliar. He moved toward her. She felt trapped on her knees and jumped up. A voice came out of her. It was the new, hard voice. Her drop-dead ironic 'frankly I haven't got the energy' voice, that would serve her well later, in her siren years. She was nearly eighteen years old. She was not, as she intended, treating him as if he were a stranger.

'You didn't answer our letters,' she said.

He stopped in his tracks as he made for her with open arms. 'Your letters?' he cried. 'I received no letters.'

She was a little shaken by this, but not much. 'When my mother died,' she said, suppressing the question mark at the end. 'And when Grandfather died too. When we were hungry, and when we left for Japan.'

His head sank on the stalk of his neck. 'Oh, it was terrible,' he said, making it his loss. 'That she was so far away and I did not hear . . .' his voice faded as he attempted to conceive of how much time he had to account for. 'Where did you send the letters?'

'Miss Hinchcliffe sent them, to Kobe.'

'Ah,' he said.

There was silence.

'Who could have believed it,' he said.

'I don't understand.'

'How much they hated me,' he said softly. 'To keep me in the dark for –'

'For?' Vera prodded. She saw his repentance but she was not ready to forgive.

'Such a very long time,' he finished. He was close enough for the embrace now and his arms were a half-circle, beseeching.

And Vera felt triumphant. She stood at nearly his height, gazing directly into his eyes.

'You are angry,' he said.

'No, I am Vera,' she said. And laughed. That new useful, hard laugh.

He reached farther with his arms. She shrank away.

325

All this was like theatre to the Headman and his muscular sons and gracious daughter, who had enacted no such dramas, ever, in their small house. They understood no English. But they understood the drama of the prodigal father returning home and felt the tragedy of it. They enjoyed it. They hid, in downturned faces, the rounded eyes of the audience at the opera.

Vera watched as Hamilton's arms slowly dropped to his sides.

'All right,' he said, quietly. 'You need time. To get used to me, of course. That's fair.'

Vera questioned herself. Was she angry, as he said? She did not feel angry. She felt powerful. She felt nothing. The two were the same. She was blasé but determined to get away from him, which was perhaps not consistent. This confused her and made her uneasy. She stepped back and looked away, at the Headman.

'Your father,' said the Headman, a little late but performing introductions as if he'd been taught. His face lit by a large smile.

'Vera,' said Hamilton, trying again, and his face now radiated the joy of a creature that cared for its offspring, reunited with same.

Vera faltered but remained cold. 'Why did you come now?'

'Why did I come now? Because I discovered where you were.'

Because you thought there was some advantage in it for you, Vera thought. And was ashamed, and confused that she had thought it. But already tears had weighted her lower lids. She wondered what she really knew about her father. In her growing-up years her grandfather had spoken ill of him. 'Hamilton – he'll do what's good for him,' he'd say. Or, 'Hamilton wants it all, but he won't take responsibility.' When hearing that he was off on another trip, her grandfather would snort. 'The Crown Prince has more fun than the King,' James Lowinger would say. 'Or he'd like to.' When Vera was very young, her mother defended her husband. But later when he had been gone too long, she stopped. She was sad; there was no joy in her. This man had stolen her spirit. Vera knew Belle had loved him, and missed him, and even died of sadness for him.

326

'You discovered just now? How?' she asked.

'Hinchcliffe,' he said. 'The letters were in her desk.'

Vera repressed a sob of frustration, remembering how that long but short time ago when they buried her grandfather she could not get past the solid body at his secretary's desk. Tears burned in her throat as a part of her was thinking: but if he did *not* receive the letters, why was he so quick to understand that Miss Hinchcliffe had them?

'Is Hinchcliffe still there, in the office?' Vera asked.

'She was there,' he said, 'until I found out how she treated you.' He paused and then said, as an afterthought, it seemed: 'And Keiko. It was terrible how she treated you and Keiko.' He flashed a smile at the Headman. 'How good Keiko has been to you. I could not be more grateful. I am so eager to see Keiko to thank her.'

This more than anything rattled the foundations of Vera's hostility. 'Why did you come here?'

'I came to bring you home. I am your father. Your only living relative.'

Despite how often she had wanted to go home, now Vera rebelled. Home? She laughed a little bitterly.

'This is my home now.'

'My dear, we are on the brink of war. I cannot leave you here.'

War. That word was the only weapon he had. The Headman nodded eagerly.

'I am not ready,' said Vera. That was all.

And so the meeting ended. There was no embrace. Vera bowed to the Headman and backed out of the hut.

For several days life continued as if he had never come. Hamilton Drew slept in the house of one of the Headman's sons, and spent his days watching people work. He watched them paint the banners that would be held up on poles for the festival. He visited the women who inspected the fishing nets. He tried to help the men who were stacking flat rocks on the roofs of the huts, but they were too polite to allow him. His tall thin shape could be picked out, here and there on the island where nothing rose above six feet but the masts of the little boats.

In the *amagoya*, on their breaks, the *ama* women talked about Hamilton Drew. They remembered when the Englishman came to the summer island, and Keiko went away with him. That was a shocking thing. *Ama* marry their own kind. Still, *ama* women are strong and know their own minds. Keiko chose and they did not question her, unlike some others in the village. Hamilton Drew had been here then and looked the whole place over with his trader's eye and did not see anything of value, and so he had left. Now he had come back and wanted Vera.

True, he was Vera's father. But Vera did not know him any more. Vera was now part of the summer island, part of the *ama* village. Keiko had adopted her and come home bringing her, and now the *ama* had adopted her. They had taught Vera and she dived with them.

It was a dilemma.

Their conclusion was that Hamilton Drew should stay on the summer island for a time, until Vera knew him better.

Keiko cleared her face of all expression and hid her eyes. She brought up the matter of war. Perhaps because of the war, Vera should go.

Setsu believed that Vera was safer here with them if this war was also coming to her land, to Canada, so far away.

And Maiko said, 'We are losing our young ones.'

'Why has he come?' Vera cried. 'What does he want?'

'I believe that he has come for you.' Ikkanshi sat with her in his new room, which had become hers.

'But why should he come for me? He never came for me before.'

'Perhaps,' the sword polisher said, 'there has been a current event.' They used to joke about this term but she did not laugh today. 'Perhaps,' he said, 'the war will come closer to our island.' And he told her a little of what he knew. Britain and her allies had declared war on Germany. Japan would have greater enemies now, and might not be as close to victory as the people believed. Perhaps Vera's father felt a responsibility to take her away from this danger, and this deprivation. He did not know exactly if this were true. He tried to be fair.

In a few minutes Keiko joined them. They all sat together like parents and child. It was as if there had been another death. 'When you dive,' said Keiko, 'you overcome your fear and you enter a new world. When you rise again you wish to bring something of it back with you. That is the most difficult task. Even when you succeed, you can be changed. Sometimes you cannot return to what you left. You are different, or the place is different.'

Ikkanshi reached out and put his hand on Keiko's thigh. It was the first time they had touched in front of Vera.

'He is your father,' she said. 'That is one reason. We are in danger, that is another. Canada is your country. The bones of your mother are there. That is the final reason.'

Vera could go back to her world; that was most important. Who she went with mattered less.

'Vera must go away,' Keiko said. 'I am the one who brought her here and I am the one to say she must go.' Now the decision was made.

They knelt, there in the empty room, as if before the inevitable.

Vera did not cry. She was pale, very pale, and quiet and hard. She wondered if Keiko loved her. A part of her had wanted to go home, since Hana drowned. They used that word; she used it herself, although Vera did not know the meaning of home, now. She held in her mind the possibility of another life she might have led, might still lead. Her father had appeared in answer to her dreaming and her begging, and now he was here.

But also she did not want to go. Hamilton was new to her. She had no love for her father, instilled from childhood, stored in her as a programmatic thing. These pieties, these traditions were not a part of her and had never been. It was what made the sword polisher and Keiko love her and fear her too. She had become part of life on the island. And there was Tamio. She would have to leave Tamio.

But in the end she agreed that she should go. Keiko was the one to speak. She was right: she had brought Vera here and when Keiko said so, Vera would leave.

They talked about the sea. About the tide and its rhythms. How people were born on one tide and die on another. How even if she went to the other side of the Pacific Ocean, she would still be on the sea.

Vera said only one thing: she wanted to dive again, before she went to Hamilton Drew. Keiko walked away then, in the moon glow and darkness, away from the houses and the preparations for *O-Bon* that had begun in the temple. Perhaps she cried, but Vera did not see it.

Teru walked alone along the water in the dark. From time to time a man or boy approached to speak to him, but he shook his head and plodded on.

Alone too, Tamio worked on his boat, where he had waited for Vera after dinner each night, as before. But she did not come. He cleaned the boat and folded the sail; he rubbed oil into the wood of the rudder, as she walked unseen by him to the far, higher end of the path. For several nights it was like this: Vera went alone to the High Place and looked out to sea. Tamio sat in his boat, caulking, and sanding, and whistling a tune that came from a radio, a long time ago. In the days, because the wind was high, the women dived *kachido* with their baskets from shore on the far side of the island.

But on the fourth night, it changed.

That night Vera came to see Tamio in the harbour. His boat was usually pulled up with all the others on the draining mud and sand, but he had moved it away, farther down, to the end of the line. None of the flickering oil lamps of the village reached here. The sea was tame; its flat tongues licked their feet, and then withdrew. The sky was alight with stars. Tamio's hand was as strong as a clamp on Vera's. His passion was silent and furious.

330

But she was the one with the power: here was a man's life for her to crush, or keep.

She tried to explain to him. 'Keiko says I must go.' To herself she thought that when she left the summer island, Tamio would be the easiest to forget. That is what she thought. She would miss the women and Hana, she would be *sabishi* without the smell of the sea and the long days of sun, the hot and the cold of diving. But Tamio, this man attached to her hand with the grip of an octopus, what was he?

So a man with food scoffs at the idea of famine. In the heat of summer we cannot believe in the pain of cold. Vera had Tamio's comfort and therefore she felt she had little need of it. She could embrace him at will. And let him embrace her. She could tangle her legs in his, wrap them around his thighs, squeeze, bringing his hard body in to the concave place at her centre. She accepted his importuning, his sweet smell and his eagerness as if they were hers by right. She could not know what it would be to lose it all. Because he was the first she did not understand longing.

'It is for you,' Tamio said, and she did not know if he meant his heart that was beating so visibly in his chest. She put her hand – their hands, the fist that they'd made of their two hands – on it.

'No,' he said, and pushed their hands away.

She did not understand.

'It is for you,' he repeated. This in English. Someone had taught him to say that. Who? she wondered. He did not speak her language well or easily. He had gone and deliberately learned this phrase.

'It is for you,' he insisted, almost crying.

Not his heart.

She brought his hand up to her mouth.

He tugged it from her. Not his hand.

'What is?' she asked.

And he gestured all around, to the water and the silent street of small greying houses.

331

'The summer island?' she guessed.

'No, not,' he said. 'To know. Not Keiko. For you to say.' He made the gesture of speaking with his hand, but still she didn't understand.

He walked away from her, and then waited for her to catch up to him. A breeze moved in from beyond the harbour, bringing cooler air. There was no one in sight but a woman with the *ama* kerchief on her head. He walked beside her, staring at the sheen that had overcome the sand. But he only repeated what he had said. 'It is for you.'

So that she understood what he meant: it was for her to decide. The decision was hers: whether she would go away, or whether she would stay.


*O-Bon* began the next day.

The people said that the dead came back from the water where they abide. They said that this year Hanako would not come; it was too soon. She would not be developed yet as a spirit. How ironic that the voyage – a voyage the *ama* made over and over, daily, all summer long, flitting from the bottom of the sea up to the bottom of the boat, and back again – was judged too dangerous for her.

At first light the women came out of their homes with their washcloths and buckets to converge at the well. The sea was dimpled and orange with dawn. They washed soberly, thoroughly, and went home dripping. After breakfast they appeared in bright *yakata*. They put clothing on the children too, for the first time since summer began, and tied their hair up on the tops of their heads.

The boats were lined up on the shore, decorated with banners that snapped briskly, one above the other, on the rising wind. Red and white pieces of rag were woven into the ropes.

The women went one by one down the path to the temple. They were beating with sticks on small hand-drums like tambourines. The priest gathered them around him, while he played his flute. Its song was soon lost to the wind, and the purple robes he wore flapped around his legs. The shrine did not resemble a shrine at all, but a fort of old stone walls to break the sea-wind. There was a timber shed behind it that creaked in the wind. When he had finished playing his song the priest opened the shed to reveal treasures normally unseen. There were portraits of the Emperor and the Empress. They had been in the dark all year and now their eyes looked astonished to be in the air in front of living folk. The women all fell to their knees. Vera didn't understand. These were the same old pictures that everyone had in their houses. There were also relics of a sailing ship that had sunk, and old books of poetry that probably only Ikkanshi-san read.

But what filled the shed was the great chariot. It was called the *mikoshi*, and weighed six hundred pounds. It had no wheels, but long handles at the front and back, so that it had to be carried. There were curtains at the windows so that if anyone were inside it, he or she could not be seen. But no one was inside, except, perhaps, a spirit. It was newly lacquered in gold – a gift from Mikimoto Taisho himself.

The men and boys came shouting along the path, pushing the bearers out in front of them. As they had been the year before, and the year before that, these young men were dressed as women. They made round Os out of their lipsticked mouths, and minced in tightly-wrapped kimonos. Vera remembered the pictures she had stared at in the warehouse of Lowinger and McBean, where she could not tell the men from the women. Tamio was one of them, and looked like a stranger to her.

'Why do the men dress up as women?' Vera had asked Keiko every year.

And every year Keiko said that she didn't know. It was the old way. Once there must have been a reason for it.

Then the young men shouted and their low voices gave them away. The women, watching, laughed with their hands over their mouths. The priest handed another bottle of sake around. The men and boys took many drinks.

In the early afternoon, the parade formed. The chariot was

pulled out into the sun where it shone wickedly. The bearers surrounded it and hoisted it onto their shoulders. It was heavy; walking together, they could only manage it for a few dozen paces. Each year, their task was to carry it down the length of the island to the far end, past the smaller shrine, and dip it in the water – perhaps it would greet the dead as they returned? Vera did not know. Then they had to take it back to its home.

'Thirsty work!' The old man laughed, to cheer them on, and handed in a sake bottle.

The sake was intended to bolster their strength. They shifted, staggered a bit, and then walked on. After twenty or thirty paces, one stopped to accept a drink from a bottle offered by a crowd member.

Vera was reeling: the heat of the sun, the baffling wind, exhausted her. She could sometimes catch sight of Tamio, in his blue patterned costume, and sometimes not. Tamio shouldered the burden along with his friends, and laughed with them, and staggered, too, when he'd had his fourth or fifth sake break. His black eye-paint ran down his cheeks, so that he looked like a sad clown. He put his back to the work, and grunted with the rest. But he seemed to Vera to be in another place in his mind, and not wholly present in these rituals.

The wind from the sea gusted in and out of the procession, so that sometimes the songs carried full voice, and sometimes the voices were blown off and nothing remained but the rushing waves and the strange feminine progression of the men.

Everyone was there, from the Headman and his sons and daughter, to the schoolteacher, to the oldest crippled great grand-father, to the fattest baby. The day was hot and the path was narrow. The chariot wobbled its square way along, and the men sweated and strained as if they had never done this before. Then there was more sake, and the bearers hoisted their burden again. Vera walked beside Tamio and poured water into his mouth – his hands were occupied. He flashed his eyes at her but did not speak.

Down the path they went, through the straggling houses, past the bath, onto the uneven ground from the far end of the town where the temple was, and into the bamboo grass. It was a long way, and a poor path. The wind was rising, and made their task more difficult.

An hour passed, and then an hour and a half. The men were sweating, and their feet were not so sure on the stones. The square chariot lurched this way and that, and each time it lurched, it imperilled the procession. People screamed in delighted mock terror and ran out of the way. The wind lifted sand into their eyes.

Tamio's make-up was nearly gone: black lines ran from his temples to his jawbone. The lipstick had become a ring around his lips, where he drank the sake. The white paint was still there, chalky, but in patches it was thin, and Vera could see that he was actually red in the face. He was hot, and drunk too.

The farther they walked, the more drunk they became; the more difficult their task, and the greater the enjoyment of the crowd. These women-who-had-been-men yesterday, and today were not either women nor men but some grotesque being in between, were a mockery of both strength and delicacy. The sun was still hot. The drinking went on. Tamio's face was distorted. Sweat made black lines of the make-up, so that he looked like one of the faces in the old prints, huge, exaggerated, his expressions classic – rage, sadness, fear – each one extreme.

Finally the sun began to sink. The bearers were drunk now; they could hardly stand up. The leader staggered and fell to his knee, sending his comrades into paroxysms of laughter. One and then another found his robe too constricting, or ripped it with a carelessly placed foot. Half naked, staggering, swearing, tripping, the fourteen boys and men approached the small Buddhist shrine. Perhaps they would stop here until tomorrow. But the old men strongly disagreed. Eventually it was decided: they would carry on into the night and dip the *mikoshi* in the sea, as they had always done. A few families separated from the crowd and went home. Most remained to cheer the bearers.

Vera turned back to the well in the centre of the now empty

town. Ikkanshi-san's door was ajar. She looked in. He was there, seated before his grinding stones. But he was not grinding. He held a light fabric between his forefinger and his thumb; it was saturated with reddish oil.

'Why are you not at the procession?'

'I am putting another final polish on the cutting edge.'

The polish was a whitish colour and he told her it was called *boshi*. 'Do you remember which is the *ha*? That is the part that cuts.' He showed her the sharpness. He was being very careful because he could ruin it at any time. He dipped the edge of his cloth in the *nugui*. 'Do you see the waving grain of the steel that is like wood, with layers, as if it had once been living? That is the *jihada*. The grain of the steel. It is now that the spirit of the blade begins to reveal itself. This is the most exciting part of my work.'

'What do you think of your blade now? What is the spirit?'

'I am not certain,' he replied. 'But I am waiting. I hope it will speak to me.' He said this so quietly she did not know if he was addressing her, or himself. 'It could be an angry spirit.'

'Where will the sword go now?' she asked. 'Will the basket maker take it away?'

'Someone will come.' For him or for the sword; he did not say which.

'Why did you agree to give it to them?'

'I did not agree or disagree. I had to trust the sword. I could not protect it.'

There was a long silence then.

'And your friend Hanako,' he said heavily, 'has she come back for *O-Bon*?'

'No' said Vera. 'The *ama* say the journey will be too difficult for her. But I don't see why, because she knows the water better than anyone.'

'That is what they believe,' said Ikkanshi. 'But you might believe otherwise.'

Vera went back to see the end of the procession. The sun was nearly down, an orange ball glowering on the horizon. The fierce

336

winds that had bedevilled the flags all day now put out the lanterns. The men were roaring with pain and staggering. They looked like little creatures on whom some inhuman golden monster had landed. One man set his end down entirely and the others stumbled around to keep the whole thing from overturning in the wind. Each shouted directions at the other; no one was heard. At last the bearers reached the edge of the sea. The sky was almost dark. The gold of the chariot winked on and off, reflecting a man here, a candle there, a ray of sunset orange there. The white make-up revealed, in a crooked row, a line of exhausted, slick faces.

At first she couldn't see Tamio. She feared he might be crushed under the great gold box. She hung back, making herself invisible, until the bearers of the chariot lay sprawled, exhausted on the beach. Along the way they had abandoned their women's clothes, and wore only loincloths as usual, their short, thick, strong legs exposed. Some were laughing. Some were snoring. The chariot sat on the beach looking out to sea. Tomorrow they would dip it in the water and carry it all the way back to the temple. Vera looked for Tamio's face, but in the gloom she could not tell which one was him. She was afraid of these drunken men, and she left them.

Alone, she looped past them to the back of the island. She climbed up and over to the black rocks. These were the ones that flowed like lava, and had hardened in lips, the ones she had hated until Hana and she had played there. She sat, and remembered the manta ray that had come to the light. Hana had flashed her light into the water looking for the green things that the manta ray liked to eat. Tonight Vera flashed her lantern. Would Hana come? She did not believe it. She lay flat on the lip of the rock and let the light play in the water. She thought about the spirits of the dead, who were supposed to be coming, and wondered when they would arrive, and if she would feel them. If Hana came, she would say to her, 'Who are you now? What are you? Where do you sleep? What sort of life do you live, is it really under the water?'

Tamio came up behind her and put his hands over her eyes. She cried out. 'You frightened me!'

He spoke in rapid Japanese. 'You are not frightened,' he said. 'You are angry.'

'You are drunk.'

'And angry too,' he said. He put his arms around her.

'Why?' she asked.

'Because it will have to end.'

Vera leaned on his chest and let the tears that had been with her all day fall.

He switched to English. 'I gave me to you.' He pounded on his heart. 'But you give you to father? I make mistake,' he said bitterly.

'Mistake? But you love me. I know you do.'

He pressed his face into the side of her neck. She could feel his tears.

'I don't belong here,' she said. 'Should I stay on the summer island even when I don't belong?'

He lifted his face to her and she could see he did not understand what she had said.

'I don't belong here.'

'No,' he said. 'Not you.'

She cried harder.

'But you come to stay.'

'I saw you at the shrine,' Vera said. 'I saw you in the procession.' Crying, she was laughing too, thinking of his costume. But it was not funny. 'You don't belong here either.'

'I hate this,' he said. Swinging his arm around the whole world of the island, from their side to the other. 'I hate.'

Now Vera understood. She was what made Tamio different, and she was going away. Who would he be, then?

Tamio pulled away from her and she heard hoarse sobbing as he climbed up the rocks. Then he was gone.

The night was very dark: there was no moon, and the stars were not out yet. The water lapped curiously below her; the pale green phosphorescence rose up to the surface. It was a sickly colour, the colour of death. The little creatures had come. Or a spirit. Hana had made her tremble. She thought she heard Tamio returning behind her, and she was afraid.

Afraid that he would hurt her? It could not be true, and yet it was. Something had turned, had turned sharp and cold and ugly between them. She realised that they might never make love the way they had: how could they now, how could it be the same?

The men would drum all night. She heard the pounding carried on the wind. She heard voices gusting over the centre of the island, and then the voices were gone. She felt the wind behind her. If she felt it here, on the protected side, it must be a gale on the open side. Some day the waves would get so big that they would overtake the island, smash the lighthouse off its stone perch, flood the lost green lake, splash down the black-lipped rocks at her back and wash her into the sea.

She walked back along the path by herself. The grass was bent in graceful arcs and its light was just visible, though all else had vanished. The rain came then, heaving, like water thrown before her. It laid the grass, and drenched her, so that she was instantly cold, her hair stuck to her head and dripping.

In the village, the women had disappeared. This hour of the night belonged to the men. The drums were louder here, pounding and pounding in riffs, in rolls, four or five of them, speaking to each other. There were shouts and chants too but she did not see anyone. The wind was louder too. There was no rain here yet.

She walked along the beach looking for Tamio. It was not difficult to find him. It was as if they were the only two people left on the island, although that was not true at all: there were voices and fires, music from all directions. But here, she could feel his presence. He lay on the beach. He had drunk more sake; she could see the bottle.

Her sand-covered ankles rubbed against his cheek. He did not move. She knelt beside him, and placed a hand on his forehead. His cheek was dark; the pillar of the chariot had bruised it, probably. He looked terrible. She thought he was not conscious until he spoke. When he spoke it was with the voice of the island men.

'Go inside,' he said. 'It is not good for women to be outside now.'

'Will you come to Vancouver with me?' said Vera. 'I will ask my father to bring you too. I want to be with you.'

He turned his face the other way. 'Not true,' he said.

She lay down beside him. She tried to hold him against her but he twisted aside. Her beautiful beautiful boy, his face in ruins, his body aching, his voice raw. 'I love you,' she said. 'I love you, I love you.'

When she touched him he roared with rage. She was frightened then and ran away in the dark.

The next morning the old women were up at dawn. The wind had settled into a pure howl and grey clouds covered the sky in all directions. The men who put out the nets had taken the night off to celebrate. Instead of spreading them on the water, they had left the nets lying along the shore, twisted together, in long ropes. Yards and yards of them, like a long snake. With the men still sleeping off their long night of sake and drumming, the women came out to unroll them.

'Aih, aih, aih!' came the cry.

It was repeated all along the shore.

It rose up the path to each little house on the slope. Keiko woke, and came to the door, and looked and heard, and then began the alarm.

'Aih, aih, aih!'

Vera woke too, in the empty room: she had half hoped, half feared that Tamio would come to find her. He had not. Instead, Keiko stood above her. Vera sat up. Keiko was telling her to get up.

'Aih, aih aih!'

She pulled on her *yakata*.

'Ikkanshi-san?' Vera said. 'Tamio?'

340

'He is not here,' said Keiko.

They ran out into the street.

The old women who had raised the cry stood legs akimbo on top of the long thick snake of nets. There were a dozen of them or more staged along the length of the nets. They had pulled the nets open, wide. It was easy to see why they were screaming. Great jagged holes were ripped in the pattern. The careful knots of thin rope, fully mended and dyed, were cut apart. The expansive, intricate pattern was broken again and again. The nets had been slashed repeatedly, all through, with a sharp knife. They were destroyed.

Now the men emerged from the houses, dark-faced, hung over, and angry. They walked forward and backward along the stretch of tied strings. They poked their toes at a hole here, a rent there. Some raised their hands to the sky in lamentation. Some said nothing, disgusted.

The priest came panting down the path. Children ran to him.

'The nets are cut. The nets are cut!'

'Who would do such a thing?'

'Who would endanger us this way?'

The cry moved like a storm through the assembled crowd. How could they fish? They would go hungry without the nets. The season was nearly over. They needed every pound of fish they could get. Who would have done this?

Now Vera saw Ikkanshi. He came up the path from the back beach. He stood, arms folded, expressionless.

She did not know where else to look. Could it have been he who cut the nets? Her breath came in short gasps. But Vera saw by the sword polisher's face that he understood, as she understood, and as Keiko understood, but did not want to understand. It was not the sword polisher who had cut them.

The crowd gathered, as angry as it had been hilarious only hours before. There was crying and shouting. The priest tried to calm people but they would not be calm.

The Headman strode from his house at the top of the street. His sons trotted behind him. He saw everything at once, the nets, the angry people, the white girl with Keiko, her face blanched, the *katanatogi* with his knowledge.

He roared words Vera did not understand, to quiet them. The people were beating the air with their fists.

'Is it the dead who have done this? Who has angered them?'

'I saw him,' said an old woman. 'I was not sleeping and I came to the well. He came out of the water. An evil spirit. He was wearing an awabi shell over his face, as a mask.'

The Headman turned on the old woman. 'He came out of the water? He wore a mask? An awabi shell?'

'He danced in front of the nets,' an old man said, 'calling down evil on us.'

The people all moved restlessly. Even Keiko stiffened, and murmured under her breath. She took Vera's hand.

'What has angered them?' came another voice.

'We do not know who has done this,' the Headman began. 'Who was it among the dead? Our dead have all been here and were well looked after.'

Panic seemed to take the old people.

The men shifted and mumbled. Vera felt the wind against her. It seemed to come from everywhere. She put out her hand to hold her hair down, as it was flying out in a stream. She was afraid. She did not understand what was happening.

'It is not the dead,' said Ikkanshi-san. He was the only one who spoke up to the Headman. 'It is not a spirit.'

There were voices of assent.

'Such spirits are not real.' His voice was calm, and easy, a voice of reason.

'It is true,' said Keiko, and others agreed.

'It is one among the living. Who is the one who is not here?'

No one answered. Perhaps they did not know. Perhaps they did.

'Tamio is not here,' said Ikkanshi-san.

Vera looked away. She hated the sword polisher then, for his betrayal of Tamio. But what the boy had done could not be hidden.

The old woman spoke again. 'He came from the water. He was

lying in the sand. He put a shell on his face. He pulled out his knife and ran along stabbing into the nets, over and over. And then he ran away.'

'You said you knew him.'

'Who saw him?'

'I saw him,' said the old woman. 'Even with the shell over his face, I recognised him. It was Tamio.'

Tamio! The word passed along the line.

The aunt and uncle's faces were stopped with fear.

'I do not believe it,' said Keiko.

But others believed it.

No one spoke. The people seemed to close in on themselves. Then Hamilton Drew came down the path. Late, as always. His face was full of sleep. Everyone stared at him. His presence hung over them. Perhaps it was his fault. He had come from the other side of the ocean. He had come to disturb the peace. The fragile peace that his daughter had already disturbed. The peace that, years ago, Keiko had disturbed, when she went with the old Englishman and started it all.

The Headman appeared to consider all of this. And more and more, from the crowd, the name Tamio was spoken.

It had to be Tamio. He was angry enough. He was drunk enough. Where had he gone? His little boat was still in its place. He had not left the island.

Vera sat with Ikkanshi in the new room. They both looked out of the window at the beaten down grass on the path to the back of the island. In time, one of the Headman's sons walked down it, through the indentations that had been Vera's and Tamio's footsteps.

'Why did you say his name?'

'I could not protect him,' said Ikkanshi.

They waited.

In time the Headman's son came back, leading Tamio. He was bruised and dirty. They did not touch his tear-stained face but led him to the beach in front of them all. He stared sullenly away and did not look at Vera's window.

The priest beat a gong, and it pealed insistently, summoning the people out of their houses. Vera held Ikkanshi's arm. Keiko was on the other side, and stood with her head high, but her eyes did not meet anyone's. The aunt and uncle were crying.

The Headman spoke to the young man who stood alone, hanging his head.

'You have hurt us all and hurt the way we live. Cutting the nets has endangered us. Because of this you have lost your place with the people. You must go and live somewhere else. You may take your boat. Your parents may give you one parcel of food. Then you must go.'

And he turned to go back to his house.

Over the heads of all the people, he spoke: 'And no one may help him.'

Tamio said nothing in his defence. He stared at them, and through them. He kicked the sand, and then turned toward his boat.

The rain began and fell like lead.

The basket maker came to the door of Ikkanshi's house.

The sword polisher made certain that at the time of the messenger's arrival he was sawing a board.

'Greetings,' said the basket maker. 'I see you are at work.'

'I am always at work but I am never too busy to speak with a friend,' Ikkanshi replied. And he continued the long smooth strokes with his saw.

'I have come to collect the *meito*,' the basket maker said. And he sat down.

344

'Would you like to look at it?'

Ikkanshi stood in the beginning stance, with the sword at his left hip. He drew the blade out of its *saya*. He held it before his eyes, edge inward, and bowed to it. The blade was a sliver of sky light, its pattern a small, glowing landscape from a world he had never seen. The handle, the *hamon*, the woven wrapping, all of it was perfected. Then, with a quick flash of light, he replaced the sword in its *saya*, *noto*, bent to brush the skirt of his *hakama* away from his knees, and knelt.

In *seiza*, Ikkanshi placed his right hand forward, then his left, making between his forefingers of left and right and his thumbs, a small triangle. He bent his head then, and leant his forehead into that small space on the floor of his house. And he bowed. In a moment he sat up and with no expression at all on his face lifted the handle, sliding the ties alongside the blade, and tucking it to his left side. Then he stood.

The basket maker stood also; he had a long bundle in his hand.

And Ikkanshi bowed.

'I bow to the inevitable,' he said in English.

The basket maker did not understand. He made reference to the Emperor, and the cause of Japan.

Ikkanshi saw him to the door.

The sword must go to its fate.

The boy, and the girl too.

Hamilton Drew took Vera away with him. She said goodbye to Keiko at the ferry, each giving the other a strained, formal hug, each one with her face over the other's shoulder, and devoid of expression. Ikkanshi stood back, with his arms folded in front of him.

They left the island on the ferry, with all the people lined up waving to them. Keiko stood alone on the dock. Her eyes were red but she was not crying. Vera was confused, because now she was leaving, and she mourned it, when all the while she had longed to go. Hana was gone. Tamio was gone too. He had vanished across the sea, in his boat, with his packet of food.

'He will survive,' Ikkanshi-san had said. 'He is good in that boat. He will go to another island. Or he will go to a city, and get work. There are many jobs he can do.'

'But the rain. The wind –'

'It will end.'

He did not say what they all feared: that he would join the army. But of course he likely would have in any case. It was surprising that he had not been called up yet.

No one ever said that it was her fault. But Vera knew that he had taken his first steps away from the people in her arms.

Vera and her father arrived in Toba. They stayed in a little inn there, where the people knew Vera and were polite to her father. It was shimmering in September sun and beautiful: you could look onto the bay and see the pearl rafts floating on the quiet water. Hamilton Drew wanted to present himself to Mikimoto Taisho. He said that Vera should thank Mikimoto Taisho for protecting her, because that was what he had done.

'From what?' she said.

'You were living amongst the enemy. You don't understand at all the danger you have been in.'

They took a ferry to Tatoku Island. In the icy wind on the deck he put his arm around her shoulders and squeezed her. It was an experimental hug. She was nearly as tall as he was.

On the island, the *ama* in their head-wraps were balancing on the bamboo rafts. They waved to Vera as she walked into the house. A woman answered: Mikimoto Taisho was doing his exercises in the bath. They had to wait. Then she returned and said that she was very sorry, that he had got out of her sight and that he was in the boat. She pointed along the shore. There was a short, thickset man, his age showing only in his white hair, leaning into the single oar. Standing, he sculled it outward. They walked along and waved to him, and he turned around to come ashore. When he stepped out of the boat, his face was pink and smooth.

'I have come to say goodbye,' said Vera. 'And to thank you for being kind. This is my father.'

Hamilton Drew made one of his stiff bows. Then the white-haired little man in his *hakama* stretched out his hand. He wanted to show that he leaned toward the west.

'I am James Lowinger's son-in-law,' Hamiton said. 'And I represent Lowinger and McBean.'

'I believe you tried before this to make some business with me,' said Mikimoto. 'James Lowinger was not happy.'

There were a few seconds of curious silence. Hamilton Drew's face clouded over. Vera remembered then, what her grandfather had said: 'What did he take? He took my name, my reputation . . .'

'Not good then. Maybe not good now too,' said Mikimoto pleasantly. He spoke to Vera. 'It is good that you go home. It is war now.'

They walked together up the beach. The wind was cold and wet across their faces.

'I understand you can no longer import the mother-of-pearl you need from China,' said Hamilton Drew.

'Of course not. We are at war with China, still.' He turned to Vera. 'We will miss you,' said Mikimoto Taisho. 'But you must come back.' He did not like to mix business with the personal lives of his employees, which he took very seriously.

'I can get it for you in Canada.'

Mikimoto-san turned his eyes back to Hamilton Drew.

'You speak of mother-of-pearl?' he said. 'I am buying it now from the United States of America. Now I have one concern. I must keep the operations open. I must keep the people in work when times are difficult.'

347

'I believe we have great untapped sources in Canada,' said Hamilton Drew.

Mikimoto-san tossed up the sleeves of his coat and a ball came out of the right one, rolled around in his left palm, and disappeared again. He made it come down again and he gave it to Vera.

'Just so,' he said. He strolled more quickly and turned his gaze out to sea.

'Ask him what he hears from the military government,' prodded Hamilton.

Vera was dressed in a travelling suit that her father had brought her. The jacket was too loose around her body, and the skirt was too short. Besides, the western style felt strange to her. Her hair was wound around itself into a knot, which sat at the nape of her neck. Despite the cold, her skin felt hot.

'I cannot ask him that, Father.'

They were to sail in a Canadian Pacific liner from Yokohama. She'd been there only once, that day she and Keiko had arrived, the day of the attempted coup. But this was the town where her mother was born. She saw the Grand Hotel; her grandfather had stayed there. She wanted to stay there too and, as there was still a festive feeling between them – united! After so long! The adored missing child and father! – they did stay there. It was ten days before the boat sailed. On each of the days they walked the Bund; they looked down on Homura. They visited the church where Sophia and James were married, and Hamilton was only mildly amused: although his two in-laws rarely agreed on anything, they had agreed to disapprove of him. The *Mayasaki*, the pleasure quarter, was closed to them.

Vera searched out the printmakers' shops. The good ones were very expensive. But you could still find the old *ukiyo-e* in the bookshops. She looked at the pictures and exclaimed over them: how different was their world than the Japan she had come to! And yet there was sameness. She knew so much more, now that she was older. But she had no money to buy things. Her father stood outside the doors, edgily looking down the street. It seemed as if he were very anxious to be gone.

'This country is not the same,' he muttered.

'Not the same as what?' she asked. Japan had finally become believable to her. When the police stopped them she could speak in simple Japanese. She could tell them that she and her father were leaving on the next boat for Vancouver.

'Did you live in Kobe after all?' she asked him when they stopped for tea.

'No,' he said. 'I never lived in Kobe for long.' He could not even remember the address he'd had there. 'I lived in Hong Kong for a couple of years. Then I was in Indonesia. I travelled a lot. Okinawa. Did you know that Mikimoto has started operations there?'

'What were you doing there?' she asked.

'Looking for opportunities,' he replied. 'Something your grandfather never gave me.' Mostly he told her stories of his business deals, deals that were thwarted, or went wrong. 'What we need to dream up,' he said, including her, 'is something that thrives on war, that doesn't just lie down and die because of it.'

Passersby looked hungry and sick. These were the city folk who took the trains to the villages on weekends, in order to try to find food. They gathered around the newsstands to look at the headlines, but they did not buy the newspapers. They stood and murmured, as if their standing would force the news out into the air.


The day their ship was to leave, Vera's eye fell on a magazine with a glossy cover. It was more like an American magazine than others she had seen, and she wondered where it had come from. On the cover was a picture of two men: one was a Japanese, and the other was Hitler. They were beaming happily as the Japanese man presented the Führer with a *katana*. It was pulled out of its *saya* for show.

Hitler: she had often seen the Führer's picture in the papers since coming here. Even Horace Calder had shown her his pictures in the American paper he wrote for. She recognised his face, so she was not surprised. The Japanese man: who was he? But the sword. It was the sword she recognised.

There it was, the beautiful *meito*, Ikkanshi-san's pride and joy. The sharpest blade, oiled to perfection. The *jihada* a graceful line of waves. The *hamon*, and very clearly, held up to the light, the *horimono*. The god Fudo was engraved on the *hamon*, the god with his sword and his rope: '*the rope to bind the emotions and the sword to cut down evil*,' that was what Ikkannshi-san had said.

The blood drained out of her head. She thought she might faint.

'Please, I need money!' Vera said to her father.

He passed her a handful of yen and she pushed to the centre of the clutch of people and bought a copy. She held it against her chest. It felt like a stone there. She held it away from her and looked at the magazine: the Japanese was presenting the sword to Hitler. It was a special gift. There was no mistaking it. The sword was the *meito* that Ikkanshi had worked on so hard.

People stood on the shore to watch the boat pull away. They had spools of paper in their hands. Passengers on deck held the other ends of the paper, lucky people, like herself, Japanese, or American, Italian or German or Canadian, who were leaving. The boat's engines were fired and it began to pull back. The people held out their hands and the spools of paper spun around their fingers, letting out more and more lengths of the white, fluttering reels. People waved, and cried, and blew kisses. No one waved to her, or to Hamilton Drew. At the last minute, she felt the awful pull of her love for Keiko.

Eventually they had gone too far and one by one the ribbons of paper were stretched tight, and broke, and both ends, separated, fluttered down to the surface, and in a minute, sank.

Vera fell into her bunk, and pretending to be seasick (an *ama*! Seasick! How absurd that her father had believed her!) she looked at the magazine and wept.

Hitler was holding it, wrongly, you can be sure, with the blade directed outward, rather than inward, as etiquette decreed. But

350

he was looking pleased with himself. She understood by reading that this famous Japanese *katana* had been presented to the German leader as a gift and to emphasise their great friendship, by the Japanese Ambassador to Germany, General Oshima.

It was made in the Shinto period, Ikkanshi-san had said, by Nagasone.

She remembered, she remembered it all.

He had lied to her. He had said that the sword was not for this war.

He had also said the sword must go to its fate.

Its fate was Oshima, Berlin, and Hitler.

But he must have known that. He had made the sword for Hitler. She felt so cold. Who was Ikkanshi-san?

'There are many ways a sword can cut,' he had said.

She heard her father's voice, saying that she had been in danger, and that she did not understand. And Mikimoto too had said that it was good she was going home. It all made sense now. They had all been evil, Tamio and her *sensei* too.

Vera's father, Hamilton Drew, was a slim, red-haired Scot with a moustache that added years to his boyish face. He was tall – that was where Vera's height came from – and perhaps because he didn't hear well, or perhaps simply because he wanted to be particularly attentive when she spoke, he leaned over her. It was fun to be with him and to notice these inherited likenesses. The bending, the attentions to others, gave him a certain charm. Perhaps it was studied. Charm was not what the Scots were known for. Charm was English, her mother had told her; a manufactured trait and not to be fallen for. Never trust a man with two first names, Belle had said as well. Meaning, whose first name and surname could each have been a first name.

'What is the problem with two first names?' Vera had asked, when once her mother had pronounced this homily after a salesman named James Martin, or perhaps Scott Morris, had called.

And Belle had puckered up her forehead trying to remember the reason. 'My mother told me. She was psychic, you know. She thought that a man with two first names might not be who he pretended to be.'

Vera hadn't listened. But apparently Belle hadn't listened either. She married Hamilton Drew, who had two first names.

A man with two first names was suspect because maybe he had got into trouble in another place and had dropped his last name so as not to be traced. In other words, maybe he was Jack Martin Finch, she had said, laughing, naming birds she liked. And he'd got run out of town. Then he'd be just Jack Martin in the next place, do you see?

Vera's mother had been afraid of everything. Even afraid of a name. Therefore Vera could be afraid of nothing.

Hamilton Drew had watery blue eyes and blondish-red eyebrows that stood out, brush-like, half of the hairs going up and half going down. The brows were fascinating and moved of their own accord, giving emphasis to certain phrases: 'The point is,' he would say, and the right brow would jump when he hit the explosive P of point, while the left one would flatten into a straight line on the verb, as he drew it out. Vera was not sure whether these theatrical expressions were voluntary or not, and she didn't feel she could ask him. 'Hey Dad, are you aware that your eyebrows are dancing?' was not possible. The years they'd been separate (when exactly had they been together? She was vague on that) precluded these kind of intimacies.

As a speaker, he could not fail to attract attention. He was intense and engaging; he seemed to mean what he said. But his voice was soft, so soft that you had to concentrate to follow his words, and perhaps this too was intentional. But for all his animation in public, he was a quiet man in private. There was no hallooing and slamming of doors, no whistling as he returned. He moved softly and efficiently, like a large cat, but without sensuality. He seemed strong, although he never exercised. He walked on shipboard, walked and walked the decks as if his life depended on it, and Vera had to skip and scuttle to keep up. If there was a love interest in his life, meaning a woman, he had not seen fit to confide this to his daughter. His real love was his plans. He was a man with several plans, any one of which might make him a fortune. A man whose fortune was overdue. Perhaps that was his hurry.

Hamilton, or Dad, as Vera began to call him, was close with his feelings. Back on the summer island he had loomed up, the only person taller than her, with his blue eyes oddly lit and his face alert to her every move, as if she were a treasure he was about to capture, and called her his dear darling lost daughter. Leaving with her, he had opened his arms and, tranced, she had stepped forward into them. There was hard muscle and bone there and a heart beating fast in its cage of bones. His was so unlike Tamio's cushioned, quiet embrace that Vera drew back, and blamed herself. Confusing to have a lover one minute, and the next to be taken to heart as a little girl. But over the checkerboard on ship and while passing through the Canadian immigration office, her father rewrote her like a lost diary.

'Don't tell them you were living in Japan. It might cause trouble. Tell them you went over with me.'

'You tell them,' said Vera.

'Where is her passport?' asked the immigration officer.

'In her mother's keeping, I'm sorry to say.' Hamilton grimaced handsomely.

'Where is her mother?'

'Dead, I'm afraid. The girl is now with me. I travel for a living . . .'

The officer's heart went out. 'I have to ask for her passport. I'm sorry.'

'I have the death certificate, is all.'

'Not the girl's birth certificate?'

'I can send for it. It must be somewhere. I'm sorry, I've been a little confused since –'

He pulled out the folded paper and was about to reveal its contents to the officer, but the officer waved them on. 'She's obviously yours,' he said, and smiled.

'We look alike do we?'

'Peas in a pod,' said Hamilton Drew, smiling down at her.

Vera did not know what she looked like. 'I'm blonde; your hair is red!'

'Actually yours is greenish blonde from the sea water, and the dry ends taste of salt,' said Hamilton Drew.

'And yours is only red because of your pipe tobacco!'

Vera was home, where she had longed to be. Belle's house on Ivy Street stood just as it had when Vera and Keiko had left nearly four years before. Bounced back in time, she wandered, dazed, the streets of her childhood.

She did not return to her old school: she was too old. She went to the school grounds and watched her friends from vantage points where they couldn't see her. She stood in the doorways of shops, or behind hedges, as the doors of the school burst open at four o'clock and a gaggle of girls spilled out. They had clinging skirts that flared below their knees and neat blouses that buttoned down the front and pastel sweaters that buttoned over the blouses. They held hands with their boyfriends or walked arm in arm, girls becoming women and finding a lot to laugh about in it. She was alone and on the outside all over again.

She saw her schoolteacher.

'Vera!' he greeted her. 'How wonderful that you got out of Japan. We were so worried. Are you coming back to class?'

354

'I'm working now,' she said.

Sensing her adulthood, her independence, he continued. In the schoolyard there were others who'd taken jobs, who for their own reasons couldn't be part of the crowd, the teacher told her. She should come back; she would find some others like her.

But it was late autumn now, and she had missed the beginning. The war machine had caught up to her, invading Canada too: troops were piling into train carriages to be shuttled across the great wide plains and then onto ships to Europe. There were boys becoming men and girls alone with the little ones as mothers went to work. There were more current events than you could imagine and she was on the outside, again, and in mourning, again.

Tamio had been amputated from her body. His weight and the comfort of him, and the spice of him and his thrusting; it was all gone. She felt concave and ghostly. She could not eat. There was meatloaf, delivered by neighbouring women: 'Oh what a miracle you have come home safely! We are all so happy for you and your father!' they said.

It wasn't home there, and it wasn't home here, either.

There were casseroles with ham and scalloped potatoes from the church suppers. 'You have been delivered from the enemy!' the minister said, triumphantly.

The hard rounded muscles in her legs softened up and went thin. She was shedding Japan and the summer island. Perhaps she had never gone there. Only when she woke up in the early morning, before the cars began to run their wet tyres on wet streets, could she imagine an island dawn, and remember how she used to rise and go immediately to the well, and sometimes heard the cranes cracking the silence with their raucous cries.

Hamilton didn't bother about what she did all day. She made her way to Japantown and got herself a wooden *bokkuto*. In the house behind the drawn curtains every day she would practise the cuts. Her body moved stiffly at first,

355

reluctant to follow the lessons. The ones Ikkanshi-san had taught her, so she would not forget. And she would think of Ikkanshi-san's words. She practised the duets they had done together. The idea was to take advantage of a mistake made by one partner, and win. She sobbed as she practised. He had betrayed her. Never mind. If he was the enemy, so much the better; she could do the *kata* and really mean it.

When she felt braver, she went down to the beach in the early morning and practised there beside the Pacific Ocean. The other side of the same ocean, she thought. The same water. She knew this water.

*How can you know water? It is never the same*, said Ikkanshi-san. *It may be in the same place, but it is not the water that was there yesterday. If you say you know the water what you are saying is that you know one minute of the water. The container is what you know. You don't know water at all.*

*I do know water*, said Vera. *I have learned water. I have brought back what I learned. It is the one thing I brought back. Nothing else. Water is everywhere. I can look at the surface and what is underneath becomes apparent to me. I could map the underwater sea bed; I could find anything that falls into it.*

*Tell me again: what do you know about water*, Ikkanshi-san repeated.

She told him: *I know the colour of it in every wind. I know the shorelines and the depth of it. Where the rocks are hidden under the surface and how close to the surface. If the wind blows from the west, that the top of the rock will cause a dimple, that is all, no hint of the rest, but if the wind blows from the east an ugly crag breaks the surface – in one place – I know that three feet farther there is more rock down in the darkness.*

*How do you know the darkness?* he asked, quietly.

They were sitting, now, in his new, perfect, empty room. It was, temporarily, her sleeping room, and her sword practice room. This would be one of the last times. He paid her the compliment of letting her lead. She was to do the exercise first, and he would show her if she made mistakes.

356

*I see myself in it.*

*That is good. You are learning,* he said. *When I see an opponent threatening to strike,* Ikkanshi said, *I try to transform myself into him. I then know every move he will make. If I stop even for a hair's breadth between his action and my own, between my own and the next, I am dead.*

Hamilton went off each day to the offices of Lowinger and McBean on Homer Street. He never invited her, but one day she went after him. And there it was, the frosted glass, the half door, the gold classical printed letters on the door: Lowinger and McBean. Here she thought the whole world was lost, but it was going on much as before. Well not entirely: Miss Hinchcliffe was absent as promised, her desk a mess of papers and full ashtrays, with Hamilton Drew's feet up right in the middle of it. He sat jawing on the telephone, and did not look pleased when Vera came in. It was nothing to how displeased Miss Hinchcliffe would have been, Vera thought. In her grandfather's office the Beauties still stood around the walls like a picket fence, but Hamilton had stuck pins in them, right through to the old, softening plaster walls, pins to hold up notepapers on which were scribbled numbers and addresses.

The café regulars met still and talked about the war: Kemp, and Roberta the waitress, the postman on his rounds. But now there were working women who dropped in looking important on their way to jobs making uniforms for the soldiers. And if she went to join them, she found herself sitting in the same booth where she had sat before she left, with her grandfather. And hearing the same stories but told differently, by Hamilton Drew.

In Hamilton's stories she was poor Vera, the tall girl, so pale, who'd been spirited off to Japan when poor Belle died. The girl who'd been cold and hungry and diving half naked for shellfish with the natives until her father rescued her.

'But Dad!' Vera protested. He made himself the hero. She

excused him; supposed they would all do the same given a chance.

Her father charmed her, the way he told it. How gallant he was! How gentle, as he lightly touched her back. How sensitive, as tears came to his eyes when he thought of the hut he had found her living in, on the summer island.

'Sucking on fish skeletons, wasn't she?' He patted her shoulder. She did not like to be touched, not now

'With algae growing in her hair.'

'Dad!' (Yes, it had gone green; that happens to blondes who spent all day in the sea. But he didn't say that.)

'And the native boys eyeing her.'

More than eyeing me, if you only knew Dad, she thought. She smiled modestly down into her teacup.

'Best of all, she'd taken up the sword to defend herself hadn't you? Imagine my astonishment! Taking lessons from a samurai who'd fetched up there, on the lam from the Imperial Army, wasn't he?'

'Not a samurai, Dad, a sword polisher.'

'She's got guts; you can say that for her. Not like her mother –'

Mr Kemp winked at her. 'You never know, you never know,' he said. He travelled to Japan every year to buy and sell fabrics. His warehouse was the floor above Lowinger and McBean. He was a kindly man, who ended every utterance with a chuckle of embarrassment. He was distracted by little dogs and cats, any animal that went by. Women he did not notice much, though he flirted with Vera, in a chivalrous way, winking when he came in the door, chuckling again when Vera's father went on talking about the Lowingers.

'I suppose it skips a generation. The grandmother was a terror. Forbade her daughter to marry me.'

'I'd say she showed some good sense there, Drew.'

There were hearty laughs all around the table.

'Old Captain Lowinger himself didn't like me either –'

'You never know,' concluded Mr Kemp, putting his palm flat on the table and pushing himself to his feet.

Vera's grandfather used to say that pearl-bearing oysters once lived near shore, comfortably, in warm shallow water. But oysters retreated to deeper, more secretive places because ancient people hunted them.

He made her laugh, describing a huddled tribe of refugee molluscs migrating down the sloping ocean floor, in their slow, inch by inch way; drifting on tides, tipping down inclines, shooting themselves forward on a jet of expelled air when they flexed their one and only muscle to snap the shell shut. She liked the thought of this undersea migration, silent hooded throngs of knobby, scaled, parasite-coated creatures moving, followed by those that fed on them, the starfish and the octopus and the eels. It was a slow migration, a few inches in each generation, a foot in twenty-five years. In summer, the oysters would spawn and the surface of the sea would bubble with foamy eggs. The eggs would float into contact with sperm and be fertilised. By autumn the egg would be swollen to the size of a thumbnail; over winter it would become a spat.

The spat were the clever ones in the new generation, who shrank from the shadows of boats floating over them, and dived under the sand as spears and dredges came down on them. They would tumble, shoot, drift farther down, away from the light and the glittering surface, until they came to a new shelf. Immigrants, the baby oysters would attach themselves to this shelf. After two years they would have a shell, at four years be ready to produce a pearl, at eight years they were dead. The last spawn would have moved again, set up home in some new safe haven, under an overhanging bank, where the waters were temperate, where the tides were not too violent and the storms couldn't reach.

'The shining of a fine pearl,' James Lowinger once said, 'is a half uncanny thing.' As lustrous, as eerie, as suffused with

359

moonlight or yellow flame as a pearl might appear in his palm, he would sigh and say, 'Imagine how it must have shone when it was hidden in the dark cold bottom of the sea!'

'But why would it shine brighter there, Grandfather?' Vera would ask. It wasn't logical.

'I just fancy they were brighter down there, that's all. Where they come from, where they're at home and not afraid. They can be alone and be true to themselves. There's many an unknown in the study of pearls and in the world in general, and many an answer that isn't logical, my girl,' he would say. 'They shine best for themselves alone.'

Wherever he was in his travels, all through his life after his marriage, and becoming a father, James practised a kind of tithing. When he had a cache of pearls to send to traders in Europe or New York, he would take out one, and put it away. It was his pension, his tax to himself. He didn't notice the cut from his gains, because he didn't know what the gain would be. He never took the best pearl – he was too greedy for that – but it was always far from the poorest too.

The trick was where to keep it. He had no associates. He was sleeping in grass huts and Chinese bunkhouses and over the bar at port-side hotels; sometimes he had a little house, but he was never there long enough to establish a safety deposit. He got a habit of sending the pension pearl 'home' to Sophia for safe-keeping.

This was never easy: there were taxes to avoid, and thieves in Her Majesty's Post Office. He invented a scheme of burying the pearl in a present for Belle, a kewpie doll or a pincushion or a set of fake pearl cufflinks. Miss McBean (who despite being his wife had never in spirit surrendered her maidenhead) for all her many faults was not an avaricious person, and after a few years she lost interest. It was Belle who unwrapped each pair of Chinese slippers or packet of Indian silk and knew there'd be a pearl somewhere.

That was their game and he kept up his tithing, and forgot the stash: there was always some new gem to be bought for a song and sold for an opera. Times were good. In 1912 there was a dip when the Balkan war scared the Americans and Europeans out of buying. But before the year was out, there were fresh millionaires everywhere and every one of them wanted to buy a famous pearl, to be not only rich, but elegantly, tastefully, so. Traders in Paris were cabling abroad demanding magnificent specimens for the possessor of some newly-minted fortune.

When the Great War began in 1914, everyone hid their pearls in the family safe. But by 1916, while governments that were at war were sinking, other fortunes were being made. And on it went.

But by the end of the Great War, the oysters were having their revenge. The owners were desperate, and the shell-openers devious. A good pearl had five people bidding on it. One night, James stood on the long Chinese pier on Jolo Island and stared into the sky. The dancing stars promised their piercing entry into some place of glory. The tents were folding on this particular circus, and he knew it. The wizened old women with their skinny dugs and skin sores from swimming in rotting oyster flesh had lost their charm. To stroll the beach of Pearltown, Anywhere, and watch a lugger come in with the flag at half-mast and the crew unload a dead diver quite frankly depressed him.

He returned to Japan and spared a day to visit Mikimoto. Standing on the beach, looking out at the islands that his energetic friend had colonised with hundreds of thousands of pregnant oysters, he gave a passing thought to his bride. The last time he had been on this spot, she had been at his side. It was the one time he had seen Sophia McBean at a loss for words. The *ama* had sculled in, with faces full of the joy of life and bodies like sleek mermaids. Sophia was agape. She knew she was beaten.

Beaten at one game, but not at another, by the end of the honeymoon Sophia was pregnant, and after a predictable time gave birth to the little girl they called Belle. The child was not quite two when Sophia packed herself off to England with the excuse that one could not bring up a child properly in this place. James pointed out that the Japanese did it on a regular basis. She stomped her buckled shoe: that was exactly her point. She was not Japanese and she would never be and if that was what he wanted he should just get himself a Japanese wife.

She was prescient, that woman. And indeed, in England she joined a cult of psychics, or so he heard. He never doubted she would have great success. How Sophia spent her time he did not ask. The girl went to boarding school. He often wondered how she grew, what was the colour of her hair, and what she was learning at school. For a long time he heard nothing from home.

Then one day, as if summoned by regret, Sophia cabled Yokohama, as if she knew he'd be there.

Come immediately. Paris. Hotel Drouot. Sophia.

He didn't hesitate for a moment.

Will arrive first option of travel.

He was there within sixteen days.

'You took your time,' Sophia said. She had ensconced herself in the 9th arrondissement near the Boulevard Haussman on the Rue Rossini. Antique sales were held every day at the Hotel Drouot. The bar chairs had round seats and were upholstered with a bright pink, the walls, too were pink. It was like a bordello. But he felt as if he were seeing a sister, not a wife.

'Apparently you are still in the business,' he said.

'No, I am in the business again.'

'What happened to your mind-reading?'

She smiled. 'I still practise.'

A tall, pale young woman entered the bar and came toward them. She had unsettling blue eyes and looked as if she had never seen the sun.

'This is Belle. Belle, your father.'

'My God,' said James Lowinger. It occurred to him that it had been cruel to leave the girl with the redoubtable Miss McBean all this time. Why had he done it? He was afraid of the woman, if the truth be known. It was easier to take on the bandits of Bombay.

He bent to kiss his daughter's hand. 'You are lovely, my dear,' he said.

The girl cried out and snatched her hand away. James looked at Sophia, confused. Was the girl simple?

Now Sophia had a proposal. They should be together as a family. Belle was finished at school, and no doubt before many years she would marry. They would make up for lost time, as a family. Try though James did to locate that wild passionate woman of the Kuwait houseboat in her hands, or her eyes, he could not.

James said that he would think about it.

He walked along the Boulevard Montmartre. He took a turn and found his way to the Seine. It was wide, dark and full of eddies. You could drown in there. He was afraid as he'd never been afraid before. He strolled past the bookstalls and found the printmakers. Belle caught up with him while he was studying a few *ukiyo-e* that had turned up on one of the barrows. Suddenly she was at his elbow.

'I don't remember Japan,' she said, 'although I'm told I was born there.'

He turned to her, his heart in his mouth. She took his arm and they walked together over the bridge to Notre Dame and through the flower market. They crossed again and had tea in a café overlooking the Hotel de Ville. Belle was sober and sad; he felt tender toward her. She walked without speaking much, her face lifted to the gale; brave but battling: what was she battling? Her sadness, it seemed. That was the boarding school, Sophia had said. These girls have a certain sameness, she said, as if Belle were an article of clothing turned out from a pattern.

But James lost no time in adoring her now. He was father to a supple white-haired girl so unlike her mother. Still, in moments of clarity he could say to himself, I am being reined in. This is the reining in of James Lowinger.

They had to have a home, and so they got one, a flat on the rue Rossini that was supposed to make them all happy: James, Sophia, their daughter, and an English housekeeper named Miss Hinchcliffe. Belle appeared to be content to be picturesque and walk with Miss Hinchcliffe in the filthy little parks, the way all the other marriageable young women did.

Paris was the centre of the pearl world. It had no right to be: France had no pearl grounds in its empire and never had. But never mind: it had style, and experts. The buyers came here and so too did the sellers. The rue du Bac was the heart of it. The dealers stood outside on the pavement. Everybody came to them, the rich ladies and their husbands, the gem merchants who wanted to buy wholesale and the guys who'd bought gems from the markets in Dubai and wanted to sell. They clustered like flies on the kerb. Every so often the French cops would tell them to make way. But they just gathered again.

They spoke French, but they weren't French. They were all trying to get their nationality down on paper, sitting down with the French officials to try to get a passport. They came from the sub-continent, from Spain, the Arab world or Russia.

James took a little office, upstairs from the Café Scosso, just a room with a carpet from the desert and a wide flat table on which a perfect pearl would roll for ever, if given a nudge, and an imperfect pearl would stall, and give itself away. On the corner of the desk he placed his sieves, for sizing, and his corn tongs.

From his window, he watched the street. The dealers paced. They had the goods and had to sell. Or they had to make a snap decision on the value, and bid. The brokers slid between buyer and seller, in an oily way, and made the transaction work. They had the gift of the gab, whatever their native language.

The traders handed around paper packets, little bundles wrapped up with pearls in them. There were no receipts; everyone was watching. Sooner or later, egged on by a broker, one of the dealers pulled out a roll of banknotes and peeled off a few. He gave some to the other dealer, some to the broker. Then he went farther along the kerb to call a taxi, one arm raised – *Voiture! Voiture!* His buyer was somewhere, waiting.

James decided that it was best to keep to the high ground, in his office. In the family were two of the oldest English pearling names. So Lowinger and McBean was born. He had it painted on the door. The firm took on the big gems, the risks, and the tricky sales no one else could make.

And this was the way it worked. A dealer made his way up in the lift with his questionable packet. 'I can get . . .' he began.

James put a magnifying lens in his eye.

'Can't offer you any more for this, my dear sir –'

'I wouldn't even consider it but I need the money quickly –'

'You're in the wrong business, I have to say then, with all respect. You know you can't unload a perfect pearl on the first merchant you find with cash.'

'With respect, that's why I came to you, the pre-eminent, the largest, the only one, frankly, I know, who could afford to pay cash for such a find –'

'Then may I assume I have the luxury of naming my price?'

James asked to keep the pearl for two hours and took a taxi to the flat. Sophia worked the estate auctions. Whenever a countess or a film star died, jewellery came under the hammer. 'You are home, my dear,' he'd say, surprised every time.

'The general public got into the bidding, so it was time to get out,' she would grumble.

'What do you think of this?'

She would roll the pearl between her fingers. She would put the pearl in the palm of her hand, and hold the palm at the level of her eyes and gaze steadily into the centre of the pearl with her lips pursed. It was as if the pearl were a feather and she could blow it into the air. She held it to her eye, she put it beside her ear and rolled it some more, which he considered an affectation, because what could you hear in a pearl?

'Where did this pearl come from?'

'The Arabian Gulf, I'm told, by way of Bombay.'

'I sense pain. I hear wailing.'

That was safe. They always wailed, those Arabs.

'And weariness, great weariness. This is an old pearl.'

Hokey and phooey, thought James Lowinger, though he never said so. The door between their two rooms remained firmly closed. Occasionally he wondered if she had any sexual feelings at all. Usually he decided not, and that she was a crackpot. But she was never wrong about the value of a pearl.

'What do they want?'

'Five hundred.'

'What is it? Fifty grains?'

'A little more.' Actually, she had it just about exactly right.

'Buy it,' she would say. 'You can sell it for one thousand francs, just now. Sell it quickly. I have a feeling of haste.'

She would stand and walk with her arms crossed, hugging her waist.

'How so?' he'd say.

'Something's coming,' she would say. 'Some disaster. I feel it.'

'Monsoons in the Straits of Manaar?'

'No,' she would say.

There were rumours that the Japanese pearls would soon hit the market. 'This is going to kill us,' she would say, whenever the topic came up.

The year was 1920. Pearls were in fashion and fashion was ruthless. Women wore them on their necks and wrists and fingers and ankles; they made cocktail dresses of them and handbags and shoes. Happy or tragic as the events of the day were, they could only help the pearl market. Every key event had its echo in sales. Insurrection, invasion or stock-market slump was reflected a few months later in the business. Pearls were luxury items, and on top of that, they couldn't be traced.

The Persian Gulf produced by itself forty to fifty million pearls, one quarter of all the production. The big French jewellers were out in Bahrain trying to buy direct from the fishers without going through Bombay. The maharajas and mandarins were selling the treasures from their family sepulchres. Hundreds of pounds of big pearls were coming out of Panama and Costa Rica. Even freshwater pearls from America, that had only been on the market a few years, and used to be had for a few thousand francs a sack, were expensive. Still James couldn't get enough of them.

How long could it last? And why didn't the benefits make their way into the oceans? You would think the lot of the poor divers would improve. But the very opposite was the case. Still the fishers of pearls died poor and died of hunger when the fishing was poor. These fishermen would not stand it for ever. The oyster population would not stand it for ever.

# 12

## *Nuki-uchi*
### Drawing upward, cutting down

Mikimoto's pearl farm first sent gems to London for sale in 1919 at a discount of twenty-five per cent because they were not natural. They were of faultless colour, shape and lustre. They caused a furore. The next year Japanese pearls went to France.

James's colleagues on the rue du Bac were spitting with venom. They offered their views, in the coffee shops along the street, and on the pavement.

'Does this man Miki – what is it? – Mikimo – think he can domesticate the oysters, discipline the spat and ask them to make pearls at fixed hours, according to his will?' one of them asked. 'He hasn't got a hope.'

'If you saw the women who do the domesticating, you might think again,' James said.

'So he has succeeded in provoking the oyster by inserting an irritant into its belly. Is it a pearl the oyster produces? No, it is a little ball of pearly matter that looks like a pearl, but it is not a pearl.'

'The pearl is the victim of science.'

Connoisseurs ventured that the lustre was 'false', that it was 'anti-natural' and that it 'deceived' the eye. All of this James Lowinger enjoyed; he only wished he could come upon dear Mikimoto himself balancing his umbrella upright on the tip of his chin, to have a chat about it. He sat in his office while the other dealers and the brokers came in to complain.

368

'It will be the end of us,' said the man with the smashed nose he'd got buying shell in a back alley in Broome. 'No one could tell the difference between a natural and a cultured pearl without cutting one in half.

'Mikimoto never actually said they were the same. He is perfectly straightforward about the way they're grown,' said James.

Some dealers swore there was a difference in the colour. But the Japanese could make them in greenish yellow, whitish gold, rosee and pure white. Others swore the perfection of the sphere was a giveaway. Nature rarely created a perfectly round pearl. They said you could tell the difference: but the only difference was in the core and that, even an X-ray could not determine. The nucleus was laid down in a shell, not on a grain. So that, instead of being spherical, it is flat at right angles. There were ways invented to see this by drilling a hole and passing a mirror through, but once you were done you'd ruined the pearl.

The only person who seemed to know was Sophia McBean. Sophia could tell with the naked eye. And she was never wrong. She went through her usual routine of holding a pearl to her eye, in the palm of her hand, and then to her ear. From the real pearls she heard tempests and screams of agony or songs of love. From the cultured pearl she heard nothing but a bland contentment.

The price of pearls was sinking like a stone.

The matter got into the newspapers.

The real issue, said the editorial writers, was the war. France had emerged with a huge debt. The franc fell to one-fifth of its former value. Strangely, the only commodity that held its value was the jewel. The value of a gem was five times in francs the value it had been before the war. In other words, it was the same, to the rest of the world, but to France, it had been magnified by the figure of twenty-five. For example, the three-strand necklace of one hundred and fifty pearls had been worth 20,000 francs before; now it was 100,000. But now, to a Frenchman, that meant 500,000 francs.

The French considered themselves sophisticated. Luxuries were their stock in trade. Jewels were part of the *patrimoine sacré*. Selling false, or fabricated stones was to attack the *patrimoine*. To suggest you could make a pearl on a little farm in Japan was treason, a campaign against the national wealth. There were no man-made pearls, only balls of nacre raised in an oyster. The rallying cry went up. Everyone who loved France should guard against the invasion of the cultured pearls, in order to prevent catastrophe, shame and grief.

The Minister of Agriculture named a committee of experts to opine. The committee examined natural and Japanese pearls. The verdict was that the cultured pearl must not be confused with the wild pearl but could be imported, and sold, in its own way – i.e. cheaply. But here the French launched another offensive. The Japanese pearl had been classified in France, and so was a French artefact.

The Japanese claimed a win; so did the French.

The Japanese appealed.

They won. Cultured pearls were permitted into the country.

This was seen as an attack on the sacred French pearl, spawning an outpouring of passion.

The pearl was the Queen of the Seas. 'Radiant, eternally beautiful, defiantly impervious to time's passing,' said one newspaper. 'Born to decorate the throats of goddesses, the rarest marvel of all,' said another.

Temporarily, business improved.

The diehards in the business called the cultured pearls 'cuckoo pearls'. If you had risked your life in Borneo, or fought off an assailant with a two-foot machete in a back alley of Hong Kong, or even withstood the rigours of the rue du Bac, you would too. But you might feel the winds of time on the back of your neck.

And then came Hamilton Drew.

Sophia attracted him first. He hung around the auction house wanting to learn about gems. Sophia, with her squarish jaw, severe dark eyebrows, and fearful eye was his unusual target. He was a tall young man with freckles and red hair and a stoop that prematurely aged him. After Sophia bid on a gem and swept to the door, he came to her side: 'Madam, may I congratulate you on your purchase.' She would have passed him by except that he appealed to her vanity. 'You have an extraordinary sense of the true worth of gems.'

'Experience, my dear boy,' she said.

They had tea in the bar. James came upon them by accident. From the first moment he did not care for the young man. Perhaps it was seeing him there with his wife. Perhaps it was his over-eager ways, and the grin that sought to win favour.

In the next few weeks he and Sophia became constant companions. Together they attended the estate auctions and bid on the old pearls. James sat in the Café Scosso most of the day now. He took some time out to find the young man and warn him that his wife was not available. Hamilton wrung his hands and wondered how he could possibly have given offence.

Then the inevitable happened. Hamilton Drew saw Belle one day, in the Hotel Druot. She was waiting, where all the English had tea, to meet her father, seated at the table with a little book open in her lap.

'James,' – he always called him James as if the older man didn't know his own name and had to be reminded of it – 'James, I would be horrified if you misunderstood my friendship with your wife. But if you think I have interests in your family you are right,' said Hamilton. 'I saw your daughter. And I said to myself, there is a girl who's had enough of travelling and maybe even had enough of the world.'

James was annoyed. 'She's hardly travelled anywhere except across the English Channel, and she knows nothing of the world and that is the way I intend to keep her.'

That was a mistake: he could not keep her.

'I mean, sir,' said Hamilton Drew, 'she's beautiful and she wants to hide. Brought out something in me, it did. That sort of timidity.'

James Lowinger just looked at him. Such an idiot would never merit his daughter's slightest glance, and that was his only comfort.

371

But he was wrong. When he saw them, head to head at a café table with their spoons in the same cup of berries and cream, he knew. Suddenly Belle was not sad. A pale, shy smile was on her face. And as the days went by the smile appeared more often. Then, when Hamilton came to the door, Belle flew toward him, and they went out.

'She could do worse,' said Sophia with complacency.

'Is it really Belle he is in love with?' James asked.

'Who else would it be?' said Sophia.

'Why you, my dear.'

'Ridiculous. Preposterous.' But he could tell Sophia was pleased.

'It's you he does business with.'

'I beg your pardon?'

'Well, whose money is he buying with? He has none of his own.'

Sophia pretended that she did not hear.

'Or perhaps, it's the business he's in love with.'

That provoked Sophia to dropping her paper. 'My, how you do underestimate your daughter.'

And he fell silent, and vowed to fend Hamilton off.

James did not wish to do business with the young man for several reasons. One, Hamilton knew nothing. Two, he was too smooth and had come upon James indirectly, through the affections of both his wife and his daughter. And three, James Lowinger was not sure he wished to do business at all any more. 'How could she fall for such a sap?' said James crossly to Sophia.

But apparently this too was his fault. Poor Belle had no confidence, his wife said, because she'd been brought up without a father to adore her.

And Hamilton found his way. Before James knew it, it was all arranged. The two would marry.

Belle's face was heartbreakingly beautiful when she smiled. A father could not say no. The light that came from her eyes filled him with fear.

Hamilton would join Lowinger and McBean. He would travel,

as James didn't, any more. This was Sophia's idea. In fact James had never tired of travelling, and was only staying put to suit her whims. Now she had 'trained', as she said, this young man, Hamilton would be the one who went to Jolo and Hong Kong. He would call on James's old acquaintances. James enjoyed the thought of this. They all still had their guns at the door. Perhaps he'd get shot. One could hope.

They were sitting at home one night smoking, the ladies playing cards, when Hamilton pressed for James's view on the Japanese pearls. Until now he'd amused himself, hearing from and sympathising with both factions. But he had to admit, finally, that despite his affection for their nursemaids, James had begun to dislike those maddening, perfect, white, staring Japanese pearls. He said so.

'If you hate them, it's only because you didn't think of it first,' said Hamilton.

Hamilton was impudent now that the wedding date grew near. Sophia slapped an ace on Belle's queen. Belle squeaked and laughed. She paid no attention to anything but Hamilton.

'These Japanese trinkets will take the magic away from pearls,' Sophia said, darkly.

'Oh, I doubt it,' said Hamilton. 'They will become accessible to so many more people. The business will grow a hundredfold. Trust me, in the long term, the only game is going to be Mikimoto's.'

The trouble was, James Lowinger didn't. Trust him, that was.

James Lowinger could feel the future coming toward him fast, and he could only stand on the side and watch in considerable awe.

As the date of the wedding neared, Sophia and James discussed a gift. The pair of freshwater rosées she had bought those many years ago in Kuwait would be perfect for earrings. Then there were the tithed pearls, James's pension pearls: despite the protests of the French, it was not clear that wild pearls were going to hold their value. Sophia had the feeling it was time to sell them. James didn't want to give them to Belle, because giving money to Belle meant giving it to Hamilton.

'The fact is, the pearls are hers, and have been since she dug them out of their hiding places,' said Sophia.

She took it up with her daughter.

'Belle darling,' said Sophia, 'shall we make you a lovely necklace out of your father's pearls? Or perhaps sell them, now?'

Belle demurred.

Another day, another week, Sophia tried again. She had no success.

James took Belle for a walk. She hardly seemed to know he was there, but her feet trod lightly on the pavement. She was wrapped in love and he clapped his hands for her. Finally he asked her outright about the tithed pearls, the pension pearls.

'Oh, Hamilton has them,' said Belle absently.

'My child,' he said, taking her hand, 'those will be my wedding present to you. They must be. They are all I have.'

'I'll ask,' Belle said.

She came back to answer that Hamilton had taken them to be made into a necklace. 'Isn't that the sweetest gift?' she said.

James thought it strange that she seemed to have forgotten the pearls belonged to the family in the first place, but at least they'd see them again.

'But why didn't he ask me? I know the best jewellers. I'd have it done for nothing,' he said.

Belle looked blank. 'He wanted to surprise me.'

'When do we see the necklace?' James asked.

The moment of presentation was postponed and postponed again. But it could not be postponed for ever. Hamilton brought the necklace in a black velvet box with a pink satin ribbon on it. Ceremoniously and with many kisses he pulled out the necklace and held it to the light. Belle cried tears of joy and even James was moved. Hamilton made as if to put the clasp around the back of Belle's neck.

'May I see?' asked Sophia.

Those were the last peaceful words spoken in the household, ever.

Hamilton hesitated. 'You may see them on your daughter,' he said.

'No,' said Sophia. 'I will see them now.'

No one remembered them, exactly. James had bought the pearls long ago, and sent them away; he'd never looked at them again. Maybe Belle had taken her little bag of them and looked at the growing number over the years. But Sophia seemed to know. She took the pearls in hand. She levered her hand up and down as if to weigh them. She held them in the light to see the lustre. She rolled each one beside her ear.

'Nothing,' she said. 'I hear nothing. Perhaps a little snoring is all. These are not they,' she said.

And stared at Hamilton Drew. He did not quake.

'These are cuckoo pearls.'

'My dear Sophia, you can't possibly mean –'

'Oh yes I can,' she said. 'You have stolen the real pearls.'

Sophia was beside herself with rage at being tricked by Hamilton Drew.

'And why didn't your second sight tell you he'd do this?' James confronted her.

'It did tell me. How do you think I knew?'

'Sooner, I mean.'

She didn't deign to answer.

James was unhappy, but not devastated. He hadn't liked Hamilton in the first place. He'd seen pearls disappear all too often. He wasn't even certain the necklace didn't contain the pearls he'd sent home. Belle insisted indignantly that they were the pearls she'd given Hamilton to string. Hamilton had gone silent and sullen with the affront of it all. Sophia and Hamilton glared at each other on every meeting. Occasionally, James wondered if it wasn't the pearls at all, but some sort of magnetism turned back on the two of them; there was that night in Kuwait, but perhaps a night like that only came to Miss McBean once every thirty years.

But on balance he sided with Sophia. The pearls, his pension pearls, his tithed pearls, had most likely been supplanted with cuckoo facsimiles. He was almost calm. But whatever they were, they were Belle's. If that was the first lesson her new husband taught her, then he hoped she was a fast learner.

He was not angry enough to suit his wife however. Sophia could find no one to blame so she blamed him. 'I hate you,' she cried. 'I hate you and him too. I will see this wedding through and I will be gone from this place and I will never, ever, speak to you, or to him, again.'

The lovers were married, with James Lowinger standing at his daughter's side. The two freshwater rosées from the spring in the sea off Kuwait were drilled and set at her ears. The necklace, cuckoo or not, encircled her neck. The plan was made for Hamilton and Belle to go to Vancouver to establish an office of Lowinger and McBean there. As an effort to protect Belle, and to provoke Hamilton, Sophia decided to send along Miss Hinchcliffe, who was longing to work in an office.

On Vera's birthday Hamilton took her for dinner at the Hotel Vancouver. They sat at a table in the window, with a thick ivory linen cloth and a view over the city. Hamilton ordered a sherry, 'for the young lady'. He was elegant in his dark suit, she thought: she felt proud and adult, sitting with him. He ordered a bottle of champagne to celebrate. She didn't like the taste, so he set out to drink it all himself.

In the window their reflections were imposed on the lights below. Vera smiled at her bare arms and pale pink satin dress and darkening blonde hair wrapped in a knot at the nape of her neck.

'What will you do now, Vera dear?' he asked.

She liked that about her father, his almost disinterested curiosity in her: he appeared to have no ambition to tell her what she should do.

'I thought I might enlist,' she said. 'Or work in the war effort.' The idea had just come to her.

He raised a glass. 'It is what all the young people are doing, I suppose,' he said doubtfully. 'This war –' he left the sentence unfinished, with a question mark at the end. Was the war really worth it, he seemed to mean. 'You'd have to fight your friends the Japanese.'

'They're not my friends.'

'No?' He looked thoughtful.

She set her chin out: no one was to see into her heart.

'I can't help but think there are fortunes to be made.'

He told her all about his scheme to harvest pig-toe mussels and sell the shell to Mikimoto. 'Remember that the war in China disrupted the supply of mother-of-pearl for the nucleus of his pearls? And he had to get shell from the United States?'

In the big window a man with greying temples leaned forward over the table speaking earnestly to the young woman with long arms and thin hands. She, Vera, stiffened. She could see the vertebrae in her back. She wondered what her mother would have said to her on this day, when she was at last no longer a child, and not only in her own but in the world's eyes a woman. Hamilton never talked about Belle. She might have died twenty years before, not five.

The trouble with the pig-toe mussels was that there didn't seem to be any in the rivers of Canada. But that didn't matter. He could grow them.

'If the Americans can do it so can I. My father-in-law knew Mikimoto.'

'I knew him too, Dad,' said Vera.

'Of course, of course you did. That's why you are so important. Thanks to you, I know Mikimoto myself!'

He had an eye on an old fishing camp on a tributary of the Fraser River. He had drawn plans and set prices. He had looked at trawlers and dredgers that would get the mussels up off the bottom. He needed investors, though.

'You know, Vera, in Arkansas when they found pearls in the Black River they just waded out to the mussel beds and grabbed the shells. But when the shallow beds were gone they had to go deeper. They developed long-handled tongs that could reach down fourteen feet.'

'Arkansas? When were you there?'

He never answered when she asked where he had been. She didn't want to talk business. She thought they might dance. There was a band with trombones. 'Will you dance with me, Dad?' she asked. 'I've never danced with a man.'

'I would be delighted.'

In the open ring of his arms she swayed on the floor. She kept her arms a little stiff, feeling awkward about being too close to her father. Hamilton hummed in her ear. Sometimes, she thought, he forgot which girl she was. He chortled in her ear and hummed, and every few bars, tightened his grip on her.

'You are a wonderful girl,' he said, his lips loosened by the fizzy drink. 'I think we can be partners.'


It was in the pursuit of investors that Hamilton took Vera to a meeting in a big hotel in Chicago. A banner was strung across the lobby: International Association of Pearl Producing and Trading Nations. There were scientists and jewellers showing charts of weights and values, and delegations from the South Seas of men with tattooed cheekbones wearing gowns. The Europeans were not there, nor the Japanese. An American politician stood up and said that the pearl industry must not be shut down. Beautiful women must be served, even in war. Especially in war. To keep the spirits up. The symbol of the pearl was more potent than ever:

purity; the sacred; innocence. He was booed by one loud voice from the back.

Hamilton had a booth for his Fraser Valley Pearl Shell Operations. He held Vera's elbow and introduced her as his daughter who had lived in Japan and become a pearl diver. Men stared and stopped to talk. Hamilton kept a close eye on her. But he wasn't looking when a man strolled up with his hands in his pockets, with an Italian hat and a trench coat caught back behind his elbows.

'Well I'll be darned. I've just remembered where I met you before,' the man said, as if they'd already been talking for half an hour.

'You did? You do?' Vera said. The crowd was confusing.

'You gave tours in English to Mikimoto's Pearl Museum in Toba.'

He gave her his hand, and there was a card in it. She pulled the card out of his palm. It was familiar. She had kept one just like it near her bed at Keiko's house, and sometimes looked at it. His name was Horace Calder.

'Remember me? I'm the guy who told you to get out of Japan. I see you followed my advice.'

'That was you!' Once he'd been a link to home. Now he was a link to there. She grasped it. 'He came for me,' she said, lifting her chin in the direction of her father.

'Your father tells me you dove for pearls?'

'I didn't,' she said. 'I dove for shellfish.'

'You must be very brave,' he continued.

She thought he was making fun of her.

'Not so brave as I had to be,' she said. Talking to him made her lonely for Japan. She missed Tamio. Her body ached at night. She missed Hana, and could not cry.

'It was sure strange to see you there! At the time I thought maybe you'd been kidnapped and hustled off to Japan.'

'Maybe I was kidnapped and hustled off home,' she said.

'You don't mean that,' Horace said. He adjusted the glasses on his nose.

She wanted to tell him things she told no one. How strange it was. 'Maybe I do.'

He was a large man, with puffy hands. Under the long, loose coat his big chest looked soft, and kind. He was bigger, and more solid than Hamilton, whose eyes were so quick to judge, and whose mind spun dreams faster than he drew breath.

'Catch you later!' he said. She watched him move off through the crowd. He was quick on his feet. But he paid attention to everything he looked at.

For the evening parties, Hamilton bought her a long, narrow black dress that clung to her hip bones and her thighs and she was self-conscious, more so than when she was naked; it felt obscene. She wrapped her arms across her breasts and stood with her head hanging down. Horace Calder was there again. Hamilton tried to introduce them.

'Have you met my daughter, who apprenticed to the *ama*? They go down forty-five feet.'

'I know all about it,' said Horace, easily extending his large paw. He had lovely eyes and he chose his words with care, spoke them with elegance.

'In winter they work for Mikimoto,' said Hamilton to the men who clustered around. 'The divers stand on bamboo rafts that ride on the waves. Their job is to pull up the oyster shells and scrub off the parasites.'

'I didn't do that, Dad, I worked indoors.'

After the men moved on, Hamilton turned on Vera. 'You didn't have to say that. Let him think you worked on the rafts, OK? I had that man, I had him; don't you see how good it looks to have you as my partner?'

Horace Calder had been listening. He waggled his fingers at her and moved on.

'I've got a deadline,' he said. 'I'll catch you later,' he said again, over his shoulder.

'You said that before,' she said, mostly to keep him there. 'I'm not a fish.'

'And I mean much later, when you've grown big enough to keep.'

Vera kept her mouth shut for the rest of the night. There were more people interested in Hamilton's Fraser River project. One wanted to know how he got his contract with Mikimoto. 'Personal contact,' said Hamilton. Another said that Vera looked young to be a spy.

The next day they were back in the booth. The journalist returned.

'It's not much later and I'm still under the legal limit,' said Vera.

He asked her if she would like to go for a drink.

They sat in the hotel lobby outside the bar. He twirled his hat on his lap. Without his hat he looked like an old man. He said he was thirty-five. She ordered two Cokes. He said he was a columnist for the *Chicago Sun-Times*.

'May I have an interview, Miss Drew?' he asked.

'I don't know why,' she said.

'You're a curiosity. Diving for pearls. I mean it,' he said. 'You are going to become a sensation.' And then he whispered, 'Give me your whereabouts in Vancouver.' Then he pulled up his camera from a leather strap over his shoulder and snapped her picture. 'I'm a two-way man,' he said.

His article appeared under the cut-line 'Canadian girl dove for Japanese Pearl King', with a picture of her in her black dress. It had its sensational bits too. The women dove naked, he had written. She was humiliated. Now, she saw his name in print and thought she would never forget it.

When she came back to Vancouver, she bumped into Mr Kemp.

'How are you doing, our Vera?' he said, using her grandfather's phrase. He seemed a friendly face and she tagged along with him. 'So you are going to harvest shell, are you?'

'I don't know anything about it,' complained Vera.

'That never stopped Hamilton.'

Vera smiled uncertainly. Since her dad had come back into her life she had tried very hard to forget everything her grandfather and his friends had said about him.

That was how, in 1940, Vera and Hamilton Drew came to live at the camp on the Blind River in the Fraser Valley. Theirs was a primitive operation. They devised a drag based on the one used in Arkansas; it had wire hooks below to cause the molluscs to clamp on as it passed over their bed. The trouble was there weren't many mussels, and the pigtoe had to be brought in. And she was not diving for pearls but planting mussels. It might have worked. But it was a long, wet winter.

She wrote to Horace and he wrote back, sending the funny pages from the Chicago paper. He also sent her pictures of Hitler and Oshima when the Japanese and Germans signed the Axis pact.

They were at Blind River on December 7, 1941. The Japanese attacked Pearl Harbor. Japan was officially the enemy now. She knew because Horace Calder wrote to her. She went into town for supplies and there in the post box was one of his bulging envelopes. It had press clippings in it. He had not forgotten to send the funnies too. Was she expected to laugh over them?

She went home and had the first of her fights with her father. He wanted her to get into the water and dive twelve feet to inspect the mussel beds. She said the water was still too cold. He stood in the doorway and threatened her: 'I'll walk out. You'll never see me again!'

'What am I supposed to do in this place without you?' she asked.

The *Vancouver Sun* said that Japantown was closed down and boarded up. The Americans had done the same thing, Horace wrote. She had the draining, fainting experience again, that she'd had when her father appeared on the summer island. This time she thought about Keiko's friend, the dressmaker, and the fishmonger. What would become of them?

There were a dozen other fights with her father before she packed her bag and called the local taxi from Blind River. She left Hamilton to his mussel shells and went to Vancouver. Horace convinced his paper to send him to see the evacuation of the Japanese Canadians. He said he was tired of gangsters anyway.

They went together to Japantown. She found the boarded-up front of the tailor's shop. They went together and saw the trains boarding and the women crying, the silent, silent men. She searched for faces she knew but recognised no one. She stayed in his hotel room; together they went out to see the trains, the confiscated houses, the fishing boats tied up at the docks with large warning signs on them. She could not feel; they were not her friends, she repeated. She lay in the bathtub and moved the layer of water back and forth over her naked belly. Her nerves were awakening after the cold.

Horace was not Tamio of the perfect skin and wide apart eyes; he did not moan when he touched her. But he was kind. He was safe, somehow; his mostly amused, sometimes concerned expression seemed to say that he knew the world, and forgave it. His mind was full of bad news; it was the war. But when his eyes lit on hers they were full of delight. She could make him happy.

The newspaper let Horace stay in Vancouver. He and Vera got a little house to live in, in the West End. Horace brought her war dispatches. He was like a sieve, a strainer – the news ran all through him like a bloodstream. They went to the cinema at the Verity, her mother's favourite theatre. He made her watch the newsreels: current events. That was the thing about living with a journalist. He knew everything. He had seen it all. He was not afraid to impute the littlest motives to the largest people. And he was never wrong.

She married him, the man in the fedora, the deadline man, byline man, Horace Calder. She had no friend to stand with her at City Hall, amongst the men in uniform who'd come home to marry before going back overseas. They asked one of the other couples who were waiting to be witnesses. Horace held her hand tightly and quizzed all the soldiers on what they'd seen.

Waiters stopped saying she was too young to drink in bars. Vera and Horace went to one every night. It was a great way to find out what was happening, Vera didn't have a job. Other women's husbands were at war. Or they had babies. She was Horace's baby. Hard-bitten to everyone else; the lost girl to him. He let her be; that was the good thing.

The war went on. At Lowinger and McBean the door was closed and locked. But Vera had a key; she opened the office, and dusted all the desks. There wasn't much there, just a jumble of papers with her father's names and numbers, written and crossed out, sideways and upside down, notes and reminders. Vera looked at an envelope on which he had scrawled and suddenly it was clear; her father was mad. Hamilton would never harvest pearl shell.

One day, she saw Mr Kemp on the staircase.

'I understand that you are now a married woman.'

Vera told him she had left her father's venture and was going to sort out some old pictures that her grandfather had had in the office.

'That will be a welcome sign of life, my dear.' He took a long time to get his wallet out of his inside suit pocket. It was there under the dog biscuits. 'You haven't signed anything, have you?'

'Only the marriage licence.'

He laughed. 'That's not what I meant. You didn't sign anything about the company?'

'No one has asked me to sign anything.'

Well, that wasn't quite true. Sometimes her father muttered about the holdings of Lowinger and McBean.

'I have something for you.'

He had found the piece of paper. It had an address on it. 'Miss Hinchcliffe,' he said, 'asked me to give this to you.'

It was only a small piece of paper.

'She said that there were things you didn't know, and that when you were twenty-one, she would tell you.' And he handed Vera the piece of paper. The words constituted nothing more than a house number: 157 Vermeer Place.

Spring, 1945: the war was still on. Vera was long past twenty-one, nearly twenty-four. She had, until now no desire to find 157 Vermeer Place. But then one day, she did. This was how she came to understand things now. It was as if she had walked a long, flat road, without knowing what was at the end or if it would end, and then came upon a turn, and took it; yes, of course the road would turn. Once she had turned those years behind her were lost from view, at least from the particular view that had been hers.

It was a neat, small house, with a hectic garden of multicoloured tulips, hyacinth, and daffodils. The scent from the garden pervaded the air as she walked up the pavement. She looked down at the piece of paper she'd kept. Yes, this was the place. Vera stood on the porch, and rang the bell. Perennials. The person who worked this garden had a view for the long run.

She came to the door, Miss Hinchcliffe, with a smile Vera had never seen in the office.

'My name is Lesley,' she said. She was on her home ground and she must have known Vera would come eventually. The front room was no less livid with fleshy bloom, these ones violets with furry leaves that seemed vaguely carnivorous. 'It is kind of you to drop by,' she said, and went to put the kettle on.

Vera could not define the nature of this visit. Had she come to see an old friend, or an old enemy? Was Hinchcliffe, *Lesley*, as a retainer of her grandfather's, somehow her charge, or was she hers, still? Her words – *kind of you* – implied that she required something of Vera. The wordless, contained clatter of crockery from the kitchen and then her inclined head as she sat across the room from Vera, the tea tray on a cart, implied a hearing, an airing of cases. Miss Hinchcliffe had the confidence of a woman who had done her job, and done it well.

Vera remembered how, in the days that now seemed long ago, when her mother died, and then her grandfather, she had hated Hinchcliffe. The fury was gone. Now she felt sad.

Vera sat looking at a painting on the wall. It was of a beach; sky, sand and sea defined it. The sand was sepia and pervasive, and went almost halfway up the canvas. All along the beach were little highly animated figures; it was a great massing of people. They were in turbans and bowler hats, in Her Majesty's uniforms, in saris, and in rags, in nothing at all. Over this was a merciless hot sun. In the very centre of the painting, the throngs parted and there, in a space by herself, was a child in a ruffled dress holding a red umbrella.

Miss Hinchcliffe saw her staring at it. She smiled.

'It's somewhere in India, I believe,' she said.

'Ceylon,' Vera said. 'Condatchey Bay.'

'My employer painted it herself. She said it was a memory.'

'Who is your employer?' Vera asked. It came back to her then, the mysterious, and irrefutable instructions that Hinchcliffe had alluded to. 'It's a *she*? Who is she?'

'You'd know if you thought about it,' said Miss Hinchcliffe again, smiling. 'She's your grandmother. Sophia McBean.'

Then Vera understood. At last. There is no Mr McBean, Hinchcliffe had said. And there wasn't. There was a Miss McBean.

'She was his partner all along? And in her maiden name?'

'Sophia sent me here to keep an eye on the men. Both of them, really – your father and your grandfather. She made me promise to keep the money safe from Hamilton

Drew. We thought he was a little, shall we say "fast"? Your grandfather – he had no head for business – he was just feckless.' Vera sat looking at the picture.

That little girl was her grandmother.

How would James Lowinger have told the story had he lived long enough to tell it?

'I always assumed that my grandmother was dead.'

'She is – now. She died at the beginning of the war.'

There was Vera's bitterness again.

'You mean she could have helped us when my mother died?'

'I did let her know. But – no. She said she'd never speak to her daughter again, after Belle married. She kept her word, but it killed her. She was very religious, in the end,' said Hinchcliffe.

Vera looked at the little girl in the picture, with her red umbrella and her white dress. The redoubtable Miss Sophia McBean could have come to them at any time. She knew where Vera was although Vera, the child, had known nothing of her. She grieved for herself as a girl. She grieved for Belle.

'She must have been awful,' she burst out, 'to let a fight, to let my father, whatever they didn't like about him, to let that get in the way.'

Hinchcliffe did not disagree.

She too looked wordlessly up at the painted girl. 'She wasn't very lucid, near the end. But she had an eye for a pearl,' she murmured.

They sat very quietly, looking at the canvas.

'When did she paint it?'

'In the years when Belle was at boarding school. I believe she was lonely, with your grandfather at sea.'

Vera took her eyes deliberately off the picture. 'How did you get it?'

'Sophia gave it to me. She grew to dislike it. I suppose you should have it,' said Hinchcliffe dubiously.

But what was the explanation for Hinchcliffe's

summoning her here? Perhaps, Vera thought, she intended to apologise. But she did not. They sat and drank their tea. Curiosity was too much for Vera.

'Why did you never send my father the letters?'

'I did send them.'

'But he said he never got them.'

'I can't speak to that,' said Lesley Hinchcliffe. 'I can only say that I sent them.'

No villains.

But there was a purpose to the visit and Hinchcliffe could not avoid it anymore. Vera could see the woman had no more liking of this task than she did of Vera. She was merely an employee, carrying out her function. James Lowinger had been right about that. But Hinchcliffe was nothing if not responsible. Vera waited for her to speak.

'I have something for you,' she said. 'James left it with me.' She left the room and returned with a brown folding file with elastic around it. 'I haven't retyped it, but I think you can make it out. He pecked away on it a few words at a time on that old Remington beside his desk that he never seemed to use.' She looked glad to see it leave her hand. 'He was the only one of the bunch that I could halfway see the heart in.'


## LAST WILL AND TESTAMENT OF
## JAMES LOWINGER

In my peripatetic life, I learned one thing: far adventurers are the most obstinate of homebodies. The more they travel, the more powerful is their longing to return to the place where they began. To me the homeward urge came late in life and with a vengeance.

But I *had* no home; the England where I grew up was a

distant splotch on the map, and Paris was one square mile with memories of salad days and super abundance, money made and money lost. I couldn't return like Odysseus to Sophia McBean for God's sake, we'd long ceased contact. And in any case I had a new wife or wife substitute, one I should have been with all along, except that she wasn't even born until I was fifty.

I suppose I had not forgotten that last quarrel with Hamilton Drew over his cuckoo pearls, the way after, I said no, finally no, I won't do business with you, how he'd given me a glance I could not interpret except perhaps to say that even a cad has a human side, and occasionally that love creeps into his greedy heart, 'Your daughter is sad. She misses you.' Oh, my deaf ears.

But not entirely deaf. Therefore the ticket to Vancouver, the telegram to Belle saying 'I'm on my way!' Only Belle was dead. Now here was an opportunity for desperate lamentation and grief – *drop drop dropping slow* as Ben Jonson said. But I could not dissolve like a pearl in vinegar for there was this child of my child, this waif, standing on the quay, looking up as my ship sailed in. A sugar-haired wretch waiting, and I was all she had.

So for once I did my duty, or tried to, staying with her, and giving her my beautiful diving woman until the old ship-master gave signals that I had to peg out.

Vera Lowinger Drew, you are the right and proper heir. This may not excite you overmuch when you learn the second part of the message which is, essentially, that there is naught, or nought, or nougat, however you write that – to inherit.

And I will tell you why.

The elusive pearl: a short dissertation. Perfectly round is genuinely rare. And unnaturally hard to hang on to. There are far more baroques and buttons and drop shapes than the law of averages allows. That is because the round ones, the ones that roll, have rolled away. They roll out of the oyster shells and they roll out of the hands of traders. Men have blunt fingers, and calloused thumbs. In the Café Scosso the one who opens the envelope to show a perfect sphere is a fool. They jump, like Mexican beans. And they are gone. It is as if they wanted to escape. I've seen it happen on the deck of a ship. I've seen it in a maharajah's tent when every single eye in the place is on it. The perfect pearl is there, and then it is gone.

The pearls of the oyster are divine. And they are found in the dimmest, deepest place in the world, under the scabbiest, tightest lid. That is their magic. There is a term we use: the quickening. It is a quality of lustre, one that comes alive in the light. It is intimate, and shy, but brilliant. This once-aliveness, this secrecy, this creature light, is the pearl's true value. But the fortunes made with pearls are as slippery as the creature that mothers them.

Men who moil for pearls all had dreams of making a fortune. They were pitiful dreams, to do with finding a perfectly spherical cream rosée twenty grain pearl, buying it for a song from a deluded diver, selling it for a hundred thousand pounds, and cutting loose. Trouble was *if* a man found the pearl, and *if* he sold it at profit, it only made him want more. Consider him on a carousel – sometimes up, and sometimes down. It's hard to get off when you're up and harder when you're down: you can see the rise coming around the bend. The problem was a thing they now call ego. I think the Greeks called it hubris. Whatever its name, I'd recognise it at midnight in a dark tunnel.

Most of us got off at about the same place we got on. It felt familiar.

I intended to leave on an upswing. After the debacle in Paris I made one last journey to Bombay where, in a bazaar, I found a pearl the size of a blackberry. It was the shape of one too. I forked it over, all of it, my entire life, my future, my past. It was only a fraction of what the pearl would be worth.

Next stop Hong Kong and a pearl doctor I knew. He walked with an umbrella, gingerly, peering right and left, as if he were a house pet taking himself for a stroll. He was said to be the illegitimate son of a princess who kept him alive on the condition that he spend his whole life under wraps. He looked as if he had. He had long feathery fingers and a monk-like air. He looked just the type who could, with his tiny scalpel, his brush, and his pick, shave off the bumps layer by layer and turn the blackberry into a perfect sphere and my fortune.

He weighed the pearl and held it to his ear, in a gesture eerily reminiscent of Sophia. He held it to the light and ran his fingertip around the bottom of it, laid it in his palm and thoughtfully pushed it one way and then the other, as a cat might a dead mouse.

Pearl doctors can take a cut of the proceeds, which means that if the proceeds are nil their wages are nil, or they can be paid a fee, and take no risk: they are paid no matter what. He said he'd like to have a percentage cut of the increase in value he brought to it, and I said no thank you. That would be mine. I would pay him any fee he named.

His fee was steep.

I agreed to pay.

He said he would like to work on it at home under a stronger light and without the din of the street to mar his concentration.

Being a suspicious man, I could envision a scenario where my pearl was perfected and then spirited away, after which he would me give a sob story and a piece of dung. I said if he wanted to retreat to his inner sanctum I would be there.

I sat in his den on floor cushions smoking a pipe. The artist worked away with files and his brush. The pearl lost one skin and was better. There was still a flat bit at the bottom. He worked away another skin; another year of life in the groin of an oyster fell to the floor. Now it was crushingly near perfect. The pearl that had been worth five hundred was worth fifty thousand.

A Chinese matron emerged from the wall behind my skinner, his nanny probably. She pointed here and there: the lustre is not good. One year the oyster went hungry. She recommended they take off one layer more: then you will have a gem that none can surpass, he said. Set fee, you remember, nothing in it for them but the pursuit of truth and beauty, as Keats said.

I agreed. The pearl winked and lolled on the tabletop, seductive as hell. The street din was small and far away. An hour went by and he had removed yet another skin from the pearl. Now what we saw was a tad less beautiful than what we had before. But the pearl was still large, very large, and we felt we owed it to ourselves to take off one more layer and see what we could get.

Vera dear, you can imagine the rest. It was more terrifying with each skin we discarded: the pearl would grow lustrous but bruised, then fair but dull, then smooth but flattened: it went through a dozen phases and each was close but none was right. It was like attending a slow beheading. I thought I might embarrass myself by shitting or crying out; that all manner of nasty elements of my personality might come to the fore. My monkish skinner was sweating from his brow and temples and his hand was shaking. I felt as if this were happening in a dream, as if it had been foretold. Yet on we went. The pearl that was worth fifty thousand was now worth ten thousand. Neither one of us suggested we should accept defeat.

A strange thing happened then; my awareness lifted up and out of my head and I seemed to be watching from a place in the silk-draped ceiling. The skinner took greater and greater care with his work. We had become quite jolly. He took one last crack with it, and the whole piece collapsed into dust. The doctor yelped and called for his nanny; we all stood and gaped at the rubble. The pearl that was worth ten thousand was now utterly worthless.

And I had to pay him.

I gave him a promissory note as that was all I had. I walked out into the sweaty Hong Kong night. I went to the bird market and strolled dizzily between the cages. I heard bird call from the caged ones for sale all around me and I thought, I am free and they are not.

Thus I ended my pearl trading days without a fortune and in fact without a bean. Or a McBean. Lowinger and Nobody.

Let me offer you an apology for my life, dear: I begin to ask what it was worth. I confess a fondness for this place, this Gastown. Perhaps it was all leading me here.

Vancouver was handy to the Orient. We came to it, English by name but farther back a muddle of Jew and Cossack, who knows. We found it open for business and we set about weaving it into the rest of the world. You'll not find me on your honour role of pioneers, farmers or town builders, but I did something and that was to make it interesting. We kept the store open. And you were born there, with your links to older spots on the planet.

You might think me a lascivious old fool bringing home a woman approximately one-third of my age. I fell in love. How could I not? A naked dive to the bottom of the sea was an augury of a short life. But in Japan the radiant *ama* women young and old set off with their lunch boxes and made a day of it, ferrying contentedly back and forth from the depths a dozen times an hour. I watched the *ama* women for years before I found Keiko. She was not a woman of twenty-eight, to me. She was a woman of the ages, strong, brave, beautiful, and straight as her plunge to the sea bed. Men love a woman who dives deep. Even though they might not follow.

I trust you to her and her to you. She's all I have to give.

393

As for The Redoubtable Miss McBean, I never doubted she would outlive me. I heard she became religious and that the fortune she made buying jewellery at auctions she gave to some charity, the Society for the Prevention of Cruelty to Molluscs, no doubt, just to thwart me. The pair of fine rosees from the freshwater spring in the bottom of the sea, Belle's wedding pearls, had gone somewhere, no doubt on with their mischief.

And so I leave you all of it, which is nothing.

Oh one thing. You'll have the pictures. Among the objects of the world, they were what I loved.

The document was signed, 'Your loving Grandfather, James Lowinger.'

There was a poem Vera liked to read:

> *What thou lovest well remains,*
> *the rest is dross*
> *What thou lov'st well shall not be reft from thee*
> *What thou lov'st well is thy true heritage . . .*

Ezra Pound wrote it, one man from this big continent of North America who loved the small archipelago of the East.

But then he was mad.

In the years following the war, countless Westerners fell in love with oriental ways, and tried to explain them. They searched Vera out, often wanting to tell her some tale of their own. The wisdom was that east-seekers were only looking for a better view of themselves, that a mirror stood on the horizon just where the sun rose. That's why it blinded the eyes.

She didn't really go to the East, she said. She went to an island off the mainland, any island, it could have been, off any main-land.

'What was it like?' the professor would say, eyes all over her. She told him, or her.

Island life is measured life. Between the arrival and the departure, that is the time you have. All you will have is what you bring from the outside world, and what grows there. The longer you stay on the island the more you begin to match yourself to the food that is there, the seaweed, the little shellfish, the fish. Some try to garden, but nothing much grows. You are allowed no excesses. The portions are small and always weighed against what remains. You soon learn to control your greed.

Island life is a resignation. The ferry comes once a week, and leaves promptly on schedule. First you long for it; then you feel a mild pleasure on the day it will arrive. Then you forget to look for it. Eventually you fear what it will bring from the outside world to disrupt your harmonies.

There were no letters from Keiko, during the war.

And Vera could not go to Japantown and find her friends to ask them what was happening. Japan was cut off from the world, cut away from the flesh. Or perhaps Vancouver was cut off. There was no fighting; there was just the news, the news and the cocktail bars where she sat with Horace. The cocktail bars and the warehouse, where Vera began to sort the pictures.

And she thought about her father. She wondered if Hamilton Drew was indeed her enemy. He came to see her, bitter that she had left and blaming the collapse of his Blind River empire on her defection. As suddenly as it had begun, their father-daughter romance, the one the poets say must be had, was extinguished. And she couldn't hate him, not the way the others had. He seemed a little fragile. His dreams were running him ragged.

But already he was talking about Labrador. He'd found a passage in an old book alleging that in the Ungava Region of the Province of Quebec, pearls had been found by trappers and fishermen from Montreal. They were white and of good lustre. No one had ever searched for them, but Indians and Eskimos – 'Many,' he said – knew their location. Recently, he told her, two beautifully matched pink pearls, weighing about fourteen grains each, were found in one Ungava mussel. He was going to get some. That was if the Hudson Bay traders hadn't beat him to it.

The end of the war came. Vera saw the atom bomb on the newsreels. There was the aeroplane's wing, the instant white, soaring cloud like a godhead. There was flattened landscape after that. Red sky, red earth, bones and dust: cities pulverised. There were living figures in swaddling, their staring eyes that did not accuse, or even seem to understand. There were the doctors, before long, taking off the bandages, to show that healing was possible. They saw the layers being peeled off, or picked off, and wet, angry flesh.

Then there was the arrival of the Americans. Horace was cynical about that: he could afford to be; he was one. There was a marine standing shoulder to shoulder with the Japanese policeman who directed traffic, watching his hand signals, and mimicking them. When MacArthur arrived, his motorcade went down the empty street. All the people stood with their backs to him. Horace whistled through his teeth. How do they dare show their hatred? he asked. Vera understood: it is not disrespect, but courtesy. The victor had great power, which might blind them.

Suddenly the public was full of pity for these enemy people. Send me food or send me bullets, the General roared: the people are starving. Vera saw cheering children outside General MacArthur's residence singing happy birthday. Women voting and even being elected. Farmlands taken from the big landlords and divided. The military establishment destroying the weapons arsenal.

She saw Hiroshima, what was left of it: streetcars running through a cremated landscape. She saw the now-human Emperor shaking hands: there had been a decision not to implicate him. He was a strange little man, near-sighted, with thick, round glasses, not at all like his picture in the shrine at the summer island. He was trotted out and stood up before crowds. Vera remembered when he had owned her lunch, and the clothes on her back.

She closed her mind, as she had closed it since leaving Yokohama, to what had happened to the ones who had cared for her. The sword polisher had fooled her: she hated to be fooled, she hated not knowing. All the while he had been working for Hitler. If Keiko was his lover, she must have been just as bad. She had compassion only for Tamio – they had sent him away to die in his boat. That was the worst of it.

Horace was a good man: he helped her. 'There are many meanings of a gift sword,' he told her. 'Suppose Ikkanshi had a reason for what he did. Suppose he was forced.'

Another time he would try, 'And Keiko, she was like your mother.'

'She was not! I had a mother, not at all like that.'

'All right then, Keiko was the older sister you never had. She was the one adult who had stayed with you, and protected you.'

'She sent me away.'

He'd give a wry smile. 'You know about the Judgement of Paris? She was the one adult who was wise enough to give you up.'

Vera heard about the terrible pain of keloid scars. She saw footage of life in Japan, life going on; there were still temples and monks tolling bells and scrubbing floors. There were pictures of Marilyn Monroe visiting Tokyo. Of smiling Japanese women in madras shirtwaists with vacuum cleaners. Still, in the background, she could catch sight of hurried tiny people in crowds, people sitting on streets begging, hiding their faces. They could be people she knew. But transformed by current events their faces were not those of her friends. She looked at every account she could find, but she never saw the sea, never the fishing people.

Horace told her when Mikimoto started up his pearl farms again. He found some pictures of Japanese fisherwomen in head-scarves. She knew she had to return to the summer island. But she did not go. She was not ready.

And then one day he showed her the article in the magazine with the sword in the picture. That friend of your sword polisher?

The one who was Ambassador to Berlin? He's being tried in Tokyo.

Vera was a woman of thirty, a dealer in objects of beauty. But if you asked her, she would tell you differently. She was a simple girl in a dangerous trade living by her wits and what strength she could muster, an *ama* diver in Ago Bay, the Sea of Kumano Nada, facing the Pacific Ocean.

They say no man is an island. Vera said we all were.

*Simplify that*, the sword polisher would say.

Every man and woman is an island.

*That is too big. Simplify again. Nothing extra. Nothing assumed. Only what is necessary and what you know.*

I am an island.

·

The war went on and on, like a long, long winter. One cold morning, Pearl Harbor screamed from the radio into his new room where, by then, Ikkanshi was accustomed to being alone, reading and thinking. A surprise attack, yes. They had been taught to seize the advantage.

He stood outside and looked above him to the huge empty sky. How beautiful it was, blue and silent. It fooled him into thinking he was apart from it all. But he knew now that from that same sky, remonstrance would come.

In the final year there were bombers over the island. The pilots enjoyed strafing the people on their way to or from dropping their gift on the mainland. They came so low it was like a greeting. Once in a while, looking up, Ikkanshi could see the face of the enemy, a young man doing his patriotic duty.

When Vera had first come she asked him if he were a

398

prisoner there. He was not a prisoner, not on the island. But he was a prisoner, of sorts, in his country. He was suspected of being against the war and as the suspicion grew, and the war grew, he *was* against it. After he had written to Oshima that he knew of no man worthy of the *meito*, Ikkanshi imagined the police would come for him. He had insulted the Ambassador to Germany. He had insulted Hitler, whom Oshima had in mind as the recipient. True, he had given up the *meito* when the basket maker came for it. But he had no reason to keep it. The sword would go to its purpose.

The police did not come for him.

The basket maker did.

He had a small package. He was exceedingly formal. He bowed to the floor presenting this short weapon wrapped in its fine embroidered cloth. It was a *wakizashi*. Ikkanshi understood the message. He was to disembowel himself.

He thanked Bamboo and put the package away.

He had a great deal of time to reflect. The massacre of Nanking stayed with him. The Imperial Army's crack troops had overrun the river to reach the town, row after row of soldiers following each other to drown in the mud, so that the last ones could run over the drowned one's backs and reach the opposite shore, and achieve the advantage.

He puzzled over why a people would launch their nation into a world-wide blood bath against impossible odds, at the behest of a remote, superior Emperor. He concluded that they had the minds of slaves, not slaves of the Emperor, but of their own ideas. They were honour-bound but their honour was based on appearance and not on true meaning. In consideration of how it would be seen, one was to die uselessly. In consideration of disgrace in military eyes, he was to dispatch himself from this earth.

Once he understood this, he no longer had the mind of a slave. To change was at the same time very difficult and very simple. He had to think for himself, be fearless in quite a different way. He thought about resistance and how it had always been there, slow and silent, sometimes laughing, not seen.

In time of crisis the people were obedient to the Headman. Take the banishment of Tamio: the people did what they believed was for the best of all. A 'Headman' ruled in families too; women were obedient to husband or father. On the summer island it was different. No one spoke about this difference, but it was there. The *ama* divers were a force, by virtue of their diving skill. Their labour earned the village keep.

The women did not agree with sending Tamio away. But they had not raised a voice against the Headman. They achieved their rebellion in small ways. Tamio's boat was strong enough for him to reach land. But he had no fuel. Keiko removed a precious can that Ikkanshi used to power his generator. Ikkanshi knew but said nothing.

The diving women knew the empty islands between here and the mainland. Perhaps Tamio stopped on one. Perhaps they brought water and food. It was not spoken of.

After the next winter Keiko returned with news: Tamio had been seen in a nearby village. So the Headman was defied. But it did not seem to matter. Tamio was soon absorbed in the war machine.

They thought about Vera, but again: what was there to say? Letters were prohibited. Keiko needed all her wits to stay alive. Each winter, her absence seemed longer.

Soon after Pearl Harbor Mikimoto's factory was ordered closed. Most of the people of Toba were out of work. The government wanted to make a war industry there, but Mikimoto refused to give up his property. By the end Mikimoto was in a bomb shelter. Keiko's house was bombed, leaving her with nothing. She moved in with her brother, who had also lost his house. They were cooking rice out of an airman's helmet that had been found on a dead body.

The last winter he asked her to stay on the island with him and she agreed.

Days after the surrender, Ikkanshi was seized with elation. He wanted to sing, to babble, to tell everyone his private feelings. Of course it was crazy. The country was in ruins. They had been peppered with bombs. And then, the bomb. Hundreds of thousands lay dead and unburied. People were dazed, as the truth entered their heads.

And yet. And yet.

It was over. He was alive.

He had spent nearly a decade hiding, by being in the open. He had had to keep his thoughts silent. Now, he spoke freely.

He left the island. Keiko stayed to dive; it was the best place for her. He went to Hiroshima Prefecture. For six months the sword polisher worked hauling water, building houses, burying the dead. There were so many soldiers returning from Russia, China, and the South Seas, who had lost home and family. He searched. He hoped to hear of Tamio, but he did not.

The Occupation forces again outlawed the sword. Ikkanshi moved to the island of Amakusa, where the people were poorest. There was a library, which had been closed for years. Everywhere people were hungry for knowledge. He put up a sign on the door offering a class in English literature. One hundred people came: they sat shoulder to shoulder, filling the room. He discovered himself as a teacher. It was very popular at the time, this English literature. He made comparisons with Japanese literature and encouraged the people to think about what Japan had done. He questioned obedience. He used the old warrior myths for examples of trickery, slavery, and behaving boldly only for the benefit of others.

He often thought of Vera the child woman, and hoped that she was safe. One day, he was reading Shakespeare in class. He came upon Othello: 'Think of me as one,' he said to his students, 'who loved not wisely but too well.' And into his mind came Vera, the girl who slunk like a wild cat. He remembered the name of that warehouse on Homer Street where her father did business, and finally he wrote a letter to tell her that he and Keiko had survived the war.

When Oshima was on trial, Ikkanshi visited. The prison was bare, but clean, and they spoke in a courtyard with guards at either end with their backs discreetly turned. This was a mark of respect for Oshima's rank and achievements. He was not at all shamed. He told Ikkanshi that Hitler had been pleased with the *katana* Oshima had given him. He told him what a high opinion Hitler had of him.

'He confided in me in advance that he was going to attack the Soviet Union,' he said proudly. 'He always said of me: Oshima has a very good brain.'

Ikkanshi pitied Oshima, but Oshima did not pity himself. He was in a dream of glory. He had stayed with Hitler until the very end. Ikkanshi asked if Hitler had had the courage to use the *meito*, or have someone use it on him.

'That was not in his tradition,' said the officer.

No one knew what had become of the sword. For a time Oshima and his delegation had stayed in a hotel in the Austrian mountains. Then the Americans had come to shake them out.

'Hiroshi,' the sword polisher said, 'you may be sentenced to death.'

'I sincerely hope so,' he told his old friend.

But as the months passed Oshima grew more sanguine. 'We were on opposite sides, old friend. How did you survive, those last years? Where did you hide?'

'My shield was the people. I did not hide,' the sword polisher replied.

The letter was addressed to Vera Lowinger Drew, Lowinger Warehouse, Homer Street.

She showed it to Horace. 'Should I read it?'

'If you don't, I will.'

He scanned it first, and left it on the table for her. 'Keiko and your sword polisher are alive.'

Still, she did not write back to him.

Horace Calder, seventeen years older than Vera, but still a young man, and a happy drunk, developed a heart condition. He had to give up drinking. But, he said, he would rather not live, than not drink. When he was only forty-five he died of a heart attack. It was 1950, a time of families, and small children. Vera had no family, no one. But she fitted in, among the many young war widows. In a way, she was one.

She spent time in bars, and she met men. They were discontented men; they felt familiar to her. But she made sure she always woke alone. Her dreams were important. When she woke with a lover she could never remember her dreams, much less drag them to the surface.

*Never?* said the sword polisher. *Was that the lover's doing?*

Whenever she woke with a lover she gave up her dreams. The orange Hiroshige sky, and peacock-blue ink water, the gentle rocking of the *konachi*, the slop slop of the sea on its wooden sides, the smell of the charcoal burner, the slap of *ama* hands on *ama* skin, the laughter of women circled together, the hands reaching over the side of the boat to pull her up, and the cup of tea in her hands.

And one day, finally, it was time. Vera returned to Japan. Perhaps it was one of those dreams where Tamio sailed his boat. Or one of those nights she thought she saw Hana on the street. Maybe it was because Hamilton Drew came to see her and asked what she had heard. She shook her head.

'But they were your friends,' he said.

Yes, they were.

It was simpler now. Without thinking, without forcing herself or refusing herself, she walked into the Canada Pacific Steamship Lines office and bought a ticket.

She expected to recognise Tokyo as the Edo of her woodcut prints. But nothing was standing, there was no bridge, no pleasure quarter, no lanterns, no banners, no parades. She took the train to Nagoya, and then to Toba. It was the most beautiful place on earth. She had a room in the little *ryokan* she had stayed in with her father, with windows looking over the inlet. The water was marked out with pearling rafts, and the hills with patchy, khaki earth and clumps of cedar, pine and even cherry trees that rose directly from the narrow beaches all around.

The innkeeper gave her *sakura* tea – cherry blossoms – its salty, sweet thick taste a balm. She ate a magnificent, endless meal, of which the highlight was local lobster with sesame sauce. The cooks came in and knelt, and bowed with their faces to the floor.

She found the village little changed.

She walked the street that twisted against the slope, above the harbour. It was springtime, and the ground was wet, and there were men on the beach working on their boats. They had motors now, many of them, given to them by the Americans, she supposed. She had lost touch with everyone, first through war and then through trying to forget and then because she thought the news, if she should get it, would be unbearable. But still she looked at the backs of the men bent over the sides of their boats. She would know the shape of Tamio's anywhere. She saw the Pearl Museum, and an aquarium where her old friend the octopus was well represented. At the Pearl Museum there were *ama*, now dressed from head to toe in white, and waving to the crowd.

She felt old. She had changed immeasurably; she wore a tailored suit with wide pleated trousers and she had darker hair, cut short. Near the harbour she went to an *udon* shop. It was not the uncle's *udon* shop, but one much like it. She ordered lunch; the words in Japanese coming back when she looked at the food. The sea had not failed the people. The tiny molluscs with their thumb-sized burden of meat, soft shellfish that you ate whole, seaweed salad, red snapper, squid in its wine-red soup, the soup of the fermented soy bean, and finally rice. She stood up satisfied and somehow reassured, as if the process of remembering might begin with her digestion. She walked and found the streets of her lonely walks to the market, and finally, the hillside road – hardly wider than a path – that led to Keiko's house. But she did not go there.

Instead she turned and walked back out into the street and who did she see there, walking with his bad leg and bent under his backpack of tools, but the basket maker.

'Bamboo!' she stopped him.

He looked at her and not a flicker of surprise moved his weathered face, the eyes, though sunk in folds, so bright and unclouded that he might have been an immortal. He bowed his greeting.

'That was not my name,' he said. 'My name is Ishihara, Kamesuke. And you are the pearl girl.'

She bowed too. 'How did you know me?' She began to speak in halting Japanese.

'It is not at all difficult to know you,' he said. 'People stay the same. And we remember you, because you have entered the stories. I told you that you would.'

She took this as a hopeful sign, but could not put her question into words.

'Where have they put you and how long will you stay?' he asked, somewhat anxiously.

She laughed through her tears at the question because it was the same one – polite, but telling – that the people addressed to all the strangers in their midst.

'No one has put me anywhere. I came on my own.' She pointed out the hotel, and said she would stay until she found the people she was looking for, or found out where they might be. 'You are just my man, Ishihara-san,' she said. 'You must know all their stories.'

'No,' he said, 'no one knows all of the stories. I only know one or two.'

'Mikimoto Taisho,' she said, starting at the easy ones.

He said the King was well and back in business. 'Bigger than ever. He welcomed the Americans with his arms open,' he said.

'Setsu,' she said.

He pointed toward the water. 'Diving,' he said.

'Still?'

'Indeed. Others?' he said, with his grin even more gap-toothed than before. How could she ask about Keiko and Ikkanshi-san? She did not want to hear of them, from him.

The next day a delegation to see her arrived at the *ryokan*. It consisted of the Headman's two sons, grey-haired now, and an official from the town who she did not recognise, a man with a cropped GI haircut and a wide, and 'open for business' grin. He was Teru and he produced from behind him a pretty but wordless woman for whom she too, had

406

no words, because she had taken Hana's place. There was much bowing, murmuring and smiling. But no one hugged her, not until Maiko appeared.

She looked so foreign at first Vera did not know her, but then as soon as her eyes got used to her she saw Hana's mother had changed only a little. She might have been Vera's age when Vera had lived in her house as her daughter. Now she was fifty-three. She was rounded and dark skinned like a seal, firm-fleshed, quick and lively like any cold-water creature. Her face was open and she smiled, cried and laughed in Vera's arms and Vera in hers. Vera did not feel she herself had grown until she held that wise woman against her breast.

It was not *risshun*, yet. The *ama* were still in their land disguise, riding bicycles with bonnets over their heads, the brims long and trained like the blinkers on a horse so that they only saw the ground in front of their wheels. An *amagoya* had been built for them at the shore. The new government wanted to extend the season: they would dive from here from the twenty-first of March until May. But if the wind were too high or it rained, they would not dive. They were going the next day.

That morning, Vera walked, picking her way in leather-soled shoes when she should have been barefoot. She saw the Quonset hut on the beach.

'No one is allowed there,' said an American soldier, gesturing with a weapon at which she glanced askance as she veered off the pathway toward the gravelly beach. He must be kidding.

'Who does this allowing?' she asked him, already a few steps down the slope.

'That is the house of the diving girls,' he told her, not really answering, and so she continued.

'I know it well,' she said, 'because I am one of them, or was, before the war.' She did not stay to hear his reply.

She bent to enter the doorway.

The place was dark, how dark she had forgotten. The *irori* gave its lingering smell of charred wood, and touches of pink edged the grey ash just as a sunrise will light up the edges of cloud before dawn. On the shelf behind sat the tools, the knives and prising tools, the goggles and caps. The small forms around the square of the hearth seemed almost inanimate until their faces turned to her, making the pathway of light from the open door and then blocking it. They laughed, their faces split open like fruit gashed; they glistened there in the darkness and she stood in confusion wondering what was so funny.

'You have not stopped,' one said, and the other said, 'She did not stop did she?'

'Stopped what?'

'Growing!' they said. And they all laughed and she remembered that laugh, how it scalded her and comforted her and kept her within their strong company when she was such a lonely girl. *Sabishi*.

One reached her hand up to point out where her head was, nearly in the rounded top of the hut. Maiko patted the space beside her. They offered her tea and very dry biscuits. Their bicycles were parked outside. They were in their clubhouse and they were girls together.

'How is the fishing?'

'Oh it is good, very good,' they said in their cagey way. Now Vera laughed.

'How much do you get on a good day?'

'Oh the same; it is very good,' each one said modestly ducking her head and with eyes sliding slightly to the side.

'Not so good,' barked Setsu, and when she spoke, because she was the eldest, the others were quiet. 'The awabi are fewer now and not so easy to find. It was the war. The soldiers dropped their blowing-up things in the sea and killed the fishes.'

'It was not so,' said another. 'It was the fishermen. And the boats with the dredge.'

'Now they are not allowed. Awabi are saved for *ama*. *Ama* must live. Keep the village alive.'

Vera looked for the girls the age she had been. There were one or two and now they had the bellies of mothers. If Hanako had been alive, her daughter would have been diving.

'You, children?' said Maiko, prodding her.

'No,' she said. 'I would have liked to, but it has not happened.'

'It is the war,' said Setsu, offering comfort. 'The blowing-up things make the wombs go dry and no children are born, and if they are born they are' – she shook her head – 'not good, not right.' Neither her eyes nor her voice wandered off, but looked directly at Vera. Did she believe that she had gone only a small distance and remained in Japan?

'I cannot blame the war,' Vera said. 'I had a husband, but he was older and he died.'

'Find another one,' said Setsu.

Vera said she had been looking. 'I have not found the right man.'

'The right man?' said Yuriko, and cracked up laughing as if it were a ludicrous concept. Bawdy laughs all around in which Vera had to share.

And now the ease of trading stories and names, catching up. Once she'd been there, nothing had removed Vera from the scene, even twenty years of not seeing. The questions sent her back to those days so that she could see with her own eyes just the way it was. She could not tell them how happy it made her and how sad at the same time. She had worried they would somehow blame her for the war; they had worried that her life was endangered by knowing them, the enemy. And she had to ask the questions.

'Keiko?' she said.

'Gone to Hiroshima.' Very long faces. 'With *katanatogi*.'

So they had been together when they went. But

Ikkanshisan? To Hiroshima? There had been no return address on the letter. Surely Hiroshima was a place people ran from, not to, if they had legs to run, she thought. 'When?' she asked.

'Soon after,' they said.

She did not ask for anyone else.

She felt ashamed, about Tamio. She was afraid to ask as she was afraid to know. Her intemperance, her great love, her innocent passion, had brought trouble on him and on the summer island. She feared he had met a terrible fate. She dreamed of him falling out of an aeroplane. She dreamed of him standing before a great white shroud that was also a sail, with black characters written on it, in lovely lines that she could not read, but she believed he was sailing to the world of the spirits. 'Oh where do you go, and what are you?' she said in her dream. 'And what will happen to you if I do not dream you any more?'

No one else spoke of him.

Then Maiko said, 'We do not use the rope any more.'

'No?'

'Diving is good. Only the rope, that was what made it dangerous.'

They said nothing for a moment and someone she did not know passed tea.

'And you,' said Maiko. 'Have you been afraid?'

What a question. 'Who has not been afraid?'

'Have you been brave?' Maiko asked.

And she said she hoped she had been.

'Your father?' Maiko inquired, and they all sat, bright-eyed, inquisitive about this man. Vera believed they recalled the very cut of his coat at that moment.

'He is well,' she said firmly and shortly, although she was not exactly certain of his health as their communications had ceased for the moment.

'He traded the mother-of-pearl shell with Mikimoto,' said Maiko. They knew as much as Vera knew.

'Do you still work there?' Vera asked.

'Oh yes. And the young ones, they work for him.' They nodded, polite, polite. 'The *ama* dive for the tourists now.' They laughed.

More little cups of cooling tea and the sun dragging its heels on the floor, but soon they would go and get their families' dinners. Vera looked at Maiko and she must have read her mind.

'Yes you can ask,' she said. 'It is a long time ago.'

'And Tamio?' Vera said it as if it were just one in a string of curiosities she came with. She could not say it idly and she could not say it with great intention. No one was fooled by her act.

'Oh Tamio,' said Setsu. *'Ta-mi-o!'*

The others giggled a little. Vera thought it cruel. The strange brutality of the summer island crossed her like a shadow. Did they still hate him so much for cutting the nets? He had endangered them, she understood. But perhaps, she thought, they had forgiven now, that they saw with clear eyes, after the war, where they had been carried on the words of the schoolbooks, the Emperor, the Headman. But she had misunderstood.

'We helped him.'

The older ones, who remembered, giggled again.

'Headman said we must not, but we do.'

'How?' Vera asked. It was so long ago.

'Keiko found him fuel, for his motorboat. He stayed on an empty island. We got him food. And some awabi he sold to get money. In time he got to the mainland.' These women were past age, really, energetic, sprightly, beyond embarrassment, beyond anyone's power but their own. That was what it meant to cross the frontier ninety times a day, between air and ocean bed.

'Do you know what became of him? Did he ever come back?'

'Oh no, he did not come back,' said Maiko.

411

'He could not come back,' corrected Setsu. Those who remembered, laughed over her romance. Others looked only mildly interested, and sat, as if knowing the conversation had to move on to something of import soon. The younger ones, who might have been twenty, or sixteen, she could not tell, those who were beautiful and learning, watched Vera open-eyed.

'He drank too much sake at the *O-Bon*,' said Setsu. 'And he performed this evil deed.'

There would be no forgiveness?

'We were in danger then.'

'But where did he go?'

'To war,' said Maiko. 'Of course to war. It was only a matter of time. All the boys went to war.'

'And his parents?'

Silence.

Maiko again. 'We do not speak of Tamio's parents. They are dead now.'

The old aunt and uncle: they had been kind to her.

Maiko patted her hand. 'Father died in bombing. Mother killed herself. No one there to help her. It is not so unusual.'

Vera took a train to Hiroshima.

She knew how to find Ikkanshi-san.

She went to a shop that sold antiques. Stone lanterns. Iron teapots. Baskets, not as beautiful as those made by Bamboo. She thought that such a shop would carry swords, but she could find nothing, no helmet, no braided armour. She knew that to carry a sword was illegal, and the men who had sold them were gone away. In the market she at last found an art shop. The shop sold *ukiyo-e*. She spent a long time looking at the pictures and found one or two she liked: a pillar-print by Kitiagawa Utamaro of a courtesan and her gallant rescuer, and a beautiful little print by Choki depicting a mother and child catching fireflies. As she approached the counter to pay, she took a risk. In the

412

back was old armour, and helmets. She tried her rusty Japanese.

'*Katana?*' she said.

'No.'

'Where can I buy them?'

'You cannot.' He spoke in English.

'I am a collector,' she said. 'From Canada.'

He only stared at her and shook his head.

'Destroyed,' he finally offered.

She stepped closer. 'I am not looking for a *katana*, but for a *katanatogi*,' she said. 'His name is Ikkanshi-san.'

'Oh, very great *katanatogi*,' said the man and smiled non-committally.

'He lives in Hiroshima.'

'No, he does not,' said the shopkeeper, and now she knew she had him.

'He does not? If you know that perhaps you know where he lives.'

'Actually, Ikkanshi-san not *katanatogi*.'

She repeated in Japanese that she was a friend, that she had been told he had come to Hiroshima.

'Prefecture,' insisted the shopkeeper. 'Not city. No one come to Hiroshima City. Crazy.' He laughed as if he were in fact crazy.

'But you know him.'

'He is famous.'

'I knew him,' she said, 'when I was a child, before the war. He lived on an island then.'

'Famous, but not for *katanatogi*. He makes no swords. No one makes swords now.'

'Then what is he famous for now?' she asked.

'Teacher. And wife makes pots.'

'Where?' Vera persisted. If he was a famous teacher he must be alive.

And the man did not know. Where did he live? He did once know, could not recall. Had no idea how he had heard

413

of this famous teacher with his wife and her pots. Vera was so angry she leaned on his counter and threatened him, like a crazy woman. Of course it was the wrong thing to do and produced an effect remarkably like that of an oyster shutting its shell. There was no crack, there was no way of getting in, the shopkeeper's face became blank with determination to give nothing. *Shiran kao*. In the end she left the market.

She went to Nagasaki.

There was just as much destruction, from the second bomb. She went to the part of town where the foreigners had come those centuries ago and where the traders in beautiful things still were clustered. Or were clustered again, because surely they too had fled these parts. And now she asked a different question, again in Japanese.

'Pots,' she said. 'I hear there are very beautiful pots made here.'

'On the island of Amakusa,' said the shopkeeper. 'There are many potters there.'

'Why are the potters there?' she asked.

'It is the soil. Very good. And the island is so far away that the people are left alone and the potters who make these beautiful things must be left alone to do that.'

Vera took the ferry from the far side of Nagasaki to the island of Amakusa. As the boat drew in she saw the fisherwomen wading in the tidal flats, their baskets floating behind them, with pennants flying – turquoise, yellow, lime. Their bonnets poked forward as they stared, intently, into the muddy sway of the edge of the sea. She saw them flip the eels from the ends of their hooks, over their shoulders into the baskets and she laughed, she loved the gesture so. That was who Hana would be, not the girl with the dog, window-shopping on Robson Street.

The tide was out and the blue-grey sky was soft over the water and the darker hills. She set off walking up the road.

There was nothing else to do. It was a beautiful place, and a mournful one. She heard soft wings overhead: eagles. They must have come for the fish from some sea stack farther off.

She was certain why Ikkanshi and Keiko had come here. The black steep rocks and the flat sandy coves were like the summer island. The hollowed out, faded bamboo tubes that floated in on the tide were the same, and the wild cats that minced along the narrow stone ledges. It was, in a way, a place of hiding. There were old grey wooden huts, and a few new houses, climbing the hillsides.

A man with a rickshaw stopped her. Where would she like to go?

Vera said she was in search of a man who was a teacher. And taking a chance, she said, he used to be a famous sword polisher. And his wife is a potter.

'I know,' he said.

They were in a little town on the sharp side of the hill, a few hours' walk: he showed her how the road wound and how to carry on walking. When she came to the outside of a little settlement there would be houses and one would be the house of these people.

'They are your friends?' he asked. Or was she a buyer, a trader for the pottery?

In this case he wanted to share Vera. The people were poor. He offered to carry her a little of the way, but she said no. She stopped and removed her town shoes. She had brought with her a pair of straw sandals, and put them on her feet. But she was unaccustomed to them and after a mile of climbing, her feet were sore.

Vera felt no hurry so she sat to rest her feet. There was a ruined castle on the horizon. A winding road. The sound of a hidden creek, making its way down the hill. Otherwise it was silent there, except for birdsong, and in the distance, when the wind blew, the sound of the sea. There was rain or mist in the hills. The moss was thick on the slippery stones.

415

She saw an old red torii arch, a series of arches, climbing a hill. The red was freshly painted, but the stones were ancient, mossy, the doorways of the buildings at the top made from old grey and ridged wood. She climbed the foot-softened steps and sat at the top on a bench. The eagles circled above her again. It was very peaceful. Although she had never been there before, she felt she had found her way back.

The hills, the air, and the ground pressed closely on her senses. She could feel the old simple concentration coming back. He had taught her that: what greater gift? It began to rain but there was sun somewhere in the clouds of fog that swam in and out, because she could see light falling, now on this hill, now on that rice paddy, now on an old face.

We abandon the landscapes of our lives, and then return, beaten back by love, and hate, bearing our small triumphs and hiding our wounds, and expect to be recognised, expect to be embraced and to feel as we once felt. But the land too has suffered. Sometimes there is nothing there. Sometimes, like that day at the torii arches, the very signs of neglect and decay are words, and magic.

Vera heard a sound, coming up the steps. It was the sound of a straw broom. A caretaker or an old priest was probably coming. She wiped her eyes and prepared to look like an interested tourist. The man appeared, absorbed in his work. He had the white and blue fisherman's headscarf tied over his head, and knotted at the nape of his neck. It was pulled very tight and revealed a beautifully shaped dome of a head. He was not an old man but he stepped haltingly. She could see that one leg was giving him trouble. But the other, the back of him, his waist – she knew it before he turned around to face her. And there were the deep-set, oval eyes.

She stood.

'Tamio,' she said.

*  *  *

They walked back down the road the way she had come, to the docks of the town. He had a new fibreglass motorboat. He was so proud of it. He put her in and pulled the throttle and they putted out from the land a little faster and more noisily than they once had. He was gentle with her as if it were Vera who had been banished, who had been at war, burned so deeply that one leg was thin and withered.

She asked about Keiko and Ikkanshi-san. She asked about their son.

'Not their son,' he said. Then he smiled, brilliantly. 'My son.' He took the boat into another dock, farther along. From here they had to climb. It was a narrow road that came close to the cliff many times; she would have been afraid to drive a car. Walking up the road she wore the sandals because, although they hurt, they felt right. As she climbed she thought, who owns the past? Is it mine? Or his? Or no-one's? And where does it go so that, when we try to grasp it, it eludes, but dances back with its smells and sounds, remembered voices, only to prove its power, and then retreat.

'You have a son?' Vera said. Or had he meant that he was their son now?

'Yes I have a son,' he smiled. And again he eyed her carefully. 'I had a wife also.'

The house was set up high where the trees made it dark, with the small glimmering pools of rice paddies adding light from the terraces. It was surrounded by vines and growing things; someone worked hard to encourage them. He showed her the little hut with the kiln and Keiko's pottery studio.

There were no other women who did this, he said, and from time to time foreigners did come to look and buy. Keiko would see that they were there waiting, and come out to greet them, thinking Vera was one of those tourists.

'She'll be surprised,' said Vera.

'No, not surprised. But she will be very happy.'

Yes, she would be happy. Suddenly Vera could not wait

417

to put her arms around Keiko. What had James Lowinger called her? Woman of the ages. She who did not want gratitude and who did not abandon Vera, but set her free. She would be happy and she would not have doubted that they would be reunited one day.

Then they stood. Vera and Tamio stood. No, I stood – the woman who was Vera, who was me, stood with Tamio – and we waited, loved ones and strangers together, in front of the house on the narrow road, for someone to appear.

*Saya no uchi no kachi saya*: to win the victory without drawing the sword.

# Acknowledgements

I want to mention first the extraordinary hospitality and helpfulness of the many people who helped me in Japan.

To begin with, Mr Terry Greenberg, then Canadian Counsel in Nagoya, put me in touch with the people I wanted to meet. Mrs Priam Greenberg and Ms Shuko Nagasi were interested and good company, and acted as translators.

Mr Teru Nakanishi in Mie Prefecture facilitated my visit and toured me around tirelessly, helping me find the information I was seeking. At the Toba Aquarium, Yukihiro Nakamura was generous with his knowledge; at the Mikimoto Pearl Museum, Curator Kiyoo Matsumoto provided an excellent tour and historical overview, which he followed with a loan of research materials. Civic officials in Toba arranged for me to meet with *ama* divers.

I was privileged to meet the *ama* women—Akiyo Yamamoto, Teruko Higashikawa, Tokumi Oota, and Setsu Hamaguchi—who allowed me into their *amagoya*, overcame their customary shyness, and spoke candidly about their diving, and their lives.

I also wish to acknowledge a debt to the following books:

*The Island of the Fisherwomen* by Fosco Maraini, which, with text and transcendent photographs, gives an account of *ama* life. *Pearls and Pearling Life* by Edwin Streeter is a long-lost memoir about pearl trading, and a great read. Similarly, *The Pearl Trader* (1937) by Louis Kornitzer, and *The Book of the Pearl* (1908) by George Frederick Kunz and Charles Hugh Stevenson, provided valuable information.

*The Pearl King* (1956) by Robert Eunson, which appears to be the only book-length portrait in English of Mikimoto, made the man come alive. My account of pearling in Kuwait was informed by *Pearling in the Arabian Gulf: A Kuwaiti Memoir* by Saif Marzooq al-Shamlan, translated by Peter Clark. I was helped in my understanding of the Japanese Imperial Army by *Soldiers of the Sun* by Meirion Harries and *Hitler's Japanese Confidant: General Oshima Hiroshi and MAGIC Intelligence* 1941–1945 by Carl Boyd. My description of Ceylon was informed by *An Account of the Island of Ceylon* (1803) by Robert Percival. What understanding I have of sword practices and *iai* comes from my study with Sensei Patrice Williams in Toronto: mistakes are my own. Much gratitude, Sensei.

And, as before, I thank Yusuke Tanaka for his translation, and Lanny Messervey for inputting and web work, as well as my agent, Helen Heller, for finding good homes for this book.

Next to last, I feel lucky to be with Iris Tupholme and the hardworking and enthusiastic staff at HarperCollins; it has been such a pleasure to work with you. And finally—at home and always—Nick. You are the best.